To Meli,

Some food for thought for my friend who has provided much food for me

God bless,

PJ

The Last BACHELOR of ALES

Journey to Purpose

Peter T Elliott

Suite 300 - 990 Fort St
Victoria, BC, V8V 3K2
Canada

www.friesenpress.com

First Edition — 2019

ISBN
978-1-5255-5396-7 (Hardcover)
978-1-5255-5397-4 (Paperback)
978-1-5255-5398-1 (eBook)

1. FICTION

Distributed to the trade by The Ingram Book Company

The Last Bachelor

Jason Johnstone's text went unanswered. The Bachelors of Ales, born in an alcoholic haze six years ago would not pass any resolutions tonight. Jason couldn't decide whether to stay or leave as he thought about the society's first resolution: "This society will take hours instead of minutes, from six p.m. until closing, to be precise." One brother was absent from that first meeting and one was present for what Jason guessed may be the last. So much for the oath each bachelor had sworn: "I will remain a BA in spite of my pending PhD and in spite of any spouse I may attain. I will attend all weekly meetings and participate actively in all raucous behaviour and lewd discussions. So help me, Dionysus." In truth, their meetings at The Tinker's Table pub were never raucous and not particularly lewd; earth's ills were discussed frivolously and remedied with ludicrous resolutions. Much despair was avoided at the expense of serious enquiry—puns being much preferable to solutions.

Over the years, members left to further their careers or tend their families, but Jason and Charles had remained steadfast. Now baby Linda was driving a deadly spike into the heart of the society; a newborn daughter was taking precedence over a freshly tapped pint. His text remained unanswered. Jason, very sombrely, drained the last of his lager and silently presented his motion, "Let it be resolved that the Bachelors of Ales be dissolved." It was time to leave.

Then things went from bad to worse. A tall, shoulder-length grey-haired, full-bearded man in a long tattered coat, with patches over patches, a pint of ale in each hand, was barring his exit. It was the old man who always sat in the corner by himself.

"Name's Moses," he said. "Can I join you?"

Charlton Heston rendition, thought Jason. *A bit worse for wear and minus the staff. One pint and I'll excuse myself.* He was too polite to refuse and could think of nothing else to do anyway.

"Jason," he said, offering a nod. He slid along the booth a bit further than he guessed any bugs might be able to jump.

"I know it's not your usual quaff," Moses said as he placed a tankard in front of Jason, "but my guess is you drink that rot precisely because it's usual. I hope to convince you that a little of what's better is much better than plenty of what's usual."

Jason had been drinking the same beer since before he should have been drinking at all. Habit was as good a reason as any. "This stuff's a bit bitter," he declared after the first sip.

"Don't judge it yet. Wait till you're almost through. It's much like life," Moses said. "You'll find the end much sweeter when the present's a bit bitter."

"I'm happy enough with my lager," Jason protested. "Why change a good thing?"

"Is it a good thing? Or do you just keep drinking lager upon lager without truly noticing what you're drinking until you no longer care what you're drinking. Again; much like life. Are you happy with it? Is it enough?"

"Well, I'm happy with my lager, and I'm happy with my life." Jason was becoming annoyed. "And what do you know of having enough? You don't even have decent clothes."

"These clothes may not be fancy," Moses said, "but they're decent and they're enough."

"You're idea of enough differs from mine. How are those rags you wear enough?"

"They fulfill their purpose; they keep me warm and they keep me covered. I have some to wear, some to wash and some to mend. That's enough."

"How can you respect yourself, dressed in rags?" Jason asked.

"Much more in these rags than when I dressed in three-piece suits and drove a Rolls. Then I valued things and sold my soul to get them. I've far more now than I ever did then."

"So what is it you have that's so valuable?" Jason asked.

"A purpose," Moses replied.

"Sounds like rationalization for having nothing."

"Tell me, then, why I'm content with nothing, as you say, while you're not content with more things than you could ever use?"

Jason was more uncomfortable than he'd been in ages. He didn't understand what was troubling him, but he knew Moses was right. He could think of no appropriate response, so he recalled the evening the Bachelors of Ales voted to repeal the law of gravity and hoped this fellow would, accordingly, float away. Jason simply asked, "Why?"

"Because you have a purpose," Moses answered. "But you don't know your purpose because you haven't stopped to think that you have a purpose. You're so distracted by chasing the ever-elusive boundary between need and greed, the boundary that rises each time it's met, that you don't stop to consider why you chase it at all. All you get from that harrying race are more means but never an end. And those means will all be wasted, never spent for their end. Until you accept that you have a purpose and stop to find that purpose, you'll keep coming here to hide from that purpose so you can continue to deny you're wasting your time, merely spinning a treadwheel attached to nothing but its axle."

Jason didn't want to stay and he didn't want to leave. He wasn't comfortable here but knew he wouldn't be comfortable anywhere. Right now he both hated and needed Moses. "Right now, my purpose is to drink this... whatever you brought me."

"That elixir, my friend, is a balm for the brain. It lubricates thoughts as they wind through your mind, unlike that slop you slurp that merely hides un-thought thoughts under a blanket of fog."

"We had many thoughts about many things," Jason countered. "The world we built in our mugs far surpassed the world outside but there is no way to bring it to life. And what has this to do with purpose anyway?"

"You had silly thoughts about silly things. You charged head-on against what is, mad that it isn't, instead of steering a course within your bounds. All the while avoiding the why, rueing what is and ignoring what ought."

"There are many things that should be yet aren't and many more that shouldn't but are," Jason said. "What can a few pawns like us do about any of it? Crying in our beers is just as effective as protesting to the deaf ears of the powers that be. Powers that be... sometimes I think there's no longer anyone in charge. The system has become a self-perpetuating monster no one can put a leash on. Crying in our beer is something we can do, and I like my beer better with a little salt."

"So you continue to do as you do though you know it's folly," Moses said. "You do as you do so you can stay as you are, though you like neither what you do nor who you are. You fear not to be as you don't wish to be."

"What else can any of us be other than hamsters on the treadwheel of life? There are no safe landing places to jump off onto. Life spins so fast we'd likely break our necks if we tried."

"So you keep working and eating and sleeping and buying just so you can work and eat and sleep and buy some more. If you're diligent and lucky, you'll be able to buy more, buy bigger and buy better, but you'll never have the most, the biggest or the best. You'll never have all you want, my friend, until you want nothing at all."

"So what's your answer?" Jason asked. "We'll never succeed, so don't try? Should we just stop pretending there's a future worth having? If that's so, why shouldn't we just cease to be?"

"No, my friend, do not die and do not let truth, beauty or goodness die. Grab a small piece of truth and hang on. Live that truth and let it grow. It will lead you to your purpose, and beauty and goodness will flower."

"And what small bit of truth can I grasp?"

"I am," Moses answered. "Know that you are. Ask how. Ask why. Know that all about you is and ask again how, why. These are small seeds; seeds that will grow. Everywhere people roam until their end, rather than toward their end. They know no purpose. They merely produce and consume because they must, but they don't know why."

"I'm reasonably sure that I am, so let's agree I've passed that point. How will the how and why give me purpose?"

"They don't give you purpose. I am has already provided your purpose. When you know how, you'll know just how small and insignificant you are. When you know why, you'll know just how great and important you are." Moses drained his pint, rose and offered Jason his hand. "I must be off now. It's been a pleasure."

Jason grasped the old man's hand hesitantly but firmly. "I don't suppose you'd like to be inducted into the Bachelors of Ales Society? We meet here weekly, at six p.m." He watched blankly as Moses left, wondering who had recruited whom.

The Bitter Drink

Jason sat quietly, staring at his pint, it was still bitter but he was beginning to enjoy the bitterness. He knew he'd heard something important but was trying to hide from it.

"Who doesn't know that they are?" he asked out loud, scornfully. "Purpose... my purpose is to be. I eat, I drink and I breathe so I can keep being. It's so obvious that it's nonsense! Everything everyone does is so that they can be." Jason finished the ale Moses had brought, brooding on the fact that everyone and everything so obviously *is* because he feared how and why.

Jason defiantly ordered a pint of his usual lager He noticed how plain it tasted after the ale. That irked him all the more because 'how' and 'why' refused to dissipate into its alcoholic haze, the haze that inevitably arrives somewhere within the fourth pint and is able to dissolve even the worst of life's ills. Yet *how* and *why* persisted, tugging ever more firmly on his thoughts. No puns or witticisms were emerging to banish the pain.

He regretted accepting Moses' offer yet wished the odd fellow was back. He was mad that Charles hadn't shown up, yet knew that phase of his life was gone, which both scared him and beckoned him. *How before why or why before how*, he mused, no longer denying the inevitable. The seeds were planted and watered with bitter ale, and they had germinated. How and why were invasive weeds that could not be eradicated; they needed to be tended and pruned or they'd choke the fertile soil of his mind.

Jason settled his tab, left half his pint unfinished and headed for his short walk home. Things were getting crazy. *Why should I care how?* he asked himself. *How can I know why?* He had no idea where to start—he was oblivious to the fact that he had already started. *What does it mean to be?* Jason couldn't remember feeling this confused and exhausted in a very long time. His hot shower did nothing to ease his confusion, and he dropped, face first, onto his bed.

His alarm sounded much too soon. Toast, coffee and his morning commute to work were so occupied with thoughts of his newfound quest that the daily puzzles in the morning paper remained untouched. Jason brought the paper with him to the cafeteria for lunch knowing that it would remain unopened. Charles was there waiting and finally provided some much needed relief.

"How much beer did you drink last night?" Charles asked. "You look hungover, bro!"

"I didn't even finish my fourth."

"Are you sick?"

"Maybe crazy," Jason replied. "I think I caught it from that old guy who's always sitting in the corner at Tink's."

"Yeah, you're sounding a little crazy. What happened?"

"Just as I gave up on you showing, he came over with two pints of ale and I didn't have the heart to brush him off."

"You think you caught something from him?"

"No, we kind of talked about life and what's important, how much is enough."

"What would that bum know about enough?"

"Exactly what I asked him. He said you can never have enough things, that you have to have a purpose, or more that you do have a purpose and you'll have enough when you know your purpose."

"He just doesn't want to admit he doesn't have anything."

"Exactly what I said, but then he asked why he's happy and we're not."

"You weren't happy because you were there alone. I warned you that Rachel was getting exhausted with Linda's colic. We've been best friends almost forever, bro, but wives and kids... if they're not first priority they become ex-wives and visitation rights. I'm not going there—ever."

"It's not that. I know I was being selfish and it wasn't fair to pressure you that way," Jason admitted. "Bachelors of Ales is gone. I was there alone; all my friends have grown up and I haven't. All of that's true, but

Moses was saying more than that. All of our stuff is just stuff; it's not real, not in any deep sense. Moses is right. We won't find meaning in our life by getting more things."

"Moses? You and that bum are buds now?"

"He's not a bum; he just prefers simple. It seems like we said more over one beer last night than the bachelors have said over many years. We said things so we didn't have to think about them. We did things just to do them. Moses is right. There should be a why."

"What's wrong with because it's fun? What's better than fun?"

"Maybe right."

"Right smite. My right, your right, someone else's right. Whose right is better and are any of them really right?"

"Moses said that am and is are real, and we should think about how and why."

"So Moses is your new guru?"

"When he was 'the guy who always sits in the corner,' he just seemed a bit weird, but when we drank ale together, he seemed much wiser."

"Much wiser than a crazy homeless guy?"

"No, much wiser than us."

"Right now, we should be wise enough to get back to work," Charles said as he collected his garbage and headed out, "before we wind up broke and homeless like him."

"I don't think he is broke or homeless," Jason said as he followed Charles into the elevator. "I think he just prefers simple."

What needed to be said had been said, so Jason and Charles just watched the numbers light up as the elevator ascended.

"Later," Charles said as they exited.

"Yeah."

The rest of Jason's day was filled with work; he was so exhausted by five o'clock his mind turned completely blank and he slept on the train, nearly missing his stop. As soon as he got home he crashed on his couch and didn't wake until morning.

The First Date

Colleen was waiting by the elevator at work. They had been eyeing each other for ages and occasionally engaged in very small talk; perhaps it was time.

"Would you like to grab coffee after work today?" Jason wondered if he'd ever have to admit he asked her out on their first date just to avoid thinking.

Colleen blushed deeply. She turned to face him, smiled and said, "Yes." Her heart was pounding and she couldn't say more.

"Great, we'll meet here at five-ish."

"Great! Five-ish."

Jason's hasty intervention worked well; all day he thought of Colleen and forgot about why, how and being. Instead, he thought of her pretty face, the way her eyes lit up when she smiled, and her perfume. He thought about the clothes, which flattered her without revealing more than was proper. He imagined she had good parents. How ironic it was that he finally worked up the courage to ask her out because he was afraid to think about Moses' questions. Maybe it was time to think about a serious relationship. He didn't believe in God but couldn't help wondering if Moses was God's way of nudging him toward maturity. Or was it the solitary meeting of the Bachelors of Ales, the fact that he was the only bachelor who hadn't moved on from university pranks and silliness? Everyone else had become seriously committed to career and family but he hadn't become serious about anything. Was it time? Was it Colleen? Why hadn't he asked her out sooner?

It was nearly five and Jason had avoided how and why all day. He slipped into the men's room, freshened up and was in the lobby by five minutes past five. Colleen showed up two minutes later. They approached each other awkwardly, both hinting at a hug but settling for a handshake. "Let's make it pub grub instead. I have a favourite place that serves really decent burgers." Jason had no idea why he suddenly switched plans and instantly felt like an idiot.

It was Friday and Colleen had nothing else to do. She had fantasized about dating Jason for quite some time. They arrived for work in the same building at the same time almost every day and usually rode the elevator together (along with many other people). Sometimes they met in the elevator going down after work.

"I can't stay out too long tonight," she said, "but a quick bite would be fine."

Jason offered Colleen his arm and led her to the metro station. From their occasional conversations on the elevator, he knew she was an accountant and she knew he was an engineer. Other than that, they both knew sun is better than rain, snow is better elsewhere, and summers were not invented with business attire in mind.

"What kind of accounting do you do?" Jason asked.

"I don't actually do much accounting," Colleen answered. "I advise on new product development. I tell people what they need to find out and how to present it, and other people actually search up the data and crunch the numbers. I review business cases and plans more for format and completeness than accuracy. How about you? What kind of engineering do you do?"

"Pretty high-level stuff. I look at trends and forecasts. I work on strategy a lot more than application or implementation. Our industry's very competitive and we have to stay ahead of technology. My title is manager of R and D. Most of the time I'm in meetings either holding someone's hand or giving them a swift kick in the pants. The unknown is a very scary place for people, and my job's mostly about who needs to be dragged and who needs to be pushed." It struck Jason that this statement could apply to both his encounter with Moses and his relationship with Colleen. Moses had dragged him to a point that pushed him toward Colleen.

The train arrived, and Jason and Colleen found seats at the back. As the rush-hour crowd packed in, they were pressed tight against each other. Neither could be heard over the background din so they just sat quietly, thinking. Jason offered his hand and Colleen took it, resting it on her knee.

Jason wondered why he suggested bringing Colleen to his pub. What if she didn't like The Tinker's Table? Did he invite her so he wouldn't be alone? Was he inviting her or just someone, anyone? What if she liked Tink's and he didn't like her? What if he found he didn't want to share his pub after all? Why didn't he just settle for coffee? The Bachelors of Ales had adopted a no-dates policy for a reason, though Jason couldn't recall how many beers had gone down before the topic came up.

Colleen wondered why she agreed to go to a pub; she didn't like pubs. TVs with soccer, football or hockey; Keno screens; loud patrons, all drinking too much. Coffee shops were quieter. You could hold a conversation, get to know each other better. Coffee could be long or short, depending on how it was going. Here she was, holding hands with an almost-stranger, going who knows where to eat and drink in a pub. What was she thinking? How much would she regret this? She hadn't even arranged a rescue call from her friend Stacey.

Both regretted their rash behaviour yet felt an unfamiliar warmth and comfort in the hand they were holding.

"This is our stop," Jason said. "Tink's is about seven blocks from the station. Do you mind walking?" They got off the train and exited on Quitman Street, still holding hands. "I've been coming here since I started university," Jason said. "We'd either study or just be silly, depending on how close exams were."

"So, is it mostly university students?"

"No, Tink's was our place away from other students. The boys' exclusive domain."

"Who else goes there?"

"Mostly older people, but we never mixed." They'd arrived. Jason held the door for Colleen. She was pleasantly surprised. There were no screens; it was lit with an amber hue and surprisingly quiet for a full pub. Colleen looked around at tables of mostly older people talking to each other. All of the tables were filled. An arm went up in the corner beckoning them. Jason placed his hand behind Colleen's waist and led her to the corner booth.

"Hi, Moses," he said. "Moses... Colleen."

"Far more fetching, she is, than the company you usually keep. What brings you here on a Friday?" Moses asked.

"We're here to get a little better acquainted than we can on an elevator for ten floors."

"Then sit yourselves down and I'll ensure you get off to a good start," Moses said, gesturing in invitation.

Aware this was most inappropriate but not knowing how to decline Moses' invitation, Jason took off his jacket and hung it on the hook at the end of the booth. He helped Colleen with her coat and hung it over his. Colleen slid into the booth and Jason slid in beside her. Colleen wondered why Jason would agree to sit with this stranger on their first date, even if there were no empty tables available.

"So, how long have you two known each other?" Moses asked.

"We don't really," Colleen answered. "We just see each other on the elevator occasionally."

"Well, Jason, this is a bold move for you then," Moses said. "I predict this will be either the start of an enduring relationship or the end of a short one."

The waitress appeared with menus for Colleen and Jason. "Today's special is Irish stew with dumplings and it's very popular. What would you like to drink?"

"Two of mine, please Maria, and a pinot grigio for the lady," Moses replied, looking to Colleen who nodded. Jason also accepted that Moses was right.

Moses then turned to Colleen and asked, "What do you want out of life, Miss Colleen?"

That's a very odd question, Colleen thought. "I want to help people do things that are important to them and to society," she answered. "I help people present proposals for new products to investors and promoters."

"I suppose that's as good an endeavour as the product and a fine place to be," Moses said, "and possibly a proper means to a good end. It seems why is not a complete stranger to you."

"To tell you the truth, I don't think as much about why now as I did in university," Colleen said. "I'm too busy doing what's given to me. Sometimes I wonder why my client wants to make their product, but it's not my job to care."

Jason hadn't anticipated how the evening might go but he was sure this wasn't it. "Business is directed by the bottom line: if it's profitable, it's worth doing. There's no other why today."

"Yes, profit has become the end for many today," Moses said, "and if we're not careful it will be the end of us all."

"What other end can a business have?"

"None, if business becomes master, but it does not become man."

"Investors weigh risk and return," Colleen contributed. "They don't really care what a product is as long as there's a market and preferably not much competition."

Maria arrived with their drinks. "Have you decided on food?" she asked.

"Stew all round," Moses answered. Jason never had anything at Tink's except burgers but he was not about to argue; Colleen grew up on Irish stew and never tired of it.

When Maria left with their orders, Colleen added, "Most of our clients look for a niche where demand is good, but not big enough to interest larger companies. There seem to be fewer and fewer opportunities for individuals and small enterprises, as multinationals and conglomerates become more efficient."

"Big companies are very efficient at producing goods and providing services that grow ever further from the actual wants and needs of the customer," Moses said. "It's not possible to mass produce tailored suits so the fit becomes more relaxed as prices decrease and profits increase."

"But the customer benefits," Jason countered.

"In sense of cost," Colleen said, "but not in sense of product. We wind up accepting what we are offered because what we want isn't available. That's where niches open up."

"Things must be available and affordable," Jason argued. "Even when exactly what we want is available, we might only be able to afford something that approximates what we want."

"And when one invests all their fortune in what they believe they want, they may have to forego what they need," Moses said.

"Or get a better job," Jason said. "We need food, clothing and shelter. I want T-bones, Calvin Klein and my own townhouse; therefore, I also need my high-paying job."

"Needs have quantity and quality," Colleen said.

"And hierarchy—psych 101," Jason added.

Maria arrived with three steaming plates of Irish stew and dumplings. "This will satisfy the food tier," Jason said as he passed a plate to Colleen.

"And surpass minimum in both quantity and quality," Moses said.

The conversation paused while they ate. "Don't tell my mom," Colleen finally said, "but the stew is every bit as good as hers and the dumplings are lighter."

"Food for the mind and food for the belly with appropriate libation to complement them both," Moses said. "A better blend none could request. I'm having a splendid time. Save room for the Triple Chocolate Lava Cake."

"We'll have to share one, Jason," Colleen said.

The evening was going far better than either Jason or Colleen had thought possible and better, too, than any of the Bachelors of Ales meetings, though in a much different manner.

The lava cake was included in the daily special so Maria traded three fresh plates for the soiled ones just as Colleen set her knife and fork down in surrender. "It goes very well with coffee," Maria said. "Decaf if you must."

"Okay, decaf," Colleen agreed.

"Regular for me," Jason ordered. He wanted to stay awake and remember the evening. His opinion of Moses was much higher than it had been on Wednesday.

Moses didn't need to say anything; Maria knew his preference.

The cake was very good, but too much for Colleen to finish.

"We've made great strides on wanting and needing," Moses said. "I enjoyed the conversation as much as the excellent meal. Miss Colleen, it has been a real pleasure to meet you. I pray it won't be our last encounter."

"Well, I've never liked pubs and definitely questioned my sanity at so rashly accepting Jason's invitation," Colleen said, "but this has turned out very well."

Moses had subtly brought the evening to a close, which Jason didn't want but also didn't know how to counter. It was the right time to leave but he was eager to remain. "How will you get home?" he asked Colleen.

"Actually, I don't live terribly far from here," she replied. "It's a nice evening; we could walk."

Jason's heart leapt at this invitation; his time with Colleen would be extended. He got up and helped Colleen with her coat. "We've had a very good time; thank you, Moses," Jason said, forgetting all about the bill.

Jason guided Colleen to the door with his arm around her waist. Outside, they held hands. "This way," Colleen said, gently tugging Jason to the right. "I really am having a wonderful time."

Jason blushed noticeably. "Yes."

"Your friend is very nice."

"Yes."

"And the pub is very much like Great-Uncle Glynn's local in Ireland." Colleen's brogue was emerging. "I spent a month with him after graduating. 'You should remember your real home,' he'd always tell me."

"So were you born in Ireland?"

"No, my family has been here for generations."

They strolled down Quitman to the track at Northside High. "Wait here," Colleen said and disappeared behind the fieldhouse. She re-emerged holding her shoes and stuffing her pantyhose into her pocket. "These are good for work but not for walking." Colleen looped one strap through the other and hung her shoes over her shoulder. "Not my first time." She took Jason's hand again and they resumed walking. "You're much different than I thought."

"Turns out I'm different than I thought too," Jason admitted. "The me I am is not the me I was not long ago."

"How so?"

"Less angry, happier." He squeezed Colleen's hand a bit.

"What brought this change?"

"Why."

"Just small talk, I guess."

"No, why is what brought the change," Jason said. "I stopped being angry that things are as they are. I'm too pre-occupied now with why they are, why I am and why anything is."

"Did you study philosophy in school?"

"Nope. Psych and anthropology were guaranteed A's but the philosophy profs were all a bit dodgy. Only weirdos took philosophy classes."

"I loved philosophy! Tonight reminded me. That's part of why I'm enjoying myself so much."

"And the company?"

Colleen smacked him playfully with her free hand. "I like Moses, the way he sort of teases things out of us."

"And me?"

"I came with you and I left with you," Colleen reminded Jason. They reached the far corner of the track and she pointed north. "I think I'm with you on some sort of journey."

"And where does this journey lead? Just home, or much further?"

"Maybe to life," she said. "I feel like I became trapped in work and I forgot to live. Moses seems different. He seems wise. His eyes are always sparkling."

They both were silent in their own thoughts for the next couple of blocks until Colleen stopped at a white house with green trim. "This is me," she said, turning to Jason and taking his free hand. They stood there holding hands and staring in each other's eyes.

"So can we find life together?" Jason asked. "Can we walk together on this journey for a while?"

"I'd like that," Colleen replied. "See you tomorrow... I mean Monday."

They gave each other a proper hug and Colleen went inside.

The Weekend

The walk back to Tink's was longer than Jason remembered. He was lost in his thoughts, picturing Colleen, her bright blue eyes, her smile, her dimples. He was smitten. He shook his head in wonder at himself. "Life together!" He knew it was too early to talk about that. Why was he in such a rush? Tink's instead of coffee! Life together! Nothing he was doing was appropriate, yet he sensed it was right. He didn't even really know her, for heaven's sake. Yet he wanted her. And he wanted her to want him.

Was this a crush? Was he a teenager? Was this because he never had a crush? He knew he was being silly but he couldn't stop himself. *She was being silly too.* The thought scared him. Was she some kind of crazy person? *Impossible!* Did she never have a crush before? Why now, after years of seeing each other on the elevator? *It must be destiny! Wishful thinking.* They'd both wake up regretting the night. They'd both wake up wanting each other more. They were both crazy; he knew they were both acting crazy. *It was all a dream!* He didn't want to wake up.

Jason was too confused to just go home so he went back to Tink's. He sat at the first empty table. "He does that to you," Maria said as she placed a pint of ale in front of Jason. "You're not the first."

Jason knew he would not be drinking lager again. He was different. Moses had made him different. *Colleen.* He sipped his tankard slowly, staring blankly and time passed... a lot of time. The people, the noise, Tink's—all were gone—and he was alone. He was floating in nothingness and thinking nothing very deeply. His ale slowly vanished and he woke as he drained the last sip; he woke though he hadn't been sleeping.

"Yup," Maria said as she collected his mug. "Moses. That girl seemed very nice too."

Jason felt warm again. "Yes, she works in the same building I do."

"So have you given up on the boys?"

"We may have all become men."

"I seriously doubt that!" Maria scoffed.

"Life goes on and we must too," Jason said. In truth, he was thinking that life for him might just be beginning. "So Moses has this effect on other people?"

"Usually takes longer. I sit with him sometimes, when work is slow. Sometimes he orders me chablis and sometimes chardonnay, even though I prefer beer. He says I should be a lady; he's old."

"But you still sit with him."

"He makes you think. He's a good person to sit with."

Jason paid, leaving a good tip, and went home. Maria was quite nice. He hadn't noticed before because the bachelors were always too frivolous. They thought of Maria as an attractive older woman who was probably quite wild in her younger days. They all imagined Maria could be very fun and each of them, on occasion and quite improperly, imagined what it might be like to be with her, not stopping to consider if she'd ever want to be with any of them. Jason began to regret some of the unwarranted comments that had been made about her.

While Jason showered, he imagined walking in the rain with Colleen. She wasn't the same pretty as Maria. She had a mysterious beauty. This really was silly! He was setting himself up for the mother of all heartbreaks. *You're basically an idiot and it won't take her long to find out. You have nothing real to offer such a classy lady. Better quit while you're ahead.* It wasn't working... the eyes, the dimples, that long brown hair with just enough curl, those legs. He imagined her taking off her stockings behind the changing rooms at the track. What did she see in him? Was it really Moses who had made the evening? *Definitely.* Could there be an evening without Moses? "Why" was becoming more important than ever. *Philosophy!*

"You're here so that I can love you," his mom told him as she tickled his tummy with her nose and kissed him and kissed him. That was what he remembered most about his mom, and that was really the last time he'd thought about such a silly question until now.

Was Colleen here so that he could love her? *Stop it, you idiot!* He was falling too fast. *Why? Oh, my gosh, another why. Life's not fair!* He was thinking silly thoughts again, much different silly thoughts, but silly thoughts that somehow didn't seem quite so silly. *Focus. Why am I?* The legs, the eyes, the hair. It was no use.

"It's not fair! Why, Moses? Why did you come over?" Jason yelled at the ceiling.

Jason dried himself and readied for bed. *Stop thinking, stop thinking.* But he couldn't. He lay down on top of the covers unable to sleep. Not realizing that he did.

***

Colleen was back on his mind, and Moses was there too. He opened his eyes to the brightness of morning. He turned to face the clock; it was already ten thirty. He didn't remember setting his coffee maker, but the beckoning aroma assured him he had. He peeled himself out of bed and downed his coffee thinking only of the night before. Jason phoned Charles; he needed a distraction.

"Hey, Charles, what's up?"

"Diapers. Rachel's gone out for a break with her sister."

"Want some company?"

"Know how to change diapers?"

"I could learn."

There was a pause. "What happened to you? You'd better come over."

Jason dressed and headed out. Soon he was knocking on Charles' door.

It took a while, but Charles eventually greeted him, crying baby on hip. "I'm afraid Linda is not too *linda* right now. She's like this when Mom goes out. It's been a half hour or so."

"Let me try," Jason said as he reached for the baby. He took her and began rocking her in his arms, quite adeptly for a bachelor.

"Man, what happened to you?"

"You know that girl at the elevator?"

"The accountant you've been eyeing for-ev-er?"

"Her name's Colleen. We went out last night."

"Baby fever already? Are you sure she's not some voodoo princess or something?"

"It's not baby fever. It's more like a high school crush. It's crazy!" Linda stopped crying.

Charles was amazed. "Maybe it should be baby fever. She never stops crying that fast."

"She's asleep."

"She never sleeps that fast. Dude!" Charles took Linda and laid her gently in her crib, covered her with her blankie and raised the side. "Tippy-toes, dude, let's get out of here while we can."

"Just leave her?"

"Baby monitor. Coffee's downstairs. I haven't had mine yet. Poop and mush and crying."

Charles grabbed the other end of the baby monitor from the family room and they both headed for the kitchen. "First few months are rough, man. No sleep, no proper meals, no me-time. It's all about mama and baby. Anytime I get even close to Rachel, she just falls asleep. She's so tired she's angry." Charles raised his hands and snapped at imaginary flies. "Snap, snap, snap. Like a turtle. So, what about you, man?" he asked. "You went out? With a girl! That's so not you. You're boring."

"Thanks, that's just what I came here to hear."

"No, man! I mean, you hold your own at Tink's. You're a founding bachelor! But 'no dates allowed,' that was you, man."

"The Bachelors of Ales is done."

"True that, but man, who let the tiger out?"

"I'm not exactly a tiger, more of a mouse, a lemming actually. I think I'm headed for the cliff. Was that really me? No dates?"

"Absolutely, with unanimous approval. It meant Wednesdays to us, but we all thought it meant ever for you."

"Not really, but the BAs are gone, ergo the resolution is gone, ergo I went on a date last night."

"Where did you take her?"

"Tink's."

Charles clutched his heart and fell back into his chair. "Sacrosanct! Blasphemy! Say it isn't so!"

"It is."

"You can't take dates there! You're done, man. Lose her number. Seriously."

"She liked it. I walked her home and we talked. We connected."

"Did you kiss her?"

"She's not like that. We held hands and we... hugged."

"Dude! She's totally like that. She's hot! Even dressed like my momma, she can't hide those curves. You totally should have kissed her."

"Why am I talking to you? You and Rachel are all hands."

"Our hands are full of baby now, man."

"But you're not my go-to for relationship advice."

"The relationship advice you need is how to find the start button because there ain't never been any relationship to 'advice' you on!"

"I don't know if this really is a relationship," Jason confessed, "but I want it to be."

"Did you feel fire in your belly?"

"More like a warm glow in my heart, all over, but mostly my heart."

Charles made a descending whistle and slumped toward the table. "You're done, dude. Toast. Another one bites the dust. Tuxedo time."

"I came here to stop thinking about all this!"

"'All this? There's more 'this'?" Charles asked. "What 'this'?"

"You know... Moses."

"No, no, no, dude! Tell me you didn't do that. Moses was not there!"

"It was the only free table."

"I know I always tell you you're waiting too long, but this is one time you ought to have waited. Dude! No wonder it feels like a high school crush. It was a high school date. Papa Moses was there. Oh, man."

"We connected."

"You're done, dude. Toast. This ain't never gonna work."

"You think?"

"I know. Double date high school." Charles spread his fingers and wobbled his hand. "Maybe. Double date grownup." Charles grimaced. "Sketchy. Threesome." Charles gave thumbs down and shook his head. "No chance. Lose her number."

"I don't have her number—"

"Told ya."

"But we agreed to go out again."

"She said. Good luck on that one."

"Why am I listening to you anyway?" Jason said. "I came here specifically not to talk about this."

"Good plan. If I were you, I wouldn't talk about this ever. Unless you're alone in a closet... with the door closed... and you whisper."

"That bad?"

"Worse. More worse."

"Do you remember our philosophy profs?" Jason asked.

"Not."

"Why didn't any of us take philosophy?"

"Class average equals fifty-seven."

"Who took philosophy?"

"Weird kids, who probably still live with their parents."

"How weird?"

"Arts-major weird."

"What do you think they're doing now?"

"Living with their parents."

"Why do you think they took philosophy?" Jason asked.

"Dude. Weird!"

"Why did Texas A&M even offer philosophy?"

"I guess so all those weird kids living at home with their parents could have jobs."

"What else could they do?"

"Flip burgers; drive garbage trucks."

"Government clerks."

"Dude, you nailed it." Charles leaned back in his chair and gave two thumbs up. "PhD in philosophy. That's how they can come up with forms nobody understands that you have to fill out in triplicate before they tell you you're in the wrong department."

"If it were easier to get A's, do you think we would have taken it?"

"Dude! Weirdos. Philosophy and business don't mix."

"Why?" There it was again.

"Because if you sit and think too much, you won't get nothin' done."

Jason and Charles heard a loud squirt over the baby monitor. "That one probably blew right by the leg holes." Charles shuddered. "Come see what you're missing. You might feel better about blowing your chance with the elevator babe."

A distinctive aroma reached the top of the stairs before Jason and Charles did. "Oh, man! I'll probably have to wash her blankie now—and a bunch of other stuff."

It was very messy and Jason stood well back. "You're definitely mama's girl right now. My little girl could never do that," Charles said. He finished changing Linda, held her up, face to face, and asked, "Are you sure you're not the neighbour's little girl? That was nasty."

"I don't know why she's not crying right now," Charles said to Jason. "You should come over more often. I'd let you hold her if she wasn't being so good."

They brought Linda downstairs and Charles sat bouncing her on his knee. "Pour us more coffee. I bought doughnuts last night. They're in the fridge."

Jason served coffee and doughnuts and sat watching Charles play with Linda.

"Don't get your hopes up. This ain't going to last very long. She's just doing this to trick you. You know, babysitting. If she was her usual self, there'd be no chance of that. Zip, nil, nada."

"She looks a lot like Rachel, but she has your hair."

"Yea, yea, yea. Hardy har har. It's common for a baby's hair not to grow in for a few months. She's going to have hair like that girl in the elevator when she grows up."

"You noticed too?"

"Dude, she could be a shampoo commercial. I don't know what she sees in you. Too bad you already blew it."

"I can always count on you for support. I don't think I blew it yet."

"She must be nicer than I thought. She's letting you down real easy. Most girls, you'd be here with a flaming arrow through your heart. Three's a crowd, dude. Didn't your daddy teach you nothing?"

"Splitsville—no dad—remember?"

"Even your momma should have taught you that."

"By six years old? Do you think that's why I've never met anyone? No dad. Mom died early?"

"You're just plain weird. I'm surprised you didn't take philosophy."

"I'm not weird enough to want a fifty-seven percent."

"Maybe that's because only weird people take that stuff. Maybe normal people would get normal grades."

"You're forgetting your stats. Class average is normal, by definition."

"Maybe normal for normal people would be higher than normal for weird people."

"I guess that would depend on which end of weird they're on." Jason was starting to realize that last Wednesday's Bachelors of Ales meeting had only been tabled until now. He was glad he wasn't obsessing about Colleen, but he was beginning to see that their Wednesday frivolities had always been a distraction to avoid the truth that they had nothing to do. "What was philosophy all about any way?"

"Dude, school's done. You won't get any percent now."

"But did we miss something?"

"No hot chicks in there, man. None. Long skirts and thick glasses." Charles faked a shudder.

The conversation was boring. It had all been said before, many iterations and variations, but nothing new. "Are we wasting our lives?" Jason asked sadly.

"Not me, dude. I've got a wife, a kid, a house, a car, a mortgage, a big mortgage, a huge mortgage. I haven't got time to waste my life."

This conversation would—could—only go where it had always gone. It was boring.

"I'm going to head. Say hi to Rachel."

"She'll be sorry she missed you," Charles lied. Charles knew the conversation wasn't done. They were in the middle. But there was only a middle to that conversation. It was a huge conversation that never led to an end; it went better with beer, anyway. It was too sobering to have without beer. *We're best friends*, Charles thought, *but we're different. Jason probably should have taken philosophy.*

Jason couldn't quite remember what he and Colleen had discussed but he knew it was much more meaningful than this. He remembered her looks and decided that, even if the conversation weren't any better, it would be better with her. He remembered her bare feet and the legs that looked just as good without stockings—better. He felt a bit jealous that Charles had noticed her hair before he did.

Jason walked. He wound up at Northside High and sat on the bleachers behind the baseball diamond. He took off his shoes and socks. Life had changed. There was no going back, and forward scared him. *Limbo is much easier,* he thought. *At least I know her.* It grew dark while he sat there.

Jason didn't want to go to Tink's even though he wanted a Tink's Tower Burger. He settled for a TV dinner and beer at home. He pledged to find a six pack of good ale at the liquor exchange, swearing off the type of beer found at CornerMart. Jason was surprised that thoughts of Colleen were second to thoughts of "who am I?"

I am a man. I am a business area analyst. I am shallow. Where did that come from? I am a Texas A&M alumnus. I am a PhD. Am I what I do? Am I what I have done? Am I what I will do? I am my parent's son. I am a son whose dad left him. I am a son whose mom died. Am I a virtual orphan? Am I at all? If I'm not, is anything? These thoughts would have seemed silly last week; they never would have occurred to him. But now they seemed important. They were important to Colleen too; he knew it. He fell asleep with many such thoughts.

***

The next morning, Jason decided to visit his mom. He made toast and coffee, stopped at CornerMart for flowers, walked over to Elysian Street and caught the bus to the Golden Gate Cemetery.

"Why did you leave, mom? I'm still not ready. How do I talk to girls? What do women want?" Jason knelt down and cleared some dried leaves and weeds from around the gravestone as he spoke. "What do you think about Colleen? Were you there? Where are you? Are you?" Jason leaned back on his heels. He was crying—he always cried—but this was a different cry. His thoughts felt like they meant more now.

He stayed there all day. Things were different; he was scared. He wanted someone to advise him, but he didn't have anyone. *Maybe Moses could.* That thought was even scarier. His mom should still be here. His dad should never have left. Maybe it was better that he had left. *What kind of advice would come from someone who could do that?* Maybe some dads had good cause to leave their families, but not his dad. Did his dad ever think of him?

Moses or no Moses, I want a Tink's Tower with fries and gravy, Jason decided.

He entered Tink's cautiously and looked over to the corner.

"You're safe. He already left," Maria said as she followed Jason to an empty table. She already had his ale. "No more lager for you, I'm guessing. Tower and fries?"

"With gravy, and you're right."

"Ale is much better for thinking," Maria said.

It was the little things like that that made everyone like Maria. She was always attentive, always polite and always cheerful. She was a little older but still very attractive. She liked teasing people but was sensitive to their limits. She knew that, tonight, Jason needed to think so she left him to it.

Jason enjoyed his dinner and another tankard of ale. Maria brought him a piece of Triple Chocolate Lava Cake on the house. The fresh breeze at the cemetery and all of his thinking exhausted Jason. He went home, showered and was soon asleep.

Monday

Jason got up without hitting the snooze button, ate quickly and made sure he would be at the office early enough so he wouldn't miss Colleen. She was already there, awkwardly trying not to be obvious. What can one do in such a sparse lobby other than take the elevator? She smiled broadly, blushing beautifully, when she saw Jason.

"I see we both had the same plan," Jason said. "Coffee after work?"

"Not Tink's?"

"Coffee. Just you and me, a quiet place, the two of us."

"Five-ish?"

"Five-ish."

They were both earlier than anyone else so they had ten floors to hold hands. Jason held the door open and leaned out to watch Colleen walk down the hall. "Five-ish," he called out.

Colleen turned, smiling, "Five-ish," and blew him a kiss.

The solitary ride for the remaining twenty-two floors was very sweet. Jason didn't think of work until he opened his office door and saw the red light on his phone flashing furiously. Most of the messages were merely reminders of issues already on agendas for the usual slew of Monday meetings. Some offered pertinent information. One requested his presence at the board meeting. He would have to reschedule two meetings and brief his co-chair of a third in order to attend.

I hope this isn't as big a waste of time as the last one, he thought. *Not even an agenda.* Previous times he was given background for the item he would be addressing. Usually he sat idly in the anteroom for most of the meeting. He wondered why they couldn't schedule the meeting so the issues they needed him for were addressed earlier and then dismiss him.

Why keep me hanging around after they've heard my report? "All my answers are clear, concise and complete," he said to his notepad. "Ten minutes to talk and three hours to twiddle my thumbs."

Gail knocked on his door and opened it. "You're early today."

Jason blushed. "Busy Monday," he said. "As usual, the directors have given me plenty of notice to appear at their board meeting. You'll have to reschedule my eleven and my one. Charles can chair the ten, but you'll have to bring him up to speed on the stuff we went over last Thursday. I should be back for two but you can cancel if I'm not. It's just a touch base."

"Right, do you need background?"

"I might if I knew what for."

"Another one of those?"

"Probably."

"Anything else?"

"Contact InSyst," Jason instructed. "They've got a slew of upgrades in the pipe for their I-Systems package. We need to stay ahead of this one. See if we can do some beta on any of it with our test banks."

"Should I schedule a meeting with Rasoul?"

"If he thinks he has enough. But no lunch unless InSyst picks up the tab."

Jason was where he hated most: no time to do anything but wait. He had too much to do to sit idle but too short a window between now and the directors' meeting. *They don't have a full bag of brains between the lot of them. Five-year plan that changes monthly. Always more to do and always fewer resources to do it with. 'Leaner and meaner'!*

"We get leaner and they get meaner," Jason said as he shuffled some files on his desk. "They move motions and expect us to move mountains."

Gail opened the door and leaned in. "McCrrrossun's uff tee Scotland feerrr a farrrtneet teemarrrew." Her brogue was awful. "He's critical for your one. Can I swap him in at three and bump your three to four?"

"I'm committed to something at five and my three's at three because it might run over. Do them sometime tomorrow morning."

"Breaking your own rules?"

"More like directors breaking my back." Jason decided the moment required pacing so he walked over to the water cooler, poured a cup and took it back to his desk; there were usually three or four full cups of water on his desk for the janitor. He looked at his watch. If he preened a bit in front of the mirror and took the stairs slowly, he wouldn't be too early. Besides, the carpet on the thirty-fifth floor was softer for pacing and the view was spectacular.

"Good morning," Jason said to Miss Grimm. She was aptly named. She always wore grey, never smiled and never returned a greeting. She just sat there, hunched over, scrawling away on her notepad. She would only raise her eyes to peer over her glasses, pull out the top drawer, turn a little with pen in hand and make a mark somewhere in the drawer. No one knew her first name.

"They'll call you," she always said.

It didn't matter if you sat or paced or tried to make small talk; she just sat there, hunched and scrawling. Charles once suggested she was writing romance novels. Jason choked and spilled his coffee. It was the only time she acknowledged anyone in the room. The coffee maker was gone the next day. It was replaced by a vase of plastic flowers that were almost as dull as Miss Grimm's suits.

Jason stared out the window, wondering what was coming. He wanted to think about Colleen but couldn't; Miss Grimm's cloud wouldn't let bright thoughts through. He had no idea what lay on the other side of the door. Suddenly he wondered, *Has my paycheque become too fat for this lean department?* He tried to convince himself that it couldn't but only succeeded in convincing himself. *This department has become too lean for my fat paycheque.*

The whole room became gloomy. The thirty-fifth floor view became a swamp of offices, a sea of businesses, none of them with research departments. He couldn't pace. The more he stood staring, the surer he was that he was being let go and the darker Miss Grimm's cloud became. A light flashed on Miss Grimm's desk. "Go in," she said without interrupting her scrawling.

"Jason!" Mr. Rosenthal called out. As Jason entered, his boss rose, strode over and grasped his hand, shaking it vigorously. He led Jason to the plush chair on the near end of the long table where the board members were seated. He pulled it out and swivelled it a bit, saying, "Sit!" Jason sat and was pushed to position. The chair was very comfortable, much more comfortable than Jason. What did this mean?

John Patrick Burkeman Senior, informally known as J.P., sat across the table looking intently at Jason. He owned TechSys Corp and a great many other things.

The board members began to speak. "Do you have any investments other than your annual options?" Bruce Martins asked.

"No," Jason answered.

"Make sure your position doesn't change in any Burkeman-associated companies. It could be construed as insider trading. What we say here cannot leave this room. It's all classified and any mention will contravene your non-disclosure agreement."

"Okay," Jason accepted cautiously. At least he wasn't being fired... yet.

"We're about to become the target of a hostile takeover," J.P. said. "You know this company better than they know it themselves."

"InSyst," Jason intuited.

"InSyst's parent, technically," J.P. replied. "But, yes, this will be an epic battle. We didn't choose it, but we're in it."

"What do you want from me?"

"Mr. Rosenthal here is retiring," he said, gesturing to Sal. "You'll replace him as director of information technology."

"You're a critical success factor for both sides and we need you to be our CSF," Sal explained. "By joining the board, you'll be bound by the non-competition clause in your new contract. Ergo, no longer part of the package in a takeover."

"I'm a pawn," Jason declared evenly. "You're putting me on the board to take me off the board."

"To keep you on our board, more precisely," Patricia Avila said. "You play for our team or not at all. We can't afford to trade you; that's the big leagues!"

"News of your appointment will be released shortly," John Junior said. "You're about to find out just how rough the big boys play. We all believe you can stand toe to toe... but only because we have to."

"Any questions?" Sal asked.

"Do I have a choice?" Jason asked.

"Not practically. See Janice on your way out. She has some papers for you."

"Miss Grimm," Jason deduced.

"The romance novelist. She's not so bad once you're on this side of the door. You might even grow to like her."

Jason blushed. "You knew?"

"We're directors," Marco Lorenz said matter-of-factly. "Janice thought it was quite hilarious, actually.

"You can go now," Sal said. "We start at seven thirty up here, which means breakfast at six thirty. Don't stay out too late. Not a word to anyone... not even Colleen."

Jason gave Sal an astonished look. "Is there anything you don't know?"

"You've been well vetted," Sal said as he gathered some papers, curling them a bit and tapping the short edge on the table. "Relax."

"Think about what Pet said," Sandra Hetherington warned, nodding toward Patricia Avila. "Our team or no team. Cedric, our chauffeur, will be in the lobby at five to take you for a celebration dinner. Colleen will like it."

Jason's head was swimming as he sank into the couch in his new office; it was very comfy. He was alone—he needed to be. *What did I just do? Why didn't I ask more questions?* "They didn't give me time to think of any."

The phone rang, rousing him from his haze. He was the only one there so he answered. "It's four forty-five," Janice said. "You'll want to get ready. Don't keep Colleen waiting."

By the time Jason got to the lobby, Cedric had already collected Colleen. "What's going on?" she asked. "Friday was supposed to be coffee and wound up Tink's. Today, coffee's turning into something quite different. I'm not use to this kind of thing and I'm not sure I should go."

"Actually," Jason answered, "I had no idea about this, this morning. I got a promotion and this is a congratulation dinner for us."

After five more minutes of assurances and promises, Colleen acquiesced. Cedric opened the door to the TechSys limo and helped her in. Jason got in and sat across from her. Colleen was scared but excited. She felt very strange. *What's going on? I don't like it. I don't want it... Yes, I do.*

"I promise you," Jason said as he rubbed his palm nervously. "I'm not like this. I'm actually pretty boring."

Colleen looked at Jason with her big blue eyes, leaned forward, took his hand and stroked it tenderly. She sensed that Jason was just as uncomfortable as she was. Somehow that comforted her. "I like boring." She felt strange in a very different way. "But we're here now, so let's try to enjoy it."

Jason squeezed Colleen's hand and smiled. He was looking at her from no more than four feet away yet his gaze extended much further into a distant space—they were here, but where was here? "Yes," he said, "we're here. But so is today." He squeezed her hand again.

Cedric stopped in front of the Regency Club. He got out, ran round to the curb, opened the door and helped Colleen out. "You'll need this," he said to Jason and offered him a card.

It was a Regency Club membership card with his name on it. He showed the card to the doorman who ushered them in. Jason offered his elbow to Colleen and led her into very posh surroundings that he was definitely not familiar with.

The maître d' approached them. "Miss Grimm called with your reservation. This way, sir." He led them to a small private room. "All has been arranged."

There was a bottle of Veuve Clicquot in an ice bucket beside a table set for two. The maître d' pulled out the chair for Colleen and seated her; Jason sat in the other chair. Their waiter appeared promptly with two watercress salads.

"Pierre," he said with a deep bow. "Pardon my haste with the champagne and salad, but I was informed that you would be retiring early as you have a busy schedule tomorrow."

The salad was delicious. They were both still too overwhelmed to say anything. Next came filet mignon with black truffles, roast baby potatoes and asparagus, also delicious.

"Don't get use to this," Jason warned. "I'm more of a Tink's person."

"This is very nice," Colleen said, "but I'm also more Tinkish."

Jason was hooked, and scared. Colleen was supposed to be consolation for the death of his teenaged past. This wasn't his plan. None of this was his plan! It was too much and too fast. There was no plan! This would have been perfect if he had planned it first and slowed it down. The comfortable distant life he seldom dreamed about was becoming a chaotic present. He didn't want to let the Colleen part go, and he couldn't let the work part go.

Neither of them needed champagne to make their heads spin, but they enjoyed it all the same. They managed to coo just a few words before the chocolate mousse arrived.

"Anything else?" Pierre asked. "Coffee, tea, digestif?"

"Nothing," Jason said.

"It was very nice, thank you," Colleen added.

Pierre left and they finished their dessert. Jason reached across the table with both hands. Colleen took them. "I'm sorry," he said.

"I'm glad," Colleen replied. "This was nice to experience, but I'm glad it's not us." They looked into each other's eyes until Jason broke the spell. He rose and led her out. Cedric was waiting.

They took Colleen home first and Jason escorted her to her door. There, they kissed. Jason would always remember that kiss. In all the craziness of that day, he would always remember that kiss. It would always be 'that kiss.' He thought of nothing but that kiss all the way home.

Jason thanked Cedric and went inside. It was definitely a long-soak-in-the-tub day. There was so much to think about that he thought of nothing. He was being pushed and pulled into a now that should be a far distant horizon. He wasn't ready to go. He wasn't willing to go. But go he must... no map, no helmet, no parachute.

Breakfast

Jason entered the executive lounge at six fifteen (he understood what six thirty meant). Sal was already seated. He beckoned Jason to join him.

"I will be your mentor," Sal said. "You've been plucked from an executive position you haven't fully experienced and tossed into a directorship you shouldn't face until you've survived not just a few skirmishes but some brutal and decisive battles. Don't think anyone is doing you any favours. You're here because we're desperate. I can't join this battle because I have a past; it's a past I'll never talk about and never admit to. You will have such a past if you don't want to wind up dead, not corporally but corporately. If you lose this battle, your career will be dead; you won't even be able to be a janitor anywhere. We didn't start this battle; they did. Because they think they'll win. You've been recruited for the front line on a suicide mission. To be fair, fate chose you more than J.P. did."

"All that before coffee?" Jason asked.

"Keep that humour. It'll serve you well. But beware of others' humour—don't believe any of it," Sal warned. "From here on, nothing will be humorous. It will all be serious. Deadly serious. Humour will just be a means of concealing a blindside attack."

"This is ominous. Not humorous at all."

"It needs to be! I was dealt a rotten hand even though I didn't ante. The hand I was dealt must be played and, since I was kept out of the game, you must be my proxy. Everyone considers you a sacrificial pawn. You must foster that illusion. In front of our board. In front of our opponents. But mostly, in the back of your mind. I know your true role. J.P.

knows your true role. And you must come to know your true role."

"Which is not the skirmish between two tech companies that the other directors think it is," Jason calculated.

"Exactly. Our battle must be waged on a different field. If we win our battle, we win theirs. But we have little chance of success if anyone else even has a clue before it's too late for them to counter. There's a lot for you to know and no time for you to learn it. It's natural that I should transition my successor; I must familiarize you with the day-to-day routine. There's no time for that. You must intuit that on your own. I must launch you up to the dizzying heights that most will never know even exist. This is a battle of titans.

"John Patrick Burkeman is a member of the Circle. Until one is in the Circle, the Circle is just a rumour. Even I shouldn't know about it, but J.P. and I were not just Tri-D roommates; we did everything together. From the time I lined up behind him during our first registration at Harvard, I've been behind him in everything. I've had his back and what I did—which I will never admit to—I did so he wouldn't have to. They would have destroyed him. But they were so busy watching him that they didn't see me coming until it was too late. I know that got him into the Circle."

"So why tell me?" Jason asked. "If what you're telling me is true, you can't tell me."

"Because you are me. You must be me," Sal stressed. "If I cannot make you me, we will lose. Someone played a trump card that put me out of the game. I need to be in the game but I'm dead now. You are my spectre."

"So... if I'm you, I already know who our opponent is."

"Once I tell you, there is no retreat. You are accepting that your life is no longer yours. You will be me, doing what I do."

Jason was afraid to agree but knew he'd been sucked into a black hole. Old Jason was being ripped apart at the threshold, and new Jason would exist in a void no one could know. "What about Colleen?"

"She slipped in by mistake. J.P. will try to accustom her to your new lifestyle; she's already tasted it. She will be one more nail in your coffin. She'll want what we give you so you'll have to stay if you want to keep her. She'll also be good defence against any honeypot traps our enemies might arrange."

"So, I'm being used and she's being used. Neither of us has any say?"

"Very little," Sal stated honestly. "There's always a chance you'll die, but failing that, no."

"I see my past is dead. Does hers have to be?"

"Your past self still wants to rescue her, but your new self can't. You'll be glad in the end, if you survive."

"If I survive!"

"Don't worry. You must survive. I always do."

"I'm beginning to hate you right now."

"You'll come to hate me more until you realize this is all a game that someone else is controlling."

"Is anyone really controlling it?"

"The Circle Boys," Sal said. "But who knows how or why."

"What about Tink's?" It was the only other thing Jason truly cared about.

"It's a good cover. Keep it," Sal allowed. "But it won't be Tink's anymore. Everything will be this."

Jason was sorry that Colleen was being dragged into this, but convinced himself he wasn't responsible. Tink's, on the other hand... Tink's he knew well. How dare they take that from him! . "Colleen likes Tink's," Jason said. "I'm glad we don't have to take Tink's from her."

It was a sweet sentiment that scared Sal and he frowned. "Yes, at least we can spare her that."

Jason mistook Sal's frown for concern about Colleen. It actually betrayed Sal's true thoughts. *I would not have such concerns. You are me so you cannot have such concerns.*

Sal abruptly got back to the business at hand. "You can talk to me, and you can talk to J.P. when he makes himself available. Do not mention anything to anyone else until you learn the limits for each of them. They all have limits and each limit is different. I have officially stepped down, but during our transition, I will be beside you at all of your meetings. Don't be surprised to find bruises on your shin; the kicks will be cues that you're about to venture too far. Mostly, let them talk to you. If you need someone to do something, make them come up with the idea."

"Where do we start?"

"Go to my office; it's ours now. There's no need to remove anything because you are me. I won't need to take anything with me to the Bahamas where I'll be put out to pasture with Myriam, my wife. That's the official version; the one I'll stick to. Self-deception can be a great thing. Perhaps you'll survive long enough to pretend to do the same thing. I doubt it. I'm still not sure I will." Sal's honesty and openness was scarier than the black hole Jason was spiralling into. "I will release a few files to you. Study them carefully. Go deeply into them. Become them."

Sal got up and left. He accepted his situation but would never like it. He would lie to himself for Myriam's sake but he would always know he lost. He hated Jason, yet Jason was Sal's one chance at retribution. If Jason survived, Sal would be vindicated and Sal's foes would be vanquished.

Sal exited and, as if by cue, others began arriving. Patricia took Sal's spot. "Now that you're on the board, you may call me Pet. We've decided to call you Onesie. See me in my office; you have papers to sign. Corporate insurance documents, code of conduct, that stuff." Her look was condescending. *How does this puppy not realize what a fool he is?* She would sit with him through breakfast for appearance sake, but really, it was beneath her. *Colleen is naive to the max! The two deserve each other.* These two had been handed on a silver platter everything she'd worked so hard for, and they were too innocent to even know what they had.

Pet raised her hand toward the valet. "Eggs Florentine for both of us." She wasn't about to let whatever Jason might order spoil her appetite. *There are limits to my generosity, and they can't expect me to take this that far.*

"So where did you go to school?" she asked, intending to rub her Harvard education in his face.

"Texas A&M," Jason replied obliviously.

Too stupid to realize I'm dissing him. "What house were you?" She knew there was no Tri Delta at Texas A&M. *He can't be too stupid to miss this one.*

"There are no frats there," Jason replied innocently. "There are dorms, but most students are local, still living at home or sharing basement suites."

Right over his head. Unbelievable! How dumb can he be?

It wasn't over his head at all, but this was the game. "Charles' parents let me stay at their place. Charles Jackson. Works here in architecture."

"Really? Who started here first?" Of course Pet knew all this, but she couldn't resist another not-so-subtle jab.

"Charles. Actually, he got me my first job here. I bet he never thought then that I'd wind up being his boss."

"Probably not." Pet was too proud to think of Jason as anything other than a sheep about to get shorn—very short! *Jason and the Golden Fleece,* she thought smugly, not knowing anything more than the title. *He's going to get a golden fleecing alright!* Pet was too smart to realize how ignorant she was.

Their breakfast arrived: yolks done to perfection, not too runny but not firm at all; two rashers of bacon, crispy but not burnt; cubed hashed browns, golden crispy and soft inside; three Roma tomato slices and a glass of fresh-squeezed grapefruit juice. The chef was Cordon Bleu.

Jason enjoyed the breakfast and portraying the yokel much better than the company. They ate quietly, eyeing each other. Jason wondered how Pet fit into the puzzle, and Pet wondered how they would pass off the idiot as a bona fide board member.

They both finished about the same time. "I'll see you in my office to sign those papers," Pet said. "Soon." She wasn't about to relinquish any control.

"Right away," Jason agreed. He wasn't about to agitate the hostility he sensed.

"In one hour. I've got a few things to do first," Pet lied. She had to establish the pecking order.

That suited Jason just fine; he had time to find out a bit more about Pet before their meeting.

Pet got up to leave. As she opened the door, she turned back to Jason. "One hour!"

Well, then, Jason thought as he dabbed the corners of his mouth with the linen napkin. He laid the napkin neatly beside his plate, sipped down the last of his coffee and rose as the waiter came to collect the dishes. "What's your name?" Jason asked him.

"José," the waiter said, "but I come for however. They are mostly just do this." He held up his index finger and wiggled it.

"Thank you, José," Jason said, nodding to him. "And what's the chef's name?"

"See-mone," José answered. "Don't to ever call him Sigh-mon," he warned.

"Thank you, Simon," Jason called out toward the swinging door, not sure that Simon could hear. "That was an excellent breakfast."

"You're welcome, Mr. Johnstone," a very French accent responded. "*Mon plaisir.*"

The Rest of the Day

Jason had to weave through a maze of workmen and loose wires as he made his way to the elevator. TechSys was restricted to the top five floors by existing lease agreements when they bought the building but now, with the expiry of two tenant companies' leases, the rest of the TechSys workers were migrating over from Burkeman Tower and communication wiring was being installed. *I miss my construction days,* Jason thought. *Everything was so much simpler.*

In the elevator, Jason pressed thirty-five. His new office was at the end of the hall on the thirty-fifth floor, the corner next to J.P.'s. The other directors wondered how long it would be before the shuffle; surely that office was John Junior's destiny. Bruce and Pet both felt they would be awarded J.J.'s old corner and Onesie would wind up in the vacated middle office.

"What did you learn from Pet?" Sal asked in greeting.

"Don't turn my back."

"Good," Sal assessed. "She's vicious and she's capable. She's Delta Sigma Chi, but J.J. and Brew, being devout Tri Deltas, claim only the Delta counts. Collectively, they're referred to as the Junior Deltas; J.P. and I are the Senior Deltas. Marco and Sandy got here by ability so there's mutual resentment and hostility. It's childish, but it's also fact. Bonds formed in hazing and drunken toga parties will never be broken. I'm just as guilty of that. The last vestige of our childhood innocence we'll take to our death. A desperate attempt to cling to that which has been ripped from us by the harsh realities of the corporate world."

Although Sal's words were still sinking in, they were already ominous. "I'm not sure what part of that I like least," Jason said. Sal continued on;

he obviously considered understanding the players to be more important than understanding the business. Jason looked at his watch. "I have to sign some papers with Pet," he said as he headed to the door.

"That should only take five minutes," Sal guessed. "I'll have these files ready by the time you get back." Jason left the room.

Sal finished just as Jason returned. "Read these carefully. All these people are your enemies, but the friendliest of your enemies. Be consoled that they are also each other's enemy, even the Deltas, when push comes to shove. Form alliances carefully and always keep me at your back. No one but you and J.P. know I'm in play. Trust no one except me."

"And why should I trust you?"

"Because the only way I survive is if you survive. I'm not backing you; I'm backing myself."

"And how can I trust that?"

"There has to be trust somewhere." That was an eternal truth and a good place to pause. Sal got up and opened J.J.'s file on the computer. "May as well start at the top. J.J. hasn't inherited any of his dad's finesse. He'll turn on you in a flash. Never go down dark alleys with him."

The file went back to J.J.'s childhood, incidents that gave insight to his reactions, his scars, his dashed hopes. There was a series of surveillance reports from a detective. *Who authorizes clandestine observation of the boss' son?* wondered Jason. It was all there: his marriages, his kids, his affairs, more kids, drunken holidays, anything that might provide leverage.

There were similar files on every board member and every top executive, even J.P. The only exception was Sal. *This is Sal's arsenal. Perhaps a little trust is warranted.* There were also folders with files on other companies. Jason's enemies were all here. Some of the disclosures were horrendous and shocking; others were only embarrassing. But all were ammunition. Jason was becoming aware that all allegiances were strategic and none were sincere. *What a world.*

Jason was completely absorbed by the files when Sal said, "It's approaching five o'clock." It was important to his plan that Jason's rendezvous with Colleen be kept promptly.

Jason finished the paragraph and shut down the computer as Sal instructed. "Sleep mode is not safe enough; shut it down. There are a lot of very capable techies on both sides and you shouldn't trust any of them. This absolutely cannot get into anyone's hands. Unplug the damn thing!" Jason switched off the power bar.

Jason beat Colleen to the lobby by three minutes. *I'm desperate, Colleen. I need you! I think I love you. Regardless, I can't do this without you and I will love you.* Jason was panicking as calmly as he could; Colleen was the part of his new life that terrified him the least. The elevator door opened and she appeared. They walked toward each other and Jason embraced her. *Sanctuary!*

"I'm in the mood for Tink's tonight," Colleen said.

"Good! I am too."

"It would be nice if Moses was there," Colleen said. "He's an odd sort of character but there's something I really like about him. He makes me strangely comfortable."

"He's very odd," Jason agreed. "He made me uncomfortable at first; I think because he pointed out things that I should think about but never had. Now I can't stop them from popping up at the oddest times. They're distracting."

"Do I pop up? Am I distracting?"

Jason blushed. He would never admit the truth about that question. "How could you not pop into my mind? Of course I find you distracting, in the most delightful sort of way." He pecked her on the cheek.

"Is that the best kiss you've got for me?" Colleen teased.

"Yes, if you still want to make it to Tink's sometime today."

"Okay. After Tink's."

Jason blushed a deeper red. "After Tink's."

Jason and Colleen snuggled all through their train ride. They held hands and swung them slowly during the short walk from Quitman Station to Tink's. Neither said a word; both were thinking about after Tink's.

Moses was seated, as usual, in the corner booth. He smiled warmly and motioned them over as if he'd been waiting for them. "My favourite couple!" he said as Jason and Colleen slid into the booth. "Are you officially a couple yet? You will be, you know."

Jason and Colleen looked at each other, smiled identical broad smiles and blushed. “Yes,” they both said softly.

“Good, good,” Moses said. “It’s too soon, in the strictest sense of things, but about time for this old man. Love is the best thing in the world and it’s best expressed between two youngsters like you. It may ebb and flow, but it will tide you over through the worst of times if you do it.”

“The last time we saw you, it was actually our first date.” Jason had no idea why he said it; he regretted saying it.

“Strange thing to do on a first date,” Moses said, “sitting with a stranger.”

“Well,” Jason replied, “they were the only seats available, and you weren’t completely a stranger.”

“I’m stranger than most, I have to admit, but at least you’ll have a good tale to tell your kids. You will have kids?”

Colleen blushed. “It’s too soon, in the strictest sense of things,” she teased, “to talk of such things.” She didn’t want to admit, even to herself, that she had thought of such things.

“But they are the true fruit of love. You will never know love fully without them. They will bring you deeper in sorrow and higher in joy than all else. There is no love until there are two, and it is not complete until there are three, and the third must be of the two.”

“We’ve only just started to be a couple,” Jason said.

“You will be one if you choose to be one,” Moses said. “The stars in your eyes don’t lie.”

Maria arrived with a pint of ale and a pinot grigio, and Jason was thankful for the distraction. Moses and Sal agreed, for very different reasons, on Jason and Colleen’s fate. That worried Jason, even though he desperately wanted them to be right. He felt a lack of control over everything in his life. “I wonder if we truly chose anything,” Jason said.

“Free will or destiny,” Moses said. “A question for the ages. Is this universe a giant clock that has been wound and left to run down? Are our deeds action or reaction, choice or consequence? Are we master or puppet?”

“Free will is an illusion,” Jason said. “I’m being shown that more and more these days.”

"Think carefully before you commit," Moses warned. "Especially in front of your lady. If you cannot choose, you do not love."

"I don't follow."

"If you are doing as you must do and can do no other, there is no love, no hate, no right, no wrong. There just is, no merit, no guilt," Moses said. "You are until you're not, and that is that."

"That may be," Jason said.

"You've just robbed yourself of purpose and conscience," Moses warned. "If that's your life, why live?"

Colleen understood the implication. "But my choice may not be your choice. What then?"

"We cannot choose what others won't let us choose," Jason said. "No matter how much we want or don't want something, we can't have it or prevent it by ourselves."

"We can choose only from what's there," Moses said.

"Sometimes we're robbed of our free will," Jason said. "It's not free; it's dependent."

"Communal," Colleen said.

"We choose to be with those who choose as we do," Jason said.

"Society in a nutshell," Moses said. "Freedom of association."

"The pilgrims," Jason said.

"My ancestors who fled the British and blighted potatoes," Colleen said.

"Your Bachelors of Ales," Moses said.

"But even so, everyone will not always agree," Jason said.

"Democracy," Colleen said.

"Dictatorship," Jason said. "Coercion."

"Education and detente," Moses said.

"Carrot and stick," Colleen said.

"Choices that allow choices," Moses said.

"But we can't always choose," Jason said. "Is it choice when there's only one option? Sometimes it's not for us to choose, only to do as others choose."

"Or stay or go," Colleen reminded him.

"It's not always possible to go."

Maria arrived to take their order. "Steak and mushroom pie today."

"Sounds yummy," Colleen said.

"Two," Jason said.

"Three it is, then," Maria said.

"Thank you, Maria," Moses confirmed, "and another round."

"Of course."

"So this is a fine society, then," Moses joked. "We all chose the same choice!"

"But how can we know the best choice?" Colleen asked.

"Know who you are, what you are, and choose to be that," Moses replied.

"Who, if you please," Colleen protested.

"But what is a 'who'?" Moses asked.

"A person," Colleen said, "with a unique identity."

"And what is a person?" Moses continued. "What makes a person a person?"

"A body, a mind, a soul," Colleen answered.

"And a heart," Moses added. "But where do they come from? Who made body, mind, heart and soul? Who chose which body, mind, heart and soul would become which person?"

"God, I suppose," Colleen said.

"Where is this going?" Jason asked.

"Just this," Moses said. "There is creator and there is created. What is created is determined by the creator. No man is his own creator; no man can put himself in his mother's womb."

"That's just a biological process," Jason said.

"That may be so for the body," Moses conceded. "But what of the mind, the heart and the soul?"

"So are you some kind of priest?" Colleen asked.

"Far from it," Moses confessed. "I'm a man who stopped to think, who was forced to think."

"And what did you think?" Jason asked.

"I miss love. I want it back."

"And that got you here?"

"Yes, because there's no love in random," Moses replied. "Love must be a choice, ergo will, ergo intelligence, ergo purpose."

Maria arrived with their steak and mushroom pies. They were served with garlic mashed potatoes and a side garden salad with house dressing.

"Ah! Something I can digest," Jason joked.

"Is this the type of thing you always think about?" Colleen asked.

"Truth, beauty, goodness and love," Moses answered. "It's what we desire and what we must think of, whether we recognize it or not. What they are. Where they are. How to get them."

"You forgot pleasure," Jason said. "That's a big one."

"Pleasure is the petulant child of goodness," Moses said. "It's very hard to keep him in his place."

"Those are all very big topics," Colleen said. "Where does one start?"

"There is but one true end. There are many paths that lead there and many more that lead to a false end," Moses said. "The best place to start is at the end."

"Which end might you recommend?" Jason asked.

"Love. It is the end and it is the way," Moses claimed. "To know love will put you on your path. To lose sight of love will mean you have strayed from your path."

"Do you have any other advice that I won't understand?" Jason joked.

"Learn who you are and be who you are," Moses said. "Know where you came from and why."

"That would be it," Jason said.

"You have skills and abilities. You have interests and desires," Moses explained. "Their sum is you. Their unique combination will point to your purpose, and your purpose to your path."

"You sound like my career planning prof."

"Did you keep your notes?"

"For twelve years?"

"Are you still pursuing the same course?" Colleen asked.

"Yes, actually," Jason said, a bit surprised himself, "with a bit of a jag yesterday."

"So I read," Moses revealed.

"Where?" Jason asked.

"Business section of any newspaper," Moses said. "It's news when J.P.

Burkeman announces anything... but board appointments. That's big."

"I didn't know you followed business," Jason said.

"You don't know yourself yet," Moses teased. "What makes you think you might know me?"

"Don't judge a man by his cover," Colleen quipped.

Dessert arrived. "Pardon the interruption, but if I don't bring it now, you'll be having vanilla ice cream," Maria explained. "We're almost out of lava cake."

"Thank you!" Moses said. "What would I do without you?"

"I suppose whatever you did before me."

"That's what scares me."

"Were you that bad?" Jason asked.

"I was who others expected me to be," Moses said. "I measured success with dollars and trinkets."

"Is that such a bad measure?"

"It was for me. It stoked my ego, which was already far too large. My ego grew and my *raison d'être* receded."

"And Maria helped you change?" Colleen asked.

"I grew much too big for me and bet too much on who I tried to be. I was gone; in my place stood the man I was expected to be. He dealt the cards in a game I shouldn't have been playing and I lost him. I was devastated," Moses said. "I hid from my shame in a pit of anger and hatred, but Maria dug me out and helped me find myself."

"How did she do that?" Jason asked, more because he liked the story than understood it.

"Maria is Maria," Moses said. "She is always Maria, little Maria. No pretentions. She serves, she smiles and she cares. She does her work and she loves her patrons. She doesn't try to be more than she is. She's happy, always joyful. I was happy each time I thought I had more, but more kept leaping further away. Each goal I met merely led to another goal, a further goal. The chase was the joy, and achievement just ended the chase. The more I got, the less I liked. The bigger I got, the bigger I needed to be. Then, pop! Maria noticed; Maria cared. Maria sat with me, and Maria was Maria. She helped me become little Moses." He stopped.

"Little Moses?" Jason wanted more.

"Yes, little Moses. I am who I am. No pomp, no pretense. The Moses you see is the Moses that is. I have all that I need and more to spare. This is the Moses that loves."

"But you must have loved before this," Colleen insisted.

"I loved taking, which is very perverse," Moses said, "because true love is giving."

They all paused to think.

Moses watched Jason and Colleen think while he finished his Triple Chocolate Lava Cake. "Well, my friends," Moses said as he shuffled over and rose from the booth. "I'm taking again... your time! I'm sure a young couple like you has better things to do."

Jason remembered after-Tink's and blushed. Colleen was blushing too. Jason waved Maria over.

"It's already paid," Maria said.

Jason walked Colleen home. They had their after-Tink's on the baseball bleachers at Northside High. They sat, cuddling, and watched the stars. They were content. Jason wanted to stay longer but knew tomorrow would start very early. "I'd better get you home."

They had another after-Tink's at Colleen's door before she went in. Jason waited until Colleen's light came on before he left. A few paces later he turned and saw Colleen at the window, watching him. He blew her a kiss; she sent one in return and waved. Jason looked back again just before turning the corner. Colleen was still watching. Both waved once more.

Preparing for Battle

Jason arrived at six sharp the next morning; Sal was waiting for him in the executive lounge. "How did you do with J.J.'s file?" Sal asked.

"He's a bit of a flake and a definite cad."

"He's J.P.'s son."

"Even so, he must contribute something."

"He fills up space. He remembers what's said almost as well as a digital recorder and he trusts Daddy."

"So his primary function is to hear what's said when J.P.'s not there," Jason summarized.

"What is said when J.P. is not there often differs significantly from what is said when J.P. is there. He's also a solid Delta, and the other Junior Deltas confide in him. They're not aware just how much gets back to Senior; that's our secret. We don't let on that we know what they scheme behind our backs. We allow them a few successes."

"He's a mole," Jason said.

"He knows his place when it comes to his father; he doesn't know it relative to anyone else. He believes his heritage is enough. J.P. will never retire and, once he's gone, J.J. will find out just how savage this game is. His friends will turn on him just like that." Sal snapped his fingers.

"So he's my perfect first target. Very powerful, as long as J.P. is in control, and easy to snare."

"You've seen how many secrets he's hiding; more come regularly. It will be effort well spent to continue updating his file. Many of the items in there also work, to a lesser degree, on J.P.—primarily the ones that may dilute his legacy,"

"How much of this do the other directors know?"

"Very little. Even J.P. doesn't know all that's in here," Sal said. "He certainly doesn't know that I know."

"Yet, I do."

"And you'd better not let on that you do. I told you, you are me," Sal reiterated. "You must be and you must know that you are. You will be wealthier than you can imagine if this succeeds, but you'll be scrubbing toilets if it doesn't."

"I have a good imagination."

"I suggest you focus more on toilets and less on wealthy for the time being," Sal advised. "We're not out of the gate yet and most people are betting on other horses. You're not even on the card; you're still a sacrificial lamb to all but J.P. and me."

"I still don't understand why."

"Because they play with money, and we play with people," Sal explained. "They're talking to bankers, stock promoters and traders. InSyst caught us by surprise and they're currently well ahead. The best Sandy, Marco and the Junior Deltas hope for is badly bruised survival; they're also preparing in case they lose. Either way, they're fattening you up to be their scapegoat."

"Hence, Onesie," Jason said. "And you and J.P.?"

"We intend to win," Sal said. "There's no chance of a draw, and we refuse to lose."

"And me?"

"InSyst owns the framework; TechSys owns all the stuff that fills in the little frames. They need us and we need them. We can reverse engineer everything they have; we have reverse engineered it. They can reverse engineer everything we have; I'm sure they have. Everything except the dynamic link security and encryption registry, the module you coded. We've tried several times to reverse engineer that. It always ends in a loop—two mirrors looking at each other. When we gutted SecTech, we kept you and we kept that module, but the original code disappeared when SecTech mysteriously went up in flames. Only you know that algorithm." Sal rose to leave. "I chose you because InSyst can't have you."

The Junior Deltas came in but had no interest in sitting with Jason; they sat at a table far from him. "Normal?" José asked them. They all agreed. José relayed the order to Simon.

Jason got up and opened the swinging door a bit. "What's good today, Simon?"

"My good or Nigaud's good?" Simon asked.

"I imagine the Eggs Florentine were your good," Jason complimented. "So let's try José's."

"One heartburn it is!"

Jason held out his cup for José to refill. He took it over to a table closer to the windows and closer to the Delta trio. He stared out the window and listened; they were really nasty.

"Table for Onesie," Pet mocked quietly to her group.

"Even the relic left him alone," Brew said.

"Don't alienate him completely," J.J. said. "We need him to believe he's one of us until he gets introduced to the shears."

"You're right, at least enough that he doesn't give up our game to the InSyst group," Brew conceded. "We can do this at the office, but he can't play with any of my toys."

"Hey, Onesie," Pet called, "get over here! Be one of the boys!" She teasingly adjusted her blouse as if to say *Even with these, I'm more one of the boys than you'll ever be!*

Their breakfasts arrived: one eggs Florentine; two steak and eggs, rare; and one *huevos rancheros* with green chilli, refried beans and corn bread. "What's that?" J.J. asked. "Did they steal José's lunch and heat it up for you?"

"No meetings with me today," Brew said. "I know what those beans do!"

"Have you signed the insurance papers yet?" Pet asked. "If not, you better get down to HR PDQ. I'd say the odds aren't in your favour."

"I signed the papers yesterday, remember?" Jason played innocent. "One hour after breakfast."

"So how are you settling in?" J.J. asked.

"It will take a while to figure out all the things you folks do around here." The Deltas had no idea of the true meaning of that statement!

"Keep plugging away." Pet offered a double rah-rah with her fist. "We're rootin' for you!"

"Thanks, guys... and gal," Jason said. "I'm sure you'll all be a great help. I'm looking forward to working with you." He saw how far down their guards were. "Well, back to my nice office." He couldn't resist the dig, knowing how much each of them resented him having that office. "Lots of studying to do."

Jason left wishing he could hear how badly they'd talk about him now. *Well, Sal, they haven't caught on yet,* he thought. Once in his office, he switched on the power bar and the computer. Jason typed in Sal's password and the left quarter of the screen filled with file icons. Jason clicked on the TechSys one, expanded the board folder and selected the Pet folder. She had most irked him this morning, so he decided to start with her family file.

The first pages showed her extensive family tree. Hovering the cursor over a name prompted a short bio to pop up. Patricia Avila was a black sheep with a high Mexican pedigree: business magnates, politicians, diplomats, judges, doctors, lawyers and professors, even priests, nuns and a bishop.

Next Jason opened the picture file. The lead thumbnail showed Patricia down on her hands and knees wearing a leash and not much more. J.J. held the leash in one hand and a beer in the other. Brew held a beer aloft in each hand. He appeared to be dancing. *J.J. and Brew must know about the picture. Who else? Where is it? Does that same leash still restrain Pet?*

The second image was of a handwritten poem:

The Victim's Song

Down, down to the bitter dregs
Where high and mighty prowl at night
I prance about and bare my legs,
Sad, ogling men to delight.
They care less for what I know
They're only there for what I show.
As first light reveals the day
I venture on to Ivory Tower;
Teachers there reveal a way

To leave my past, find my power.
My tests and papers surely show
To value me for what I know.
Back each night I face my fate;
Just a toy, I bump and grind
Lustful lurid minds to sate
Until my past I can unbind.
I'm stuck in here and I know
To these pigs I'm just a show.
How long, how long will it be?
I study hard and read my books
Certain they will set me free,
Make me more than just my looks.
A part of me I have to show;
The part of me I shouldn't know.
You, dear uncle, put me here!
They trusted you when truth was mine.
Distressed, betrayed, a single tear
Weren't enough, they missed the sign.
A daughter that they didn't know
A truth so plain just couldn't show.
A man they dealt with every day?
Deny his guilt, his lies believe!
A daughter, close, yet far away?
Cast off, cast off, leave her to grieve.
Console her not but to him show
His truth, not hers, you will know.
The time will come, pray it be soon,
When you will face a price that's high;
The pipes will play a different tune!
At last note you will wish to die.
But live you will and come to know
That I, at last, the truth did show.

This was Patricia, filled with hate and vengeance poured into her by a family that neglected and rejected her.

Jason did not understand the significance of the third frame: a younger Patricia outside a health clinic. Other photos showed her working as a singing telegram and a night club dancer. None of them were as revealing or indelible as the first picture.

Jason had a coffee maker in his office but opted to stretch his legs. He needed to let his brain think; there was too much data to process intentionally.

"Hello, Mr. Johnstone!" José greeted him with a broad, genuine smile.

"Hello, José!" It was nearly lunch time. "Reuben with fries, please."

"And a nice cup of fresh black Mexican coffee? I make new pot!"

Jason would have been happier with old coffee, now, but didn't want to offend José.

José brought the coffee over as soon as it was ready. "The other ones, they can to drink old coffee; I no care," he whispered as he poured.

Jason didn't know how he had earned José's friendship. He took a sip. "Thanks, José, this is good coffee." Jason sat and mulled things over.

José soon delivered a Monte Cristo. "Simon say you will like this one better; I think is French. Simon like only French food mostly."

No one else was in the lounge so Jason called out loudly, "*Merci*, Simon!"

"*Mon plaisir!*"

The Monte Cristo was very good. Jason enjoyed it slowly as he sat and thought. He was very tired.

"Don't the others eat lunch here?" he asked José.

"Mostly they go restaurant, so they get drink to expense account. Simon and me, we mostly alonely. Is okay. He make for us good food. Sometimes there big meeting, then we busy. Mostly is too easy here. Sometime breakfast busy once to a while."

José brought over a bowl of bread pudding with cranberries. "This my favourite dessert," he said. "You try it."

José watched and smiled as Jason tried it. "My wife no make it; I only have here. Mostly every day more than one. Very good, no?"

The sour cranberries countered the sweet custard nicely. *A little like work and Colleen,* Jason thought. He finished his pudding and had another coffee. "Thank you both very much," he said loudly.

Back in his office, Jason waded deeper into Pet's past. *Her life should have been easier than this,* he thought. She had excellent grades, which dropped slightly in her final year at high school. Then she travelled for a year before tackling Harvard with a vengeance. She paid her own tuition. *Her choice or her family's?* Jason wondered. *Or both? The singing telegrams and night club dancing... rebellion or banishment?* Pet and her Delta Sigma Chi roommate, Connie Mason, got into mischief regularly, but of such minor nature that Jason missed the significance. Her post-grad studies were co-op. She moved out of sorority into a little apartment; all mischief ceased. Pet held a master's degree in organizational behaviour and a doctorate in business economics.

Pet was parachuted into the TechSys board shortly after graduation. There wasn't anything in her dossier to explain why. Certainly, she had a PhD and a decent GPA, but her somewhat tenuous connection to J.J. and Brew seemed more a minus than a plus. *There must be a reason. Where is it?* He flipped through the screens, forward and back, but saw nothing.

Our Place

It was already past five o'clock. Jason switched off the computer and the power bar. He used the men's room quickly and called the elevator. *Five twenty-five; she'll be gone!*

The doors opened and there she was beside the front doors looking out. He rushed over, "Colleen!"

She turned and they hugged politely. "Busy day?" she asked.

"Busy day! How 'bout you?"

"Brutal." She straightened his tie. "I hope it's not over."

"All but the fun part," Jason said.

"Where are you taking me?"

"To the moon. Are you coming?"

"Can we stop by Tink's first?"

"While they fuel our rocket?"

"While they fuel our rocket."

"You like Tink's."

"I met someone nice there."

"Someone nice?"

"Two someone nice."

"Two?"

"Yes, Moses and Maria."

"Moses and Maria?"

"Yes! And one really nice."

"Do I know him?"

"Not very well."

"I think that's what Moses tried to tell me once."

"Was he right?"

"That depends."

"On what?"

"On whether he meant my business-me or my me-me."

"And which one do you know?"

"My you-me."

"So I met five nice people at Tink's."

"Three nice, one really nice and one that's becoming nasty."

"One really nice?"

"My you-me."

Jason and Colleen were boarding their train by the time they finished cooing. They sat quietly, holding hands and snuggling close, until they got to Quitman Station.

"Can Tink's be ours?" Colleen asked.

"I'd like that."

They walked slowly, arms linked and leaning into each other. They entered Tink's and there was Moses. He seemed to be waiting for them. They didn't even think about another table, though there were several.

Jason nodded to Moses. "Evening."

"Sit yourselves down, my fair couple." Then he called out, "Maria! Drinks! Don't dare bring menus." Leaning over slightly, he said to Colleen, "It's coddle tonight."

"I haven't had coddle since my mum! Jason, you'll love it!"

Jason had serious doubts. *Coddle is some way of cooking eggs with vinegar that I don't like,* he remembered incorrectly. *At least he's right about this ale; much better than my lager.*

"Good food is on the way," Jason said, after Maria had brought them drinks. "Time for some good talk."

"I'll toast to that." Colleen raised her glass to Jason's mug and then Moses'.

"So, fairest child among we three," Moses began, "I know your name and not much more. Save the love your glow betrays. Tell us who sits behind that name?"

"My ancestors came here during the Great Potato Famine in eighteen forty-eight," Colleen revealed. "I'm seventh-generation progeny of a shipboard romance. Patrick and Colleen—yes, my namesake—were just children when they met at sea. They pledged themselves to one another and were true to their troth even though they were separated. Patrick's family stayed in New York and Colleen's moved to Boston. They chanced to meet again when Patrick accompanied his nephew to settle in at Harvard. They recognized each other at once and that was that! It's a much longer tale, but that's the gist."

"Well, I was raised by my nana and granddad," Jason said. "My father's name was Cliff Johnstone and that's all anyone cared to say about him. He abandoned Mom and me very early, leaving nothing but his name. My mom died when I was six. Cancer. I barely remember her. I can't truly say whether I know her or I know what Nana told me about her. Granddad never talked much; he tolerated me. After Charles moved next door, midsummer before ninth grade, I spent more time at his house than at Nana and Granddad's. His parents were great."

"That's so sad." Colleen took Jason's hand and caressed it. "How about you, Moses?"

"I am the scion of Texas aristocracy." Moses never spoke of his past. "I had all I wanted except more. I chased and I chased, but more lay always just beyond my grasp. I came to be a brutal competitor. Invincible! I learned the hard way that the higher one soars, the further one falls."

"Three-piece suits and Rolls," Jason recalled.

"Exactly," Moses said. "Now it's three not-quite suits that fit me much better. But past is past and will ever be. Who are you now?"

"That's a thing Jason and I were discussing on the way here," Colleen said. "It depends on which you you mean, work-you or not-work-you."

"I'd prefer not slicing you up," Moses said. "But, if slice you must, slice away!"

"I'm very ordinary and quite predictable," Colleen said. "I get up at seven, have one cup of black coffee and a toasted bagel with cream cheese, read the *Chronicle*, shower, dress, and I'm off to work by eight fifteen. I'm done work at five and, until recently, headed straight home to reheat a meal, which I prepare ahead on weekends. I watch the news while eating and a couple of TV shows after that. I wash my dishes and set the coffee for the morning and I'm in bed by eleven. That's the usual routine, but sometimes I go out with friends and I often talk to my mum and sisters on the phone. My brother doesn't often call, but his wife sometimes does. That's the boring me, before Jason finally asked me out."

"Finally?" Jason said.

"I've been waiting patiently and hoping every time we talked on the elevator."

"I wish I knew," Jason said. "I was too scared to ask."

"What happened?" Colleen asked.

"More, 'who' happened," Jason said. "Charles' baby and Moses, here."

"Moses?"

"He asked me how and why. It got me confused," Jason said. "I'm not accustomed to thinking."

"So when you started to think, you thought about me?" Colleen asked.

Jason had painted himself into a corner. "May as well think of something nice."

"Something nice?"

"Someone nice," Jason said. "Oh look! Here's our dinner!"

"I think it worked out for the best. Don't let what brought you together tear you apart," Moses said. "'How' is oft best left a mystery."

"But that was one of the three," Jason complained. "Who I am, how I am and why I am."

"In regards to being, yes," Moses said. "In regards to doing, how is merely technical."

"So we're really back to who we are," Jason said. "This is good! Where are the eggs? I thought coddle was a way to cook eggs."

"Coddle means gently steamed," Colleen explained, "and this is gently steamed bacon, sausages, potatoes and onions."

"Bacon is bacon; sausages, sausages; potatoes, potatoes; and onions, onions. Together this way, they are coddle. Alone they are food and together they are food," Moses said. "It is in this manner I ask, 'Who are you?' I once answered by what I have. You have answered by what you do. Man is man. I refer to species, not gender." Moses nodded to Colleen. "Earthling, American, Texan or individual, and ask again, 'Who are you?'"

"I see your point," Colleen said. "Our being, not our having or doing."

"In a broad sense, you are man. More precisely, you, Jason, are man and you, Colleen, are woman."

"But hasn't society outgrown those distinctions?" Jason asked.

"By my eyes, no!" Moses said. "And in truth, it can't. Man did not decide man should be thus and woman thus else; rather, each was observed and their traits were discerned. It is not by choice that they differ, and by choice they cannot be made the same. Who one is must be discerned, not decided. So now, again, who are you?"

"But surely, we are free to choose. Our choices make us who we are," Jason protested.

"It's folly to think we may be other than as we are. Valid choices may only be made between available options. One may choose to be a bird but they will not fly. They may desire with all their heart to be a bird but will never lay a single egg."

"But I may choose to be an engineer, a lawyer or a doctor," Jason said.

"You may choose to do as you're able or as you're not, but success will be found in the former, not the latter," Moses said.

"Persistence and effort will always yield progress," Colleen protested.

"Progress, yes," Moses conceded, "but not necessarily success."

"So what do you suggest?" Jason asked.

"We are a basket of interests and aptitudes," Moses answered. "Most are average and some exceptional. Some to the good and some to the bad. If one has no interest, they will not choose unless coerced; if no aptitude, they have more chance of despair than success. Pull from your basket that which you like and that which you can; do it with heart and will."

"'Who are you?' is a summary of our interests and aptitudes," Colleen said.

"Ah! Dessert," Moses said.

"He does that to me too," Maria said. "It's time to think."

"Ponder," Jason said, "over another beer."

"Ale," Maria corrected.

"Yes," Moses said, "ale is much better for pondering."

Jason, Colleen and Moses sat and pondered over dessert, thoughts lubricated by ale and wine.

"'Who am I?'" Jason said at last, "should resemble what I do."

"Should determine," Moses said, "once you know."

"More pondering," Colleen said.

They pondered. "It's late," Moses said as he got up. He bowed to Colleen and to Jason, before backing up, turning and leaving.

Jason and Colleen finished their drinks quietly, holding hands, pondering. Jason nodded to Maria. "It's been settled," she said.

"We can't let him always pay," Colleen said as Jason helped her with her coat.

"No," Jason said as they exited, "I offered. Next time I'll arrange it with Maria."

Jason and Colleen pondered all the way to Northside High. They sat and had a long after-Tink's then held hands and pondered some more. "Will we see each other after work every day?" Jason asked as they resumed their amble to Colleen's house.

"Too much?" Colleen asked.

"Not enough," Jason answered.

Colleen smiled, Jason smiled, and no more was said as they strolled hand in hand. They had another after-Tink's at Colleen's door and said goodnight. Jason thought more of Colleen than of who he was.

The Outsiders

Jason was back in the executive lounge by six. Sal, as usual, was already there. Sandy and Marco were also there, preparing for a meeting. Sal led Jason over to their table. "Mind if we join you?" he asked.

Sandy and Marco both knew yes was not an option. "We're about as prepped as we can be," Marco answered; he rose and pulled out a chair for Sal.

José rushed out of the kitchen still buttoning his shirt. "Sorry I keep you to wait."

"Bacon, over easy, brown," Marco ordered.

"Benedict, medium soft," Sandy said. "Easy on the béarnaise."

"Good morning, José," Jason said.

"Good morning, Mr. Johnstone!"

"You name my poison this morning. Surprise me."

"It might be poison," Marco warned.

"You've never been to the Texas A&M cafeteria," Jason countered. "Gastronomical immunity."

"That bad?" Sandy asked.

"Worse."

Sal frowned at Jason, obviously perturbed by the banter. He lifted himself from his chair and headed for the door. "Fill him in on his duties," Sal said as he left.

"Keep your eyes on the horizon," Marco said.

"Over the horizon," Sandy said.

Marco and Sandy took turns instructing Jason to do things that he already did. There were no additional duties, nor was there mention of products or customer support. These were definitely bottom-line people.

Worse. Stockholder people, he thought. *Why did Sal arrange this?*

For the rest of breakfast Jason may as well have been at a different table. It was obvious that Sandy and Marco were friends as much as TechSys directors. They knew each other's families, where they lived, where they vacationed and where they partied. Both complained about their spouse with no concern that Jason would hear. It was obvious they held little regard for him.

Enough of this, Jason thought and excused himself. "Thanks, José. Breakfast was great, Simon," he called out as he left.

"Come early for lunch," Simon said. "The meeting will come here at twelve thirty. You try it first. It will be very good!"

"Thanks, Simon. I will."

Jason wanted to know Sandy and Marco while breakfast was fresh in his mind. He opened Marco's portfolio first. He came from a poor family and, even with Marco's scholarship and student loans, his dad worked two jobs and his mom worked part time to get him through school. Jason was a bit surprised to find that Marco's PhD was in electrical engineering. He was founder and president of Book Me Dyno, an online calendar that wasn't Google's. Marco joined the TechSys board in a deal that absorbed his company.

It was time to go for early lunch; Jason didn't want to disappoint Simon. Jason thought about the life lessons Mr. Jackson used to tell him and Charles almost every day. "Don't count out us little people; we're the ones that does all the doin'. This world would be a much better place if more workers actually worked! All those boss men can plan till the sun comes home but nothin' gets done till us workers gets our hands dirty. Too much plannin' and bossin'! Moving things from here to there and back again, stuffin' their pockets every time it passes by. The watchin' guy gets more than the doin' guy."

On his way up to receive his PhD, Jason vowed always to remember Mr. Jackson's dinner-table advice; he renewed that vow now, on his way to the executive lounge.

All the tables were set with linen table cloths and napkins, cut-orchid centre pieces and real silverware. "*Bonjour*, Simon," Jason called at the swinging door.

"Monsieur Johnstone," Simon replied. "Good you came! I have you're portion here. I'll prepare it right away."

"*Merci*, Simone."

"What about your friend, José?" José asked as he came rushing out.

"*Ola, mi amigo*," Jason answered, "I didn't want to greet you through a door when I knew I'd see you out here. *Como esta?*"

José smiled broadly. "Very well, Mr. Johnstone. Thank you, sir. Sit. I will bring coffee! I make it early because I know you come soon."

Lunch was more like dinner: bacon-wrapped scallops, endive salad, fillet medallion, roast squash, asparagus and chocolate mousse for dessert.

"Wow," Jason said as José refilled his coffee after delivering the mousse.

"Don't worry," José said. "Me and Simon have table in kitchen. We try everything!"

"Excellent," Jason called to Simon as he passed by the kitchen door. He left early so José would have plenty of time to reset his table.

"*Merci!*" Simon replied.

Back in his office, Jason focused on the technical aspects of Book Me Dyno. He guessed that it must use algorithms at least a little similar to his security and encryption module, yet Marco claimed it relied on a variation of algorithms he learned while writing his MSc thesis on electronic switchboards. Jason couldn't find the similarity. Jason called Charles. "Got time for coffee? Outside? My expense account?"

"Any room for lunch on that account?" Charles asked.

"I just ate," Jason said. "But sure, you can."

"In that case, I'm in. Lobby in five."

Charles caught the same elevator as Jason. They went around the corner to Java With Jas.

"Hi, Jas!" Charles called out. "Expense account! I'll have a macchiato, ham and Swiss, and a dark chocolate tart."

"Big spender on someone else's dime," Jas said.

"Medium dark roast," Jason ordered.

"You're not on the expense account?" Jas asked.

"My expense account," Jason answered.

"Still," Jas persisted.

"Why here?" Charles asked as he headed to the table. "Can't be seen mixing with us common folk?"

"I don't want anyone to overhear us," Jason answered. "You know our calendar module?"

"Interactive scheduler?"

"That one."

"I'd better know it."

"That's supposed to be Marco Lorenz' baby," Jason said. "He supposedly developed it before he came here."

"Supposedly?"

"I don't think he knows enough about it to have done that. I read a transcript of his negotiations with TechSys where he claimed it was based on electronic switching technology."

"No way. That's strictly binary tree stuff. Way too old school."

"That's what I thought," Jason said. "So there's no way?"

"It's more like your security and encryption."

"Exactly what I thought."

"You already knew he's lying," Charles said. "Why am I really here?"

"Because I can't believe what I do believe."

"Pops always told us they're all liars," Charles reminded him. "A pack of vipers waiting to bite you in the back. So what now? What are we going to do about it?"

"I don't know. I'll see how things develop," Jason said. "I just need someone I can trust."

"I'm here, bro."

Jason watched Charles finish his lunch and they returned to work. "Later, bro," Charles said as he got off the elevator. "I've got your back."

Jason's spirit dropped as his new reality sank in. He opened Sandy's portfolio. Her parents were both accountants and her younger brother was an accountant. Her older brother was a plumber. *Black sheep*, Jason thought. Sandy had been with Book Me Dyno right from the start. She and Marco were both part of the takeover package.

Sal came in. "Jason, how am I doing?"

"Hi, Sal," Jason said. "What are you doing here?"

"I went to lunch. You should have seen them when they saw me! Want some daggers?" He turned his back to Jason. "Take as many as you want."

"I don't see J.P's there."

"Just wait," Sal said. "It will be. Your back or mine. No difference."

Jason was desperate to trust Sal but wasn't quite there yet. "Anything interesting?"

"Some new faces. Don't know who yet; didn't get introductions," Sal said. "I'm on it though."

"Who did you sit with?" Jason asked.

"Me... I heard you were in earlier."

"Yes."

"You're more like me than I knew."

"Oh?"

"José thinks you're nice."

"So, you're nice?"

"José thinks I am."

"And Simon?"

"He'd think I was nicer if I had the smattering of French you do."

"But he talks to you?"

"There's always more on the menu than just food. Sit at the kitchen table with them sometimes; just don't get caught." Sal stepped closer to look over Jason's shoulder. "How are you making out?"

"Well, J.J. puts too much faith in Delta loyalty. The Junior Deltas are just waiting for their chance. Once Senior is gone, Junior had better watch out. Brew and Pet will be at each other's throat. Marco and Sandra are really tight and much more capable than the others."

"Gooood!" Sal congratulated. "How will I play them?"

"I'm only getting to know the players," Jason said. "I don't know the game."

"Well, you're starting to understand how the players play each other. Go see Colleen."

And how are you playing me? Jason thought. "I'd like to spend a bit more time with you," Jason said as he logged off the computer and switched off the power bar.

"I can't let you get dependent on me," Sal cautioned. "You have to be quick on your feet, a master at improvisation. You have many roles: you and the deal, you and the Junior Deltas, you and the Book Me's, you and me."

"I thought you-and-me was real."

"It is real and it's a role. Life is a role."

"What about Onesie and J.P.?"

"Not even on his radar, my boy. Not even on his radar. Go have fun. I need it!"

Rocks

Jason got to the lobby before Colleen. *There should be at least a few chairs and a table,* he thought. *It's uncomfortable and very conspicuous to stand around a completely empty lobby waiting.*

He leaned against the wall beside the elevators, waiting. Colleen finally arrived. She rushed out, looking about anxiously, but didn't see Jason. She shrieked and turned as he grabbed her waist from behind.

"You scared me!" She smacked him playfully. They hugged politely.

"Sorry, Love," he said. *Will that be my pet name for her?* Jason blushed.

"Love?" Colleen blushed.

"Tink's again?" Jason said, evading her question as they began their stroll toward Central Station. "It won't be too much Tink's?"

"Never. I love it there," Colleen said. "Our Tink's."

"And Moses? He'll probably be there. Do we need some just-us time?"

"He's sweet," Colleen said. "I like him. You could come back to my place for coffee after. We'll have some just-us time there."

"Coffee?"

"Or tea."

"Or tea?"

"Or tea," Colleen insisted. "I don't trust myself with any after-Tink's there."

Colleen and Jason walked quietly, deep in thought, both wondering where they were headed.

"I'm totally smitten," Jason admitted as they found their seats on the train. "You must know that. Still, it's too soon. Things are very complicated right now. Very complicated."

"Smitten is my concern too," Colleen said. "I had a boyfriend before...

for a long time. We were never smitten. We were more... expected. We were together because our friends thought we should be together more than because we thought we should be together. I never felt the way I do with you; with him I was comfortable. With you... well, with you... I'm scared. I'm scared it's too fast. I'm scared it's too much. I'm scared it's not real. And mostly, I'm scared it won't last."

"Things seem fast to me too. Charles' dad says a dog that poops fast doesn't poop long. Not the most elegant way of phrasing the sentiment, but I don't think that's us."

"Are we the real thing, Jason?" Colleen asked. "Or will we get pooped out?"

"My heart says we're the real thing, and my mind wants us to be the real thing, but it keeps hollering 'Woah!' When I'm with you, I'm in a dream and I don't want to wake up. When we're together, I know it's right, but when we're apart, my brain says 'Slow down!'... And then there's work—" Jason stopped abruptly.

"What about work?"

"I want to tell you but I can't tell you."

"Confidentiality?" Colleen guessed.

"Yes," Jason said, "and fear."

"Why, Jason?"

"So much happening. So vicious. I don't want you to be a part of it."

Colleen didn't understand and didn't know what to say. She stroked Jason's hand. "You just got promoted," she prompted.

"For now... for what?" was all Jason could muster.

Colleen kept stroking tenderly, watching him as he stared into space. "Well, we're together right now."

Jason turned to look in Colleen's eyes. He had a tremendous urge to kiss her passionately, right then, but there were too many people on the train. Jason's heart pounded. *After Tink's will be nothing compared to after now!* Jason's heart knew their future would be long and there was nothing his mind could do to stop it.

Colleen saw Jason's look and blushed. "This is our stop. Come on. Tink's."

Jason and Colleen held hands as they made their way from Quitman

Station to Tink's. Jason cornered Maria as soon as they entered. "Make sure I get the bill today."

"No need," Maria said. "Moses' bill, and anyone else who sits with him, is always covered by the owner."

"You're sure?"

"I'm sure."

"Can we thank the owner?" Colleen asked.

"The owner's shy about it," Maria said. "But I'll make sure the owner knows you're grateful."

Moses was waiting expectantly. "My favourite couple!"

"Do you have any other favourite couples?" Jason asked.

"No, no," Moses replied. "Apart from you two and Maria, I don't have any favourite people at all. There are a few others I like, but three favourites are enough for anyone. If one has too many favourites, then favourite isn't very special."

"How about the owner?" Jason asked.

"Maybe we can include the owner in favourites," Moses said.

"You have room for a fourth," Colleen said.

"I have room for dinner. Let's eat!"

The special was steak and kidney pie. Colleen and Moses were both delighted; Jason was hesitant. "Do you know what kidneys do?" he asked.

"They stopped doing it long before they got baked into the pie," Moses replied. "The taste is far better than the thought."

"Maybe I'll just try some of Colleen's this time round," Jason said. "I'll have a Tower."

"Gravy on the fries?" Maria asked.

"Please."

"Well, then," Moses said. "Business is done! Give me some thoughts for this ale to wash down."

"By which you mean, who are we?" Jason asked.

"Yes, Jason. And how and why. But, ladies first."

"Well," Colleen started, "interests and abilities, if I recall."

"Yes, my dear," Moses said. "But back a bit to the start. You plan to find attributes, but attributes must attach to something."

"Well, me," Colleen said.

"So you seek to describe the me that is you. It's not the me that is Jason or the me that is me?"

"Yes," Colleen said. "The me that is me... Colleen."

"And need that me be?"

"Well... yes if I mean to define myself."

"Is there that which would not be if that me were not? Must it be for the rest to be?"

"Um... no," Colleen said uncomfortably.

"Yes!" Jason interceded. "This conversation could not be. We could not be."

"Could we not put Maria in her chair?" Moses asked. "Could we not still have this conversation?"

"It wouldn't be the same conversation," Jason said. "We wouldn't be the same us, and the we that is Colleen and me wouldn't be at all."

Colleen smiled at her knight in shining armour and blushed. "Well," Colleen said, pointing to other patrons in the pub, "they would still be they. Their table would still be their table. This table would still be this table. This place," she waved her hands over her head, "would still be this place."

"No," Jason said, "this Tink's is not the Tink's before you."

"So, some as they are, some as they're not and some not at all," Moses said. "There's that of which she's not a part, that of which she's an incidental part, that of which she's an integral part and that which she is."

"But I don't think anyone can set clear boundaries," Colleen said.

"So, Colleen is very complicated!" Moses said. "And we may be too simple to know her well. Let's start with something much simpler and see how that goes."

"Such as?" Jason asked.

"A rock," Moses suggested. "They seem simple. What is a rock?"

"A lump of something hard," Jason said.

"Ahh!" Moses said. "So last week's dinner roll is a rock?"

"Or penicillin," Colleen joked.

"A lump of mineral," Jason said. "You know, twenty questions: animal, vegetable or mineral? Not living."

"So this?" Moses held up his mug.

"Not man-made," Jason added. "Rocks occur naturally."

"This is man-made and supernatural," Maria said, serving their food, "and woman-delivered."

"And much better than rocks," Jason said.

"Here, try this so you'll know what you're missing." Colleen offered Jason a forkful. "And I made sure to include a lump of kidney."

"You're sure that's not a rock?" Jason joked. "It looks a bit like a rock."

"No kidney stones here," Colleen replied. "I'm sure it's animal."

"What's wrong with steak and mushroom?" Jason had already decided not to like it. He accepted the mouthful hesitantly. "But I suppose one could acquire a taste for this." He wouldn't admit that he enjoyed it.

"Unless concept outweighs percept," Moses said.

"I'll concede that it's better than rocks—that's our topic," Jason dodged.

"Lumps neither living nor man-made," Colleen recapped.

"And that's the best definition we can come up with?" Moses asked.

"I guess a geologist would have a better one," Jason said. "But why? When I see a rock, or you or Colleen or anyone here, I know it's a rock."

"Why would a geologist have a better definition?" Moses asked.

"Because they work with them every day," Jason said. "They need to know the different types and what to do with them."

"And you work with you every day," Moses said. "So perhaps you should have a better definition of you and what to do with you."

"Well, I'm a man," Jason said. "So I live. I can move about, I can think and I can plan."

"So you can already define yourself better than a lump of animal," Moses said. "You know yourself better than you know rocks."

"And he can love," Colleen said, blushing again.

"But not steak and kidney pie."

"So man has traits that are special among animals," Moses said. "And what are they?"

"He can make ale!" Jason raised his mug.

"And wine," Colleen added.

"And what do animals other than man lack that prohibits them from making ale and wine?" Moses asked. "At a basic level."

"Recipes?" Jason half answered, half asked.

"And what are recipes?"

"Instructions of how to make something," Colleen answered.

"And what are instructions?"

"A list of ingredients to use and steps to take to make something." Colleen was sure this would be a sufficient answer.

"And now a question we often forget to ask," Moses said. "Why?"

"Because they didn't want to forget how to do it," Jason said.

"Or they wanted to tell someone else how to do it," Colleen added.

"This is getting interesting," Moses said.

Or not, Jason thought, but he still wanted to listen.

"Someone made a list of ingredients and steps required to make something so that they or someone else could make it again," Moses recapped. "Why?"

"Because it tasted good," Jason said.

"Like steak and kidney pie?" Moses asked.

"I guess it must have tasted good to someone," Jason said just as Maria arrived with their dessert. "Unlike this Triple Chocolate Lava Cake, which tastes good to everyone! Thank you, Maria."

"Thank Larry," Maria said. "He baked it."

"He also made the steak and kidney pie," Jason said. "The jury is still out."

"And the Tink's Tower?" Maria reminded.

"Okay," Jason conceded, "you may thank Larry for me."

"For all of us," Colleen added.

"So if someone made a recipe for cement, say," Moses said, returning to their conversation, "it would be because it tasted good?"

"In that case," Jason said, "it would be because it was useful."

"So can we say, then," Moses summarized, "that someone made a list of ingredients and steps required for someone to make something that fills a need or desire?"

"Yes," Jason agreed.

"And what are ingredients?"

Colleen had a sense of how this would go. "Particular items from a person's environment," she said, "and steps are actions that alter or combine those items."

"Very good, my dear! A recipe is a list of items to use and actions to take in order to fill a need or desire," Moses said. "Now, let's enjoy our cake! Coffee, anyone?"

"Well, actually," Colleen said, "we planned to have coffee at my place. Jason and I."

"Good! Good," Moses said. "It's just as well. I don't need more help not sleeping; I can do that very well without the coffee."

They finished their cake quietly. Jason and Colleen looked at each other and smiled. They looked at Moses and wondered if they had offended him.

Moses rose. "Well, I have steak and kidney to digest, and 'recipe' to digest. I've had a pint to assist with each and one more for good measure. All in all, a good evening's work and a good night to you both." He doffed his pretend hat, bowed deeply for his age and left. "Good night, Maria!" he called from the door.

"He's really quite a character," Maria said. "We love him here."

"How long have you known him?" Colleen asked.

"I don't think anyone really knows him," Maria said, "but he's been coming here since before it was Tink's."

"Before it was Tink's?" Jason asked.

"It used to be Diablo's Den. It was much different then. Moses was much different. I was much different."

"Much different?" Jason pressed.

"Loud music, more drinking," Maria explained, "exotic dancers."

"Exotic dancers!" Colleen was shocked.

"Yup. Moses sat up front with his various business associates, and I danced," she confessed.

"You were an exotic dancer?" Jason was shocked. He looked Maria up and down. "I mean, not that you couldn't be!"

Colleen elbowed him in the ribs. "Jason!" she scolded.

"It's okay," Maria said. "I'm not proud of it, but I did it. It's part of a past that Moses helped me escape."

"How?" Jason asked. "Why?"

"Now you're sounding a lot like Moses," Colleen said.

"He was with some other men one night," Maria began. "They got really angry and caused a big scene. They got tossed out and Moses just sat there looking very scared. I had never seen him that way so on my next break I sat with him and we talked. He changed after that. He'd sit at the back alone, not watching. I'd go over during my breaks; we kept talking. He told me his life and I told him mine. A few months later, Diablo's closed and became Tink's. When it reopened after the renovations, Moses was gone; he stayed gone for a couple of years. When he came back I was still here but a waitress. There's a lot more to it than that, but it's painful. My past is my past and his is his; they both hurt in different ways and neither of us wants to go back there."

"Is this hard for you?" Colleen asked.

"I've come to terms with it," Maria said, "and Moses has come to terms with his past, but there is definitely a point beyond which neither of us likes to venture. The short version is enough."

"So were you two ever a thing?" Jason got another elbow to the ribs.

"Not like you and Colleen," Maria answered. "We were too busy being what we weren't to build a now or a future. He was being much more than himself and I was being much less than myself. I wonder, sometimes, but we need each other too much as we are; what we are is too precious to risk for what we might be. Pasts are hard things to escape."

It was a very sad story. "We have to go now." Colleen got up, tugging Jason's arm as she did. "Thanks, Maria," she said and gave her a hug.

Jason didn't know what to think, much less say. He settled on, "Yeah, thanks."

Colleen and Jason held hands, swinging them slowly as they walked. "That's a very surprising story," Jason said.

"Very surprising," Colleen said. "I would never have suspected that."

"I wouldn't have believed it if it hadn't been Maria telling it. I wonder what happened that night, why Moses was so scared."

"I'm glad we don't have a past like that."

"I don't know," Jason said. "I might like to see you dance." He earned a smack on his chest.

Colleen resisted as Jason attempted to turn toward their after-Tink's bleachers at Northside High. "Coffee or tea, Jason," Colleen said. "'Me' is not on the menu tonight."

Colleen rented one side of a duplex. It was quite small and very tidy, and furnished very simply. Colleen went to the dinette and pulled out one of two chairs for Jason. "No couch tonight."

Jason knew this was a very big and significant step for Colleen; he didn't want to make it more difficult than it already was. "Tea, please," he said.

Colleen smiled. She knew that Jason preferred coffee; the tea was for her. She filled the kettle and plugged it in. "I have some biscuits if you'd like."

"Thanks. Tink's was interesting tonight. We talked about stuff you wouldn't think there was anything to talk about."

"Such as?"

"Well, a rock is a rock and everyone knows what a rock is. If you show someone a rock they'll say, 'Yup, that's a rock,' but when Moses asked, it was really hard to say what a rock is. We recognize things very well without really knowing what they are. We're better at saying what something is than we are at thinking what something is."

"It seems so simple before you think about it," Colleen said. "If someone asked me, 'Would you like to talk about what a rock is?' I'd think they were crazy... before tonight, that is."

"Or even who you are," Jason said. "That was like an ice breaker for when you meet a new group of people. Now, with Moses, it seems like a serious question."

"Moses makes you—us—think differently. Things you'd think would be boring and trivial take up the whole evening."

"And they make you think. I wouldn't think about things like that at all if I hadn't met Moses."

"I'm not so sure," Colleen said. "I think we often think about who we are, just not always so consciously."

"How so?"

"Well, when we get dressed in the morning, what clothes we pick. When we go to meetings, what's my role and what's theirs. We conduct ourselves differently in different situations according to how we perceive ourselves."

"Guards and prisoners in psych 101."

"Exactly!" Colleen said. "Tonight made me think in other ways too, like... recipe!"

"Meaning?"

"Our lives," Colleen said. "Are we each items to be transformed and combined with other items to meet a need or desire? Whose need? Whose desire? Our jobs. Are they recipes for different 'us'-es? Is that what a job description is? Take one person, add this much school and this much practice, put in a business and bake until done? Us. Are we part of a social recipe or are we unique? Are people truly unique or are they pushed through a social assembly line to become one of many?"

Jason was thinking too hard to answer.

"Do I need you, Jason, or do I desire you? What is a need and what is a desire? Do you need me or do you desire me? It isn't enough to be desired and it isn't enough to be needed. Do you need someone and desire me?"

Jason got up, grabbed Colleen's shoulders, spun her around and hugged her tenderly. He looked in her eyes. "I need you and I desire you. Not someone. You."

"You say that and I want to hear that, but is that itself merely one of the steps in a recipe, and what recipe?"

"You need to hear that," Jason said. "And if it's a recipe, let's start cooking."

Colleen pushed Jason away and hit his chest with the side of her fist. "You're terrible. I'm being serious!"

"Are we serious?" Jason asked softly. "Are we past infatuated?"

"I want to be."

"What does serious mean, in the Moses sense?"

"Us is more than me or you," Colleen said. "It's still early."

"Not too early for tea and biscuits, but too early for any serious after-Tink's?"

"Serious after-Tink's is very serious. It's much too early." Colleen was a little scared.

"Good," Jason said. "I want our after-Tink's to mean more than... to be more than... infatuation."

"You desire our after-Tink's—"

"I desire it very much. But I desire it to be real much more than I desire it to be now."

They hugged again, a more permanent type of hug. "Tea and biscuits," Colleen said, nudging Jason toward the table.

"Our after-Tink's is more than I had with anyone else," Jason said. "Even though it's less," he confessed.

"The truth comes out," Colleen joked.

"It was never truth before," Jason said. "It was games. I was entertaining myself."

"The truth sinks in."

"I cared more about what I wanted and what my friends expected than what my partner wanted or expected," Jason said. "It was what everyone did."

"Everyone knows a rock is a rock."

"Exactly. And a relationship is a relationship. But this one is like a diamond. I recognize something different about it."

"Shall we go see a geologist?" Colleen asked.

"Maybe Moses is our geologist," Jason surmised. "Maybe that's why we're both attracted to him."

"Maybe that's why he likes us. Because he too sees our relationship as a diamond."

"Well, tomorrow comes early," Jason said. "As much as I love being here, I have responsibilities."

Colleen saw Jason to the door. They shared a hug and a short kiss, and she let him out. "Good night, Jason."

"A very good night." Jason walked backwards to the gate and blew Colleen a kiss as he closed it.

Colleen watched until Jason disappeared and then watched a few seconds more.

Mexicans and Poles

Jason got to the executive lounge at five forty-five. José wasn't there yet, but Simon was. "Good morning, Simon," Jason called at the kitchen door.

"*Bon matin*, Monsieur Jason."

"You're here early."

"My pastries must be ready for my patrons," Simon said. "Come in and try my raisin and custard brioche."

"It sure smells good!" Jason said as the door swung closed behind him.

"Sit." Simon set a plate of pastries on the table. "I will press you some coffee. It is better than that insipid fluid Nigaud creates with his machine."

"Oh, good morning, my friend," José said as he entered and hung his coat in his locker. "I see Simon has give you his pastries before I can bring you a real breakfast."

Simon clicked his tongue. "Good morning, Nigaud."

"Good morning, Simon!" José said jovially.

"Good morning, gentlemen," Sal said as he entered. "I see you've seated Jason at my favourite table."

"Good morning, Mr. Sal," José said.

"Yes," Simon said. "Here. Your favourite pastries!"

"Made the way no one else does," Sal said. "So what manner of treason are you three up to back here?"

"No treason," José said. "We no have time yet."

"Ah, I've arrived in time, possibly saved TechSys from a horrible fate!" Sal jested.

"Maybe just Señora Fufurufa," José said. "Maybe I put plenty hot sauce in her breakfast."

"Has she been at it again with you?"

"No again, Mr. Sal," José explained. "She never stop."

"It's more about her than about you, José," Sal assured him.

"It only about her. Always about her."

"Well, at the end of the day, she goes to her home and you go to yours."

"And she will never to come to my home!"

"This coffee is good, Simon," Jason said.

"That coffee is French," José said. "I have better Mexican coffee out there soon."

"Thank you, José," Sal said. "We'll come out when it's ready."

José left and busied himself in the lounge. "I call you when it ready!"

"Bad yesterday?" Sal asked.

"*Mon Dieu!*" Simon replied. "*Comme chien et chat!*"

"Pet?" Jason deduced.

"Incessant!" Simon sighed. "'That peon should know his place!' versus 'This is America!'"

"José's America is not Corporate America," Jason observed.

"He lives in the land of hope and promise," Sal said. "She lives in a land of intrigue and deception."

"And in which land do we live?" Jason asked, expecting the latter.

"Desperation, bordering on desolation."

"That's reassuring."

"Don't worry too much. We'll be out soon. Either vindicated or destroyed."

What Sal said was less disconcerting to Jason than the unimpassioned way he said it. It made Jason think of the end of a Monopoly game where one person holds most of the properties and the other has most of the money. *Sal knows he has the money*, Jason thought.

"J.P. today," Sal said. "By day's end you'll either trust me more or not at all."

"Is there a dossier on you?"

"Somewhere? Certainly! Here? It's buried in the others."

Back in his office, Jason opened J.P.'s portfolio and selected the family tree folder. At the top was Burkeman Holdings Corp and branching underneath, some with solid lines, some with dotted, were many subsidiary and affiliated companies. Most had fairly well-known names. *All these companies are Burkeman controlled?* Jason was awed. *It's huge!* Jason maneuvered the cursor over the screen as a placemark. At one point, over empty space, the cursor changed shape; he clicked and another file opened up. Mason Holdings. Shareholder: Solomon Rosenthal. Directors: Solomon Rosenthal, President; Constance Mason, CEO; Ricardo Gonzales, CFO. Assets: Hacienda Gonzales, Mérida, Mexico; three Range Rovers; minibus; furnishings.

Is Sal aware of this Easter egg? Jason wondered. *Who compiled these documents? Are there other copies? Where?* Jason closed the file and searched the directory. No Mason Holdings. It was a hidden file. *Are there other hidden files?* He reopened the family tree and began running the cursor across it, back and forth, top to bottom. The cursor always changed at the same spot in the middle of blank space but nowhere else. *How about in other files? They'd be virtually impossible to find. Why put it there at all?* Jason reopened Mason Holdings. Jason opened a second window and searched for Constance Mason. Nothing. Ricardo Gonzales—Pet's family tree. Pet had six distant relatives and one first cousin named Ricardo Gonzales. *One of these, probably the cousin, must be the Ricardo. Who's the Constance?* Jason wondered. He googled her name. She was concealed in a forest of Constance Masons. "Who are you, Constance Mason? I'm watching you. I'll spot you again... somewhere."

Jason needed a break so he went for lunch and a visit with José and Simon. "*Ola*, José. Slow today?"

"Yes, Mr. Johnstone, it's good you came."

"*Bonjour*, Simon behind the door. Anything good back there?"

"*Vous m'insultez*, Monsieur Johnstone. *Tout est délicieux*, except what I cook for Nigaud!"

"I'll have some of that, *s'il vous plaît*," Jason teased, "and some of your Mexican coffee, please, José."

"Of course, Mr. Johnstone!" José smiled his usual smile.

"Any other customers today?"

"No, Mr. Johnstone, only our friend Mr. Sal came to visit us in the kitchen."

Jason drank his coffee and did the daily puzzles in the newspaper.

"José," Simon called from the kitchen.

José reappeared with a cheese soufflé and croissant. "Simon say he can give you salsa if you want to make Mexican."

"This will be fine, José." It was better than fine.

After lunch, Jason opened a folder labelled HLH only because the name stood out by its brevity. There were five files: Addendum, HLH, Palomex, Synopsis and Trans Mexico. The obvious first pick was Synopsis; it gave details about a takeover brokered by J.P. himself that involved Houston Long Haul Corp and Trans Mexico, two logistics companies. HLH absorbed a few routes but most of the company was split up and sold. There wasn't any significant profit. A few land holdings acquired in the deal, including the Burkeman Mexico head office at 295 Paseo de la Reforma in Mexico City, were transferred to assorted Burkeman companies at appraised value, but the whole deal seemed more trouble than it was worth.

Addendum gave details about a nasty foray south of the border in which Palomex tried poaching several of Houston Long Haul Inc's trans-border contracts. The dispute was costly for both companies and the routes involved were barely profitable. "This is not about the money," Jason said out loud.

HLH further confused Jason. *There's nothing here that would warrant J.P.'s personal attention. This is a small-potatoes company.* "Why, J.P.?"

"Why J.P. what?" Sal asked.

Jason had been too wrapped up in his quest to notice Sal enter. "I'm looking at HLH."

"Good," Sal said. "I'll leave you to it. Breakfast tomorrow will be interesting." He turned and left.

Sal's response made Jason all the more determined to understand the significance of such a trivial matter.

Sal poked his head around the door a while later. "It's past five."

Jason hurried to log out and switch off the computer; he grabbed his jacket and put it on as he ran to the elevator. He looked at his watch several times as the elevator descended: five twenty-one, five twenty-one, five twenty-one, five twenty-two, *Sorry Colleen,* five twenty-two. The doors opened.

Colleen was looking at her watch. She looked up, saw Jason and smiled. "Busy day?"

"Busy day." Jason was relieved. "Sorry, Colleen. Tink's?"

They had a quick hug and grasped hands. "Tink's."

They said nothing as they walked to the station, just held hands and smiled. Colleen blushed whenever their quick glances met. The train was crowded so they stood for the first two stops until they could find seats together, then it was time for a silent cuddle.

Tink's that evening was crowded and two young men were sitting with Moses. Colleen and Jason looked around but saw no empty seats. "We could go to my place," Jason offered. "Order pizza or Chinese."

They looked over to wave goodbye to Moses. Instead of 'goodbye' he waved them over to his booth. "Hi, Moses. We're going to have pizza at Jason's," Colleen said.

"Nonsense!" Moses said. "I told Pawel and Stefan here to expect you. They're students from Poland."

Maria already had drinks for Colleen and Jason on her tray. "Hi, Maria," they said sheepishly.

"I can't serve you until you sit," she said. "Rules!"

"Colluding with Moses?" Colleen asked.

"It happens... occasionally."

"Our friends, here," Moses said, nodding toward Pawel and Stefan, "heard that the perogies and sausage are particularly good here."

"I didn't know it was on the menu," Jason said. "I've never had it here."

"Marek makes excellent ones," Maria said.

"The dishwasher?" Jason was surprised.

"He was a cook on a freighter," Moses explained. "Before he jumped ship."

"Perogies for five, then?" Colleen guessed.

The evening was spent discussing Pawel's and Stefan's life in Wroclaw. They described how being Polish was more cultural than political; Poland, the country, had been conquered and freed many times. It had been split up and reunited, ruled by other nations, been and stopped being. Poland, the people, had endured. They told how servitude of their bodies had not enslaved their souls, how what they did was not who they were. “Sometimes we have to do what we have to do, but we can still be who we are,” Pawel said. “I am the same man cleaning toilets or digging rocks as I am dancing or writing poetry.”

“If you say you are my master,” Stefan said, “you may be able to force me to do or not do, but you cannot force me to believe or to stop thinking.”

“Poles are Poles because of where their hearts and souls are,” Pawel said, “not where their hands and feet are.”

“Fair enough,” Jason said. “You and Stefan are going back to Poland after your studies. How about Marek, who is staying here, should he not now be American?”

“America should have more Poles,” Pawel replied. “Poles have been Poles for a thousand years; Americans today are not the Americans of two hundred years ago. Americans should learn how to really be a country again.”

“Too many Americans sacrifice their principles for dollars,” Stefan said. “They used to sacrifice their lives for their principles. Perhaps life here has become too soft and lost its value; there is much to be thankful for in a hard life.”

Time slipped by quickly as the guests talked and the others mostly listened. “It’s well past my time,” Moses said at last.

“My goodness!” Colleen looked at her watch. “Jason, you need to be up early.”

Jason and Colleen walked to her house briskly and had a quick good night before Jason rushed home to bed.

Digging Up Worms

Jason arrived at the executive lounge at eight seventeen. "*Ola*, José."

"*Ola*, Señor Johnstone. You are late! Mr. Sal and I are worry about you."

"I lost track of time last night and stayed up past my bedtime. That Mexican coffee smells especially good this morning," Jason said, then called toward the door, "*Bonjour*, Simon. I'll have what you've got today."

Sal smiled as Jason sat down. "So your sweet Colleen is keeping you out late. I'll have to have a talk with that young lady."

"Actually," Jason corrected, "it was a couple of young Polish students who kept us out late."

"I liked my version better. A wry smile would have pleased me more than your explanation."

"Truth will out."

"Sometimes it's better not to let all of it out. What did you find out yesterday?"

"I think I'm starting to put the pieces together," Jason said. "I'm not there yet, but I think today will get me much closer."

"So what pieces are you putting together?"

"This isn't about money. Something else is driving this battle."

"The pieces," Sal said, focusing Jason.

"J.P., Pet, one or more of Pet's relatives, HLH, Trans Mexico, Palomex and Constance Mason."

Sal was surprised and very pleased that Jason included Constance. "That's good. Think bigger."

"You know what I'm looking for. Why don't you just tell me?"

"I could easily explain everything and you would understand, but I need to know that you can figure this out by yourself," Sal said. "Enough of the pieces are there."

"It would be easier if you just told me."

"You need to show me you have a chance of winning; my life depends on it. The cards have been dealt. You're in my hand and you must demonstrate that you belong there before the time comes for my discard."

"So," Jason said evenly, "the hand is not fully dealt and you have other cards to consider."

"Right now you're my ace," Sal admitted. "If you want to be safe, find me another one or, better, two."

"And this is how you convince me to trust you?"

"I told you you'd either trust me more or not at all. It's not what I do that will make you trust me; it's what you do that will make me need you."

"Once you need me, I can trust that you will keep me in play?" Jason wasn't enjoying the game.

"I'm all in on this one. I have nothing left to lose."

"How about your honour?"

"I lost that many hands ago."

"And mine?"

Sal smiled a knowing smile. "Go study." He got up and left without touching his breakfast pastries.

José arrived with a shrimp and spinach omelette. "Where did Mr. Sal go?"

"He lost his appetite," Jason said. "Mine wasn't far behind, but that breakfast is bringing it back."

"Do you want some salsa? This one very good with salsa."

"Will Simon shoot me?"

"Probably." José shrugged. "What he know? He not Mexican."

"Neither am I."

"But you are very nice," José said with a big smile. "I go sneaking some."

"Thanks, José."

Think bigger, Jason thought. *I'm looking at the cards; I need to find who's playing them.*

Jason decided to enjoy his breakfast. "May I have more of that Mexican coffee, please, José?" He thanked José and Simon on his way out.

"Did you put salsa?" Simon asked.

"Would I spoil a delicious French breakfast?" Jason asked as he winked at José.

Think bigger. Jason turned on the computer. *J.P.* "It's not getting any bigger than that on this side," he said out loud. "Who are you Trans Mexico and Palomex?"

Jason's search revealed that one Enrico Gonzales had been president at the time of the HLH takeover. He recalled Pet's Gonzales relatives and opened her family tree. Uncle Enrico Gonzales was Ricardo's father! Now Palomex. Its president was Ernesto Gonzales. There were four Ernesto Gonzaleses on Pet's tree. "Not a coincidence." Further searching revealed that Palomex was a subsidiary of Groupo Avizales.

Jason didn't have to search very hard to satisfy his hunch. Groupo Avizales, 300 Paseo de la Reforma, Mexico City. "That seems familiar." He checked Burkeman Mexico's address. "Across the street," he murmured. "Definitely something." He looked a little further. President, Hector Avila. "Pet's father? Definitely something." *The head of a huge Texas conglomerate is facing off against the head of a huge Mexican conglomerate*. "Remember the Alamo."

Jason found branches or subsidiaries of Groupo Avizales spread out all over the globe. One in particular caught his eye. Harvard Properties maintained five residences in Cambridge, yet Pet was a Delta Sigma Chi. "Why, Pet, why?" Jason revisited Pet's file. Pet on a leash seemed clear enough. Family tree was obvious. Pet outside a health clinic? Jason zoomed in. Oswaldo Clinica de Mujeres. He searched online; it offered reproductive services. "Did you get pregnant in high school? Who's the father?"

Jason was rereading Pet's college history when he noticed roommate Connie Mason. "Constance! Sal has your roommate and your cousin stashed away together in Mexico." Jason looked through the pictures again. Pet outside the clinic was younger than Pet in college. *Is that why your grades dropped? You got pregnant in your senior year and had an abortion.* Jason looked with greater interest at the pictures of Pet with her roommate. He was looking at her singing telegram pictures when he noticed a mirror behind Pet; the camera was partially covering her face, but the photographer was definitely Connie. "Of course!" Jason said. "Three in the picture and a fourth taking it! You took the picture, Constance Mason."

Jason reviewed the cast. "J.P., you're battling Hector; you beat Enrico and Ernesto already. Pet, you don't get along with your family; your roommate and cousin are squirrelled away in Sal's place. Are they your friends or not?" Jason decided to let things simmer over lunch.

"*Ola*, Señor Johnstone," José said. "You look tired. I'll get you a big cup of Mexican coffee!"

"Oh, hi, José," Jason replied. "Too much thinking."

"That make José much tired also." José brought a large mug of coffee. "This is of José the good morning cup."

"Thanks, José," Jason said. He called out from his table, "*Bonjour*, Simon. *Plat du jour, s'il vous plaît*."

"*Bien sur!*" came the reply and, shortly later, a croque monsieur with roasted asparagus.

Jason was just finishing his sandwich when J.P. himself approached the table. "Sal tells me it may soon be time to talk to you. Monday, ten a.m."

"Ten sharp," Jason replied. J.P. turned and left.

"Wowee wow!" José shook his hand in front of his neck. "Oh la la!"

Jason looked confused.

"Mr. the J.P. Burkeman never come to here!" José explained.

"Eureka!" Jason said before remembering José was there. *Hector is Circle!*

Jason was reinvigorated and left for his office with very quick good-byes to José and Simon. Sal was in his office waiting. "That smile is encouraging," he said. "What have you discovered?"

"J.P. and Hector are Circle boys in a chess game," Jason answered. "J.J., Brew, Enrico and Ernesto, Connie and Ricardo, you and me, and especially Pet. We're chess pieces!"

"Okay. What was the opening move?"

"Pet got pregnant in her senior year and aborted the child. Her very Catholic family couldn't accept her choice and disowned her."

"Too simple," Sal dismissed. "Think of something more perverse."

"Uncle Enrico," Jason realized. "The poem! He was the father!"

"Consider the timeline." Sal got up to leave. "Breakfast tomorrow," he said and closed the door behind him.

Jason mentally listed the chronology of critical events as best he could: pregnancy, abortion; rebellion; Harvard, Connie, J.J., Brew; picture; Trans Mexico, J.P.; BA; Connie's gone; post grad—*Who did you co-op with?*—TechSys board, Deltas; Palomex.

Pet's transcript indicated her first co-op placement was with Campbell Consulting Corp but the performance review was submitted by DBK Associates Ltd and all subsequent placements were with DBK. Jason looked up Campbell Consulting Corp. They are a local human resources consulting company. He called them and found out that Campbell Consulting had no record of Pet's transfer to DBK. The transfer was also contrary to her terms of employment.

"You're playing the sort of game that makes you interesting. Who are you, DBK?" Jason asked as he pulled up their website. It didn't take long to find out. The opening sentence of About DBK read 'Dell Burkeman Kinder is named after its three founding partners.' The director biographies revealed that Andrew Burkeman, president, was the son of founding partner Cecil Burkeman III. Even more interesting was the vice-president, Hector Gonzales. Jason looked back to Pet's family tree. Enrico Gonzales' second son. There were no Dells or Kinders to be found anywhere.

"Okay, Pet. The pregnancy is the motive and DBK is where you made your first move. How?" It was time for Jason to act.

"Pet, do you have time for a coffee?" he asked into the phone.

"No."

"Perhaps you should."

"Why?"

"DBK."

There was a short pause. "When?"

"Now." Jason wanted to see how strongly his mention of DBK would motivate Pet. "Jas'."

"Okay."

Pet was waiting when Jason arrived. “I don’t know what you think you know, Onesie,” Pet said, “but this can of worms doesn’t make good bait for fishing.”

Well, the fish is hooked, Jason thought, *and about to be landed.*

“You’d best be careful,” she warned. “There are plenty of sharks in these waters.”

“Is one of them Uncle Enrico?” Jason knew the answer but wanted to see what type of response he’d get.

“Uncle Enrico is a little fish, a minnow. He’s already been swallowed up by the sharks.”

“And how did you get Andrew Burkeman on board?”

“Tess’ idea, actually, because of a family disagreement. Tess spawned the idea when she saw my Burkeman connection, to keep up with the metaphor.”

“Who’s Tess?” Jason asked.

“Teresa Avila, my mother. She knew how immature J.J. was. She knew we could compromise him and leverage that into his father’s help with our problem,” Pet said. “She couldn’t very well let herself be seen destroying her own brother.”

“So your mom believed your side of the story?” Jason pressed.

“I didn’t think so at first.” Pet realized her slip. “Wait! What do you know?”

“Enough,” Jason bluffed. “Go on.”

“Tell me what you know!”

The worms were working so Jason cast another line. “Your cousin Ricardo also believed you.”

“How did you find out?” Pet insisted. “No one knows.”

“Yet here we are.”

“Even J.P. He didn’t care why I set Uncle Enrico up. He was just more than ready to take advantage of the fact that I did.”

“He got his brother to finance your post grad, then parachuted you onto the TechSys board.”

Pet didn’t see any benefit in withholding this truth. “Actually, the parachute was courtesy of J.J. and Brew.”

“Which antagonized Uncle Ernesto.”

"No, that was more about him building the Avizales building across the street from Burkeman Mexico. Uncle Ernesto's *huevos* grew too big."

"So how did you compromise J.J.?" Jason knew the answer but wanted to hear Pet's version.

"We caught him in some college prank that could put him up before the disciplinary board."

"And that was enough to get J.P. to act?"

"No, that was enough to get J.J. to introduce us to his dad," Pet snapped. "Our plan got J.P. to act."

"You and Connie?"

"Who told you all this? Nobody knows all this. Some, maybe, but not all."

"And they won't," Jason assured her. "Trust me."

"Not a chance," Pet said. "Why do you know all this?"

Jason couldn't think of a good answer. Why indeed? *Time to punt.* "So I can see just how firmly you are on our side against InSyst."

"InSyst is Uncle Gus' thing," Pet revealed. "So, yea, I'm totally on side."

It fits, Jason thought. "Thanks for the coffee. We'll do it again soon."

"Real soon," Pet bit off, fuming. *Summoned and dismissed by this... upstart!* She still wasn't prepared to accept that Jason might be anywhere near her equal. *That peon is digging in the wrong field!*

Another Evening

Jason arrived back at the office just as Colleen got off the elevator. "Care to go back up?" Jason asked. "I left my coat in my office. You can see where I hang my hat in the daytime."

"I'd love to. I'll check out your secretary."

As she stepped back off the elevator, Colleen looked around. "Wow!"

"Hello, Miss Colleen," Miss Grimm said. "You seem every bit as lovely as I've heard."

"Thank you." Colleen blushed. "You must be Janice. Jason says you're much nicer than Miss Grimm!"

"I'm glad he thinks so," Janice said, "but perhaps Miss Grimm is not getting the credit she deserves."

It was Jason's turn to blush. "Come see the view from my office," he said.

"Wow!" Colleen repeated. "I can see all the way to the gulf from here!"

"Not that I get much time to look out windows."

"It's nice inside too." Colleen rubbed the leather desktop. "Who's that?" she asked of an oil portrait hanging behind the desk.

"Cecil Burkeman. Founder of Burkeman Holdings. Great-grandfather of J.P. Burkeman."

Colleen looked around at the other artwork. "Is that an original Remington oil?"

"No idea," Jason admitted. "I can tell you the computer is an original Hewlett Packard."

Colleen smacked his arm. "Uncultured brute!"

"I suspect Moses is trying to fix that. We'd better get to Tink's and give him another go."

"Did you take any art classes in Texas A&M?"

"Yes," Jason said. "Business arts." He earned another smack.

"Moses definitely has his work cut out," Colleen said. "We'd better get to Tink's quickly!"

"It was nice meeting you, Janice," Colleen said as they left. "Have a good evening!"

"I will," Janice said. "I have a good book and a glass of chardonnay waiting for me at home."

"No husband?"

"No Mr. Grimm," she assured her. "I'm married to my work."

"Janice Grimm?" Colleen blushed a deep red.

Janice smiled. "Goodnight!" she said cheerfully.

"I hope you never get married to your work," Colleen said in the elevator.

"I'm monogamous," Jason assured her.

She squeezed his arm and snuggled closer. "I'd better catch you fast."

"I'm caught. Don't let me get away."

"Honest?"

"More than I've ever been."

Their train ride was a quiet cuddle, and Jason whistled as they walked hand in hand to Tink's.

"What tune is that?" Colleen asked.

"*Could I Have This Dance*," Jason answered. "Couldn't you tell?"

"Maybe through soda crackers."

"Not my forte?"

"Not your forte."

"Can you whistle?"

"Better than that!" Colleen said. "But, no."

"That's harsh," Jason said with an exaggerated frown. "Is this the real Colleen coming out?"

"Look!" Colleen pointed just ahead. "Tink's."

"Just in time."

Moses was waiting anxiously, his coat already on. "We're going to Pawel and Stefan's for *golabki*," he said as he downed the last of his ale.

Pawel and Stefan rented a basement suite three blocks away; it was tiny with low ceilings. Pawel's bedroom was more like a closet and Stefan slept on the couch. Their table was a piece of plywood on top of four double-stacked milk crates. There were two very plain wooden chairs and three wooden crates around it. Pavel and Stefan managed to do all their cooking with a toaster oven, a microwave and an electric frying pan. The toaster oven and microwave both sat on the kitchenette counter; they had to be shuffled about to free any workspace. The frying pan was in the bathroom on top of a board resting on the tiny sink mounted to the wall. A block of wood was wedged between the board and faucet to prevent the whole thing from tipping over. "The circuits will pop if we plug them in together," Pawel explained.

Jason pointed to the top of a chest of drawers against one wall, the most obvious spot, in his mind, for a frying pan. It was reserved for two religious statues, a candle and a cross. "Why not use the frying pan there?" Jason asked. "There would be room if you put those things closer together."

"Because we need to have a space for our prayers," Stefan answered.

"The best space?" Jason asked.

"Yes," Stefan said. "To remind us of our priorities."

"More important to pray than to eat?"

"My nana always thought so," Colleen replied.

"But science is disproving all that," Jason argued.

"Science is only stopping us from thinking properly about it," Moses said. "Science cannot disprove anything which is beyond itself."

"Given time," Jason predicted, "science will reveal all things."

"Science observes directly," Moses said, "by interpolation or extrapolation. It can observe only that which is observable and known to be observable."

"Which will be all things," Jason said.

"No," Moses replied. "It must be physical, temporal and spatial, or directly relatable to something that is. And it must be limited or it cannot be observed."

"Why limited?" Colleen asked.

"Because it must be here and not there, not now as it was then, or both," Moses answered, "or we would miss it altogether."

"But all things are limited," Jason argued.

Pawel was serving dinner. "Not God!" He invited Colleen and Moses to sit in the two chairs and straightened one of the crates for Jason. Jason sat tentatively; he was not at all sure the crate would hold him.

"He cannot make a round square." Jason resorted to a stock argument.

"That is a limitation on square," Moses said, "not on God."

"Zubrowka!" Stefan pulled a bottle of vodka from under the table, divided it evenly between five glasses and passed them around the table.

"You cannot prove that God exists," Jason argued.

"We can believe without proof," Stefan said. "Pawel and I do, so we will thank Him for this meal. You may join or not, as you wish."

Pawel, Stefan, Colleen and Moses all signed themselves with a cross; the Poles recited some words and they all signed themselves again.

"You cannot prove that one plus one equals two," Moses said, returning to the previous topic, "but you can do many things if you accept that it does."

"I can do many things," Jason replied, "whether I accept that God exists or not."

"Will you know why?" Moses asked.

"I do things for many reasons. Different things for different reasons."

"Not in that sense. In the sense that things are, rather than are not, that there's order rather than chaos."

"Intelligent creator."

"That's God."

"I don't believe in God."

"So how did things come to be?" Pawel asked.

"They just did."

"You are very stubborn to believe that everything is explained by science, by action and reaction, conservation of matter and energy," Stefan said. "Yet you make us to believe that there is no first cause for everything to be."

"To be as it is," Pawel added, "with rhythm, with harmony, with patterns."

"It is natural to become chaos," Stefan said. "Yet everywhere we see beauty. This is just atoms tossed into the universe by random?"

"I thought you two were here to learn English," Jason said, changing the subject. "You seem to be doing just fine."

"We speak well of our faith," Stefan explained, "because we think of it more often and more carefully than you think of your science."

"Purpose and consequences," Pawel added. "Will you know your obligations from your science?"

"If everything is only action and reaction," Stefan said, "choosing this or that is mere deception. You can choose only so you can love."

"You will know what you love," Pawel said, "when you think about what you choose... carefully, not as a child."

"And why do some people choose to go to work when they don't love work?" Jason asked.

"Mostly because they love money," Stefan said, "which is also something they should think about carefully."

"But everyone needs money."

"What for?" Pawel asked. "To eat it?"

"People don't need money," Stefan said. "They need things they get with money."

"Sometimes they don't know what they already have," Pawel said, "because they are busy chasing money."

"Where do you live?" Stefan asked. "I bet you live in a beautiful big place with a lot of nice things."

"Yes," Jason admitted.

"And how much time do you spend there?" Stefan asked.

"I pretty much just sleep there."

"You work longer and harder to get a nicer place that you have less time to be in," Stefan said. "Do you think you enjoy being asleep in your fancy house more than Pawel and I enjoy being asleep here?"

"When our eyes are closed," Pawel added, "this place looks just the same as yours."

"And the *pierogies* are much better!" Moses intervened.

"And the vodka!" Stefan retrieved another bottle from under the table.

"All true, and I very rarely have such good company at my place," Jason conceded. "But, no thank you," he said, indicating the vodka. "I must get back home." The vodka was much stronger than ale or wine, and Jason was sure it would be too much for Colleen.

"Tomorrow starts early; Jason must keep paying his mortgage," Colleen said. "Thank you so much for having us over!"

"Yes," Jason said. "Thank you for inviting this scientist into your religious domain. I enjoyed it."

"All scientists are in God's domain," Pawel said. "They are all most welcome. Just, some... they don't know it."

Jason, Colleen and Moses shook hands with Pawel and Stefan as they left. "I have to admit," Jason said, "my place may look better, but the food is definitely better here!"

The trio passed by Tink's on the way to Colleen's. Moses bade adieu and went in; Colleen and Jason continued on. There was time for a long after-Tink's at Northside High as they pondered the evening. A quick kiss at Colleen's door and Jason was off to another short stay—with his eyes closed for most of it—in his expensive townhouse. "They have a point," he conceded as he looked around.

Jason lay in bed staring at the ceiling, his hands behind his head. *Why do I want this promotion? I was comfortable without it; I'm not now. Do I truly want this promotion? Perhaps we need a degree of discomfort to be comfortable, a bit of chaos to sort out.*

Sleep eluded Jason. *I've agreed to do something without really having any idea what that something is. Why? Because I was asked? What is it that I will do? Will I like doing it? Will it be moral? Will it be legal?* Jason had to admit that was a real concern. *Will I be able to do it when I find out what it is—technically, physically, morally, legally?*

Legally was difficult to think about. *Will I break the law? Will I get trapped like Pet with that picture? Like Sal, somehow, that's making him bow out?* Jason didn't really like the pieces in this chess game. *Maybe Sal is a bit of a charming rogue, but he's stated plainly enough that the only reason to trust him is that he needs help that can only be delivered through our mutual cooperation, through necessity, not choice. I like the pieces from my old match. Charles, Gail, Scott. Maybe I like Janice more than Miss Grimm, but that's really the only improvement. And Colleen, of course, but that's not work. Moses, Maria. Pawel and Stefan.* Eventually his worries surrendered to his fatigue and he fell asleep.

Good Fishing

Four thirty came earlier the next morning than it had in years. Jason wanted to toss his clock and roll over, but that wasn't an option in this game. *Free will is not as free as most people try to believe, and this is not a free country. Nothing is free.* He sat up in bed.

Jason chose the strongest pod he could for his Nespresso. "Do your thing, caffeine!" To appease the growling stomach gods he found a stale donut that was just passable when dunked. He switched on his eighty-eight-inch TV to listen to the news. "—reliable sources. InSyst Management Corp CIO César Gonzales called the rumors premature. TechSys Inc's spokesperson, Sandra Heatherington, declined comment. Reporting from New York, this is Pamela Stewart." Jason switched off the TV, left his unfinished coffee on the counter, grabbed his coat and rushed out.

Sal was waiting for the elevator when Jason arrived at the office. "You heard?" Sal asked.

"I just caught the tail end. You leaked the takeover!" They got in the elevator.

"Negotiations for a joint venture, actually," Sal said. "Analysts will realize that the only joint venture possible would be an updated version of one, the other or both companies' core product—in which case a takeover or merger is the more likely scenario."

"So the media business analysts will start roiling the water."

"Exactly, which will distract our foes from pointing their fingers at us."

Sal led Jason straight into the kitchen; it was too early for José. "Good morning, Simon."

"Good morning, Sal, Jason. My apple-cinnamon Danish are ready. I will press you some fresh coffee."

"Thank you, Simon."

Sal led Jason out of the kitchen. "What on earth did you do yesterday to incur such wrath from Pet?" Sal asked. "I haven't been able to get her that excited for ages."

"I presented myself as an equal. I revealed I know more than she wants me to."

"She ordered me to call off my stray dog," Sal confided. "You didn't mention the picture, did you?"

"Nor anything that could only be attributed to the picture," Jason said. "Unpleasant family history."

"Uncle Enrico?"

"Uncle Enrico."

"It worked."

"Like a charm. She confirmed all that I suspected and also revealed that InSyst is Uncle Gus."

"Augusto Gonzales," Sal clarified. "Last of the three brothers that were the 'zales' side of Avizales. J.P. has been taking them down one by one; after this it will only be Hector left."

"The 'Avi' side?"

"Exactly. Groupo Avizales will be so wounded that J.P. will have little opposition."

"So why now?" Jason asked.

"The leak?" Sal clarified.

"The leak."

"Pet was so enraged, that I knew you were ready," Sal said. "It was bold of you to approach her without checking with me first."

"Sorry."

"To the contrary, Jason, it encouraged me! You'll need to make many more such rash decisions if I'm to succeed."

"So how far, exactly, will I have to go?"

"Nobody can say, at this point. But, at minimum, well over the edge of the cliff."

Jason was sure he didn't want to be in this game, but he was even more sure he couldn't avoid it. "Is there any upside?"

"What doesn't kill you—" Sal said.

"—only makes you stronger," they said together.

"Suggestions?" Jason asked.

"Keep studying, know more, think devious. Then more devious!"

"Imagine my worst nightmare?"

"It won't be imagination much longer," Sal said. "But eventually you wake up."

"To what?"

"Victory or defeat; I make it fifty-fifty. Which is better than it was. Find more dirt."

"Where?"

"I can't say," Sal confessed. "We're pretty much up to the same speed on the Mexican side and I'm not about to help you find the dirt on our side."

Sal, Jason guessed. *The dirt I need is his.*

"*Ola*, Mr. Sal, Mr. Johnstone," José said. "You are early! I will make you some Mexican coffee. You no need to finish that ones. You eat already? No *huevos*?"

"Thanks, José," Sal said, "but it's time for me to leave."

"I'll stay for one cup," Jason promised.

Sal nodded to Pet as they passed each other in the doorway. Pet just glared back, then charged over and sat at Jason's table. "Don't you dare mention anything to anyone!"

"Tell me your version. The version I heard is probably biased."

"I saw Sal was here," Pet said. "He told you!"

"Different source," Jason claimed. "Your version?"

"Not here. Jas'. Let's go!"

"Sorry, José," Jason said. "Rain check."

"No rain, Mr. Johnstone," José said. "Are you come lunchtime?"

"*Si, amigo, hasta luego!*"

Jason and Pet left together; Brew looked twice as they passed him in the hall. "Morning, Pet, Onesie."

"Morning," Jason said.

Pet stayed silent, brooding.

They met Colleen in the lobby as they went out. "Good morning, Jason," she said sweetly.

Pet kept walking without acknowledging Colleen. "Who's that?" she asked once they were outside.

"Fifteenth floor," Jason said.

"Get me a quatro Americano," Pet ordered Jason as they entered Jas'. "I'll get us a table."

Jason didn't see any empty tables. He lined up and watched. Pet was digging in her purse as she approached a table with two people, obviously students, who were studying together. Jason couldn't hear what was said but watched Pet hand them some money. They packed their things and left.

Jas poured Jason's black dark roast before he had a chance to order. "And a quatro Americano for her highness," she said. "I'll deliver it."

"Good memory," Jason congratulated.

"Some people are worth remembering, Jason," Jas winked.

"I don't recall telling you my name."

"I asked Charles," Jas admitted. "He says you're taken."

"Very."

"I'm patient."

"How much?"

"Very!"

"The cost," Jason said, flustered.

"It's on the house."

"Thank you." Jason took his coffee to the table. "Yours is on the way."

"Who's your snitch?" Pet got straight to business.

"Confidential," Jason said. "You don't want me blabbing; they don't want me blabbing. Your version."

"The only one you need to know," Pet declared. "Uncle Enrico raped me. I aborted his spawn. He hates me. I hate him. End of story."

"But your dad believed his brother."

"Uncle Gus gave him an alibi; they both lied. Two against one."

"And your mother?"

"Tess is a Mexican wife," Pet said. "What can I say?"

"She didn't believe you either."

"I didn't think so at first, but she says Father made her support her brothers."

"So when you wound up at DBK, you saw the chance to get back at Uncle Enrico."

"I saw that chance when J.J. was in my class. DBK is when I found out Tess believed me. She's the one who thought up the Trans Mex thing. Ricardo and Hector both hate their dad for what he did to me so they were only too glad to help. Ricardo told Tess, she told me, and I told Andrew."

"So why did J.P. broker the deal?"

"Andrew didn't want Uncle Enrico catching on."

Jason noticed something in the way Pet spoke Andrew's name. "To the deal or to your affair?"

"To either!" Pet said. "He didn't want Uncle Enrico to see HLH coming and he didn't want a divorce."

"So Ricardo passed inside information to Andrew through you so that HLH could pre-empt any moves by Trans Mexico."

"Yes, and we passed false information back the other way."

"And your mother helped."

"She didn't like any of her brothers even before Uncle Enrico raped me and Uncle Gus lied about it."

"Why not?"

"Think about it," Pet said. "Tess is the eldest child, but in a Mexican family. Her father owned one of the biggest companies in Mexico yet, because she's only a girl, she was never accepted into the business. She's older and smarter and should have been the one to take over the reins but, because she's a girl, she was basically sold to my father to consummate the Gonzales-Avila merger. Tess says my uncles are petulant little boys and always will be petulant little boys."

"So, she was happy to throw Uncle Ernesto under the bus too?"

"No, he did that himself," Pet claimed. "He thought that, if J.P. couldn't stop Avizales from building their head office across the street from Burkeman Mexico's head office, he couldn't stop Palomex from poaching his business."

"You didn't help kill Palomex?"

"Uncle Ernesto didn't rape me and he didn't give Uncle Enrico his alibi," Pet said. "He stayed neutral. They were his brothers; I was only a niece."

"But you did play a part." Jason cast his net again.

"Andrew insisted. That's why I finally left him; I realized he was just using me."

"Which is when Hector was recruited to replace you." More fishing.

"No, Ricardo landed at DBK as part of the Trans Mexico deal. Hector took over when Ricardo left." Pet was letting her guard down.

Keep fishing, Jason thought. "To be with Connie," he said.

"To be with Connie," Pet confirmed. "But he made Uncle Gus believe he was switching sides again. That's why Uncle Ernesto gave him Hacienda Gonzales."

Jason paused as the new information settled in. *Uncle Gus is the alpha dog.*

Pausing wasn't something Pet did well. "I hated you yesterday," Pet admitted. "I hated you this morning. But now... I'm relieved. I've been keeping these secrets locked inside for so long; it feels good to admit them to someone. I still don't like you, but I don't hate you anymore."

"There's still more that I know," Jason bluffed, "and we have to discuss it. But for now, I have to get back to take a call I'm expecting."

"I need to get away for a while," Pet said. "I'm going for a walk at Kinder Lake."

"Soothe the guilt?" Jason fished for more insight into Pet's time at Dell Burkeman Kinder.

"He was a really nice man," Pet said. "Dell was an ass and deserved what he got, but Steve was so nice. And Barb treated me like a daughter, even after she took to Blanton's. That accident was so horrible!"

"Put your cell number in here," Jason said. "I'll call you." Jason wasn't really expecting any calls, but now he had a good reason to get back to his office. *What exactly happened to Dell, Steve and Barb? What accident?* Today's fishing yielded an excellent catch.

Pet left; Jas came over with another dark roast and sat with Jason. "Do you mind?"

"Not at all. Another one on the house?"

"My house, my rules," Jas said. "How'd you tame that one?"

"What do you mean?"

"Well, the best way to describe that one is with a word ladies shouldn't use. But she sat there with you and you were in control."

"It was business."

"Uh-uh." Jas shook her head. "That got personal. A woman can tell."

"If it was personal, I shouldn't tell."

"I don't care what she said; I just want to know how you got her to say it. You were a man in charge!"

"Whatever." Jason shrugged.

"Are you kidding me?" Jas asked. "You're not telling!"

"It was business. It would bore you."

"Uh-huh. My black butt it was business!"

"Your black butt can park itself there as long as it wants," Jason said. "Private is still private."

"I'll tell you Junior's secret."

"Cynthia?" Jason guessed. "His kids that aren't his wife's kids?"

"You're no fun at all," Jas said. "Brew's secret."

"Brew's a train wreck," Jason said. "He doesn't keep secrets."

"My secret!" Jas was desperate.

"Your silent partner?" Jason was getting good at guessing.

"But whooo is my silent partner?" Jas teased.

"Sal," Jason guessed.

Jas pushed her chair back a little in exasperation. "You're no fun at all!"

"Hey, your game."

Jas paused, looking inquisitively at Jason. "You don't know why."

Jason made a very long cast. "The accident," he said confidently.

Jas looked at him with fear in her face. "You're making me all tingly," she confessed. "I'm right about you."

"I'm expected for lunch," Jason said nonchalantly. It was the most honest he'd been since he came in.

"Don't be a stranger." She was too startled to come up with anything better. Jas was tingly, down to her toes!

Jason went straight to the executive lounge. "*Ola*, José."

"I got you burritos, Mr. Johnstone," José said excitedly. "Mr. Simon make them for me. I told him you will like them too!"

"Thank you, José," Jason said. "I haven't had good burritos since school."

"One day you will come to my house," José said. "My wife make them very better than Mr. Simon."

"I'm looking forward to it."

"You will bring your *muchacha*! I have see you with her in the downstair. She is *muy linda*! My wife will like her very much!"

"Colleen," Jason said. "You've been spying on me."

"Oh no, Mr. Johnstone. I only see you like each other very lots; you looking on each other *muy dulcemente*! You are holding together your hands."

"And kissing?" Jason teased.

"Yes, Mr. Johnstone, but José no watch that!"

"*Bonjour*, Simon," Jason called to the kitchen. "I haven't forgotten you! José is keeping me busy here."

"*Bonjour*, Monsieur Johnstone," Simon replied. "Send Nigaud here for your burritos!"

"Coming!" José said.

Jason sat at his favourite table by the window. Sal came in and sat with him. "What are you up to?" Sal asked. "She called me. She never calls me."

"Pet or Jas?" Jason asked.

"Pet, of course," Sal said. "Why would Jasmine call me?"

"She will," Jason assured him. He noted that Sal used Jas' full name.

"You're poking a hornet's nest," Sal warned.

"Pet's or yours?"

"The hornets are swarming, and they have very nasty stings."

"We both know that," Jason said, then quietly added, "I'm supposed to be you but you don't want me to know what you don't want to admit about yourself. Well, I already do."

"Jasmine didn't tell you," Sal replied just as quietly.

"No, she didn't, but she'll call you to tell you that I found out."

"How?"

"Dell Burkeman Kinder. You may as well tell me your version in case mine has errors."

"After lunch. Not here."

Sal got up and poured his own coffee. "It's okay, José," he said, raising his cup in José's direction.

Sal rejoined Jason and continued in the same hushed voice. "You're turning out to be better at this game than I ever imagined you would be. Perhaps there really is hope for me yet."

Simon's burritos were truly delicious; Jason enjoyed them. Sal sat patiently with his coffee, pondering.

I'm not quite prepared, Jason thought as he and Sal walked back to their office. *I wish he hadn't shown up so quickly. If I flinch now, he'll know I'm bluffing. Fourth and long. Hail Mary or punt?*

"Okay," Sal said as he closed the door behind him. "Where do you want me to start?"

"How much time do you have?" Jason decided to punt. "Make sure you allow time for the accident."

Sal's face reddened—Jason wasn't sure whether in anger or in shame. "Let's start with the accident. What do you know?"

Jason was forced to punt again. "The favour Andrew demanded and who delivered."

Sal slumped into a chair. "J.P. never had a stomach for it; I had to."

"You had his back." Jason stalled for time as he scanned online news reports of the Kinder accident.

"There were too many problems. This move solved the biggest one. I didn't know the exact details at the time. What else could I do?"

According to witnesses, the Kinders' chauffeur swerved to avoid a man who committed suicide by jumping from an overpass in front of them; their limousine hit an overpass pillar instead and flipped several times, killing all occupants. Police speculated, 'Unfortunately for the Kinders, the unidentified man probably waited for a larger vehicle to make his death more certain.'

"Was it really for J.P.?" Jason asked, still stalling. "If J.P. was gone, you were gone! Go over it to make sure I have the details straight."

A later report identified the jumper as Francesco Muro, who, ironically, left a typed note indicating he was despondent over the loss of his job shortly after the death of his wife and two sons in a traffic accident.

"What specifically do you want clarified?" Sal was beginning to suspect that Jason didn't really know as much as he was claiming.

"Muro." Another punt.

Sal slumped further in his chair. He was concerned more by the callous manner in which Jason was pursuing the conversation than by what was being asked. This was a very serious matter and Jason was dividing his time between it and whatever he was doing on that damn computer! It was inconceivable to him that Jason might be calling plays on the fly.

"Kumar Rampursad. Somebody I wish I'd never met," Sal confessed. "He caught Frank at the fax machine and panicked. Once Frank was dead, Kumar figured he may as well kill a second bird with the same stone."

These punts were working. "Frank was going to expose the secret."

"We might never have figured it out ourselves if Jasmine hadn't found a ream of documents still in the fax the next morning. The *Chronicle*'s number was dialled in. The EPA would have been all over it; they would have found out everything."

"Barbara could drown many things in her bourbon," Jason said, "but not that. That's why you had Frank drop in on Barb."

"No," Sal said. "Kumar told me about a conversation he'd had one night with a drunken Barbara. I mentioned that she should be discouraged from talking about such things. Kumar added two plus two and came up with ten; I didn't intend for him to do anything."

"But you couldn't report his involvement without disclosing DBK's connection."

"No. Either cover up Kumar's evil deeds or expose ours—face heavy fines, bad publicity, falling stock prices, maybe jail."

"What happened to Kumar?"

"That junkie? Probably dead by now. We had him leave town, but that's it."

"And that's your debt to Jas."

Sal cocked his head and squinted a bit. "Jas decided that exposing the truth wouldn't help anyone; no one could be brought back from the dead and the polluting had already stopped. Barbara's foundation actually made a substantial contribution to help rehabilitate contaminated land before this happened. You've become cruel; you really are becoming me. I'd hoped, for the sake of my soul, that you wouldn't."

"Isn't that what you want?"

"You're succeeding a little too well."

The phone rang, and Jason picked it up. "May I speak with Sal, please?" a voice said.

"Who's speaking?" Jason asked.

"Ricardo Gonzales."

Jason put it on speaker.

"Hello," Sal said.

"Good afternoon, Sal." Sal jumped up, snatched the phone from Jason and shut off the speaker.

Jason strained to listen but only heard Sal's contributions.

"Yes... When?... Are you sure?... Did she say?... Is it possible?... Probably... Yes, I will... Goodbye... Tomorrow."

Sal passed the phone back to Jason. "How do you think Colleen would like Mexico?"

"Why?"

"You're going tomorrow. For the weekend. I want you to take her."

"Why?"

"She'll help you realize what's most important in life while you still have the option to choose."

"Do I?" Jason asked. "Wasn't that option taken away when you slammed me onto the board?"

Sal had changed so gradually he hadn't seen it coming. Jason, on the other hand, was evolving very rapidly. It scared Sal because he could no longer deny what he was. "Time for you to get to know Colleen," he said. "Learn who she is. Who you are with her. Love her. You both need to pack tonight. I'll arrange things; the limo will be at your place by six thirty tomorrow morning."

"Make it six," Jason suggested. "If Colleen agrees, we'll have to pick her up from her house."

"She can't sleep over with you?"

"Irish Catholic!"

"Good. I wish I had been brought up with more faith."

"Other than in the dollar?"

"The dollar is only as good as what you do with it." Sal folded his hands in his lap and rolled his thumbs. "I've squandered mine. I let my dollars rob me of my time... and my wife's time..." Sal slumped down and turned his gaze from Jason toward his foot as he tapped it on the floor. "And kids."

Jason leaned back and folded his hands behind his head. He rolled his chair a few inches away from the desk. He watched for a while as Sal shrank before him. *What is this?* Jason logged out, switched off the power bar, grabbed his coat and left. "Bye, Sal." *I'm just doing what he wants, and now he doesn't seem to want it.*

An Early Night

Jason got to the lobby before Colleen. He had plenty of time to think about many things he didn't want to think about. Instead of eagerly watching the elevators as he usually did of late, Jason stared blankly out the window with his hands in his pockets.

Colleen saw his furrowed brow reflected in the window as she came up behind him. She touched his shoulder. "What's wrong?"

"Everything," Jason said, "except you."

"And Tink's," Colleen consoled. "Moses, Maria, Pawel and Stefan... Northside High."

"That's all part of you."

"Tink's and Moses were before me."

"They're not the same Tink's and Moses," Jason said. "Maria's Maria, but we know her better than I ever did."

"What happened today?"

"I got caught up in the game," Jason acknowledged. "I stopped caring about why."

"I can't believe that."

"It's as if work is just a giant jigsaw puzzle. We just keep putting all the pieces together, wherever we can make them fit. The only goal is to finish. But this puzzle keeps growing; it will never be finished. Why do people do puzzles anyway? It's not to look at the finished picture; that would be easier if no one cut it up in the first place. I guess it's good for kids. They can practice manual dexterity and spatial recognition, but old people, why do they do jigsaws? To fill time. That's what work is. No noble cause. Just idling. Filling our time and filling our pockets. Who stops nowadays to think about what they're accomplishing? Are we making the world a better place? Will anyone truly benefit from what we do? Or are we merely helping them idle along in lives similar to our own? Will anyone care?"

"Is this a Moses moment?" Colleen asked.

"Maybe a pre-Moses moment. He seems to have become discouraged and opted out. I think I'm in a period of discernment. What am I doing... and why?"

"And what will you do with the answer?"

"Nothing. Probably."

"Or go out and buy a shiny red sports car?"

"The male's ultimate signal of surrender."

"So what do we do now?" Colleen asked.

"Pack," Jason said. "I've been summoned to Mexico and you've been invited."

"As Colleen or as window dressing?"

"As Colleen. I think Sal is genuinely concerned for me... for us."

"I don't know if I'm ready," Colleen said. "Are we ready for a trip together?"

"A weekend in Mexico. Not really a trip together."

"Yes, Jason, it's a trip together. A man and woman discerning their future is not the same as a couple of college buddies on spring break. I want to do this the right way."

"That's partly my point," Jason said. "I have to go and I'd like you to come. We'll be away from the usual distractions and I'd like to talk seriously with you... about us... about you, me, work, life. What are our goals and ambitions? Do we have any? Are mine compatible with yours? I'm confused about what I'm doing at work. I don't want to be confused about what I'm doing with you."

"Separate rooms?"

"Separate rooms."

"I'll go," Colleen said. "Where, exactly, are we going?"

"I don't know. Sal arranged everything. All I know is we'll pick you up at six thirty tomorrow morning."

"So how will I know what to pack?"

"I'm sure it will be casual, business casual, and hot. There will probably be a pool."

"And bikinis?" Colleen teased.

"It's hot!" Jason defended.

"Hot bikinis?"

"And margaritas."

"We had better be quick at Tink's tonight," Colleen said, "and no Northside High. I'll need time to pack."

"It's only two days," Jason reminded her.

"It's a woman thing."

"As long as you don't forget your bikini." This earned Jason a shove. "That's a man thing."

Jason and Colleen were silent for the rest of the trip, holding hands with their arms interlocked.

"Hi, Maria," Colleen said when they came through the door of Tink's.

"Hi, you two," Maria said. "I recommend the fish and chips tonight. Fresh halibut!"

"You two look happy tonight," Moses said.

"Hi, Moses," Jason said. "We're together!"

"Young and in love. A fine pair! So, Jason, did you slay any dragons today?"

"I may have tamed one or two; it's hard to say."

"It may not be fair to slay them before you're sure they won't be tamed," Moses said. "But the finding out is often more dangerous than the beast."

"I'm finding out just how dangerous," Jason said, "and it worries me that I may be dragging Colleen into the fray."

"You're not dragging Colleen anywhere she doesn't want to be," Colleen assured him.

"And do you know just where that is?" Jason asked. "I don't."

"By your side."

Jason smiled and Colleen blushed.

"It's a dangerous place. There's a whole thunder of dragons circling about," Jason said, "and they're all breathing fire."

"Where are you in this picture?" Moses asked.

"I don't know whether I'm a dragon whelp or a

soon-to-be-crispy villager."

"Why not be the knight in shining armour?" Maria suggested as she brought their drinks.

"My knight in shining armour," Colleen said.

"Could you be content as a maiden in distress?" Jason asked.

"As a rescued maiden."

"You can't be rescued until you're in distress," Moses warned.

"Put me in chains!" Colleen said.

"Why?" Moses asked his favourite question.

"The knight can only win if there's a maiden to save. I want Jason to win."

"And live happily ever after," Maria said. "Fish and chips?"

"One piece for me," Colleen said. "Thanks, Maria."

"What dragons have you slain lately?" Jason asked.

"My dragon slaying days are over, I'm glad to say," Moses replied.

"So what do you do before Tink's time?" Colleen asked.

"Come with me tomorrow and I'll show you," Moses said. "You'll have fun."

"We can't," Colleen apologized. "We're off to Mexico."

Moses looked surprised. "Chasing dragons?"

"Getting new armour, I hope," Jason said, "and maybe a sword or two."

"Any that fit Colleen?"

"None of that for me, thank you," Colleen said. "I'll just be there to remind him what he's fighting for."

"Next week then," Moses said. "It will still be there to do."

"No clues?" Jason asked.

"I don't wish to scare you off."

"Ominous," Colleen said.

"Awesome," Moses assured her.

"That was fast," Jason said as Maria served their food.

"I had the cook put it on before I took your order," Maria confessed.

"Including my one piece?" Colleen asked.

"You're tiny," Maria said. "If you hadn't asked I would have suggested it. Where are you going?"

"Mexico," Jason said.

"Anywhere near Cancun?" Maria asked. "I have relatives there."

"I don't know exactly where," Jason admitted.

"Men don't worry about such little details!" Colleen jibed.

"The people who need to know, know," Jason said.

"Including the State Department?" Maria asked. "Some parts can be quite dangerous."

"I'm sure this part will be," Jason said, "but hopefully not for us."

"Business?" Maria asked.

"And some time for serious talk too," Colleen said.

"I'd say you two are at that point." Maria winked at Colleen.

"Serious talk and casual attire," Jason said. "I hope these skinny white legs don't scare her away."

"More often," Maria said, "it's the serious talk that scares the boys away."

"Unless I miss my guess," Moses said, "the business part will scare him closer to Colleen." He looked meaningfully at Maria.

"I remember that look." Maria patted his back and lightly brushed the top of his head. "I've got other customers. I can't be spending all my time with you."

"And we've got packing to do," Colleen said. "We'd better finish this lovely halibut and head home."

"And I've got praying to do," Moses said.

"I didn't take you for a religious man," Jason said.

"It's the surest way back up from the bottom," Moses said. "Anyone who's been in a deep enough pit either learns to pray or stays in the pit."

"Or seeks therapy," Jason said.

"Unless the therapist also knows how to pray," Moses said, "they just help you jump from pit to pit, usually deeper each time. I've had my share of that."

"No offense, Moses," Jason said, "but your God may have left you only halfway up."

"I'm grounded, Jason. It's dangerous to soar with the eagles. I see as much as I need to see from here."

"Well..." Colleen said, trying to lighten the conversation, "you always seem happy enough!"

"Joyous," Moses said. "Much better than happy."

"Is there a difference?" Jason asked.

"More peace, less pleasure. Joy helps you love the right things."

"Well, I have Colleen," Jason said. "She's the right thing for me."

"You have her now," Moses said, "but if you believe she's a thing, you won't have her long."

"Of course she's a person!"

"Body, mind, heart and soul, each part more precious than the last. The body is the easy one, especially with ladies like Maria and Colleen." Moses nodded toward Colleen. "You haven't had time to know each other's mind, and minds change. Your hearts are entwined, just now, but you must lift them above things if you want them to remain so. Souls are elusive; most people don't even know their own."

"Bodies change too," Jason said.

"If a relationship doesn't progress beyond that level," Moses said, "it won't last long enough for that change to matter."

"Something that will matter," Colleen said, "is if I don't get home in time to pack some clothes."

"That would definitely get me closer to you!" Jason earned another smack.

Maria arrived with dessert just as Jason and Colleen got up. "You're not leaving already are you?"

"Off with you, then," Moses said. "It seems I'll have three portions of lava cake to keep me entertained."

"Your body will definitely be changing!" Colleen said.

"Bye, you two," Maria said. "Have fun in Mexico. Bring me back a T-shirt."

Colleen gave Maria a hug. "Bye."

Jason and Colleen were too busy contemplating what the weekend would bring to do any talking. Outside her door, Jason gave Colleen a tender embrace. "Six thirty," he said and kissed her forehead.

Jason went home and packed. He set his coffee maker to brew at four fifty-five and his alarm clock to ring at five, and put his suitcase by the door. He showered, went to bed and slept soundly.

Priorities

Country music and the aroma of fresh coffee woke Jason from a deep sleep; he hit the snooze button, rolled over and tugged on the blankets. Music began playing for a third time before he remembered to hurry. He jumped out of bed and dashed to the shower; he washed, shaved and dressed in five minutes flat. He had his coffee and a bowl of cereal, washed the dishes and rushed down to the lobby just as the limo arrived. “Good morning, Cedric!” Jason said in greeting.

“Good morning, sir.” Cedric put Jason’s suitcase in the trunk and opened the door.

“Good morning, Jason,” Sal said.

“Oh!” Jason said. “I wasn’t expecting you. Good morning.”

“Where’s your friend’s apartment?” Cedric asked.

“Just past Northside High. North on Cochran and right on Ryon; the white one with green trim on the right.”

Colleen was waiting at the curb; still not sure she wanted to go. Jason opened the door and helped Colleen into the back as Cedric put her suitcase in the trunk. “You must be Sal. Good morning.”

“Good morning, Colleen,” Sal said. “It’s nice to finally meet you.”

“Maybe I’ll finally be able to find out where I’m going,” Colleen said.

“We’ll be staying at a small boutique hotel in Mérida.”

“Is it near the beach?”

“No, but there’s a nice pool.”

They drove onto the tarmac and right up to a Challenger jet with the BH logo on its tail. Sal introduced them to the pilot and steward as they climbed onto the jet.

They approach the runway then idled for about five minutes before the engines whirred loudly and they were pressed back into their seats. The jet climbed for about ten minutes before the engines became quieter and they levelled off. “You may unfasten your seat belts,” the pilot said.

The steward headed into the back of the plane, returning a short while later pushing a trolley with coffee, tea, orange juice and three servings of scrambled eggs, bacon and hash brown patties.

“The menu is extremely limited,” Sal said, “but deceptively good.”

“The menu here,” Jason asked, “or in Mérida?”

“We’ll keep the business to a minimum so you two will have time to explore,” Sal assured them. “I’m not your host so I won’t say more, other than I’m sure you will be well pleased.”

“Ricardo?” Jason asked.

“Constance,” Sal said. “She’s anxious to meet Colleen.”

“Who are Constance and Ricardo?” Colleen asked.

“A couple who found themselves in a situation similar to the one you two are in now,” Sal explained. “It will be worth your while to hear their candid account. There are many who don’t care a whit about what becomes of you after this fray; my wife is not one of them. You’ll also meet Myriam there.”

“Are you one of the many?” Colleen was bold enough to ask.

“At first,” Sal admitted. “Until I started studying him.”

“And now?” Jason asked.

“You care,” Sal said, “about the little people and about right and wrong.”

“Like you,” Jason said. “I see you with José and Simon.”

“Yes,” Sal said. “I’ve always cared about them; they somehow seem separate from the others. The executive lounge seems something other than the business. I am harsh and ruthless with those under me, and definitely with those against me. Simon and José have just never been part of that game. I didn’t really even think about the others as people; they were only either tools or opponents.”

“What changed?”

“I got kicked real hard in the teeth by someone who treated me the same way. I resented it. I never talked to Myriam about business but that one hurt so much. It took me completely by surprise. The person I trusted most. I didn't have anyone left to talk to so I opened up to Myriam."

"J.P.?" Jason asked.

"No, he can't kick me," Sal said. "This was someone I was sure wouldn't."

"If it wasn't J.P.," Jason asked, "why couldn't you talk to him?"

"I tried. He listened a bit, but when I paused for him to say something, he just asked, 'Is there a question in there somewhere?' Empathy and J.P. are complete strangers."

"What did you tell your wife?" Jason asked.

"Everything. Myriam told me she'd been waiting for that moment for ages. But if I wasn't prepared to tell her everything, she'd rather wait forever. I warned her that she'd probably hate me."

"What did she say?" Colleen asked.

"She told me that she'd hated what I do for a very long time but that, if she were capable of hating me, I would have seen her rather large rump heading out the door years ago. She told me that no one ever had, did or would love me like she did, least of all anyone at work."

"You didn't leave anything out?" Jason asked.

"I tried," Sal admitted, "but each time I did, she'd remind me of things I was sure she never knew. At one point I asked her why I was telling her since she already knew. She said, 'So you'll know.' She told me that unless I admitted out loud what I had done, I would never truly appreciate the gravity of my sins."

"And they were grave?" Colleen asked.

"Indeed they were."

"What happened then?" Jason asked.

"She made me promise to stop."

"And did you?" Colleen asked.

"I try," Sal confessed, "but she says I'm not allowed to sin by proxy either."

"Hence this trip?" Jason asked.

"Hence this trip," Sal confirmed, "and hence Colleen."

"No hope for me without Colleen?"

"Little. I wish there had been a Myriam for me while she and I were still Colleen and you."

Sal's phone rang. "Hello... It's for you." He passed his phone to Colleen.

"Hello... Mr. Lee! How did you know I was here?... What?... Okay... Yes." Colleen handed back Sal's phone. "That was my boss."

"Gerry agrees," Sal said, "that one weekend is too short."

"I didn't pack," Colleen said.

"I'm sure Myriam has thought of that," Sal said. "You're meant to relax."

"What will we do?" Colleen asked.

"Constance and Ricardo know the area very well; I'm sure they'll keep you busy enough. Me? I intend to sleep a lot, smoke Maduros and sip Azteca."

The jet landed and taxied to a hangar far from the main terminal; there was a Range Rover waiting there for them. "Good morning, Sal," the driver said as they stepped onto the tarmac.

"Good morning, Ricardo," Sal returned. "This is Colleen and Jason."

"Good morning, Colleen. Good morning, Jason. I've heard a lot about you."

"Good morning," Colleen and Jason said together.

Ricardo put their luggage in the back. Sal went over to speak with the pilot. When he returned, he announced, "Our return flight will leave a week Monday at three; let's see what kind of adventures you two can find until then."

Colleen squeezed Jason's arm tightly. "This is so not me!"

Sal held the back car door open for Colleen and Jason as they got in; then shut it and got in the front passenger seat. "How's Malka?" he asked Ricardo.

"Excited," Ricardo said. "More than usual."

"She has a project."

Ricardo pointed out some of the historic buildings as they drove. "That's Saint Ildephonsus Cathedral. It was finished in fifteen ninety-eight. They have Mass in English every Sunday at nine. Will you come with us? Sal does when he's here."

"I was hoping to find Mass," Colleen said. "Will you come, Jason? It's on my list of serious things."

"Well, if we're going to talk about it," Jason said, "I'd better get some idea of what we're talking about."

"Actually," Colleen squeezed his arm, "I was a bit concerned about how I would broach the subject."

"Consider it broached," Jason said. "Any more such subjects?"

"Yes," Colleen said. "When we're alone."

"We'll gang up on him to talk about family," Ricardo said.

"That hardly sounds fair," Jason objected.

"No. To protect you from Malka!" Ricardo explained. "We will be more gentle."

"Who's Malka?" Jason asked.

"That's what we call Sal's wife," Ricardo said. "It's like 'queen.' She's not about to let Colleen suffer what she did."

"Why do I feel like the bad guy?" Jason asked.

"You're not. Yet!" Sal said. "We want to help you not be."

"Group therapy," Jason said, "where the therapists are the group."

"Well," Sal said, "I'm still a patient with you."

About a half hour later, they pulled up to a grand gate. Above the gate was a sign that read Hacienda Gonzales.

"This hacienda has been in our family for generations," Ricardo explained. "We raise cattle and grow henequen. We mostly feed the cattle what's left after the sisal is stripped from the leaves. Some of the buildings have been converted to a hotel, but we still operate the farm. We have a little sisal museum and gift shop; most tourists find it fascinating."

Ricardo drove past the hotel and up to the main house. "You will stay in our guest wing."

They got out and collected their suitcases; Ricardo carried Colleen's. "This way," he directed.

They went in through the great room and down a corridor to the left. Sal disappeared into the first doorway. Ricardo opened the second. "Señorita," he invited. At the third door, he said to Jason, "This will be your room."

The room had pale yellow walls and rich coffee-coloured wood floor and furniture. Jason set his suitcase beside the chest of drawers and quickly tested the firm four-poster bed. He looked out his window to a private courtyard with a swimming pool and a sitting area under a vine-covered arbour. Ricardo was approaching two women, a young boy and a younger girl. Sal knocked on Jason's door. "Come with me," Sal said.

Sal had already collected Colleen, and he led them together out to the courtyard. "This is my wife, Myriam, and this is Connie."

"Welcome to my house," Connie said. "This is my little Maria and *el chico* over there is Luis."

"Come on, dear." Myriam took Colleen's hand. "We'll let the boys get in trouble by themselves," and she led her back to the house. Connie followed.

As the three women disappeared into the house, Sal said, "Ricardo will tell you a bit of Pet's history."

"Where to start?" Ricardo asked. "It's painful to talk about. My father is an evil man. He thinks everything in this world is there to serve him. Trish use to spend summers with us here at the hacienda; her parents didn't have much time for her. She's an only child and loved spending time with Hector and me. She's very attractive, as you know, and my mother wasn't. Arranged marriages were still common among the wealthy—more mergers than marriages—and my father was never fond of Mom.

"Two months into her final year at San Ignacio, Trish showed up one weekend. She didn't come in, just stood at the door yelling at my father. She and my father left together, and that's the last we saw her around here. Officially, Mom had a heart attack the following May, but rumours abound that my father, Trish and a bottle of pills were the true cause of her death. Hector and I were eleven and thirteen at the time, so we didn't hear the details.

"I didn't see Trish again until I went to Harvard—all our family goes to Harvard. I was surprised, one day, to see someone who looked just like Trish; it was Trish. At first she wouldn't speak to me, but after a few attempts, we met regularly in the cafeteria and a few times outside her sorority. That's how I met Connie; they were roommates.

"I found out what my father had done. It upset me, at first, and I didn't visit Trish for about a month. But after that, it started to make sense. I put the pieces together and went to tell her how sorry I was and how much I disliked my father. Connie had a job singing telegrams; she got her boss to hire Trish as well. Trish still wasn't earning enough to cover everything, but she would never accept a dime from her family. Another girl at the telegram business got Trish a job dancing in a night club. She hated it, but that was her only way of paying her Harvard expenses.

"After her BA, Trish got into a co-op program in the psych department and moved out of the sorority. I think she tried to put her past behind her because she never called Connie again and would only see me occasionally on campus. When Connie was with me, she'd ignore me completely. That Easter, Aunt Tess came to visit my father at the hacienda. I was surprised because she despises all three of her brothers. I told her about seeing Trish and she asked me to see if I could convince Trish to call. Trish told me she considered Rosa to be more her mother than Aunt Tess. After many attempts, Trish finally agreed."

"Who's Rosa?"

"Trish's *chacha*," Ricardo said.

"Nanny," Sal explained. "That's about the time J.P. and I met Pet. J.J. said he had a proposition that would be a good opportunity. J.J. and Pet made their pitch, but it turned out the opportunity was more for J.P.'s brother Andrew. So J.P. made the introduction. Andrew used that as an excuse to get J.P. back involved. It took a lot of my time and there really wasn't anything in it for J.P., not really for anyone, other than vengeance for Pet."

"Father deserved it," Ricardo said, "and I'm still glad we did it."

"It pretty much destroyed Enrico," Sal continued. "He's a pretty lonely character now."

"Nobody cares for him now," Ricardo added, "except the ones he buys tequila for. He drinks and sleeps and drinks some more, different friends every day."

"Enrico hated J.P. for taking over Trans Mexico and ripping it apart," Sal said. "But when Andrew kicked Avizales out of their head office and made it Burkeman Mexico, that was the last straw. There was no convincing him it wasn't J.P. He was so focused on J.P., he disregarded Andrew who then had free reign to pillage Enrico's other assets."

"But he didn't get this place," Jason said.

"It wasn't my father's. We stayed over there." Enrico pointed to the hotel. "This belonged to Uncle Ernesto; he lived in the grand villa where we are now."

"How did you come by it?" Jason asked.

"Aunt Tess," Ricardo explained. "She convinced Uncle Ernesto to give it to me and Connie as a wedding present if I'd come and work for him at Palomex. She said I could give him secrets about DBK."

"And did you?"

"Yes, false secrets. I was actually finding out what I could about Palomex and telling Hector, who took over my position at DBK. Trish was at DBK too, working for Andrew. But she wasn't that involved with the Palomex thing."

"Why did you go against your Uncle Ernesto?"

"I didn't really. Aunt Tess showed me a deed that put Hacienda Gonzales in Connie's name and a contract to redevelop it into what we have today. She said it would be my payment for helping with the merger of Palomex and HLH; all that was missing was the signatures. Andrew and Hector double crossed us. They got Uncle Ernesto to sign contracts based on the combined capabilities of both companies and then never delivered their share of services. When Palomex couldn't deliver, it was forced into bankruptcy; Andrew Burkeman made sure HLH was in the right position to pick up the pieces. Uncle Enrico finally signed over the deed to this place just to keep it away from Andrew. A week after the documents were finalized, he went up to Houston and hanged himself on Andrew's front gate."

"I arranged the financing to complete the construction," Sal said.

"Why?" Jason asked.

"It's a good investment," Sal said, "and it turns out Malka loves it."

"But J.P. doesn't know," Jason guessed.

"We know, Connie knows and Malka found out," Sal said.

"One of the things you were sure she didn't know?"

"Exactly."

Myriam led Connie and Colleen back into the courtyard. "Okay, men, time for a break! Pedro will serve *comida*." She clapped her hands twice and waved them about, signalling the men to change seats.

Pedro brought out tacos. "Don't eat too much," Myriam warned. "There's much more to come."

"Lunch is our main meal," Ricardo explained.

Five more courses followed; everyone was very full by the time Pedro cleared the last dishes away.

"Now, *siesta*!" Miriam declared. "No working." She led Connie and Colleen back into the big house.

Pedro appeared again with a box of Maduros and a bottle of Azteca. Sal and Ricardo accepted cigars, and all three had brandy.

"This is definitely not Houston," Jason said.

"Much more civilized," Ricardo said, "and not just Saturdays. Every day! Air conditioning spoiled things for office workers, but here on the hacienda, it's still too hot to work from noon to three."

"You don't have air conditioning here?" Jason asked.

"In thc hotel," Ricardo said, "but not our house or the workers' quarters."

"Is the farm profitable?"

"Not really," Sal answered. "But the workers are like family and the tourists like it. It would be more profitable if we leased the farming out and stop ranching altogether, but then it would be a different place."

"There's enough to go around," Ricardo said. "We're very comfortable and the workers are able to support their families well. We have a very nice community here."

The ladies came out again to use the pool. Colleen's swimsuit was conservative but still showed much more of her attractive form than Jason had seen before. Connie's swimsuit wasn't quite as conservative but was definitely less risqué than what Jason had seen in Pet's pictures. Myriam was wearing the same loose-fitting muumuu she wore earlier.

Connie and Colleen climbed onto a pair of floating chairs in the pool. Connie splashed the men. "Come on! Get your swim suits on!" After several minutes of splashing and cajoling, Jason and Ricardo surrendered and left to change into their swim trunks. Myriam went over to one of the loungers under the arbour, and Sal took the one beside hers. Jason and Ricardo were out again quickly. They cannonballed together into the pool, drenching both girls. The water was cool and refreshing. The four frolicked together until Pedro appeared with a pitcher of lemonade; then they joined Sal and Miriam under the arbour.

"So, did you men behave yourselves?" Myriam asked.

"Yes, my sweet," Sal assured her. "We had a proper siesta with no business."

"We enjoyed our cigars and brandy," Ricardo said, "and talked about life and community on Hacienda Gonzales."

"I came here originally," Myriam explained, "to get away from my beast of a husband. He had no time for me. I rattled around in our huge empty house in West U all alone, just me and Sal's nasty cat. I arrived here unannounced one very sad day and immediately felt more welcome than I ever did back in Texas."

"I didn't know where she was for more than two weeks," Sal admitted.

"He was upset I had the nerve to leave him; he wasn't upset I was gone."

"I was upset because your disappearance interfered with what I was doing, and I knew, inside, it was my fault; that made it really hard to tolerate."

"Is that why you're stepping back from TechSys?" Jason asked.

"Hardly. That was some four years ago."

"Five," Myriam insisted.

"Five. Myriam and I agreed that absence makes the heart grow fonder. We got along far better when we weren't together," Sal said. "I didn't have to interrupt my schedule for her. We talked when and if it was convenient for me."

"I will never stop loving Sal, but I hate that life and refuse to live it. I'm happy with Connie, Ricardo and all the people here. They have become my family." Myriam wiped away a tear. "I actually have responsibilities; I contribute. Back in West U, I wallowed in too much house for anyone and too much self-pity. I did nothing but order others to do what needed doing. I resented the workers for being happy. Here, no one pays any attention to me unless I'm trying unsuccessfully to do something; then they stop whatever they're doing and help me. They don't do things for me because I pay them; they do things for me because they care."

"Myriam became nice again," Sal said. "She was no longer mad at her life."

"Sal gave me a lot of things," Myriam said, "and they kept me happy for a while, but they lost their luster. I wanted Sal but he only gave me the tiny leftover bits of Sal. I sacrificed my career for Sal, and he sacrificed me for his career. I wanted to turn the clock back and find the old Sal, but we can't. Once I stopped trying, I learned to appreciate what I have."

"I'm confused," Jason said. "This is the opposite of Houston. Two completely different things."

"Yes," Sal said. "I need you to do the thing in Houston, and I pray that you'll do what you learn here. I don't want to be responsible for leading you down the same path I took."

"Can he do both?" Colleen asked.

"He's stuck with TechSys. And you seem to be stuck with him," Sal warned. "He has to continue that."

"So why are you doing this?" Colleen asked.

"I wish I could say it's because I care about you and Jason," Sal said, "but more truthfully, because I'm stuck. I played all my cards. I lost all my chips. Jason just happened to be there with some good cards, so I stole his hand and his seat."

"Andrew?" Jason tried to identify who had Sal's chips.

"No," Sal said.

"Who?"

"I wish I knew. It would be easier to anticipate what's coming."

"Why are we here then?" Colleen asked.

"Me," Myriam said. "I don't want you to lead the life I led. I thought that if you two saw this place, what we have here, it would help save you from what Sal and I are asking you to do."

"So I'm the reason Jason and I are here?" Colleen asked.

"Yes," Myriam said. "Mostly you, and Jason, but also me. I desperately want my Puki back. If he tricks you into helping us, he will still be Sal. He could, quite possibly, wind up being nobody—never for me but to himself. It's risky for us. But he can only be Puki if he reveals the whole choice you're making before you make it."

"It's actually a little late already, Jason. You've already been drawn in. But at least I can give full disclosure now," Sal said, "and as we proceed.

Necessity dictates that your immediate goal is winning the TechSys–InSyst game. Too many chips are on the table. Myriam insists I help you see what other games are being played at the same time and how they intertwine. The best thing I did in my life was marry Myriam, and the worst thing I did in my life was marry Myriam. Perhaps it's not too late to atone for the worst and retrieve the best."

"Why the worst?" Colleen asked.

"We had a chance to be a family but I squandered it, for both of us. I left Myriam behind while I chased more where it can never be had—in things. More is always just beyond where we are. We can't find more until we learn that it's hidden in less. Look at these people." Sal waved his arms indicating the whole hacienda. "They're not on that illusory merry-go-round. Connie and Ricardo chose to get off. All the workers were never allowed on. Who has more, us or them? Who smiles more?"

"Are you suggesting we shouldn't dedicate ourselves to our work?" Jason asked.

"No, everyone should dedicate themselves to their work, but only the part of themselves that work deserves. Work should not be our all, and we should not let ourselves or anyone else make it our all. I didn't realize that until I was knocked on my butt. I'm just lucky Myriam was still there to snatch me up and shake me awake. I was lured to a false god who blinded me."

"What has God got to do with work?"

A man who was working nearby, raking the flowerbeds, looked up and said, "All things are God."

"That's Juan. He came with the plantation and I think he's just about as old," Ricardo joked. "He doesn't say much, but what he says is worth hearing. Juan! Please come!"

"Señor," Juan said as he approached.

"Explain," Ricardo requested.

Juan rested on his rake for a moment, composing his thoughts. "All things are from God. If you will follow things to the little bits, there you will find God."

"So work is from God?" Jason asked.

"*Si*," Juan said. "God give us life. God give us what we need for life.

We need work, so God give us work."

"We don't need work to live," Jason said. "We need the things we buy with the money we earn from our work. Why doesn't God give us those things instead of giving us work?"

"Right now, you need the chair you sit in," Juan said. "How will God give you the chair if he will not first give someone the work to make the chair?"

"God could make the chair Himself."

"Yes, He will make a very much better one! But if God make everything for everybody, what does Jason give?"

"What do I give?"

"Yes, God give Juan seed. God give Juan work in garden. God give Juan sunshine and rain. Juan give God flower. Juan give Jason flower. If God make flower with no Juan, what will Juan give God? What will Juan give Jason?" Juan went back to raking the flower beds.

What do I give? In silence, they each contemplated Juan's words.

Myriam finally broke the silence. "Jason, think honestly about what you most want in life and how you will get it." Colleen blushed.

Sal watched Jason's gaze shift toward Colleen. "And how you might lose her."

"All right," Jason said after thinking for a bit. "We were talking about work and about being stuck before we got distracted by all this God and giving stuff. You say I'm stuck at TechSys. That implies I can't get out. If I'm not trying to get out, that's not stuck."

"If you stay based on false or incomplete information, you just don't know you're stuck," Ricardo said. "That's how I got stuck at DBK. They used the lure of a bright future to keep me in a dark place."

"Choose carefully," Connie advised. "We're very comfortable here, running the hotel. We have an elite clientele who, I've observed, are never as content as the families working here. Our guests have much more, yet appreciate much less."

"Our workers all tell us they have more than they need," Ricardo said, "and our guests all believe they need more than they have. Who is free and who is stuck?"

"Very few of them ever bring their kids," Connie said. "But they all bring their cell phones and laptops."

"And the ones who bring their kids also bring their nannies," Ricardo added.

"The kids spend more time with their nanny than with their mom and dad," Myriam observed.

"What's the point of having a family if your family can't have you?" Connie asked.

"Do you know one of the favourite activities of our guests?" Ricardo asked. "Being invited into the home of one of our families here. They are treated as our workers would treat any visitor. The guests often claim they wouldn't like to live that way, but they always enjoy that evening more than they enjoy their shopping tours or excursions."

"Why are you all convincing me not to go back to TechSys when you know I have to?" Jason asked.

"We just want you to set yourself a worthwhile goal," Myriam said. "At work, you make your five-year plans and your one-year plans, your budgets and agendas, but in life you just do whatever presents itself at the moment. You don't look any further than the weekend. Do you ever stop to think what might be further down the road?"

"I have my retirement savings plan, my pension and insurance," Jason said.

"To finance what future?" Sal asked.

"When Ricky and I met," Connie said, "we only cared about partying. We got wild and crazy every weekend, but I really liked dressing up for DBK dinners. Barbara, Mrs. Kinder, was always there and she always talked to me. I don't know why me, but she was really nice. She was also really sad. I remember always wondering how she could be sad. The night that disgruntled ex-employee jumped in front of their car was the night I started thinking. Was I going to wind up just like her? Was I destined to be sad? Ricky and I started having some really bad fights, not because anything was wrong but because nothing was really right."

"Our lives weren't going anywhere," Ricardo said. "Everything, more or less, just was. We just went with the flow."

"It got to the point where I felt I had to stop floating and start swimming," Connie said, "probably because that crash reminded me that life ends. When would mine end and where would I be? I just didn't want to be in the same place I was."

"Connie kept asking me if we were just going to keep partying until someone jumped in front of our car. I got really sick of that question until, one day, I thought about my parents, and my aunts and uncles. They had hundreds of friends but no one really likes them, not even their own families. That's the thing that got me. Connie and I never thought about having a family; we only thought about having fun. But right then, I knew I wanted a family who liked me."

"So Colleen and I are here for a week to think about where we are together in our careers and our relationship," Jason said. "Our relationship which, until recently, to be honest, consisted of commenting in the elevator how much we like sunny days and dislike rainy days."

"You two are very sweet together," Myriam said, "and I hope you decide to make more of your relationship. I'm sure if you do, it will be a good one. But no, you are here to see a community, how it works."

"Why?"

"Because here, the beginning is close enough to the end that people know why they do what they do," Sal said. "People grow food and they see who eats it. They make clothes and they see who wears them. They build houses and live in them. It is easy to see why you do things. Why do you do what you do at TechSys?"

"To get paid."

"Exactly. We do things to take and we never learn how to give."

"And what did you give?"

"Too little of what is mine," Sal admitted, "and too much of what isn't. We live in a world that's more concerned with taking. Our success is measured by how well we take."

"So you're suggesting we stop taking?"

"You two live here for a week. Look around. Wander through the workers' houses. Talk to them. Most of them speak at least a little English. We'll continue this discussion after that," Sal assured him. "Tonight, we have a party to attend!"

The Mexican Experience

I'm going to go find the kids," Connie said as she headed to the house.

"Go with her," Sal told Ricardo. "We're fine here."

Ricardo jumped up, ran over to Connie and took her hand.

"You come with me," Myriam said, leading Colleen away.

"Pedro will get you sorted out," Sal said to Jason. "Let's go find him."

Pedro was in the kitchen. "What will you like, Señor Sal?"

"Help Jason get ready for tonight, please, Pedro."

"*Si*, Señor Sal! Come on, Señor Jason. We go this way." Pedro led Jason to the laundry. "Here are lots of things the *Americanos* leave behind. We will find some for you."

Jason picked out a cotton shirt and cotton trousers. "No, Señor Jason, that *camisa* is *bueno* but we will not wear that pants. That is from *turista*. I will find you some jeans."

They were a bit short and there were holes in both front pockets, but they were okay. The rips in the knees had been earned by hard work. There was already a length of sisal rope looped through for a belt. Jason chose a pair of huaraches and was looking for a sombrero to complete his ensemble. "Why do you want sombrero?" Pedro asked. "It is night; there is no more sun."

Jason went to his room, changed into his new outfit and returned to Pedro. "Where's Colleen," he asked.

"She will be there," Pedro assured him. "You are Mexican very well!"

Pedro led Jason to the corral by the horse barn, where several plank tables and benches were set up. A hind quarter of a large cow was being slowly turned over an open fire, and a great assortment of pots full of various Mexican dishes prepared by each family filled one of the tables.

The children were playing soccer in an open area off to the side. There was beer, tequila and brandy. Jason opted for tequila; his taste in beer had strayed from lagers since he met Moses. Jason felt an urge to look behind him. He turned and saw Colleen approaching in a loose white cotton dress with colourful embroidery around the top and hem, looking lovelier than he had ever seen her. He was so taken by her looks in that simple dress that he could only stare.

"What's wrong?" Colleen asked.

Absolutely nothing! Jason wanted to say but nothing came out.

"You are too pretty for Señor Jason," Pedro said.

Jason just nodded. Colleen blushed and took his hand. "Or too much tequila?" she joked.

"Too much you," Jason said.

"Lime water?" Myriam offered.

"Thank you," Colleen said. "This all looks and smells wonderful!"

"This happens about once a month," Myriam said. "One family or another has a special event. They're always lots of fun. It doesn't help my dresses get any looser!"

"Sometimes even more bigger," Pedro said.

"The party or my dress," Myriam teased.

"Of course the party, Señora."

"We only celebrate at Thanksgiving or Christmas," Colleen said. "But not like this!"

"Oh, don't even mention that," Myriam said. "Christmas, Easter, Mardi Gras, those are something really special! This is not even close."

Connie and Ricardo came over to join them. "They know how to celebrate," Jason said.

"This is a sweet sixteen party for Conchita Rodriguez," Connie explained. "In many parts of Mexico, she might already be married and starting a family. Here at Hacienda Gonzales, there's more opportunity for the girls to finish schooling so they tend to marry later. That's one of the things I really like about this place."

"Already married?" Colleen asked incredulously.

"Yes," Connie said. "It's not uncommon for girls to marry, formally or informally, as young as eleven or twelve. They don't see much point in continuing their education when they know they'll just be raising kids and keeping house."

"It's almost the opposite of back home," Jason observed. "There, we don't let marriage and family interfere with school and career."

"We hope our girls will find a balance somewhere in between," Connie said.

"Now is very much better than before," Pedro said. "We all have every much that we need. Everybody love Señor Ricardo and Señora Connie too much."

"How about Señora Myriam?" Myriam asked.

"She is very much good friend to us too," Pedro said. "By the first, she is very *gruñona*, but now she is become happy and so we are happy too."

"What's *gruñona*?" Colleen asked.

"Grumpy," Myriam said, "and that's an understatement."

"Now she is smile very big," Pedro said, "especially she with *los niños*."

Luis came running over. "Mama! Mama! I want to go to Pablito's. Can I go? Please! Please!"

"Why isn't he here?" Connie asked.

"Grounded."

"Why?"

"I don't know," Luis said.

"You can go to ask them if they're coming to the fiesta," Ricardo consented.

"But if his parents say he's not allowed, you come straight back," Connie instructed. She gave Luis a peck on his forehead and a loving pat on his backside as he ran off.

"Is everyone invited?" Jason asked.

"Always," Myriam assured him. "Even *gruñonas*."

The hotel bus rumbled by, stirring up dust behind it. "The guests are back from today's excursion," Ricardo said. "They'll begin wandering over after they clean up. Then things will really get going. I should go back to the hotel to greet them." He and Connie headed over to the hotel, hand in hand.

Jason put his arm around Colleen's shoulders and they strolled leisurely around looking at all the happy people. "We don't have anything like this back in Houston," Colleen observed.

"Could you imagine a hind quarter roasting over an open fire in Woodland Heights?" Jason mused. They found a table at the far side of the corral and sat backwards on the outer bench, facing the henequen fields.

"Or a picnic where even strangers are invited?" Colleen added. "I like it here. Connie and Ricardo are lucky to have this place. Look at all those stars!"

"It's a bit like having Tink's all day," Jason said.

They sat cuddling and watching the stars until they heard music. They turned and saw a mariachi band leading several of the hotel guests to the party. The guests came over, got drinks and snacks, and clustered around the tables. The mariachi band went to stand close to the roasting hind quarter.

Myriam came over and brought Colleen and Jason to the table of honour. "This is Carlos and Catalina Rodriguez," she introduced, "and Tia Elena. They are the hosts tonight."

A short while later, the leader of the mariachi band announced, "Ladies and gentlemens! I will like to introducing Señor Carlos Rodriguez and his too beautiful wife Señora Catalina!"

Carlos and Catalina went over and stood by the musicians. "Welcome to everybodies," Señor Rodriguez said. "Today we thank to you, dear Lord God, for our little Conchita. She is sixteen years old and *bonita* like her mama and very smart too. Thank to you, Lord God, for her and thank to you, Lord God, for all this friends that comes to be happy with us and for all this food that we can enjoying from all your gift for us. Thank you, also too, for this mariachis and for all the hand that are prepare this foods. And we praying also too for those peoples that doesn't has so much. Bless us, Lord God, and this food. Amen! Okay, everybody, come on and eating the food!"

People filled their plates from the dishes and then went over to the fire where Sal was carving beef right from the spit. The mariachi band kept playing until everyone had their food and their seats. Then the musicians propped their instruments against the fence, got their food and sat wherever they found empty space at a table.

There was such joy and laughter. People got up for seconds, desserts and drinks. When the musicians finished eating, they got up and played some more. They went over to the Rodríguezes table to serenade Conchita with *Cielito Lindo* and wandered among the hotel guests singing other Mexican favourites.

"It's too bad nobody does this back home," Colleen lamented. "It's so much fun." She rested against Jason, holding his hand and stroking it. They both listened and smiled.

Slowly the crowd thinned. Mothers with young children left first. Most hotel guests stayed until quite late. Sal and Myriam approached, holding hands. "Come on," Sal said. "Let's go have a brandy in the great room."

Colleen and Jason walked with them over to the main house. "This is so much fun," Colleen said. "I love it here!"

"You're welcome, my dear," Myriam said. "Make sure you don't let Jason forget how life is here. Don't hope that yours may be like this, but don't let life become like Sal's and mine either."

"Come. Let's make some tea," Myriam said to Colleen and led her off to the kitchen.

Sal poured brandy for Jason and himself. Jason sat in the leather and pine loveseat; Sal sat in one of the matching armchairs and reached for a cigar from the humidor on the table beside him. "So, how are you enjoying your first day in Mexico?" Sal asked.

"I don't know if Colleen and I will want to go back to Houston," Jason said.

"After a week here, you'll be ready. You'll both be restless for home."

Colleen overheard Sal as she and Myriam returned from the kitchen with a full teapot and three cups. "I don't know that a week will be enough."

"Regardless, it's what you have. Ten days, to be precise," Sal said. "I need Jason back in Houston by then. And I'm sure Gerry will want you back too; he didn't really want you down here at all."

"I'm in the middle of three quite substantial projects," Colleen said. "I'm impressed you were able to convince him at all."

"We have history. We owe each other. And he cares about you."

"But I'll still have to catch up next week on the work I'm missing."

Colleen sat beside Jason, took his hand and looked apologetically into his eyes. "It will probably mean a few late evenings."

"Don't worry about that," Sal said. "I'm sure Jason will be very busy too. Enrico and Augusto both have eyes here at Hacienda Gonzales."

"Then they'll also know that Colleen and I are just here on vacation."

"It won't matter. They still consider the hacienda Gonzales territory and they consider Ricardo a Burkeman. Gonzales and Burkeman are worse than the Hatfields and McCoys. More Burkemans being here—even if they are Rosenthal and Johnstone ones—will infuriate them and stoke the fires under the TechSys-InSyst boiler."

"So Myriam has us here for us," Colleen observed, "and you have us here for you."

"Don't tell Myriam," Sal jested.

"No," Myriam glowered at Sal. "She wouldn't like that."

"Actually, it wasn't at all my intention. But that's how these Gonzales brothers will see it."

Ricardo caught Sal's words on his way in. "Except for one thing." He poured himself a brandy, accepted a cigar from Sal and leaned against the fireplace, one foot raised on the hearth. "Father is too busy drinking to care about anything."

"Enjoy the night, enjoy the week and prepare for battle," Sal said. "This week is for Myriam."

Ricardo lit a small fire in the fireplace. Connie came in and beckoned Ricardo to sit beside her on the sofa. Myriam poured her a cup of tea and the six of them enjoyed the quiet. Colleen and Jason sat snuggled in the loveseat longer than the others but, once they were both too tired to stay awake, they retired to their rooms. "Good night, Jason."

"Good night, Colleen." They shared a quick kiss and each headed to bed.

***

Too soon, it seemed, Ricardo was rapping on Jason's door. "Church today! Breakfast in twenty!" It was morning already.

Jason arrived at the table about five minutes before Colleen. Myriam, Sal, Connie and the aroma of fresh coffee were already there. "Good morning, Señor Jason," Pedro said as he came in from the kitchen. "I have a nice strong smelling-good coffee for you!"

Pedro served coffee for Colleen when she arrived and two minutes later appeared with tortillas, fried eggs, refried beans and green chili for everyone. "Enjoy your breakfast, everybodies!"

They all did enjoy breakfast. "Now," Ricardo said, "off to Church."

Jason thought the outside of Saint Ildephonsus Cathedral was quite plain, but the massive pillars inside were very impressive. "What's going on now?" Jason kept asking Colleen throughout the Mass.

Colleen always had the same answer. "Shhh."

Jason came away impressed with the piety of the people but not understanding Church any better. The afternoon was a lazy one, mostly sitting outside watching the two kids and their friends splash about in the pool, and sipping lemon water. It was very refreshing.

The rest of their time was spent touring Mérida; the ruins at Uxmal and along Ruta Puuc; mango groves; the town, ecological reserve and beach at Progreso; and several cenotes. They relaxed each evening at the hacienda where they were often joined by some of the workers. Despite their original intentions, they experienced Hacienda Gonzales life much more than they discussed their own.

"We'll come back often," Jason promised Colleen as they ate breakfast before packing for their trip home. Who knew whether they would? They said their farewells to Myriam, Connie and the families who came to see them off, and watched all the waving people out the back window as they drove away. They slept for most of the planc trip home.

"Feel like Tink's tonight?" Jason asked as Cedric helped Colleen out.

"It's already past six," Colleen said, "and I have to unpack—a lot more things than I brought! Maybe tomorrow's better. Thanks, Sal, for everything. It was really wonderful."

"It's truly been my pleasure," Sal replied. "Good evening, Colleen."

Back to Business

Jason slept early and woke early the next morning, awash with warm memories. As he showered, he thought of Colleen in her peasant dress. The coffee was brewed and his alarm was beeping when he got out. He sat in his robe with his coffee and looked through the mail he'd gathered from his mailbox the previous night. Nothing looked particularly urgent or interesting so he left it for later. He dressed and headed out in time to catch the five thirty-eight train. Sal, as usual, was there to greet Jason when he got to the executive lounge.

"Hi, Sal. *Hola*, José. *Bonjour*, Simon," Jason greeted everyone. "Did you miss us?"

"Of course!" Simon said. "I had only Nigaud to speak with."

"Yes, Mr. Jason!" José said. "Nobody talks to José, only Mr. Jason and Mr. Sal. Except, get me coffee! Get me this! Get me that! No nicely like you."

"We're glad to see you, too," Jason said, "and I can't wait for a cup of your Mexican coffee!"

"I ordered us omelettes," Sal said. "I hope that's okay."

"Yes, fine. So, what, besides omelettes, is on the menu today?"

"My friend, Tony, at the *Chronicle* gave me a heads-up on a story they're working on. Apparently Andrew's about to be slammed with some rather nasty allegations about his personal life, and the same reporter, he thinks, is looking into our board of directors."

Maybe it's Andrew's affair with Pet, Jason thought. *Does Sal know?* The more Jason thought about what had gone on and what was going on, the surer he became that Andrew and Pet's affair must be at least part of the big scoop. It fit perfectly. "Did he mention anything in particular?"

"It will cost us lunch to find out any more. Come with me. Cedric will be waiting out front at eleven twenty-five. Look into Andrew's folio in the meantime."

The omelettes came—shrimp, avocado and gruyère. "So what do you think of Hacienda Gonzales?" Sal asked.

"I think Connie and Ricardo are very lucky," Jason said. "That is truly a magical place."

"It's far too rare a thing when a couple can find themselves a piece of paradise like they have," Sal said. "They are in the perfect place for them."

"Maybe you and Myriam will find something similar in Bermuda."

"No. I'll just become the flag on the nineteenth hole, a bunch of pompous wannabees all listening to my lies about how I retired at the top. There won't be any of the little people. Myriam will probably still spend most of her time at the hacienda."

"Why don't you just stay there with her?"

"I'm too proud," Sal said. "I'd rather live the lie. I like dropping by every so often as the man Myriam claims me to be; it wouldn't be fair to Myriam to let them see the real me. We've made our peace with living apart. I'm far better as her fantasy than as her husband. I'll just keep pretending I'm enjoying what I'm doing."

They finished their omelettes and headed out in different directions.

***

"Welcome back," Janice said as Jason exited the elevator. "You have a couple of messages. A fellow from InSyst—Rasoul—left several and a Sam Grierson; he didn't say where he's from." Janice handed Jason two slips of pink paper, and her head followed him as he stepped past her, opened his door, and stopped short.

Pet was seated at his desk. "Why were you at the hacienda?" she demanded.

Jason closed the door. "Hello, Pet," he said. "Connie, Ricardo and the kids are fine. They send you their best."

"Why did you go there?"

"Colleen and I wanted some alone time."

"Sal was there! What were you doing?"

"We saw the ruins, the cenotes; went to Church; had a fiesta."

"Church? Really? Okay, Onesie, enough crap! Sal and you didn't go down there for a vacation. I told you everything. Why did you have to go behind my back?"

"Believe it or not, Pet, you were barely mentioned the whole time," Jason said truthfully. "There was only 'How is she?' and 'Give her our best.' They wish you well when they think of you, but they really don't think of you very often."

"I'm going to find out," Pet threatened. "I always do!"

"Okay," Jason said as she left.

Janice watched wide-eyed as Pet stormed off to her own office. She looked back to Jason and shrugged her shoulders. Jason raised his eyebrows and frowned in return. He flicked the papers in his hand. "I'll call Rasoul and Grierson." He closed the door and sat in his chair. He placed the two pink papers side by side on the desk in front of him, leaned back with his hands in his lap, and rocked a bit side to side ruminating before picking up the phone and dialling. Two rings.

"Hello."

"Mr. Grierson?"

"Uh... yes?"

"Mr. Johnstone returning your call."

"Oh, uh, Mr. Johnstone. I'm... uh... a reporter with the *Houston Chronicle*. I wonder if you'd mind answering a few questions."

This must be Tony's story, Jason thought. *How much can I find out before lunch?* "That will depend on the questions."

"I understand you worked with Virginia Malcolm at SecTech Systems."

"Ginny," Jason said, "senior analyst."

"Are you familiar with where she was before SecTech?"

How does this relate to Pet? Jason wondered. "Where?"

"Andrew Burkeman's motel room."

"That's supposed to be news?" Jason bluffed.

"Her day job was at Brewster Coal Corp."

"Will you hold for a moment?" Jason needed to stall. "I have an urgent call coming in." He typed 'Brewster Coal Corp' into the search bar and scanned the results quickly. Several old postings came up: 'Mercury

Contamination in Rio Grande,' 'Rio Grande Becomes Red River,' 'Burkeman Minerals Awarded Contract.' Bingo! He clicked. 'Burkeman Minerals Inc has been awarded the contract to develop an open-pit lignite mine after competitor Brewster Coal Corp faces bankruptcy over Terlingua cinnabar disaster.'

"Sorry, Mr. Grierson." Jason kept reading as he spoke. "Where were we?"

"Where was Ms. Malcolm?"

"If you're suggesting that Ginny had anything to do with the dam breach in Terlingua," Jason called his plays on the fly as he read the news article, "I can assure you that it would be completely out of character for the Ginny I knew."

"You knew her, then?" Sam asked. "Perhaps you can tell me why Ms. Malcolm was there with Burkeman in the TXTV spill interview."

Right story, Jason thought. *What part?* Jason wanted to find out more but knew he wasn't prepared. "I don't have time to discuss this properly right now. I'll get back to you."

"Wait!"

Jason hung up the phone and tried searching for the TXTV interview. He didn't find it. Then he had another thought, he typed 'Virginia Malcolm, PEng' into the search bar and found 'Proctor Martin Geotechnical Consulting Corp.' Jason looked up the contact information and dialled.

"Good morning, Virginia Malcolm."

"Ginny," Jason said. "How are you?"

Ginny recognized his voice. "Is that you, Jason? To what do I owe the honour?"

"I thought you should know there's a reporter digging up your past."

"SecTech? Why?"

"No, Brewster Coal."

"What about it?" Ginny sounded worried.

"Three guesses."

She only needed one. "Mercury spill. But why me?"

"Burkeman."

"How did they find that out? And why does it matter?"

"What were you doing at Brewster?"

"Remediation. We were going to dump tailings into abandoned shafts."

"What went wrong?"

"That idiot Rampursad."

"Kumar Rampursad?"

"Yes. How on earth did you know that?" she asked, surprised.

Jason tried to suppress the excitement in his voice. "What happened?"

"He parked an excavator on top of our weir just before a thunderstorm. It's a dumb place to leave an excavator and the worst time to do it. Weirs are designed to hold water, not excavators," she said. "How did you know his name?"

"It must have been in one of the news reports," he lied.

"No," Ginny said. "Nobody was allowed to mention Rampursad. His actions bordered on negligence, especially since we all knew he sometimes showed up high. Hank told us not to mention anything about him or the excavator.

"Hank?"

"Solway. Brewster's president."

"Did Burkeman ever meet Rampursad?"

"No, he steered clear of Brewster because we were competing against him for an open-pit contract."

"How did you meet Burkeman?"

"About two years before the lignite thing, the EPA ordered some remediation on our cinnabar tailings pond. We were deciding whether to contract out or use own forces. Burkeman Minerals submitted a bid. Hank said there were too many contingencies. I remember him saying, 'Brewster likes to pay cost, not cost plus.' He was so concerned about costs that he forgot about liability."

"And the liability wound up sinking his company."

"And him," Ginny said. "He was the engineer of record. I heard he had a really tough time after that."

"And you?"

"I was lucky. I started college in IT before I settled on geological engineering. I lucked into SecTech because I stayed friends with Sue. You remember her."

"Spider," Jason said. "The hair lady."

"The one and only! I think she threatened to quit if Ronnie boy didn't hire me. I did specs and she did the pages. There was plenty of geotech work around, but those were some crazy fun times at SecTech!"

"They sure were," Jason agreed. "But we digress. Was there anything suspicious about the mercury spill?"

"Hank didn't believe the excavator alone was enough to make the weir fail as catastrophically as it did. Hank wanted to find something just as much as the EPA did. He never accepted that the weir was under-built."

"What did the EPA find?"

"They concluded that there was cavitation at the weir base. I can't really see how that would happen but, hey, the weir failed."

"Did anything unusual happen between you and Andrew Burkeman around that time?"

"Other than an affair with a married man more than twice my age?"

"Yeh, other than that."

"Not really. It was a rather brief affair. We got started at the ACC conference about a month before the spill and broke up just after it."

"Why?"

"He liked sex; I liked limos and expensive jewelry. Neither of us really liked each other. He probably found some new bimbo. Time to switch channels, I guess."

"He broke it off?"

"Cold. Cancelled his cellphone; never saw him again. Didn't even say goodbye."

"So you knew him a while before the affair?"

"Close to two years, I guess."

"But you never got together before the convention?" Jason asked.

"I was never that drunk in the same room as Andrew before the convention," Ginny said.

"Drunker than you usually get?"

"Drunker than I ever get! I wasn't exactly counting my martinis, but I think it had more to do with all the late nights and stress preparing for Brewster's booth at the convention. Anyway, I got super drunk that night and I got super drunk three nights later when I agreed to meet

Andrew again specifically to tell him to stop harassing me because the first night never happened. After that it was just a thing I can't really explain. Maybe girls really do need bad boys. I just don't know. I wish it hadn't happened."

"How long did Kumar work there?"

"Rampursad? I don't know. He wasn't anyone special until after the washout; after that his butt was never allowed past our gate again. Hank personally cleared Rampursad's locker and tossed his stuff over the gate onto the road. A couple of guys drove over it before Rampursad got to it—probably on purpose. Everyone was so mad at him. I think we all knew our jobs were gone."

"Thanks, Ginny," Jason said. "It's nice talking to you."

"Same," Ginny said. "We should get together, have drinks somewhere."

"Yeah, real soon. Let's keep in touch," Jason fibbed. Even if Colleen hadn't been in the picture, Ginny was a bit too old and much too wild for Jason.

He looked at his watch, jumped up and grabbed his jacket. "I don't know how long I'll be," he said as he rushed past Janice.

"I was about to call," Sal said as Jason got out of the elevator. "Anything about Andrew jump out at you?"

Jason guessed correctly that many affairs would be documented in Andrew's portfolio. "Do you think it will be one affair in particular or just the sheer volume?"

"I'm hoping it won't be one that's not there."

"Virginia Malcolm?"

Sal looked shocked. "I've created a monster!"

"A temporary monster," Jason said. "I won't forget Mérida."

"Thank God."

"I might start doing that," Jason said.

Sal smiled. "Thank God."

Jason smiled too and then became serious again. He was pleased with how much he was able to discover through his bluffs so he tried another. "How many of these 'favours' did you do for Andrew?"

"That was the worst," Sal said. "I knew there was always more to these things than what he told me but, as long as I never found out, I could pretend there wasn't. That one went way beyond my limit. I couldn't do it anymore."

"And Kumar's job at DBK was part of his payment."

"No, that was blackmail. He was mad he lost his job and said he'd tell what happened."

"But he would have to implicate himself."

"It's a risk you run when dealing with potheads," Sal said. "They don't always think things through; they're always looking for the big score."

"Does J.P. know?"

"He refuses to. Even when he tells Andrew about a particular problem with the specific intention of making it mysteriously resolve itself, he denies the obvious. It's kind of ostrich morality."

"That seems to be an all-too-common workplace ailment," Jason said.

"And often hard to diagnose without a good mirror," Sal admitted.

"Or a timeout in Mérida."

"Or a timeout in Mérida," Sal agreed. "Especially with Myriam."

Sal and Jason arrived at Vic and Anthony's Steakhouse. "Let's see," Sal said, "if what Tony has to say is worth the price of our lunch."

Tony was already at the table. He partially rose, holding on to the table to support his substantial girth. He raised a hand in greeting as they approached. "Hello, Sal. It's been a while." Tony was already on his second bourbon and halfway through a calamari appetizer.

Sal introduced Jason as he shook Tony's hand. "Anything you want to tell me, you can say in front of him. Anything."

"Tony." Jason shook Tony's hand in turn. "Pleasure."

"You're a bit late," Tony observed. "I hope you don't mind I took the liberty."

"Not at all," Sal assured him. "Jason had some important business to finish and he needs to be here."

"Oh," Tony said. "What's your position at TechSys, Jason?"

"Sal's right hand and successor," Jason said, guessing the tenor of the meeting. "Once we can boot his sorry butt to Bermuda!"

"Myriam wants me to throw in the towel," Sal said.

"And that was how many years ago?" Tony asked. "Why now?"

"My whiskers are getting a little too grey."

"Does that mean J.P.'s not far behind?"

"Always fishing for a scoop," Sal said. "But, no, Junior's not ready, not nearly."

"Never will be," Tony said. "Cut from a different cloth than his father. More suited for the times but less suited for the game. The game is getting more ruthless and the men less. The women are taking over, I'm afraid. If you think business is harsh now, wait till women are running things!"

"They're not all as heartless as your ex," Sal said.

"No one is! God love her."

"So," Sal said, "what's up at the *Chronicle*?"

"Business first," Tony said. He waved for the waiter. "Lamb chops, wild mushrooms and asparagus, and top up the bourbon."

"Philly cheesesteak, please," Jason ordered.

"Caesar instead of fries for me, please, and a bottle of Amarone. Two glasses." Sal wasn't about to waste good wine on a bourbon-pickled sot.

"I have an excellent 2013 Monte Zovo," the waiter suggested.

"Fine. Thank you, Rafael," Sal said. "So, Tony, the scoop."

"It's not what I know," Tony confessed. "It's what I saw."

"Go on," Sal urged.

"An eight by ten," Tony continued. "Definitely Andrew Burkeman and definitely a small vial of something tipping over a drink."

"Who else?"

"Just a low-cut dress with some pretty good cleavage. She was looking sideways but she has long wavy hair."

"No face? No name?" Sal asked. "That doesn't even cover the bourbon. What else?"

"Bios of the TechSys board. I didn't have time to check everything; some guy came in so I stopped snooping. By the time I got back to the printer, I guess Sam already had it."

"Sam?" Sal asked.

"Grierson. The cover sheet was attention to her. It must be big because she wasn't biting on any hints I dropped; she's keeping it close."

"She didn't say anything?" Jason asked.

"No," Tony said. "I told her I was missing some pages I sent to the printer, asked her if they might accidentally have gotten mixed in anything of hers. She point blank denied picking up anything all day."

"I need more, Tony. You haven't even bought your lunch yet," Sal said.

"Whoever sent those papers knows Andrew dosed someone's drink. They must know whose drink. The bios have to mean TechSys ties in somehow."

Jason thought back to his conversation with Ginnie. "We need the picture," he said. "Get us the picture."

"Are you sure it was definitely with the TechSys bios?" Sal asked. "Andrew's not TechSys."

"Same pile of papers. No separate cover. Same transmission."

"Get us those papers and earn this lunch," Sal said as their meals arrived.

Rafael uncorked the bottle and poured a taste for Sal.

"Very good," Sal said. Rafael added more wine to Sal's glass and poured one for Jason.

"This is good." Jason swirled his wine, sniffed it, held it up and looked through it toward the light. "At least this lunch is not a complete waste of time."

Tony frowned, his face turning red. "It's there. I'll find it!"

"Have you heard from your kids lately?" Sal asked.

"Their mom has turned them completely against me."

"All work and no play can be good advice when it comes to co-workers," Sal rubbed.

The rest of the lunch was quiet.

"Let us know when you find something worth hearing," Sal said when Tony's plate was empty. "You're still working off this tab. Jason and I are going to enjoy our wine."

"Bye, Tony," Jason said.

Tony got up. His face was very red. "Later!"

"That was an expensive almost nothing," Sal said.

"Maybe," Jason replied.

"What do you know?"

"This is very good wine; we should enjoy it."

"You're enjoying this, aren't you?"

"It will keep till the ride back," Jason promised.

A few minutes later Rafael came back. "Your car has arrived, Mr. Rosenthal."

Jason and Sal both thanked Rafael on their way out.

"Thanks, Cedric," Sal said as he entered the limo. "Did you get things taken care of?"

"Mabel's done shoppin'," Cedric said, "and Lulu's at the doc's."

"So," Sal said, "all's quiet on the home front."

"For now."

"You really care," Jason observed.

"It's the me I prefer," Sal said. "But I can't seem to do without the other one either. So what was that maybe?"

"I'll let you know as soon as I check a couple of things," Jason said. "But don't worry; there's no headline coming."

Back in his office, Jason retrieved a pink paper from his top drawer. He switched on the computer and pulled up the *Chronicle*'s website. The phone numbers weren't even close. He pulled up Sam Grierson's picture. Probably mid-thirties, long blonde hair, markedly feminine despite her pants-and-jacket outfit. "Who are you, pink paper Sam, and what are you up to?"

He did a reverse look-up on the number: Carlos Mendoza, 4111 Mallow Street, Houston, Texas. Sunnyside. *Not the best neighbourhood in Houston.*

Jason typed 'Sam Grierson Houston Chronicle' into the search bar and found 'Gangs Strafe Sunnyside Street,' 'Willing Workers Baptist Church Launches Community Improvement Program.' He phoned the *Chronicle*. "Sam Grierson, please."

"Sam here."

"Hello, Ms. Grierson." Jason played a hunch. "I have a story you might be interested in. Do you pay for information like that?"

"We have a budget for confidential informants. You have to divulge your identity to the paper, but we'll keep it a secret."

"How does it work?"

"We could meet," Sam said. "Or you could send me enough information to convince me that the story is worth paying for."

"I'll get back to you." Jason hung up.

Jason called Sal's cellphone. "Are you good for Jas' in five?"

"Ten," Sal said.

"Ten."

Jas smiled when she saw Jason. "Dark roast or dark passion?"

"Medium," Jason said.

"Is five eight medium?"

"Five eight is more trouble than I can handle."

"I'd be glad to do the handling."

Sal came in. "How are you, Jasmine?"

"Hotter than my coffee. Can you take the counter for a while?"

"While you take Jason?" Sal asked. "Sorry, I need him."

"Kinky!"

"I'd prefer a caramel latte," Sal said.

"You guys are no fun!" Jas said.

"Come and join us," Jason said.

"Should I lock the door?"

"No," Jason said. "Seriously. I have something to ask you."

"The answer is yes," Jas said. "Whenever, wherever!"

Jason took his coffee. He and Sal went over to a table near the back. Jas made Sal's latte and brought it over.

"Jas," Jason said, "do you remember the papers you found in the fax?"

"Pretty hard to forget that episode of my life!"

"What happened to them?"

"Sal read them and shredded them, right then and there."

"Could there be copies?"

"You guys finish this up without me. I buried all this stuff, way deep." Jas excused herself and turned to leave. "I don't need to go digging it up. Ever!"

"There must be copies of most," Sal said after Jas left the table.

"What exactly were they?" Jason asked.

"Engineering documents, maps, geological reports. Things we shouldn't have had."

"Why?"

"They were mostly stuff about Burkeman Minerals, DBK and Brewster. Nothing to do with TechSys."

"So how did they get there?" Jason asked. "Who had them?"

"Frank, we know," Sal said. "But who else? Your guess is as good as mine."

"You didn't think to find out?"

"I guess I was too concerned about other people not finding things out. Murder has a strange effect on one's thinking."

"It's coming back to haunt someone," Jason said. "Who do you know who's not afraid to do a little snooping in Sunnyside?"

"Bad place," Sal said. "Why?"

"Because the Sam Grierson who left me a message while we were in Mérida is really one Carlos Mendoza of 4111 Mallow Street, Sunnyside."

"There is someone." Sal wrote the information on a napkin and put it in his breast pocket. He looked at his watch. "Just about Colleen time. We'd better go."

"Come back when you're more fun," Jas said as Jason and Sal left.

Back to Tink's

Colleen was watching the elevator; Sal and Jason startled her as they approached from behind. "Oh! I was expecting you ten minutes ago!"

"And apparently from the other direction," Sal said. "How did Gerry take your absence?"

"Mr. Lee said they barely survived without me," Colleen reported. "I doubt they missed me at all."

"I missed you," Jason said, "and it hasn't been twenty-four hours yet."

"I doubt that. You couldn't even bother to show up on time."

"Guilty," Sal said. "I've been making him catch up on missed time."

"Actually," Jason said, "I've been over flirting with Jas."

"I know which one of you was doing the flirting there," Colleen said. "Tom's always talking about her."

"Tom, huh?" Jason teased. "Should I be worried?"

Colleen smacked Jason's arm. "He's our student this term; he's barely nineteen."

"After the younger men, are you?"

The elevator doors opened. "Well, I've got things to do," Sal said. "More important than what you two are up to. Good evening."

"Evening, Sal," Colleen and Jason said in unison.

"Take care of that girl," Sal ordered. "She'll take care of you!"

Colleen and Jason headed out. "Busy day?"

"Very," Jason said, "and brutal."

"New problems or old?"

"Both, and a lot of them are turning out to be the same problem."

"As in recurring?"

"As in never resolved and linked and compounded... and festering!"

"My mother always reminded me that little sins become big sins."

"Well," Jason said, "huge sins become huger sins."

"That bad?"

"Worse. Blackmail, rape, murder, industrial espionage, sabotage."

"Are you serious?"

"Deadly. Literally!"

"Are you safe?"

"Physically? Yes. Probably. Emotionally? No."

"I'm concerned, Jason."

"I'm concerned for both of us," Jason admitted. "But the only way out seems to be through."

"How much can you tell me?"

"Less than I already have."

"Jason." Colleen grabbed his shoulders and made him look in her eyes. "You have to tell me!"

"I'm afraid I do," Jason said. "Really afraid."

"I'm a big girl."

"This is a big problem. Maybe bigger than either of us."

"But not bigger than both of us," Colleen assured him.

"It might be. It was bigger than Sal even before it got as big as it is."

"Sal tried to face it alone," Colleen said. "Now we're three."

"Even so."

"Do we have a choice?" Colleen asked.

"Maybe you still do."

"Not if you don't! Shall we skip Tink's and go to my place?"

"I need Tink's today," Jason said. "Tink's, with you."

"Moses will be there."

"That's probably a better thing than either of us knows."

***

Moses was there. "Welcome back, strangers! How did Mérida treat you?"

"How did you know?" Colleen asked.

"I don't take my friends for granted."

"Still," Jason said, "we didn't even know we were going there."

"What I know and what you know are not the same," Moses said.

"And how I know I don't always know myself."

"Well, that's plenty enough confusion to warn me off," Jason said. "I've had more than my share already today."

Maria came over with their drinks. "Hi, you two. We missed you."

"Hi, Maria, we missed you too." Colleen pulled an embroidered cotton blouse out of her bag. "We got you this. Moses, you were a very big problem. We couldn't think of anything to get for you so Jason brought this," she reached further into her bag, "little carving made by one of the men at the hacienda."

"That's as fine a memory as anyone's brought me from anywhere," Moses said taking the carving from her. "Thank you very much; I'll treasure it."

"And thank you for this blouse," Maria said. "It's just my style. I love it! Chicken pot pies today."

"Three?" Moses looked to Colleen and Jason, who nodded their agreement.

"Three it is," Maria said.

"Jason," Moses said, "you don't look as relaxed as Colleen."

"There was a giant steamroller waiting in ambush when I got back," Jason explained.

"At Tink's we make sure they stay parked outside," Moses said. "We have more important things to do in here!"

"Like why and how, if I recall," Jason said.

"Our old friends that never leave us," Moses said, "no matter how often we leave them."

"And in the end, it's simply 'because,' and 'I don't know.' Since they all end there, why don't we just start there?" Jason asked.

"Sometimes what you find along the way is better than what you find at the end," Moses said, "and if you find the right things along the way, you will find a better end."

"If the end is always the same, how can one be better than another?"

"Because. No creature can cause it to be. Who does," Moses said, "and I don't know who does."

"I don't follow," Jason said.

"No one does without being," Moses said. "He who is, is He who does.

We who are being are merely doing."

"Still don't follow."

"He who is knows who we are; we who are being know only what is done."

"I can't think like this right now," Jason said. "Can we do something else?"

"You can eat your chicken pot pies," Maria said as she set them down.

"We can do many things else," Moses said. "What do you have in mind?"

"I don't know," Jason said. "You. You always seem to be here. How do you find the time?"

"I find the time because I'm not too busy trying to find anything else."

"Fair enough, but what do you do when you're not here?"

"Many things that are worth doing and little that's not worth doing."

"Such as?"

"Such as that which I invited you two to do with me two Saturdays ago," Moses said, "and will do again next Saturday, with you if you will come or without you if you don't."

"We'd love to go with you. We can, can't we, Jason?" Colleen asked.

"Things are so hectic at work. I can't commit, right now, to anything on Saturday," Jason replied.

"Right now is exactly the time to commit to important things," Moses said. "Otherwise you will never find time to do anything important until it's too late to do it. It's like getting married or having kids; it's never the right time but it's always the best time, as long as you truly do it and don't just pretend to do it."

"Are you speaking from experience?" Colleen asked.

"The sad end of one."

"Were you ever married?"

"Engaged," Moses answered, "for far too many years, until suddenly, one day, I no longer was."

"She got tired of waiting?" Jason asked.

"Much too tired, but she still waited."

"What happened, then?" Colleen asked.

"I taught her not to trust me," Moses said, "one too many times."

"Where is she now?" Jason asked.

"A place she doesn't want to be. A place she didn't have to wait to get to. Now she's waiting to get out."

"That's sad," Colleen said.

"Very." Moses dabbed his eye with a napkin. "And sadder still, I know it's my fault, and my folly."

"Do you still see her?" Colleen asked.

"Every night in my dreams and every day in my thoughts," Moses said. "In Maria and in you, in every young girl I see laughing. I was a very foolish man; most of us men are foolish. I hope you, Jason, won't be."

"I'm afraid I must be," Jason said. "At least for a little longer."

"Little grows very quickly," Moses warned. Maria came with dessert. "As will my belly around all these Triple Chocolate Lava Cakes Maria makes sure we don't miss."

"Thank you, Maria," Colleen said. "May I have some water as well, please?"

"Of course!"

"So what did you like best in Mexico?" Moses asked.

"The people," Colleen said.

"Definitely the people," Jason seconded. "They were so cheerful. Always willing to help, to share."

"It felt like everything was ours," Colleen said. "Nothing was mine or yours; it was ours."

"They have very little by our standards," Jason said. "But they have so much more!"

"Sounds like it hasn't changed," Moses said. "Gertie loved Mexico and I couldn't leave Mexico too soon."

"You didn't like Mexico?" Colleen was amazed.

"I liked Mexico too much. I didn't get anything done there. I refused to accept that that was the point of being there. At home, there was never any me left for Gertie by the time I got to her—if I got to her! There, I was all hers all day. It scared me because I didn't know how to give. It scared me because I knew I would take myself back once we got home. And it scared me because I liked it."

"The people were best, the food was great and there was so much to do," Colleen said. "It's amazing to see things that are so much older than anything we have here."

"We went to Church in Mérida Cathedral. They finished building it in fifteen ninety-eight," Jason said. "It's the first time I've been in a Church. It felt very odd. I liked it. I didn't understand anything at all, even though it was in English, but I felt peaceful." Colleen squeezed his hand, looked in his eyes and smiled.

"In Mexico, it takes much more time for things to become old," Moses said, "and much less time for people to become wise."

"I think that's why Myriam invited us," Colleen said.

"We'd probably have more old things," Jason said, "if we didn't have as many new things."

Moses smiled. "Well, it's time for this old thing to find his old bed." He headed to the door. "Goodbye, Maria, my old friend."

"I'm not that old!" Maria said.

Colleen and Jason finished their drinks. "Good night, Maria. We'll see you tomorrow."

Colleen and Jason swung their hands slowly and watched their feet as they walked. They thought about Tink's. "Do we make the wrong things important?" Colleen asked.

"Well, we're important," Jason said, "and that's not the wrong thing."

"What about the things we do all day? Why do we do them? Just to make the world go 'round?"

"Someone has to do them."

"Do they?" Colleen asked. "Really?"

"What would happen if nobody did them?"

"Mexico," Colleen suggested. "The biggest factor in all my analysis is the marketing. If we didn't sell so much stuff, we wouldn't have to make it."

"People still need stuff."

"The way Moses does or the way we do?"

Colleen and Jason arrived at Northside High and sat on their bleachers. There was less after-Tinking and more thinking. "We are important," Colleen said, "but for how long and to who?"

"Forever," Jason assured her, "to us."

"Forever right now," Colleen said. "But will it be forever next year? Is it only for us? Is that enough?"

"Forever forever." Jason cuddled Colleen a bit tighter. "For us and our friends."

"We should be more important. All couples should be more important. They keep getting less important; work keeps getting more important. Why work if there's no one to work for?"

"We work for things."

"Why?" Colleen asked. "Aren't people more important than things? Why don't we work for people?"

"We work for our bosses," Jason said.

"We work for our bosses' things."

They thought for a few minutes more and went home.

Wanting to Know

Hola, mi amigo!" Jason was still thinking about last night. "Why do you work, José?"

"To feed my family, of course, Señor Jason," José answered, "and so my kids go to good school where they will learn God."

"That's important to you?"

"Of course, Señor Jason, God give us everything! We must give God everything too."

"You don't work for the money?"

"You are funny, Señor Jason. Money is all gone before José got it! I work for my family and for God, and for you, Señor Jason, so you will have food, and good Mexican coffee to drink." José filled Jason's cup.

"Thank you, José."

"Don't to mention it, Señor Jason. José is glad to help you. What do you like for breakfast?"

"A Mexican special."

"Okay, Señor Jason. Very well."

Jason was surprised not to see Sal. He thought about sitting in the kitchen but decided to sit alone and contemplate. Jason opened the *Chronicle* and flipped slowly through the pages without reading them. No one came in. He ate his breakfast, straightened the paper and left for his office. "Thank you, José," he said and then, "*Merci*, Simon," in a little louder voice.

"*Bonne journée!*" Simon replied.

On the way to his office, Jason decided to call Rasoul. "This is the mailbox of... Rasoul Amedi... Please leave your message... beep."

"Rasoul. Jason Johnstone returning your call."

Jason couldn't decide what to do so he thought about Colleen; could forever mean only for a while? Would forever stop being? No. Forever with Colleen had to be forever. No one else had been like Colleen. Then again, no one else had ever been like the current one. No. Colleen was definitely different! *Why? How?* "Damn, Moses!"

Jason switched on his computer and stared at it for a while. *Andrew Burkeman*, he thought at last and opened Andrew's affairs folder. Andrew was every bit the cad Jason had guessed, and worse. "What a narcissistic sociopath." Jason kept reading. It didn't get any better; it couldn't get worse! Models, cocktail waitresses, strippers, wives of business associates, unidentified. *Wow!*

The phone rang. "Good morning."

"Cedric will be out front in ten, maybe fifteen minutes," Sal said.

"Where am I going?"

"I'm with a friend," Sal said. "You'll want to see this."

"The guy who's not afraid to snoop around in Sunnyside?"

"The same."

"Beep-beep... beep-beep." It was the call-waiting tone.

"Take your call; see you soon."

"Hello, Jason Johnstone."

"Jason. Rasoul. What's going on? They told me you're not on the file anymore. Kicked upstairs or some such thing."

"Yes and no," Jason said. "I've had a promotion, but I'm still involved with InSyst. More so."

"They pulled it from me. Nothing but mumbo jumbo," Rasoul said. "Old man Gus was actually there when Bozo-boss gave me the word. I'm not supposed to even contact you. We need to meet on neutral territory. I have to swing by close to TechSys around three. Is that hot chick still at the coffee place around the corner?"

"Jas?"

"Yeah!"

"Three, then," Jason agreed.

"Yeah."

Jason looked at a few pictures in Andrew's file—mostly eye candy dripping off Andrew's arm. *His jeweller must love him.* Lined up side by side in the thumbnails, Jason noticed how similar the baubles around the well-exposed necks were. For that matter, how similar the necks were from the waist up. Andrew's taste in jewelry and women was very superficial and very expensive. Jason logged out and switched off. On his way to meet Cedric, he thought about how one right woman was so much better than countless wrong women.

Jason saw the limo approaching and went outside. The car stopped, Jason opened the front door and got in beside Cedric. "Good morning, Cedric... barely."

Cedric reached over to shake hands. "Good morning, Jason. You're a lot like Sal."

"Is that good or bad?"

"Very good. But don't let him know I said it."

"Our secret. Where are we going?"

"A place where I definitely have to stay with the car," Cedric said. "With my eyes peeled wide open."

"Sunnyside?"

"Almost."

"Do you have a family?"

"Three wives and a son."

"Three wives?"

"My wife," Cedric explained, "and two married daughters. They all think I'm their personal taxi. I'm always drivin' them here and there; sometimes they get mad when I have actual drivin' to do."

"Like now?"

"Like now," Cedric said. "My Lulu wants to be somewhere and my Bebe doesn't want to be somewhere else."

"How about your wife?"

"Right now, she wants to be where those two aren't; they're both after her butt to get after my butt to get after their rides. None of them are appreciatin' that I have to get after business."

"You looked a little more stressed than you were on Monday night."

"Between those three naggin' on me and bein' so close to the 'hood and all," Cedric said, "it's not my favourite day."

"Well, Sal and I appreciate you," Jason said, "and I'm sure your three wives will sort things out."

"Yeah, man, people oughta have more sons!"

Cedric stopped at forty-eight ten Eppes Street. A sign in the window read 'Jackso Taylor Invest gations.' Jason knocked on the front door.

"It's open."

"This is Jackson," Sal said, introducing a man.

Jason shook hands. "Mr. Jackson."

The man laughed. "First name. Everyone does it! Jackson Taylor. Pleased to meet you, Mr. Johnstone."

"Jason."

"Anything you can add that Sal, here, hasn't told me?"

"What's he told you?"

"Name and address, and I'm glad you guys didn't try to take this Mendoza cat on by yourselves," Jackson said. "This guy is one serious piece of dirt! My contact at HPD tells me he's a definite person of interest linked to six active homicides. He's mid-level in coke, not street but not too high. He's very violent and not too bright—dangerous combination."

Sal nodded toward Jackson's desk; there were six photos laid out across it. "Victim three is none other than our very own Kumar Rampursad. A little older and more used up, but definitely Rampursad."

"Did Sal tell you that we suspect Carlos has some papers we're interested in?" Jason asked.

"Not rollin' papers, I'm guessin'," Jackson said.

"Pictures and documents."

"So they'd be out of place in a crackheads den?" Jackson asked.

"Definitely," Sal said.

"My contact at the Griggs Road Station tells me Mendoza is overdue for a visit. They have plenty for a warrant. It'll cost two G's, but for that price, he wouldn't be averse to makin' sure that when they toss the place they might accidentally toss somethin'-somethin' my way."

"Two plus you?" Sal asked.

"Hey, I can't be playing both sides. A guy's got to stay on the up-and-up if he wants to survive in this game. Two plus me plus whatever Mendoza chips in is bonus."

"Done!" Sal said. "Let's go, Jason."

"You're not going to hear anything we say on the way back," Sal told Cedric.

"My ears are zipped."

"You trust Jackson?" Jason asked.

"With my life," Sal said. "People like Jackson draw a line that they don't cross."

"And people like us?"

"We keep shifting the lines, little by little, whenever they get too inconvenient for us."

"Like now?"

"Like now."

"J.P. and Andrew?"

"J.P.? He has dotted lines," Sal said. "Andrew? No lines."

"The little people have the best lines." Jason thought about his own lines, how they were definitely shifting. Could he shift them back? Would he?

Eventually his thoughts switched back to the present. "So, where are we going to get two thousand dollars?"

"I'll lend it to us," Sal said, "and Andrew will pay us back—after we have the pictures."

"And then what do we do?"

"I think we have a pretty good picture of the main players, but we still don't know the game."

"I might see a play or two when we get back," Jason said. "I'm meeting Rasoul, my contact at InSyst, at Jas' around three."

"Are you sure about Jas'?"

"His choice. Rasoul wants to ogle Jas."

"She's definitely ogle-worthy."

"And amenable to ogling," Jason said, "as long as you don't cross her line."

"*Touché!*"

"Rasoul's already on guard. Things are happening at InSyst. I have to meet him alone; he was ordered not to have contact with anyone at TechSys."

"Okay, then. I'll get our package and deliver it to Jackson so things can start moving on that end," Sal said. "I don't know how long it will take, but I'd like it to be sooner than later. I'd like a few more aces in our deck."

"Are we getting aces," Jason asked, "or are we being jokers?"

"Are you ready to fold?" Sal asked. "Do you think you're even able to?"

"No, and no."

"Then don't ask."

Cedric dropped Jason off outside Jas'. It wasn't quite three.

"Medium dark roast," Jas said, "and me." She brought out Jason's coffee, looped her arm through his and walked him over to a table at the back. She sat down with him. "We're all alone in here," she teased.

"You, me and some ugly business," Jason said.

"At least only one of us is ugly," Jas said. "Spill the beans."

"Is that a good idea in a coffee shop?"

"I do it all the time. I survive."

"How come it's so dead in here?"

"Lucky timing, I guess. Why don't you take advantage of it?" Jas flirted. "And me."

"I'm taken," Jason said.

"With this?" Jas brought her hands down her tight-fitting, low-cut top provocatively.

"My friend, Rasoul, will be here shortly. He'd be more than happy to oblige."

"Only you."

"The forbidden fruit?"

"You should try it."

Rasoul came in and noticed Jas' flirtatious pose. "Am I interrupting something?"

"I wish," Jas said. "What would you like?"

"Cinnamon latte." Rasoul looked Jas up and down. "Something spicy."

He sat down as Jas went off to get their orders. "Man, she's hot!"

"She's only teasing."

"She wants you, man! I could smell it!"

"Go for it," Jason suggested.

Rasoul called over to Jas. "What have you got that's hot and spicy?"

"I've got some beef, jalapeno and jack fajitas," Jas said. "They're good. Or chili. It's always good."

"I'll have a bowl of chili, please."

"So you got kicked upstairs with the big boys," Rasoul said. "How's the air up there?"

"Not as rare as people think. Usually it's so thick you can't even see through it."

"But you must know what's going on. I mean, being on the board of directors."

"Actually, these directors are just as protective of their turf as anyone else," Jason said. "Probably more."

"But the Integrator package must be yours," Rasoul said. "You are that package!"

"Things are still in flux."

"I'm on commission," Rasoul said. "I take a serious hit if I can't touch TechSys stuff."

"I'm afraid I can't help you there, my friend."

"Something's going on. Help me out. I have a mortgage to pay. Give me something. I'm going crazy here! I haven't been this bummed since... since forever!"

"I've got nothing," Jason said.

"That ain't true," Jas said as she delivered Rasoul's latte and chili.

"Man, your paycheque just got a bunch bigger," Rasoul said. "Mine's getting a whole lot thinner. I'm hurtin' here!"

"Why did they take you off?" Jason asked. "Were your numbers falling?"

"No, they're rock solid. It's the old man. Gus is just playing some kind of game."

"I'm still trying to find out what that game is," Jason said. "Just like you."

"You're upstairs, man! You gotta know."

"I'm just sitting in a different chair."

"I don't believe it! I'm begging you and you're just brushing me off. How many years have we been doing this? Come on, man, give me something! We're a team."

"Pump as hard as you like, Rasoul; the well is dry. You know I'd give you something if I had it. Have I ever held out on you?"

"No, man. I'm just hurtin'. I need something."

"As soon as I know anything, you'll know," Jason promised. "That's the best I can do."

"I know." Rasoul's shoulders slumped and his chin dropped. "We're good."

"Eat your chili," Jason said. "It'll give you a kick-start."

"I need one right now." Rasoul looked up, his brow furrowed. "I'm so bummed I'm not on my game. It's gonna be a lean, mean payday."

"Things will get back on track when this thing sorts itself out," Jason assured him. "You'll be okay. You'll see."

"Yeah, I guess. It better be soon." Rasoul wiped his bowl with a piece of roll to get the last of the chili. "I better go make my call. Wish me luck."

"Always. As soon as I know anything," Jason promised. "Good or bad."

"Yeah, man, take it easy." Rasoul's head drooped as he shuffled out, both hands in his coat pockets.

The coffee shop was getting busy again. Jason carried the dirty dishes over to the counter. "Thanks, Jas."

"Any time," Jas said. "Any time at all." She bumped Jason playfully with her hip as he walked by.

A Busy Night

Jason's cellphone rang before he got back to the office. "Jackson's friend in HPD doesn't mess around," Sal said. "The bust is tonight. We have to be around the corner."

"Tonight?"

"Yes. Jackson wants us at his place, now. Cedric and I will be there by the time you get down."

"I'm already out front. I just got done with Rasoul."

"Good. We'll talk in the car." Sal hung up.

Cedric arrived three minutes later. "We'd better give Jackson some specifics about what we're looking for," Sal said as soon as the limo doors closed. "He's going to be outside when the bust goes down and his HPD friend is going to give him what he finds."

"How long do you think we'll be?" Jason asked.

"I don't know. I don't even know when, exactly, HPD's going to move. I only know it's today."

Cedric pulled up in front of Jackson's house. "Am I staying?"

"Let me check," Sal said.

Sal and Jason let themselves in. "How long is this likely to take?" Sal asked.

"You better make yourselves comfortable," Jackson said. "It might get late."

"I'll tell my driver." Sal went outside.

"So, what are you two after?" Jackson asked Jason.

"Pictures of people, anything Burkeman name or logo."

Sal returned. "Your man, here, says you want pictures and Burkeman documents," Jackson said.

"We know there was an eight by ten of someone spiking a drink."

"It will likely be just one stack of papers somewhere," Jackson said. "Guys like Mendoza don't usually keep too many documents around so cops don't spend time lookin' for them. They'll be lookin' for drugs, cash, weapons, so Bert's got a good chance of grabbin' your stuff."

"So where will we be?" Sal asked.

"Here," Jackson said. "I'll be scopin' the back, watchin' for Bert's signal so I can go grab what he finds. Soon as I've got it I'll be back here and you guys scram."

"When should we call Cedric?" Sal asked.

"You got any other wheels?" Jackson asked. "That limo's a sore thumb around here, better to keep low key on this op."

"How about if we have Cedric park a couple of blocks away?" Jason asked.

"A couple o' dudes like you wouldn't last a couple o' blocks around here," Jackson said. "Not after dark!"

"I'd better call Colleen."

"She better be tougher than you dudes if she's comin' down here," Jackson advised.

"She's not getting anywhere near here!" Jason said. "I'm calling to let her know I'm busy tonight."

He pulled out his phone. "Hi, Colleen."

"Where are you?"

"Is it that time already?"

"Ten minutes ago!"

"I'm sorry," Jason said. "Sal's got me out on a mission; we're going to be a while. I don't think we'll be able to get together tonight."

"Call me when you're done. We'll see... love you."

"Love you back."

"Car, guys," Jackson reminded.

Sal phoned Cedric. "Hi, Cedric. How's Mabel?... No. Jackson's advising against the limo. Do you have access to another car?... You're sure your brother will be okay with that?... I don't know yet. Hang on."

Sal held his phone against his chest. "Jackson! What time should Cedric be here?"

Jackson constructed a timetable out loud. "HPD will start rolling up around eight. Fifteen minutes to set up their perimeter. Hit the house around eight twenty."

"What time should Cedric get here?"

"We're well away from the action. Probably eight forty-five, nine. I shouldn't be longer than that."

Sal put the cellphone to his ear again. "Cedric... Eight forty-five... Not entirely sure... Probably... Thanks. I'll see you then."

"Is there a good place to eat around here?" Sal asked.

"Do you like fish or Mediterranean?" Jackson asked.

"What do you recommend?"

"Louisiana fries up a mean catfish, or Medi Grill, if you like that stuff," Jackson said. "Both are good but I'm all about the catfish."

"Catfish it is, then," Sal said. "Will you join us, Jackson?"

Jackson looked at his watch and did the mental calculations. "I have time if we leave now." He grabbed his keys from a hook and held the door open for Sal and Jason.

Sal took a stack of tabloids off the front passenger seat of Jackson's car and handed them to Jason, who tossed them to the far side of the back seat on top of everything else. He shoved the empty drink containers and fast-food bags over the centre hump, brushed off the seat and sat down. Jackson drove a few blocks and turned into the Louisiana Seafood House parking lot.

The place inside looked more than a little tired, but as they ate, they noted the catfish was every bit as good as Jackson promised.

After dinner, Jackson drove them back, pressing the remote to open the garage door. "Make yourselves at home," he said. "I'll shoot back here soon as Bert delivers. The less time I hang there the better."

"What laws are we breaking?" Jason asked.

"Interfering with a criminal investigation, obstruction of justice, bribery, conspiracy," Sal said as he pressed the button to close the garage door. "Next will be blackmail or extortion, concealing a felony, probably a few more in there somewhere."

"Are we bad people, Sal?"

"This is definitely a dark shade of grey."

"I'm not feeling good about myself right now."

"It's going to be a long hour or two."

"It's too late to not do this, isn't it?"

"It has been for a long time. We sat down at the table with some bad players and we have to play the same game."

"It's too late to fold?" Jason asked.

"I'm afraid we're at the spindle or mutilate stage," Sal replied.

Jason wasn't familiar with the saying, but its meaning was plain enough. Time went by very slowly and there were no comfortable seats anywhere. Sal and Jason began pacing, occasionally looking at their watches and each other, neither smiling. After ages and ages, Cedric knocked at the door; his brother's Chevy was parked on the street out front.

"Come in," Sal said. "We're still waiting."

Cedric phoned Mabel. "Hi, Baby... No, everything's fine... They're still waiting... No idea. Hey, Sal, how much longer?"

"Just a few minutes, most likely."

"A few more minutes, Baby... I will... Of course... I promise... Love you too... Bye." Cedric hung up. "She's jumpier than a grasshopper."

"We're pretty restless ourselves," Sal said.

The three of them paced together some more until they heard the garage door open. They were staring anxiously as Jackson came in carrying a cardboard box. "Mission accomplished!" He handed the box to Sal.

"Wow," Sal said. "This is much more than we expected."

"Bert didn't stop to go through it," Jackson said. "He just saw that glossy on the top and handed the whole box over. I hope it's what you needed. If there's any stuff that's not yours and might help Bert, he wouldn't mind receivin' a package from an anonymous source, if you catch my drift."

Sal and Jason both looked into the box; it was not the picture they expected. Sal dug two-thirds of the way down without finding it. "Thanks, Jackson. We'll go through this and get back to you."

Cedric dialled his cellphone. "Hi, Baby, it's done... I'll just drop Sal and Jason and head home... No, no... Of course, Baby... Okay... Less than an hour... Don't do that... No need... Love you too... Bye."

"Is she okay now?" Jason asked.

"Not till I get home. So, you first and then Jason?"

"What do you think, Jason?" Sal asked. "This box is not going to the office. Do you have time tonight?"

"It's too late for Colleen," Jason said. "It's either go through this stuff with you tonight or pace my living room all night. I won't be sleeping."

"My place, Cedric. Jason will stay over. Come and get me at the usual time."

Jason phoned Colleen. "Hi Colleen, we got it."

"Did everything go as planned?"

"We got more than we expected. We're going to go to Sal's place to go through it and see what we've got."

"What time do you think you'll be done?"

"I don't know, but it's a whole box of stuff so it will be late late. I'm going to stay over at Sal's and we'll go to work together in the morning."

"Do you realize this is the first day since we started seeing each other that we haven't gone out?"

"I know, Hon, I miss you."

"Me too. I feel a little silly."

"Maybe I can sneak you into the executive lounge tomorrow morning," Jason suggested. "We can have breakfast together."

"What time?"

"Hang on," Jason said. "I'll put you on speaker. Sal, can Cedric pick Colleen up on our way to the office?"

"Will she be ready by five-fifteen?"

"Ready and waiting for my prince!" Colleen said.

"It will be Cedric," Sal said. "Is that okay, Cedric?"

"Five ten would be safer," Cedric said.

"Five ten," Colleen said. "Can't wait to see you."

"Jason, Cedric or me?" Sal teased.

"All of you!"

"But mostly Jason," Sal said.

"Mostly, and then Cedric," Colleen teased.

"I'm mortally wounded."

"Goodnight, everyone," Colleen said. "Behave!"

“We’re done all our misbehaving for the evening,” Jason said.

Sal lived in a big brick house on Robinhood Street near Wakeforest Avenue. Cedric pulled his brother’s Chevy into the driveway and up to the iron gate. “Home safe and sound.”

“After quite a day of adventure. Thanks, Cedric.” Sal got out of the car and went to his front door.

“Yes, thanks. See you in the morning,” Jason agreed, following behind with their box of loot.

Sal went in, turned on the light and switched off the alarm. “Come in, Jason. Have a seat at the dining table; I need to feed Stinky. Start spreading things out and we’ll sort through them.”

Jason went in and put the box on the table. “Who’s Stinky?”

“My cat,” Sal said. “He farts a lot; Myriam hates him.”

“Could I use the washroom?”

“Down the hall, second door. This is basically a bachelor house, with Myriam staying in Mérida. The towel may be a bit dirty.”

“As long as it’s not as dirty as today’s deed.”

“I’ll get us some wine,” Sal said. “You can start sorting the papers.”

Jason returned from the powder room and began sorting papers into piles: pictures, news clippings, handwritten notes, bank statements, typed pages, phone logs. He was starting to wonder where Sal kept his wine when Sal finally returned, pushing a tea trolley. “This is a very nice Texas Tempranillo Reserve from Pedernales.” Apparently, having wine, to Sal, included having something for the wine to go with. “It’s a bit much for fruit, so I prepared a selection of cold cuts and cheeses.” Sal poured a glass for each of them but left everything on the trolley. “We’ll let it air for five minutes. What have you found out?”

“I’ve just been sorting by type. I haven’t looked at content.”

Sal picked up the stack of pictures. “Andrew’s not the only one here. Who are the others?” He started separating the pictures into different piles. “That’s interesting. Edgar Simms. He’s a banker.” Sal sorted a few more pictures. “Hold on there. This shouldn’t be.”

Jason looked over; Sal was holding a picture of Andrew and someone else, sitting and laughing on the deck of a Grady-White sport fisher. “Who’s that?” Jason asked.

"Avizales' CFO, Pablo VeraCruz," Sal said. "He and J.P are sworn enemies."

"Here it is!" Jason found the picture of Andrew and Ginny.

Jason and Sal looked closely. The picture definitely showed white powder pouring out of a glass vial about half the size of Andrew's thumb and into a martini glass. "That's definitely Ginny," Jason said. "And that matchbook has the ACC logo on it. Ginny told me that the ACC convention is where their affair started."

"When would that be?"

"Sometime while I was doing my master's," Jason said. "Where's the clipping from the Brewster spill?" He dug through the pile and came up with it. "There!" he said, pointing out the date to Sal.

"The photo of Andrew and Pablo is definitely a lot more recent. Let's see if we can make some kind of timeline with this stuff."

"There are just a few more things in the box," Jason said. "I'll sort them first."

Sal put the plate of snacks on the table between himself and Jason, and handed Jason a glass of wine.

"Is Jackson the one who helped you with all the files I've been reading on our computer?" Jason asked.

"Cheers," Sal toasted and they clinked glasses. "He and I go way back, since before Myriam."

"Before J.P.?"

Stinky jumped up onto the table and began playing with the papers. "Off of there, you!" Sal batted Stinky off the table. "No," he said. "I didn't need anyone like Jackson before J.P. He and I were already well on our way."

"On your way where?" Jason thought Sal might have considered it a rhetorical question because he didn't answer right away.

"I guess we were just on our way to now," Sal finally said pensively. "I'm not sure where we'll go from here. I don't think J.P. will come with me."

"Now is different?"

"I've been stuck in now since shortly before you and I met. Time hasn't just kept passing by the way it always does. Now, time is forcing me to notice. Now, time is forcing me to make a decision."

"The same one you want me to make?"

"Yes, the same one I wish I had made at your age."

It was Jason's turn for silent thought. "Thank you," he finally said.

Sal smiled. "This stuff covers quite a few years."

"I've got BursaBanc statements for TGIM2K, and Prospero Bank ones for TGIT2K, both starting about fourteen years ago all the way up until August two years ago."

"The banker I spotted in the picture, he's BursaBanc," Sal said. "If we identify the others in that picture, it should reveal something."

Stinky was rubbing against Sal's leg and purring loudly; Jason found out how Stinky earned his name. "No wonder Myriam doesn't like him. That's disgusting!" Jason crinkled his nose and swept the air away with his hand. "I'll google the two account names to see if I can find out who they actually are."

Sal refilled Jason's glass. "Let's enjoy our wine and leave the paperwork for the morning."

"Suits me." Jason looked at his watch. "It almost is morning."

"This wine is from Texas," Sal said. "A small family estate that only started up in the eighties."

"You found it while thinking of now," Jason guessed.

"Next," Sal corrected. "A next Myriam might share with me."

"Do you think she would?"

"I think she's entrenched. I haven't figured out how I could bring Mexico here."

"If you could?" Jason asked.

"Not when she finds out how different her Sal is from this Sal. I think her Sal is too far distant to retrieve for more than a few days at a time." Stinky hopped up and curled into a ball on Sal's lap. "Behave yourself, you wretch, or down you go." Sal began petting and Stinky purred his very loud purr.

"How about next Sal?" Jason asked.

"I don't know him yet; I can't really say." Stinky renewed his trademark, but Sal made no move to evict the cat from his lap.

"I'm sure that, if you can endure that cat, Myriam will be able to endure next Sal."

"We'd better decide what to bring to the office with us tomorrow. I'll put the rest in my safe."

"The bank statements," Jason said. "We can reconcile them against each other."

"Follow the money," Sal said. "The police shows always say that."

"Should we bring some pictures?"

"The one with the Mexican banker," Sal suggested. "I'd like to put names to the other people."

"What else?"

"The notes and newspaper clippings. We'll sort through them, see if we can figure out what story they tell, maybe who's story."

Jason took the notes and bank statements. Sal took the pictures and news clippings, and put the rest in his safe. The doorbell rang just as Sal gave the tumblers a spin.

"I'm glad I keep a clean shirt at the office," Jason said. "I hope Colleen won't mind sitting beside me."

Breakfast for Three

Cedric opened the limo's front door for Sal, and Jason climbed in the back. "Grrrr," Colleen growled. "You look a little sexy with that five o'clock shadow."

"And it only took me an extra twelve hours to get it," Jason said.

"Did you boys find out anything interesting?"

"Besides how much I missed you?"

"I already know that," Colleen assured him. "I felt it too."

"We got some stuff that's definitely worth looking at," Jason said. "We don't know what it means yet."

"You'll tell me, won't you?"

"He'll tell you or I will," Sal assured her. "Something I learned from Myriam: you'll find out anyway. It would have been a lot easier on my ego if I'd told Myriam myself instead of finding out she knew everything anyway—absolutely everything!"

"I'll tell you," Jason said. "There's not much love if there's no trust."

Colleen squeezed his arm.

"We've got some notes, some bank statements and some news clippings with us that we're planning to sort through today," Jason said. "Sal locked the other stuff in his safe at home."

"How much stuff did you get?"

"A whole box full. About a two-inch stack of eight by tens, over ten years of bank statements from two different accounts for companies with very similar names, TGIM2K and TGIT2K."

"Thank Goodness It's Monday and Thank Goodness It's Tuesday," Colleen joked, "or Thursday."

"More like Thank Goodness I'm Mexican and Thank Goodness I'm

Texan," Jason said. "One bank is in Mexico and the other is in Texas. Anyway, we have the pictures, the statements, a bunch of newspaper clippings and some other documents, notes, letters, memos and such."

"Our job today is to try to build a story around what we've brought," Sal said. "A skeleton that we can flesh out with the other documents."

They arrived outside TechSys. "Thank you, Cedric," Sal said. "Go hang out at Discovery Green for a while. We're not likely to need you till it's time for home."

They all went up to the executive lounge. "Good morning, José," Sal said. "This is Colleen, Jason's girlfriend."

"Oh," José said, "I see you in the downstair sometime! Nice to meeting your acquaintance! I tell Señor Jason he will bring you my house; my Juanita will cook good Mexican dinner for you. We will having good time."

"I'd love to come," Colleen said. "Just let Jason know when. I'm sure your wife is lovely."

"And my *niños*," José said. "They mostly can bad only once a while."

Jason took Colleen's hand and led her to the kitchen. "*Bonjour*, Simon. This is Colleen."

"*Enchanté, mademoiselle.*" Simon bowed, crossing his feet and tracing a wide arc with his arm.

"I've heard how fabulous your meals are," Colleen said. "Nice to meet you too."

Jason held a chair next to the window for Colleen then sat across from Sal.

"I bring you a fresh good Mexican coffee," José said as he filled three cups. "Simon say he no make Mexican breakfast for nice lady, only for Mr. Jason. He say Mr. Sal will have some good French pastry he like."

"I'm sure whatever Simon prepares will be fine," Sal said. "Don't worry."

"Did you men talk about business all night?" Colleen asked.

"No," Jason said. "Actually, we spent quite a bit of time discussing the importance of including one's spouse in one's life."

"More, how I regret not having done so," Sal admitted, "and how I hope Jason won't make the same mistake."

"But you and Myriam were so sweet together," Colleen observed.

"Myriam loves the Sal of her heart. I can be him for short periods, and I enjoy him," Sal said. "But Myriam would be devastated to know the real Sal; it's better I don't force him upon her."

"Perhaps she knows the true Sal better than you do," Colleen said. "If you weren't more him than you think, you wouldn't be so concerned for her, or for Jason and me."

"Myriam is my life, my heart. I am only just now finding out how true that is. I let myself become a hideous beast and I know it has hurt her deeply. I can't keep hurting her."

"I will keep praying that you and Myriam get back together," Colleen promised, "because I've seen how you two are."

"It's a long time since I've been that nice. I've done some horribly evil things; I don't know if I have enough life left to properly atone. God only knows how bad my sins have been."

"And he sent His Son," Colleen said. "Admitting your sins is halfway to atonement."

"That's Catholic," Sal said. "I'm not."

"Christian," Colleen corrected. "And He was sent 'that all might be saved,' not just Christians."

"Okay. This is one of those things we have to talk about," Jason said. "It's a bit heavy for breakfast."

José brought a plate of pastries for Sal, crêpes Suzette for Colleen and *huevos rancheros con frijoles refritos y chile verde* for Jason. "Simon say this foods will make Jason to be savage like José!" he announced proudly.

"Tell him thank you," Colleen said. "Everything looks and smells very good!"

"Okay," José said, "I am bring you more Mexican coffee."

They were all enjoying breakfast. "You didn't bless your food," Jason observed.

"I did silently," Colleen said. "And weren't you the one who decided this discussion was too heavy for breakfast?"

"Well," Jason said, "it's nagging at me anyway; it won't go away."

"No," Sal agreed, "not once you know it's there."

"So why does it matter whether one believes in God or not? Why is it important?" Jason asked. "Why not just accept the answers science can provide and work with those? That's more than enough to get by."

"Because if we are created by an intelligent God," Colleen said, "then we are His and He gave us a purpose. He is our boss. All men are created equal. That's generally accepted even if God isn't accepted. If there is no God to be the boss and all men are created equal, who is the boss?"

"Do we really need a boss?" Jason asked.

"We need to know that we are not the boss," Sal said. "We must have a God who is greater than any man; otherwise any man could make himself God. We just fool ourselves if we believe we can do as we please; we have limits and we must live within them. Accepting God helps us accept this."

"So, do you accept God because you believe there is a God," Jason asked, "or because it is useful to have a God?"

"Because it's terrible not to have one," Sal said. "Breakfast will be over long before we settle this, so let's press on with more immediate issues."

"My immediate issue is I have to get to work," Colleen said. "We'll see each other tonight?" She looked at Jason.

"Yes," Sal said. "Jason and I will do what we can today and plan for tomorrow. But tonight, he's yours."

"I'll walk you to the elevator." Jason got up and took Colleen's hand.

"Nice to meeting you," José said. "I hope I seeing you again!"

"I'm sure we'll see each other again," Colleen said. "The crêpes were delicious, Simon," she called out. "Thank you!"

"You're welcome, Miss Colleen," Simon called back.

Whose Papers?

Sal caught up with Jason in the hallway just as the elevator door closed on Colleen. "Now. Battle room!"

Jason looked over a handwritten note labelled 'Burkeman Mole' that summarized various photos and events. It was obviously the script Mendoza used to impersonate Sam Grierson. Next, he examined the TGIT2K and TGIM2K bank statements. The accounts rose steadily until a combined amount of roughly one million dollars US was withdrawn. The withdrawals occurred between eight and eleven times a year.

Meanwhile, Sal sorted the news clippings into chronological order. He noticed several themes so he reorganized the stories into a grid, by topic across the top and by date top to bottom. The stories covering Brewster Coal Corp and the cinnabar disaster were expected; stories covering the Trans Mexico and Palomex battles weren't surprising either. The collection covering Stanford Dell's arrest, trial and conviction for embezzlement was very thorough, with clippings from many different papers. The Jacob and Barbara Kinder crash only had clippings and obituaries from the *Houston Chronicle*. A number of articles about narcotic and human trafficking involving the Machetes Motorcycle Club were much less expected. There was a long column of miscellaneous stories and a thick stack of clippings in Spanish from Mexican papers.

Jason's cellphone rang. "Hello."

"Do you think you two could bump up our zoo appointment to eleven thirty? I'd like to get into the Cypress Circle Café before the lunch rush."

"Who is this?" Jason asked.

"Jackson. Who's this?"

"Jason."

"Sorry. I must have the wrong number." Jackson hung up.

"Who was that?" Sal asked.

"Jackson. He asked if we could change our zoo appointment to eleven thirty and then pretended he had the wrong number." Jason was confused.

"He's warning us. He wants to meet us and he suspects his phone is tapped." Sal dialled his cellphone. "Hi, Cedric, how soon can you be at Jas'?"

"We're going to Jas' while we wait for Cedric to take us to a café?" Jason asked.

"Jackson obviously suspects he's under surveillance," Sal said as he collected the papers and locked them in a wall safe concealed behind Cecil Burkeman's portrait. "We may be too. I want to see if we can spot someone tailing us."

Sal looked around the lobby as they exited the elevator. "We can't make it obvious that we're checking," he said. "Watch the reflections in the windows. Stop and pretend to retie your shoelace so I can have an excuse to look back." Jason obeyed. Sal walked a few steps on and then turned to face him.

"How are you so good at this?" Jason asked quietly when he caught up to Sal.

"The thing I won't admit to."

"I still haven't guessed, have I?"

"Though you made significant progress in different directions both times you bluffed," Sal said, "it's a good thing I believed you had figured it out; otherwise we wouldn't be as far as we are."

"But I won't be able to bluff again."

"No."

They reached Jas'. Sal held the door, giving himself another chance to look behind.

"I see you brought a bodyguard," Jas said to Jason. "Have a seat; I got you guys."

Jas brought Jason's dark roast and a caramel latte for Sal. "Maybe you can give me a tip, Sal." Jas put her arm around Jason's shoulders and sidled up to him provocatively. "How can I get this guy to go out with me?"

"He wouldn't survive," Sal said, "and you wouldn't survive once Colleen found out!"

"I heard she's kind of a librarian type." Jas turned her look from Sal to Jason and ratcheted it up a few notches. "Why don't you take a walk on the wild side?"

Jason blushed. "Dark roast is about as wild as I get."

"Uh huh, I can fix that," Jas said, "if you give me a chance."

Jas' phone rang. "Excuse me, boys."

Jas returned with the phone. "It's for you, Sal."

Sal took the phone. "Hello... I don't see anyone... Okay... Yes... Five minutes." He handed it back. "Thanks Jas." He turned to Jason. "Cedric will be here in five minutes."

"Would you boys like anything else?" Jas winked at Jason.

"We're good," Jason said.

"Oh yeah?" Jas asked. "Show me." She walked off with an exaggerated sway, looked back and winked again.

"She's very good at being bad," Sal said. "You know she wouldn't do it as much if you didn't blush so easily, don't you?"

They finished their coffees about the same time Cedric arrived outside.

Sal left twenty dollars on the table. "It's the only way she'll accept anything."

"Other than what you've already given her?"

"Yes, I guess that pays for a lot of coffee."

Jas stood by the door as they left. "Come back soon!" She stepped in a bit closer and let out a soft growl as Jason passed by.

"I don't know which one of you would be more scared if she ever actually caught you," Sal said.

"Are you kidding me?" Jason asked.

"She's hiding some very deep emotional scars behind that act of hers. She only teases you so terribly, apart from you responding so predictably, because she knows you won't bite."

Sal got in the front seat and Jason the back. To their surprise, Jackson was also there. "I take it we're not meeting at the zoo," Sal said.

"No. I thought I'd throw those turkeys on a bit of a wild goose chase,"

Jackson said. "I called my sister right after you with the same story. She's gonna have a nice day at the zoo with her kid—on your tab. Those Feds can have a nice time babysittin' her. There won't be as many chasin' us."

"Who are they?" Jason asked.

"They're not local," Jackson said. "I didn't recognize anyone and it was too easy to shake my tail. I just slipped into the tunnels at Tranquility Park and had Cedric meet me outside Wells Fargo."

"Do you think they're FBI?" Jason asked.

"Probably DEA."

"Machetes?" Sal asked.

"Yeah. How'd you know," Jackson asked. "Mendoza is a wannabe."

"We found a lot of newspaper clippings about them in the box."

"We might have put Bert in a bit of a jackpot," Jackson said. "The Feds can only be on me 'cause they spotted me—"

His phone rang, and he pulled it from his pocket. "This is my hotline to the Feds. My sister's callin'."

"Choochoo... Yeah, sorry. I'm not gonna make it... I got stuck downtown and I still haven't made it to the courthouse... Kiss your kid for Uncle Jackson... Later."

"What was that?" Sal asked.

"Sandy doesn't know she's helpin' us. Better the Feds think they lost me than I ditched them."

"What are you doing at the courthouse?"

"I parked there, and I'm gonna flirt with my contact there when I get back, find out somethin' about another case I'm on."

"This time's covered," Sal promised. "We'd better see what we can do to clear Bert."

"Okay," Jackson said, "they'll have a couple of guys parked on my car. I'll use that to introduce myself. I'll find out what I find out."

"Let us know. I'm sure you could find out more from what's in the box than we'll be able to find out by ourselves; this isn't exactly accounting. See if you can meet with us later."

"Better drop me back at Wells Fargo." Jackson handed Sal a cellphone. "Here. Use this to contact me; my burner's in there under Dick. I'll call you in a couple of hours. Keep watchin' your backs for tails or trouble."

"What should we do if we spot someone following us?" Jason asked.

"Take them for a nice long walk somewhere," Jackson said. "Anywhere except where they might want to be."

"Shouldn't we just be in our office?" Sal asked. "Where one would expect us to be?"

"That might be an invitation for them to come knockin' on your door," Jackson warned. "So make sure they're not gonna find you with anything they shouldn't."

"We could probably stretch out lunch for a couple of hours if you're sure you can call us by then," Sal said. "Two hours is probably too long to sit in our office without looking at our stash of papers."

"We should invite Pet," Jason suggested. "Let her squirm a bit. She'll never believe we're just being nice."

"We aren't," Sal said. "At all! But that's not too bad an idea; we might get something. Whoever collected that box of stuff must be well connected to both Burkeman and Avizales. Even if she doesn't intend to help us, something might slip out."

"She does seem to be the common link. There isn't any connection between the two groups before her. I'll call."

Jason made the call with the speaker on. "Pet. We need to meet."

"Why?" Pet asked.

"Use your imagination and show up at Vic and Anthony's in twenty minutes."

"Thirty."

Cedric dropped Jackson off outside Wells Fargo and drove Sal and Jason to Vic and Anthony's. "Mabel's suppose ta pick up little Sally from school and watch her at Bebe's."

"Go. We'll be fine," Sal said. "We can walk back to the office."

Jason held the restaurant door open for Sal. "Hi! Twice in a week!" Rafael said. "To what do we owe this honour?"

"Hi, Rafael," Sal said. "Same game, different player. Patricia's on the menu today."

"Thanks for the warning," Rafael said. "You couldn't have picked a different place?"

"Sorry, it's definitely a Vic and Anthony's type of meeting."

Rafael sat Sal and Jason at the same corner table as before. "Would you uncork a wine for us and let it breathe?" Sal asked.

"We just brought in a 2012 Prunotto Barolo," Rafael said. "The customer who recommended it is pretty reliable."

"How about that Monte Zovo we had last time?"

"We may be out. If we are, I have a 2013 Pio Cesare Barolo I can personally vouch for."

"Vic and Anthony's is about the wine," Jason observed.

"Good food, good wine, good company," Sal said. "I come here whenever the second needs to supplement the third."

"Do you think the wine will improve Pet?"

"That would be a complete waste," Sal said. "She'll be drinking her Rossinis."

Pet came in and rushed over to the table. "What's so important!" she demanded before she even sat down.

"Hello, Pet," Sal said. "I'm fine, thanks for asking, and how are you?"

"I don't have time for all these pleasantries!"

"That's why people don't often find you pleasant," he said dryly.

"Hi, Pet," Jason said. "Thanks for joining us."

Rafael came over with three menus. "May I start you off with a drink?"

"Rossini," Pet said curtly and then turned to Sal. "Why am I here?"

"To rescue you from Irma's."

"Ha, ha," Pet said. "I like Mexican, and it's much faster than here."

"And to rescue you from the Machete Motorcycle Club," Jason said.

"It may have been my house," Pet said, "but that was my mother, not me."

"Are you sure?"

"When a gang of thugs lays siege to your house, you tend to find out why," Pet said. "I had dinner with Hector and Tess a day before it happened. Tess said their driver almost ran one of the Machetes off the road earlier that same day; we figure he followed their car to my home when their driver came to pick me up. I guess guys like that don't like being run off the road."

"That's the official police version?" Jason asked.

"Those HPD cowards didn't even get out of their cars. They just showed up with their sirens wailing and their lights flashing and waited outside my house, all safe in their cars, long enough for the bikers to get tired of their little game."

"So whose version is it?" Sal asked.

"Tess and I figured it out together. She came up from Mexico to talk about it when she found out; she actually cared," Pet revealed. "She was in the car when her driver almost hit the biker."

Rafael returned with Pet's Rossini and Sal's and Jason's wine. "Just pour it, thanks, Rafael," Sal said.

"Have you decided?" Rafael asked as he poured the wine. Pet ordered pan-roasted chicken; Sal and Jason ordered burgers.

"So you guys are running up Sal's expense account over some lame-brained concern about a bunch of over-testosteroned boys with toys?"

"No, actually," Sal said, "we'd like to ask for your help."

"Yeah, right," Pet sneered. "Tell me another one."

"Seriously," Jason said. "Someone is collecting a whole lot of information about all things Burkeman and Avizales. That connection didn't exist before you entered the picture. We'd like you to help us figure out who it is."

"Someone who got screwed by Houston Long Haul," Pet said. "There's a long list to start with."

"Can you suggest some names?" Sal asked.

"Uncle Gus is pretty pissed for starters. There's a lot of drivers, guys with empty warehouses."

"It has to be someone who works both sides of the border," Sal said. "And they understand both English and Spanish."

"So Uncle Gus is a leading candidate. Why did you have to drag me here for that?"

"We need to know more about Stanford Dell," Jason said. "We only have the official version."

"That's only a tenth of how rotten he was," Pet said. "He was worse than Uncle Ricardo."

"Did he try something with you?"

"Me and anyone under thirty wearing heels. He'd snort up his happy powder and chase the nearest skirt."

"So he began embezzling from the company to pay for his cocaine addiction?" Sal asked.

Rafael approached the table. "Chicken and another Rossini for madam... Burger with fries here... And with Caesar here. Enjoy!" He topped up Sal's glass and then Jason's.

Pet cast an angry glance at Rafael for the interruption. "All his money went up his nose," she said. "When his was gone, he needed more. He had to keep his party girls happy, five or six all the time. His place was nothing but a big party house after Jan left him."

"When did she leave?" Jason asked.

"She got out while there was still something to get," Pet said. "While I was still with Campbell Consulting Corp. Dell was a total womanizer. Jan thought anyone whose skirt was more than three inches above their knees was sleeping with Stan; only two of them actually were. He picked the rest up in strip clubs. She saw me come out of Stan's office one day and was certain I had just finished screwing him. I was actually just delivering a bunch of folders. Stan wasn't even in there!

"That, ironically, is how I met Andrew. He heard Jan ranting at me in the hallway and came out to rescue me. Andrew took me out for coffee to calm me down; we talked for a couple of hours and one thing led to another. He promised me that night he'd talk to Jan. I think that talk was the one that finally convinced her to give up on Stan."

"Could Jan be the one collecting the information?" Jason asked.

"No. There was enough in her settlement to keep her more than happy. She's quite content playing tennis and having tea. Besides, that was before the Mexican stuff."

"So Augusto is our only suspect," Jason said. "Is there any way you can find out more than we already know?"

"Not a chance!" she said. "Even if I could, I wouldn't go near that snake!"

"How about from your mom?"

"Tess only has time for me on her schedule. I only see Tess when Tess wants to see me."

"You can't think of anyone we might be able to get information from?" Jason asked.

"That line of communication is completely cut off," Pet assured him. "We are both persona non grata to each other."

"I guess we'd better just enjoy our lunch," Sal said. "We seem to have made more progress finding who it's not than who it is. No sense beating a dead horse."

"Do you think you'll ever go back to the hacienda?" Jason asked.

"That's where it happened," Pet said.

"It's much different now. It might help you get past the past to see how it is now. I'm sure Ricardo and Connie would love to have you visit."

"I'm not ready," she said. "I don't think I'll ever be. Maybe if we destroy Uncle Gus."

"Your anger may be hurting you more than he is," Sal said.

"He has enough anger over Enrico and Ernesto to keep him busy."

"Same story with a different title. You're stuck in chapter one and Uncle Gus is stuck in chapters three and five."

"And we don't yet know how many chapters there are," Jason said. "Perhaps we'll get stuck in one that hasn't been written."

The rest of the meal was very quiet. "If you think of anything, let us know," Sal said to Pet as she left.

A Bigger Picture

"This is really good wine," Jason said.

"I'm glad that I've finally found someone to enjoy my wine with," Sal said.

"How did you acquire the hobby?"

"That's painful to discuss."

"The person you least expected to betray you?"

"One and the same."

"Your chapter one?"

"No. There's not much to forgive there," Sal said. "They're doing it to save me, not hurt me. I guess I'm mostly angry because they're not letting me follow my own timetable. They're making me do what I ought sooner than I want to, which would probably be never."

"I'm guessing that's all you have to say on the subject."

"We'll probably talk about it in Mexico one day," Sal said. "You, me, Colleen and Myriam."

"I hope so."

Sal's phone rang. "Hello... I'm going to put you on speaker; start over."

"We're all good here," Jackson said. "These guys here are DEA and they want us to co-operate. Bring everything over to my place: pictures, clippings, bank statements, even the stuff you haven't looked through. We're gonna go over it all and see if we can't help each other out. When they see why I was watchin' Mendoza, they promise to cough up their side. You're gonna give up the papers to my friend Bert. He's HPD. He's here, and he's gonna make sure the DEA doesn't just scoop everything and run. He's also gonna tell us why HPD was at Mendoza's."

"Should I bring our lawyer?" Sal asked.

"No, it's still like I advised before: we don't know who's in on this and who's out, so the less people that see anything, the more we catch them by surprise and the less hidin' they do. Just Jason and you."

"Okay, but it will take me a bit to collect up the stuff from where it is. We're out of the office right now."

"Listen pal!" Neither Sal nor Jason recognized the voice. "My partner's waiting for you outside your office. He'll take you wherever you need to go, but you need to go now!"

"We're happy to co-operate," Sal said. "We have some documents that made us suspicious, but they don't prove anything and they haven't pointed to anyone in particular. We're just exercising our due diligence by investigating further, hence, Mr. Taylor. It seems you're also interested in what we've collected so we're all too pleased to share it with you. I appreciate that you're very busy, but we also have business to attend to. Our efforts will prove more fruitful if we can be civil toward one another. Do we understand each other?"

"Yes, Mr. Rosenthal." The voice became syrupy. "Agent Wyman will gladly drive you wherever you need to go to pick up the documents and bring you here."

"Thank you," Sal said. "I look forward to meeting you, Mr... Mr.—"

"Brokowicz."

Sal hung up and handed Jackson's burner to Jason. "You'd better call Colleen."

"Hi, Hon. I'm afraid I'll be late again tonight."

"Are you and Sal getting into more trouble?"

"Out, actually," Jason said. "We're meeting with some DEA agents and handing the stuff over to them."

"You're not in any trouble for the way you got it?"

"No." Jason wasn't sure whether Colleen's phone might be tapped. "We paid Kumar Rampursad for them in good faith. We don't know how he obtained them, but we obtained them legally."

"Okay," Colleen said. "Call me when you're done and let me know how things went. It doesn't matter how late; I won't be able to sleep anyway."

Once Jason was off the phone, Sal said, "Let's enjoy the rest of our wine first. Let's not rush just yet."

"Do you think that's wise?"

"We'll co-operate fully, but we won't let them bully us."

"What if they arrest us?"

"If they had cause to do that, they would have," Sal assured him. "Remain calm. We're a couple of law-abiding citizens helping out the DEA because it's our duty as citizens of this fine country."

Sal enjoyed his wine, sipping slowly, twirling it in his glass and holding it up to look through it to the light beyond. Jason saw the wheels turning in Sal's head despite his relaxed demeanour. The twelve minutes Sal spent with his nebbiolo felt like more than an hour to Jason. They finished, paid, bade Rafael goodbye and sauntered back to the office. As promised, a young DEA agent was waiting. He got out of his SUV and showed his badge as they approached. "Mr. Rosenthal? I'm Trevor Wyman."

Sal shook agent Wyman's hand. "Call me Sal. And this is Jason Johnstone. You may call him Jason. Mr. Brokowicz told us to expect you. Judging from that conversation, you're good cop and he's bad cop. It's much more a pleasure to meet you than it was to converse with your partner."

"He's a little rough around the edges and, to be fair, intimidation is a good tactic for most of the characters we meet in our line," Trevor said. "Once he gets to know you, he may mellow out a bit."

"I hope a good bit."

"You'll probably come to like him."

"It sounds as though you expect us to become well acquainted," Jason said.

"If you'll agree to what we intend to ask of you," Trevor said.

"Which is?" Sal asked.

"I don't want to steal Brok's thunder," Trevor said. "He is, after all, the senior partner."

"Fair enough," Sal said. "It wouldn't be good if our DEA agents were stealing."

"Would you like a hand with anything in there?" Trevor asked.

"No. It's probably better that we don't introduce any strange faces."

"We're probably already generating rumours by our behaviour lately," Jason said.

"I'll wait in the car then."

"You may as well wait with Trevor," Sal suggested. "I can easily handle what we've got upstairs."

Trevor got back into his SUV and Jason waited in the TechSys lobby. Sal returned shortly with the satchel he had loaned Jason that morning.

"We need to swing by my house," Sal said. "How long have you been in Houston?"

Trevor started off, not asking for an address or directions. "Actually we're just in and out; we've been operating out of Laredo for a couple of years now, but that's all you're getting out of me until we get to Taylor's place."

"He likes to go by Jackson," Sal said. "He thinks he's Action Jackson."

"Sounds like you know him fairly well."

"We use him exclusively for TechSys."

"What does TechSys need a detective for?"

"Background checks on key personnel, mostly, and fidelity checks."

"Bedroom window stuff?"

"He has done," Sal admitted. "But more in the line of protecting intellectual property, confidentiality, non-compete, anti-poaching."

"So what's he working on right now for you?"

"I think I'd rather wait till we're all together," Sal said, "so that everyone will see what cards are on the table and how they fit into the deck."

Trevor pulled up to the iron gate across Sal's driveway. Sal went in and retrieved more papers, and they drove on.

"Have you been to any of our museums," Sal couldn't help asking, "or our zoo?"

"We're not here to sightsee," Trevor said, and that was it until he parked in front of Jackson's place.

Jackson was waiting at the door. "Hi, Sal. We good?"

"We're good," Sal assured him. "Let's see what our friends have to say."

Brokowicz was huge—very broad-shouldered. Sal, though not at all short, barely reached his shoulders; Jackson topped out mid-nose. The best B-movie costume designer couldn't have done a better job of picking out Brokowicz's brown corduroy jacket and beige Eddie Bauer slacks. "Where's his fedora?" Jason whispered to Sal.

"Nice to put a face to the voice." Sal's hand disappeared into Brokowicz's. "They match very well."

Brokowicz just looked Sal up and down. Next, Jason introduced himself. "Trevor tells me you're his senior partner."

Brokowicz allowed himself half a smile. "Hmmph."

"Since you're calling the shots," Sal said, "I think it's only fair that you have first volley."

"All right," Brokowicz said. "I don't like guys whose suits cost more than my rent, and I don't like guys who play cop for a living."

"Fair warning," Sal said. "How do you like Jason?"

Brokowicz just stared.

"Okay, then," Sal said. "I'm not liking you very well either. Where's Bert?"

"Bert's busy," Brokowicz said. "He'll be back later."

Jackson looked at his watch. "There's a seafood restaurant just around the corner. We can eat while we wait for him," he suggested.

"These guys just ate," Brokowicz said, nodding toward Sal and Jason.

"We'll just have a cup of chowder." Sal offered. "You must be hungry, though, big brute like you."

Trevor watched Sal and Brokowicz eyeing each other. "I could go for seafood," he said, trying to break the mood.

"I'll drive," Jackson said. "I know the way." He quickly tidied the back seat of his car, uncrumpling a few plastic shopping bags to stuff everything into. He put the good stuff in his trunk and the garbage in the can just outside.

Brokowicz shoved his way past Sal to claim shotgun. Sal ushered Jason and then Wyman into the back before climbing in himself. "My treat," Sal offered.

"This is on the DEA. Policy!" Brokowicz insisted.

"Can't we keep this just between friends?"

"No!" Brokowicz adjusted his seat all the way back, leaving Sal with his knees around his ears.

"No wonder you drive an SUV," Sal said. "So Brokowicz will fit."

All through dinner, Sal and Brokowicz continued their game of alpha dog. There was no clear winner, but Sal definitely took the humour award. Jackson grew disgusted with Brokowicz; Trevor was embarrassed. Only Jason saw what was actually going on. Relief finally came in the form of a call from Bert.

"Bert's waiting outside my office," Jackson said.

Brokowicz made a big production of paying the bill; Sal left a huge tip. They crammed back into Jackson's Crown Victoria and drove back to his house. Bert was waiting beside the driveway; he followed them into Jackson's garage. "Hi, pal. Did I miss anything?"

"Just the big guy over there dishin' out crap," Jackson claimed.

They all went in and sat around Jackson's dinette table. "I'm here to share what we know about Carlos Mendoza," Bert said. "We all know we were all there so let's put that on the table. As a show of good faith, I'll go first. Mendoza is a mid-level cocaine distributor. We had intel that he just received a shipment so we tried to catch him dirty. DEA's turn."

"We delayed the shipment you almost got," Brokowicz admitted. "We set up a sting to try and turn someone we've been tracking, but we were spotted."

"Who? Where?" Bert demanded. "Spill."

"Machetes. Sunnyside Park. They were all set up. Something spooked them and they scattered. We don't think the exchange took place."

"Don't think?"

"They may have met somewhere else after. We picked up our guy later and tailed him to Mendoza's. He watched for a while and left. That's when we spotted Jackson, here, skulking around. We knew our guy pretty well and where he would head, so we decided to tail Jackson. Now," Brokowicz looked menacingly at Jackson, "your turn to give."

"You know I'm on a case for TechSys—Sal and Jason, here. They had me purchase some information from one Kumar Rampursad. He's a former employee of Dell Burkeman Kinder—"

"What's that to TechSys?" Brokowicz demanded.

"TechSys is J.P. Burkeman's tech company," Jackson said. "Anyway, Rampursad worked for DBK, and he contacted Sal about sellin' some information—"

"Why'd he contact Sal?" Brokowicz demanded.

"We met at DBK," Sal said.

"Anyway," Jackson continued pointedly, "after we purchased the information, Sal kinda wanted to get to know Rampursad a little better. I tailed him to Mendoza's and he went off radar. I've been watchin' Mendoza waitin' for that crackhead to show again. We think Mendoza's his supplier."

"Okay, Sal," Bert said, "your turn."

Sal pulled out the news clippings about the Machetes. "This gives us a link to the bikers." He pulled out the bank statements. "There's a considerable flow of money through these accounts. We have no idea who TGIM2K and TGIT2K belong to or where the money comes from or goes to. It may be linked to the drug trafficking, but it's just a guess." He pulled out the stack of pictures, spread them out over the table and pointed at one of the pictures. "This man is Edgar Simms; he owns the bank where the TGIM2K account is. We don't know the other people."

Brokowicz grabbed the picture and looked closely at it. "John Clarke," he said, "aka Slasher, Pete Rose and Little Billy."

"Machetes?" Bert guessed.

"Mr. Machete and his two captains," Brokowicz said. "Who are the other two?"

"As I've mentioned," Sal said, "we don't know."

Sal laid out more pictures. "This," he pointed at another picture, "is our Kumar Rampursad."

It was Bert's turn to snatch a photo. "There's a familiar face. If you want to see him in person, I'll introduce you."

"You know where he is?" Brokowicz asked.

"About ten minutes away. I don't think he's in the mood for answering questions, though; he's chilling out at the morgue. Toe tag says he's John Doe."

"How long ago?" Brokowicz asked.

"Three days."

"Two days after we got these papers," Jackson said. "No wonder I lost him."

"It appears Jackson lost him," Sal said, "just about the time Bert found him."

"Where was he found?" Trevor asked.

Bert called his colleagues at Briggs Road. "That John Doe three days ago, where did we find him?... Unh huh... Have a peak in his file for POI's... Thanks."

"So?" Brokowicz pushed.

"He was found off Incinerator Road; that's right behind Sunnyside Park. Our Carlos Mendoza is a person of interest in the case."

"The ducks are lining up," Brokowicz said.

"When we co-operate," Sal said. He laid out more pictures. "Some of these pictures seem familiar; though I can't put names to them."

"What else do you have in there?" Trevor asked.

Sal pulled out the stack of clippings from Mexican papers. "I didn't take a close look at any of these as my Spanish is not very good. Palomex and Trans Mexico are companies Houston Long Haul had dealings with."

"Houston Long Haul?" Trevor asked.

"It's another Burkeman company," Sal said. "Why?"

"We know one of their drivers. He's been having conversations with a Machete."

"That's all I have," Sal said. "I'm on the boards of both TechSys and Burkeman Holdings. Burkeman Holdings is the umbrella for all things Burkeman so, as a director, my responsibilities include due diligence in any questionable matters that may impact our companies. As I've demonstrated, I'm most willing to co-operate to my fullest with the appropriate authorities. It would be of mutual benefit for us to co-operate on any matters arising from this information. I'm quite capable of maintaining strict confidence, as is Jason. He has my full confidence. He's my right hand at TechSys, and I trust him with any information I trust myself with. I intend to retain the services of Jackson, here, to investigate this matter further. Any links to illegal activity must be thoroughly investigated for the integrity of our companies and the protection of our shareholders."

Brokowicz clapped his hands slowly three times. "A fine performance. Bravo! You may be aware that the DEA is not a civilian organization. As such, we're not in the habit of sharing information with anyone."

"And are you in the habit of operating within the city limits of Houston without informing the HPD of your activities?" Bert asked.

"We're Laredo; we just followed a few guys in and out of Houston," Brokowicz defended. "We weren't really running an operation here."

"So nothing like a stakeout at Sunnyside Park ever happened," Bert said. "If you're not going to be open and honest with us, even after our co-operation here, I think our captain should contact your handler."

"The way you're being open and honest by meeting here at Jackson's?" Brokowicz asked.

"We can take this over to the station any time!"

"Whoa! Guys, dial it back a notch!" Jackson said. "We all know we're here because nobody wants anybody to know everything. But we're gettin' somewhere here!"

"Jackson's right," Sal said. "I think we are getting somewhere. Let's review what each of us brought to the table. DEA's been following the Machetes, obviously narcotics trafficking—"

"And human trafficking," Brokowicz added.

"HPD's been tailing Mendoza, narcotics again," Sal said. "Jackson, on Burkeman's behalf, has been—was now—watching Rampursad. All three of us arrived at Mendoza's via different routes. Before this meeting, HPD had Mendoza. I'm sure they're aware of the Machetes, but the link wasn't there. DEA followed a Machete to Mendoza. Burkeman, via me, Jason and Jackson, has linked Rampursad, Mendoza and the Machetes. Burkeman has also introduced specific bank accounts at Texan and Mexican banks. A little investigation of the other documentation Burkeman obtained, and is willingly surrendering, will undoubtedly provide more leads. My concern that some people employed by at least one Burkeman company may be involved in illegal activities appears to be well founded. Our co-operation, so far, should have earned us at least a little trust. That, and the ability for us to offer timely information about any Burkeman involvement, should warrant candid disclosure of any developments in this case. We cannot assure our employees will never run afoul of the law, but we can assure we will never condone such behaviour."

"I'll give you that," Brokowicz said. "If you promise you'll keep everything completely confidential and help us with whatever we need, we'll work with you."

"We'll work with you," Sal said. "You're the experts here; this doesn't fall within our scope of expertise. We're obligated to protect the legal and moral integrity of our company but, as directors, our responsibility is to assure the right people are performing the necessary tasks and provide guidance. In this instance, the task falls to law enforcement agencies. We do not presume to tell you how to perform your work or impede you in any way from performing it. We merely ask that you promise to inform us, in a timely manner, of anything you find out about Burkeman companies or Avizales companies."

"Whoa! What's this Avizales?" Brokowicz asked. "Where have they been up to now?"

"They're a conglomerate formed by the merger of the Avila and Gonzales families in Mexico. We have a long history with them and, usually, if we find trouble, we find Avizales."

"Where are they in these papers?" Trevor asked.

"Probably all through them. Palomex and Trans Mexico both used to be Gonzales. Whatever dirt you find in this stuff, I'm one hundred percent certain their footprints will be in it. We'll be able to help you navigate through their swamp."

"I'd like to send this down to Laredo," Brokowicz said. "We have some guys who are real good at this kind of paperwork."

"It's still our paperwork," Sal said. "But Jackson will make copies for us and Bert, and you can take the originals—full co-operation."

"You've made your point," Brokowicz said. "Truce."

"No truce needed. We're on the same side. There was never any battle."

"Let me send the documents to Laredo," Brokowicz said. "I'll have our guys scan them and give you access to the scans."

"As a demonstration of trust." Sal collected all the papers and handed them over. "With our compliments, Mr. Brokowicz. Access for us and for HPD."

"I could have obtained a warrant and forced you to hand these over," Brokowicz said, "but thank you. I apologize for treating you so harshly, all of you. I'm not accustomed, in my line, to having such open and willing suspects. Call me Brok."

"You don't know how hard it was for him to spit that out." Trevor patted Brok on the back.

"Who's in for a brew?" Jackson asked. "Or are you two still on the clock?"

"To co-operation?" Jason suggested.

"I guess we can agree we're clocked out, then," Brok surrendered.

Jackson went to his kitchen and returned with a six-pack of Karbach Hopadillos. He offered one to Brok first. "Peace offering?"

"The jury's still out on you," Brok admitted. "But I'm willing to wait for it. Thanks."

"I only ask for a fair shake," Jackson said. "I may surprise you yet. You might even get to like me."

"You surprised me with this IPA," Sal said. "I was expecting a lager."

"I wanted you to drink it," Jackson said. "I hate pouring out good beer."

"Good, in beer, is relative." Sal popped the tab on his can. "To the good guys!"

Everyone raised their can. "To the good guys!"

A Short Stay

Brok and Trevor finished their beers and excused themselves. "I have one left, if you want it, Sal," Jackson offered, "and a few cans of the stuff you won't drink for Jason and me."

"No thanks, Jackson," Sal said. "It's time Jason and I were off. I'll call Cedric."

"No need, man," Jackson said. "I'll drop you where you need to go."

Jason called Colleen. "We're done here, Hon."

Colleen insisted it wasn't too late for Jason to drop by. "I'll put on some tea. We should talk."

"Can you drop me at Colleen's?" Jason asked. "She says we need to talk."

"Uh-oh," Jackson said. "You in trouble!"

"No," Jason said. "She's right."

Jackson dropped Jason off at Colleen's before taking Sal home. Jason knocked on her door. "Come in!"

"How was your day?" Colleen poured Jason some tea. "Come sit on the couch with me."

"The breakfast was great," Jason said as he and Colleen snuggled down into the couch. "The rest was confusing and scary."

"What did you accomplish?"

"Well," Jason thought for a moment, "I think we're clear of our indiscretion, Sal and me. We handed all the papers over to the DEA."

"That's one of the things I was concerned about," Colleen said. "How did the DEA get involved?"

"They were watching someone who went to see the guy who had the papers. They saw Jackson watching the HPD raid."

"Jackson is Sal's detective friend?"

"Right. Anyway, they started following Jackson and that led to our meeting. Sal told them we got the papers from Kumar legitimately so we could make sure nothing untoward was happening at TechSys. They bought it and Sal gave them the papers. They promised we could still see them."

"The papers or the DEA guys?"

"Both, actually. They're going to scan the documents and give us access, and they're going to keep us up to date and ask us to help where we can."

"You're not going to do anything dangerous, are you?"

"We already are," Jason admitted. "But, hopefully, the DEA will handle any rough stuff. I'm actually glad we don't have those papers anymore; there's some scary stuff going on."

"What will happen if they talk to Kumar?" Colleen asked. "What will he say?"

"Nothing. Mendoza murdered him."

"Murdered!"

"Probably some drug dispute. That must be how Mendoza wound up with the papers."

"He doesn't know who you are, does he?" Colleen was worried. "Or Sal?"

"No," Jason assured her. "And he's probably still locked up anyway."

"What have you gotten into?"

"As far as work—a lot more and a lot scarier stuff than I ever imagined. As far as us? That's what I want to talk about. I'm really concerned."

Colleen took Jason's arm and rubbed it reassuringly. "Why?"

"Because right now, everything Myriam invited us to Mérida for is coming true. She warned us not to let work take precedence over us. For two nights, now, I've called to cancel us so I could do work stuff. That's not what I want."

"I know, Jason, but we talked about this in Mérida too," Colleen consoled. "We knew this was coming up; we knew it was unavoidable in the short term. Our commitment is to not make it the long term."

"But these are things I don't have any control over. How can I guarantee that things like this won't keep happening?"

"I'm not sure. But it's something we'll work on together."

"And I know that your Catholic faith is important to you," Jason said. "The way I just dismissed the subject this morning bothered me when I thought about it later."

"The fact that it bothered you is a good sign. Deal with this right now and we'll deal with that when we have time."

"That's my point. I'm dealing with work now and pushing us to later; your faith is about us!"

"It's enough right now that you realize that," Colleen said. "You understand more than you know."

"I've always written off faith as vague superstitions meant to answer what people didn't understand," Jason said. "I'm not sure I think that way anymore. Not since I met you."

"See, Jason? Your attitude is changing because faithful people are around you; it's contagious! Sal, Myriam, all the people at the hacienda, Moses too. You're seeing it."

"It's not enough to see it. I know that, for there to really be any chance for us, I must know it."

"You do," Colleen said. "Everyone does. It's just that not everyone is aware they know."

"How can people know without knowing they know?"

"It's our nature," Colleen said. "The way we're made. Cats act as cats, and dogs as dogs, even though they're not aware that they do. The same way, people act as people. When things go well, it's because we're acting as God intended; when they go badly, it's because we act against God's will. People prefer things to go well so they tend to act according to God's will. It's like driving; people put gas in their cars because they want to keep going, not because they understand all the mechanics of it."

"You're sounding a lot like Moses," Jason said. "I miss Tink's."

"Me too," Colleen agreed. "It's getting late. You'd better go home now or we'll be too tired for Tink's tomorrow."

"Are we allowed to have any after-Tink's even though we didn't have any Tink's?"

Colleen gave Jason a quick kiss. "There. Now, off with you."

They got up and Colleen saw Jason to the door. “Good night.”

“One more,” Jason said. “Enough gas to get me home.”

“You’re terrible.” She gave him another quick peck. “Good night!”

Jason thought about work and Colleen all the way home... and he thought about God.

A Good Start

Sal was enjoying his French pastries by the time Jason got to the executive lounge.

"Good morning, José," Jason said, and then a little louder, "Good morning, Simon." Jason sat beside Sal. "Good morning."

"Good morning, Jason," echoed back in different languages from each respective recipient.

"Here is your good Mexican coffee," José said. "What will you like to eating?"

"Just fried eggs, over easy and buttered toast. Thanks, José."

"You didn't give them the Brewster stuff," Jason said once José was out of earshot.

"It's not the same game and it's an ace we'll keep up our sleeve," Sal said. "Let's enjoy breakfast. We'll have a nice chat, then go to our office and conspire. What did you and Colleen talk about last night?"

"I gave a brief recap of the day and then pointed out that things weren't going according to Mérida. We finished off our talk with religion."

"And what did you have to say on the matter?"

"Just that I know it's important to her, ergo us, and I no longer dismiss it as the refuge of the ignorant."

"That's a good step," Sal said. "And Colleen?"

"She claims I know more about it than I think. That we all do."

"The whole of Western society is based on Judeo-Christian philosophy," Sal said, "so most of what you know about society is also about the Judeo-Christian faith. What's the Golden Rule?"

"Always say please and thank you?"

"Uh, no. The 'do unto' one."

"Do unto others as you would have them do unto you?"

"See. You know the basis of Judeo-Christian theology."

"All men are created...?" Sal raised his hands to prompt a response.

"Equal."

"Right. Another tenet, and the basic principal beneath our legal system. People say there should be a separation between Church and state, but all laws regulate moral conduct. Where does morality come from? Not science and definitely not politics!"

José brought Jason his breakfast and refilled the coffee cups. Jason pondered Sal's words as he ate. "I guess, at the bottom of things, everyone acts as they act because they believe what they believe."

"Except nowadays people are willing to leave their beliefs on a shelf and follow orders," Sal said. "Their paycheque has become an overriding motivation. I believe X but I will do Y in order to get my paycheque. There are not many conscientious objectors in today's workforce."

"À la us," Jason said. "We left certain things in Mérida to come back and do what we say we must do."

"Faith in divine providence is at very low ebb. People used to believe that, if they did what was right, the Lord would provide. Not that things would drop from the sky, but that the means to obtain what was needed would present itself."

"I guess that makes sense. When more people believed in God, more people depended on Him to provide," Jason said. "Now people don't believe in God, so they depend on themselves to provide."

"Also because life is much easier now," Sal said, "when things are going well, people are happy to take the credit. But when things are tough or go badly, we're not so eager to take credit for it."

Jason finished his eggs. "Well, this has been pleasant," Sal said. "Now, let's lock ourselves behind closed doors where we can safely do what we ought not."

"But must," Jason said.

They got up and headed to the door. "Are you ready to put your principles on the shelf for a while?"

"Are we able not to?"

"Technically or practically?"

They both thanked José and Simon. "I suppose it's possible when you're a cook or a waiter," Sal surmised, "but not once one climbs to the higher rungs of Corporate America."

"Or corporate anywhere," Jason said. "I guess that includes governments as well."

"Probably more so," Sal assessed. "It's impossible to climb those rungs without ending up indebted to many people. Many things are decided very far from the polling booth."

Sal and Jason greeted Janice in unison. "Good morning, Janice!"

"Any messages?" Sal asked.

Janice handed Sal a pink paper. "A Mr. Brokowicz. He said you'll know who he is."

"Thank you, Janice, I do," he replied, and to Jason, "This will be interesting."

Once in the safety of their office, Jason said, "Now, on to our private share of the papers."

"Yes. Our leverage against Andrew."

"Because of that which you will not admit? You told me that our enemy was using that to force you out and that it wasn't Andrew."

"That's right," Sal said. "But what we have against Andrew will help me with the other thing. I'm sorry, but it may place you in a worse position at the same time."

"So you're increasing my risk to reduce yours?"

"Perhaps expediting yours would be the better term. You'll face this risk sooner or later whether we abandon my quest or not."

"So I don't know either the risk or the foe, or even the extent of the risk. Can't you tell me anything more?"

"The risk is probably a life of poverty and shame. Probably no physical harm."

"How about Colleen?" Jason asked. "Is she in any danger?"

"Possibly of losing you," Sal said. "I think that's what I regret most."

"So you expect me to fight a battle I don't know against a foe I don't know and risk losing the person I think I most care for so that you might win the same battle?"

"Actually, fate has drawn you into this particular battle. But if it hadn't, you would still wind up facing the same war on a different field. Who's to say whether this battle or that is the more fierce?"

"Can't I at least know who my opponent is?"

"Not the particulars," Sal said, "but greed, sociopathic greed!"

"You cover up murder, conspiracy, bribery, environmental contamination and who knows what else," Jason said, "and you say greed is the mighty foe I must face?"

"All greed in different clothing."

"Isn't putting our beliefs on the shelf while we earn our paycheque also greed?"

"You see?" Sal said. "You're in the war, and neither of us is winning that skirmish at present."

"And how is our leverage over Andrew going to affect that war?"

"It's the artillery for a battle we must choose before one chooses us. Now we must learn how powerful our weapon is, how far it will fire and where we should aim it."

"And how much collateral damage might be incurred?" Jason asked.

"And how to avoid becoming part of that damage. But first, let's find out what Brok wants."

Sal dialled Brok. "Good morning, Brok... Yes, he's here now... We could do that... When and where?... I'll call you back within fifteen minutes if we can't."

"We're going to meet Brok and Trevor at the DEA building," Sal announced. "Can you print a copy of Pet's family tree to bring with us?"

"What's up?"

"Apparently their team in Laredo is having a field day with the papers they sent down." Sal dialled as he talked. "They're asking for our help in connecting the Avizales dots."

Sal held up his hand, palm forward, asking for a pause. "Cedric, can you pick up Jackson and meet us out front?... Let me know when you're on your way."

"We should have an hour or so before Cedric gets here," Sal said as he walked to the safe behind Cecil Burkeman. "Let's do some digging in the Brewster cinnabar mine."

Jason noticed that the papers inside the safe were neatly filed. "When did you have time to do that?"

"While my conscience denied me sleep. I hope this quest doesn't bring your conscience to the same state."

Sal brought two folders to the desk. He spread the contents of one across the desk—pictures taken at the ACC convention. "Do you recognize anyone?"

Jason's eyes went immediately to the picture of Andrew spiking Ginny's drink. "That's the one we expected to find." Jason slid over a picture of six diners at a table; he framed a portion of it with his thumbs and forefingers. "It's part of this one! That's the Andrew and Ginny eight by ten," and then pointed to one of the other diners. "This guy watching Andrew. I've seen him somewhere."

"You're right," Sal said. "He's John Hartmann, our chief stationary engineer."

"A janitor? What's he doing at an ACC conference?"

"And how's he pulling down a six-figure salary here?"

"Hundred-thousand-a-year janitor?" Jason was astounded.

"Plus," Sal stressed. "Why? And why here? Why not with Andrew?"

"Who are the others?"

"That very large man is Hank Solway."

"Brewster's president. Why is he sitting with Andrew?" Jason asked. "Wasn't this while they were competing for the open pit?"

"The fellow beside Hank is Robert Tajima. He was managing engineer for Burkeman Minerals. He passed away about three years ago."

"Who's the sixth guy? He looks about three sheets to the wind."

"That's Andrew and J.P.'s brother-in-law," Sal said. "On his good behaviour."

"Where is he now?"

"I won't know until eleven o'clock. That's when the bars open. Let's not talk about Tim anymore; he's out of the picture now."

"What about the rest of the pictures?"

"We can tell they're all from the ACC convention," Sal observed. "Maybe if we figure out who collected all this stuff, we'll have a better idea why they kept them and what to look for."

Sal opened the second folder; it contained surveillance photos of

Ginny and Andrew in various places and various states of undress. Sal handed the stack of pictures to Jason, who looked at each in turn and then put it on the bottom of the stack. "Wait," he said, looking at a picture of Andrew and Ginny having dinner in a restaurant. "Look at this guy!" He turned the picture toward Sal. "Isn't that Hartmann?"

Sal looked closely at a table three over from Andrew and Ginny's. "You're right. I hadn't noticed."

"Coincidence?"

"Perhaps we should ask him. But let's figure out more of the story first."

Cedric phoned to say he'd arrive in ten minutes. "Any more details your sharp eyes can pick out?" Sal asked Jason.

"Some birthmarks we shouldn't know about," Jason confessed. "You ought to stamp an R on the front of that folder!"

Sal returned the pictures to their folders, and the folders to the safe. "We'd better go down to meet Cedric."

A Better Middle

Sal, Jason, Cedric and Jackson exchanged greetings. Cedric took the scenic route to the DEA parkade while the three men in the back talked.

"I've been putting my ear to the ground about the Machetes," Jackson said. "They're some hard-assed dudes! You'd best leave anything to do with them to me and the DEA."

"We've no intention of doing otherwise," Sal assured him. "The farther we stay away from them, the better I'll like it."

"I'm guessing it won't be as far as you want it to be," Jackson said. "Some of my contacts get all jumpy when I put certain names in the same sentence."

"Such as?"

"It's too early to tell you. This is just kind of a 'keep your eyes open behind your back' warning. Some of the good guys you think you know... not so good."

"So this is one of those 'don't trust anyone' moments you see in the movies?" Jason suggested.

"This is one of those 'don't trust anyone in your life' moments," Jackson said, "except in the car. We're the good guys. Everyone else is a bad guy until we make sure they're not."

Jackson's warning was genuine; his tone conveyed more to Jason and Sal than his words did. "What about Brok and Trevor?" Sal asked.

"Maybe they're playing us. Maybe they still think we're bad guys," Jackson said, "which means they're still bad guys until we're absolutely sure they don't know what we did."

"And how will we know?" Jason asked.

"We have to find out if they showed up at Mendoza's before I put the box in my car or after. They tailed a Machete to Mendoza's. If we find out when he showed up, we find out when they showed up."

"I think we're safe there," Sal said. "If they saw you get the box, they would know who gave it to you, and if they knew that, I'm pretty sure they'd be all over Bert and wouldn't be bothering with us."

"Maybe. But I won't be comfortable until I'm more sure than I am. This is my licence and my friend. If they saw Bert hand off the box, I'm done and he's done."

"What else should we be trying to find out?" Sal asked.

"Where they picked up the Machete and how much stuff they have on them. How they got on to the Machetes in the first place."

"Why do we want to know all this?" Jason asked. "It's incidental to what we want to know. We've got the Andrew and Ginny picture. We've got all the Brewster stuff."

"Sins are like snowballs," Sal said. "Once they start rolling downhill, they keep picking up more sins. We need to know whether this other stuff is just more layers that got built up onto the original sin as it rolled along."

"Why?" Jason asked. "Why not just hold on to our ace and let everything else run its course?"

"Because if they keep peeling the layers away and find our ace, we won't have it any more."

"But they'll still have theirs," Jason said, "the one you won't admit."

"That keeps me awake at night," Sal said.

"Well, here we are!" Jackson said as they pulled into the parking lot. "We better put our best game faces on!"

"We'll just be as honest as we can be," Sal said. "Brok said they want our help identifying people connected to Avizales, so we'll help as much as we can."

The trio introduced themselves at the front desk, and the receptionist offered them seats in the lobby. Brok and Trevor came down ten minutes later and escorted them to an interview room. They sat around a table, Sal and Jackson on one side, Jason and Trevor on the other, Brok at the head operating the controls for a TV at the other end.

"Thank you all for coming," Brok said. "Today we'll be looking at people we've identified from the information you brought us. Our goal is to identify relationships between the various parties."

"We brought these," Sal said and handed out copies. "This is a family tree of the Avizales group. You'll see the Gonzales relatives to the left, Hector and Teresa Avila at the intersection, and the Avila family to the right. There are a lot of Guillermo and Rodriguez relatives on the Gonzales side and a lot of Sanchez and Hernandez relatives on the Avila side."

"I'd like to caution everyone," Brok said, "that just because we identify someone from our research as having the same name as someone in this family tree, it doesn't mean they're one and the same person. We must also remember that associating with a criminal doesn't necessarily make one a criminal. Much of what we have here may be legitimate business activity; the origins and purpose of collecting these documents is not known. That's part of what we're attempting to determine. Okay, let's begin.

"This first slide is, as far as we can establish, the earliest transaction. We've identified Pedro and Francisco Gonzales." Brok used an on-screen cursor to point out the individuals. "This is David Barker, an American, and the fourth person is unknown. David Barker died in an unsolved homicide in New York City. No motive was ever determined. We're off to an auspicious start."

Pet's family tree listed Pedro and Francisco as the elder and younger brothers of Pablo, father of Teresa, Augusto, Ernesto and Enrico. Brok's presentation showed how the pictures and news clippings all spread out from the first one. Pedro or Francisco would be associated to others, and then those others would be associated with still more. Most names of the Mexicans could be found in the Gonzales side of Pet's family tree. "You may remember this one," Brok said when he was halfway through the presentation. It was the picture of Edgar Simms, John Clarke (aka Slasher, Pete Rose, Little Billy) and two others. "We've identified the other two as Chico Rodriguez and Hector Avila. A trend our researchers noticed is that prior to this picture, the Americans involved were from New York, Boston and Chicago. After this picture, the Americans are all from Texas and Arizona."

"So do you think the Avilas were connected to the southern states and the Gonzales clan shifted to a closer group of American partners?" Jackson asked.

"We can't come to that conclusion," Brok said. "Our take is that whoever was compiling this information was concerned with the southern US connection and not the northern. This doesn't guarantee that the Gonzales group discontinued their association with the northern US. We still need to know who's compiling—or was compiling—this information to determine the significance of the lack of northerners subsequent to the introduction of the Machetes."

"And the introduction of Hector Avila," Sal said.

"And Hector Avila," Brok conceded. The picture show continued building connections between various Avilas and Machetes with growing involvement from the Gonzales family.

"Could I see those last few slides again?" Sal asked. "Who are those people again?"

"Simms and Rose. Your banker friend and the Machetes second-in-charge." The slide show ended with a surprise. "This is Hector Gonzales with three Machetes." Jason and Sal recognized him from a photo at the hacienda.

"Do you guys want to break for lunch in the cafeteria?" Brok asked. "Our treat."

"I'm highly inclined to believe," Brok said on the way to the cafeteria, "that whoever compiled these documents was interested in the, let's say, shady activities of the Gonzales and Avila families. Can you think of anyone who it might be?"

"I think it must be someone from either Texas or Arizona," Sal said. "Otherwise I think the northern connection would have continued to be followed."

"I tend to agree. In my experience, that type of relationship is none too easy to break off. The types of people who form those kinds of connections like to either keep them or eliminate them all together."

"À la David Barker," Jackson said.

"À la several of the people we saw," Trevor said. "Why did you single him out?"

"I guess his name was easy to remember."

The five men ordered various burgers with fries from the cafeteria and discussed possible motives for collecting the type of information they'd just reviewed. All agreed there must have been a triggering event to motivate whoever collected the information and that event must have occurred before the initial New York meeting. No motives or suspects sprang to anyone's mind by the end of lunch, but they agreed significant progress had been made. They decided to call it a day, so Sal called Cedric to come and pick them up. A cup of coffee later, Brok and Trevor accompanied Sal, Jason and Jackson to the parkade door; they all shook hands and agreed to keep in touch.

A Worse End

In the car, Sal, Jason and Jackson were able to talk more freely. "Why was David Barker's name easy to remember?" Sal asked.

"He may have died in New York," Jackson said, "but he did most everything else in these parts. I investigate lots of things for lots of people, and David Barker showed up in more than one place, mostly after normal business hours."

"What was he up to?"

"He dealt in trade secrets. He used to trade secrets for cash. I bought more than one sealed manila envelope from him and I watched lots of them get burned; somehow he knew lots of things other people, including one Andrew Burkeman, wanted kept secret. I'm guessing someone wanted to be sure one thing he knew got taken to his grave."

"Sal," Jason said, "since we're being candid, why were you so interested in the pictures of Simms and Rose?"

"It wasn't so much Simms and Rose as where they were," Sal said. "The boardroom at DBK."

"A banker, a biker and a Burkeman," Jason said. "They weren't likely there to write nursery rhymes."

"Probably not," Sal said. "I'm starting to wonder how involved dear Andrew is in all this."

"And I'm wondering whether the Brewster incident could be the start of it," Jason said.

"The timing is right," Sal agreed, "and Andrew seems to be in the thick of it. So, if that's the case, who?"

"Hank Solway?" Jason suggested. "He seems the type who might."

"That's what we were forgetting," Sal said. "Yes, we can assume the

Brewster thing is part of it—a part we kept from the DEA—but Hank must be out of the picture precisely because he's in the picture."

"Maybe we should talk to him anyway," Jason said. "Even if he didn't collect this stuff, he'd probably be in favour of it. If he thinks we're after Andrew, he might be glad to help."

"If he's still alive," Sal said. "Jackson, do you think you could locate Hank for us?"

"That's what I do!" Jackson said. "Above the ground or under it, I'll find him."

"How about Ginny?" Sal asked. "Do you think there's more information we could get from her?"

"I think she's told me all she knows," Jason said, "and I think it's just as well we let her believe it was alcohol that led to her lack of discretion."

"At times it's better not to know the truth," Sal agreed.

"Maybe I can ask around in my circles to see if I can find out what kind of pie Barker had his fingers in when he got burned," Jackson said.

"That might be useful information," Sal said, "but we don't really know when Barker was shot relative to when the picture was shot. It may have been much later."

"Or even if it was the same time," Jason said. "We can't be sure it was related to the picture."

"I'm as happy finding it's not related as it is," Jackson said. "We know more or less when the picture was. I sort of remember it's about the same time I stopped seeing Barker around anymore. I can easily find out when he got buried. If it is close, I'll see what other kind of bones I dig up."

Cedric pulled up in front of TechSys. "Why don't you come up to the office for a bit," Sal suggested to Jackson.

The trio went up to Sal and Jason's office. "Oh! Hello, Jackson," Janice said in greeting. "It's been a very long while!"

"You haven't changed a bit," Jackson said. "Still as beautiful as ever. When do I get that first kiss?"

"Still in your dreams. You haven't changed either."

Jason switched on the computer and logged in while Jackson and Janice bantered. He typed 'David Barker' into the search bar. Several David Barkers came up. He added 'murder' to the search. Several David

Barkers had apparently murdered several people.

Jackson came in and saw what Jason was up to. "This is why you do what you do and pay me to do what I do." He took over the keyboard and in short order had the obituary of David Barker, who'd died suddenly and violently in New York City at about the same time the photo was taken.

"There. Look at the date," Jackson said. "My Spidey senses are tingling!"

"Okay," Sal said. "But finding Hank is higher priority."

Jackson sat at the computer typing, waiting and reading, then typing, waiting and reading again. He made a call. "May I speak with Mr. Solway, please... I see... Could you give him a message please?... Ask him to call Mr. Taylor." Jackson left his burner number.

"Hank Solway is currently employed by Oaxaca Corp," Jackson said. "Right now he's out doing field work; they'll leave a message for him to call me."

"Where exactly is he doing his field work?" Sal asked.

"She didn't say. I always find it's better to say too little than too much on first contact; don't want to raise suspicions."

"When he calls back," Sal said, "find out when and where we can all meet him."

"I will. But for now, I should get back onto the streets with my ears on."

Jackson was no sooner gone than the intercom buzzed. "My office now!" It was J.P. "Bring your whelp with you."

"Good luck," Janice offered as they passed by. "Sounds like he's more than a little upset. What have you two been up to?"

"I'm sure we're about to find out," Sal replied.

"Andrew's been onto me about you two poking your noses into things that are none of TechSys' business," J.P. said even before the door had time to close behind Sal and Jason.

"What things?" Sal asked, feigning innocence.

"Andrew claims it's his personal business. He told me to call off the hounds and I have no clue what he's on about. That can only mean this is you!"

"I'm just busy trying to make sure Jason knows his way around," Sal said. "Whatever Andrew is upset about can't be our fault."

"Cut the crap, Sal," J.P. said. "I know you too well, and I also know Jackson. There's something going on that has my brother upset, and when he's upset, he has a knack for making me upset. Focus on InSyst and leave my brother alone."

"I assure you, what we're doing is very relevant to InSyst. Perhaps if Andrew is upset, it's because he's poking around where he ought not to. The InSyst acquisition is TechSys. TechSys is J.P. Burkeman, not Andrew Burkeman."

"I appreciate your loyalty," J.P. said, "but InSyst is Avizales, and anything Avizales is open season for all Burkemans."

"So you knew this was Avizales all along," Sal said. "It might have been nice if you'd mentioned that earlier. Maybe Andrew wouldn't be so mad now."

"I'm only mentioning it now because it seems you already know," J.P. said. "You really shouldn't need to know."

"I thought we didn't have secrets. You know that nothing Avizales stays just business."

"Andrew insisted it stay secret, not me."

"Are there any more secrets Andrew doesn't want shared with me?"

"Family's family."

"So the short answer is yes. I can't do this for you if you withhold relevant information from me. I don't expect access to your bedrooms or your peccadillos," Sal said, "but things as pertinent as Big Gus owning InSyst need to come out. What else is there?"

"You're planning to leave me here to fend for myself while you go play golf in Bermuda," J.P. said. "So excuse me if I decide to withhold a thing or two from you!"

"While I'm still here, you'd better let me know about such minor details if you expect there to be anything left to fend for!"

"I did you a favour to get Jason here, and I can undo that favour just as easily. Andrew says that what you're doing must stop, so stop!"

"He hasn't even told you what it is he thinks we're doing, has he? You don't even care to know what you're asking us to stop."

"Andrew will still be here when you're gone," J.P. pointed out, "so I need to know that he's happy more than I need to know why, so just stop!"

"Even if you don't need to know, isn't there anything you would like to know?"

"How's Myriam?"

"How's Myriam?" Sal said. "Nice segue! How can you go straight from ordering me to stop straight to 'How's Myriam'?"

J.P. shrugged and said, "I like Myriam."

"I'm beginning to think she's right in not particularly liking you," Sal said. "I always thought I was your best friend. Lately it's becoming abundantly clear that John Patrick Burkeman is your one and only best friend. Now that my departure seems imminent, you're prepared to throw me under whatever bus Andrew happens to be driving!"

"He's staying and you're not," J.P. said. "Who do you suggest I ally myself with?"

"They say the apple doesn't fall far from the tree. I'm getting a good idea of what type of tree Cecil James Burkeman the third was. Perhaps Cecil James Burkeman the fourth was the lucky brother."

"I'm going to forget you said that," J.P. said, "but I think you should get out now—and I know you should stop!"

"You'll never forget what I said," Sal retorted, "because you never forget that type of thing. I can't stop because it's not me who's chasing Andrew. I'd watch your tail, if I were you, because I can't watch it for you this time!"

"Right now I want to watch your tail as it heads out my door!" J.P. said.

"Let's go, Jason." Sal turned and guided Jason out the door by his elbow.

"Wow," Jason said. "That happened!"

"It wasn't what it looked like," Sal said. "That storm has been brewing since before you got here. Tomorrow will be the same as yesterday. I quite rightly claimed that J.P. will never forget what I said, but he's known it was coming—or something like it—for a very long time."

"What was that about Cecil the fourth?"

"J.P. and Andrew's older brother. He died in a car crash at five years old. They blame their mom for that accident, and that accident for their mother's OxyContin addiction. I have a different version, one more strewn with neglect and emotional abuse. Sue was headed down addiction road well before the accident, and no one did anything to help her navigate it after the accident."

"Where is she now?"

"Officially? She's in a seniors' care home. In reality? She's in a convenient closet, out of sight of any guests."

"That's sad," Jason said. "Where does all this leave us?"

"No change, really. Just keep on doing what we're doing. We don't have much choice."

"So you're going to ignore Andrew?"

"Of course not. I'm just going to pay attention in a different way than he thinks. I'm more sure now than ever that he's very involved."

"Can we try to stay a little further below the radar?"

"We'll try. Right now, go see Colleen. It's that time."

"I need that right now!"

Good God

Jason got to the lobby before Colleen; she smiled brightly when she saw him. "It's a good thing you showed up today," Colleen teased. "You know what they say, 'three strikes you're out.' You missed two already this week."

"Maybe I'll hit a home run tonight," Jason shot back.

Colleen smiled, blushed and smacked his arm. "Maybe we'll have time to talk about that if we don't stay too long at Tink's."

"It's part of the Catholic talk, isn't it?"

"It's a talk that should be expected when you date a good Catholic girl."

"Some of my friends warned me about Catholic girls. I'm glad I didn't listen."

"I'm glad too. But you'd better listen now."

"To this good Catholic girl?" Jason asked. "Can't you be a little bit bad?"

"Mom told me, if someone is willing to be bad before the wedding, don't be surprised to find they're bad after the wedding. We have only one chance to do things right. Once it's gone, it's gone. I want my marriage to be like Mom and Dad's."

"It's important to you, so that makes it important to me. We'll both be good, even though I've already been bad."

"I have to admit that I suspected as much, the way things are today."

"In my defence," Jason said, "at the time, I thought it was good."

"Not too good, I hope," Colleen teased.

"I thought it was too bad every time they ended," Jason squeezed Colleen's arm, "but now I'm glad they did."

"I felt quite reckless, the way I got into this. But now, I think this really might work. It's still early in our relationship, but it doesn't feel that early."

"It's the same for me," Jason said. "It's strange the way something so new can feel so old—old in a good way."

"It's still scary for me," Colleen admitted. "I've never felt so comfortable with anyone before but, at the same time, we keep seeing how many things must change for this to stay the same."

"I don't think it will stay the same. I think it will grow, and I think it's the one thing that will give me the courage to change the other things."

"But how much can they change? And what can they change into that will allow this to be?"

"Perhaps that question is best left to your Catholic faith."

Jason and Colleen pondered that thought the rest of the way to Tink's. Maria was just inside the door when they arrived. "Hello, you two," she said in greeting. "Nice to see you again!"

"Hello, Maria," Colleen said. "Jason has been busy with work, and I've been busy pining. On the plus side, my house is much tidier, finally!"

"It's nice to see you back. Perhaps his nibs, over there," Maria nodded toward Moses, "will be less grumpy."

"I can't imagine Moses grumpy," Colleen said. "He's always so pleasant."

"It's been just him and his beer," Maria said. "He likes to talk and his beer doesn't."

"His ale," Jason corrected. "There are a lot of other people here. I'm sure some of them like to talk."

"About sports and girls. You two are different, and Pawel and Stefan too."

"And you," Colleen added.

"But I can't sit there with him," Maria said. "You'd better go now; look how anxiously he's waiting!"

Moses sat bolt upright, holding his mug in both hands. He stared intently at Jason and Colleen; they could feel his 'hello' yearning to leap out. "Hello, Moses!" Jason said as they approached. "We're finally back."

"Aye, and it's a long while since you were back." Moses' frown turned to a smile and he relaxed. "But that just makes now even more pleasant than it might have been yesterday."

"We've truly missed you," Colleen said.

"By your choice," Moses said, "not by mine."

"By our choice," Jason admitted. "But a choice that was coerced."

"Well, my boy, I see you've made progress in your absence."

"I have three mentors, you, Sal and Colleen."

Colleen blushed and looked down. "I thought you were going to say Myriam."

"Four mentors," Jason corrected.

Maria brought Colleen and Jason their drinks. "I ordered pot pies, all around, for you."

"What has sweet Colleen been mentoring you about?" Moses asked.

"Her Catholic faith, mostly," Jason said, "though I'm not so sure God exists."

"Does God exist? It's a difficult question," Moses said, "and people have very different answers, mostly because they're answering very different questions."

"It's three simple words," Jason said, "with three simple answers: yes, no or I don't know."

"Those are simple answers, I'll grant you that. Too simple! But I'll only grant that the first of the three words is simple."

"We're listening," Jason assured him.

"I'm not wise enough to speak definitively about God, so I'll start with something I know more about." Moses pulled a dollar from his pocket and placed it on the table. "Does this dollar exist?"

"Yes." Jason pointed at it. "It's right there!"

Maria served their pot pies. "Is that my tip?" she joked. "You'd better add a few more."

"That was close," Jason said. "If that was ten dollars, it might be gone; since it's only one, it's still there."

"Is it now?" Moses asked. "Is the actual dollar there, or is it just a piece of paper that's there, one with the right type of printing to represent the dollar?"

"I see your point. I guess it's not the actual dollar, but the dollar still exists."

"There was a time when each dollar was backed by gold," Moses went on. "Each note represented a specific portion of gold held in a vault. Each note could be redeemed—in theory, at least—for a measure of that gold. What about today? Can the note on this table be redeemed for any particular thing? Is there a dollar that rightly exists? Now it's just a concept, an idea. It exists only because we agree it exists. How much is it worth? Not the same today as it will be tomorrow or was last week."

"So you're suggesting that God exists in the same manner as the dollar," Jason said.

"In one sense, yes. A sense that no one can deny, for if that is the essence of God, as long as two minds share the same thought of Him, He exists. But even in that sense, there are many answers, for God may be to one 'He who created the universe' and to another 'that which I desire most.' Which God is it then who exists? Both ideas exist and both are God, yet there can be but one God."

"Why can there be only one God?" Jason asked.

"Because all must proceed from one," Moses said. "There can be only one first and there can be only one greatest, and the one may not change or greater would be either before or after."

"I'll have to think more about that," Jason admitted. "But let's say I accept that there's one God—or don't accept it—either way, why is that important?"

"Let's not distract ourselves with that yet," Moses said. "Let's first agree He is or He isn't, and worry about one or more later. So... will you agree that, in the same sense as the dollar, God exists at least for some?"

"Yes," Jason said, "God exists as an idea in the minds of some people."

"So if we find an idea in your mind that you can agree is God, will you agree that God exists?"

"To the same extent I agree that a dollar exists, yes."

"Do you believe in science?"

"I believe in the scientific method of examination," Jason said cautiously.

"So what is Newton's third law of motion?"

"Give me a hint."

"For every action..."

"There is an equal and opposite reaction."

"So you believe that fully; there are no exceptions?" Moses asked.

"Absolutely," Jason claimed.

"And can one calculate it forwards and backwards?"

"Yes."

"And how far backwards can one calculate it?"

"To the initial action, I guess."

"So there was an initial action?"

"I guess."

"What initiated that initial action? If it occurred spontaneously, what else might occur spontaneously? If that's the case, how can you trust your science?"

"Whatever happened," Jason said, "it happened so long ago that it no longer matters."

"Perhaps that's so, and perhaps it's not," Moses said. "Most certainly, it was a long while ago. Less certain is whether it matters or not. If there was no purpose, I would tend toward 'not,' but since I tend toward purpose, I tend toward 'matters.'"

"Even if a purpose was intended," Jason said, "that purpose may have been achieved or it may have failed. In either of those instances, it would no longer matter."

"If some power is capable of and interested in taking the trouble of creating our universe, I prefer to believe they would not be so callous as to let it drift aimlessly once they're done with it. As such, I prefer to act as though that is the case."

"Though it may not be," Jason pointed out.

"It may not be true, but I must act as if I believe it to be true," Moses said. "And even if I'm uncertain, prudence would dictate acting according to the positive while determining its truth. If there's no purpose, either choice is as good. If there is purpose, it ought to be sought."

"Okay. Say I'm prepared to accept that there is a God, though I'm not yet firm in that belief, and don't quite know what it means, what, then, do I make of that?"

"Who, what, when, where, why and how," Moses suggested. "Come to know Him!"

"How?"

"If you accept that He is God of the universe, its creator," Moses said, "observe what He created. You cannot observe Him directly, but you cannot get 'what is' from 'what isn't.' Look about you and see what is; God is all that and more."

"What about evil?" Jason asked. "Lately I've been seeing a lot of evil. Are you suggesting God is evil?"

"He is no more evil than He is dark. Evil is the absence of good, just as dark is the absence of light. You will yet find God where nothing is, but 'nothing' cannot be God; it is nothing."

Maria brought their chocolate lava cake. "I'm sure we'll be able to find God in this," Jason said. "This is nothing if not good!"

"This will be the end of our dinner," Moses said, "and, I sense, the end of our talk. Talking too much about good can turn it bad... So what have you been up to this past while?"

"Trying to find out what others have been up to," Jason said, "and who's been up to the things we've found out."

"And I've just been waiting to find out what they're trying to find out," Colleen said.

"I hope you'll find out it's worth the wait!" Moses said.

They finished their desserts. Jason and Colleen excused themselves, said goodbye to Maria and walked out holding hands. "How do you feel about God now?" Colleen asked.

"I guess I've always accepted that He exists as an idea in some people's minds," Jason answered, "though now I wonder whether He's only that idea. Is God something because we agree He is, or is He something whether we agree He is or not?"

"But either way," Colleen said, "you agree He is."

"Yes," Jason said, "but if He exists in the same sense as money. If He exists only because we say He does, then He exists in the way we say He does. If He exists whether we agree He does or not, then He is as He is and perhaps we exist only as He says we do. That's a very big difference."

"Where did everything come from if not from God? It had to come from somewhere."

"There must have been something or there would still be nothing. But was it God?"

"It was if you say it was," Colleen said. "Whatever it was that must have been, call it God."

"But does it help me to call something I know nothing about God?"

"As Moses said, if everything in the universe came from God, then everything, to some degree, reveals who He is."

"Even if I agree to all that, why is it so important?"

"Because God is God and I am not and you are not," Colleen said. "We believe that God is intelligent and He creates for a purpose; He knows the purpose and we don't. Once we accept that, we have a basis for respecting what He's created because He, in his infinite wisdom, has decided it should be as it is. That's the whole reason to respect one another. God made you in the best way He could. He made me in the best way He could. He made each and every one of us in the best way He could. He has infinite wisdom and we don't; therefore, we should accept that everyone should be as they are. I'm not better than you. You're not better than me. No one is better than anyone. Everyone is as they are because that's the absolute best way they could be, according to God's infinite wisdom. That's the reason to believe that everyone is created equal. If we don't believe that, then we're adversaries; it's nothing but survival of the fittest, and that's a very cruel world. That's not my world, and I won't let it be."

"Where did that all come from?" Jason asked.

"Too much?"

"It was impressive. I'm not there yet, but I'm willing to try."

They approached Northside High. "There's our bleachers; shall we sit a while?" Jason asked.

"Would you rather have tea at my place?" Colleen asked.

"Tonight, I'd rather look at the stars. The few one sees from the city. They are so much clearer down in Mérida at the hacienda. I want to marvel at God's creation and wonder what God could create it."

"A lot of things are clearer at the hacienda." Colleen squeezed Jason's hand a little tighter. "But since we're here, let's watch the stars we can see."

They sat and watched for a long while, saying nothing. Colleen reclined and rested her head in Jason's lap. They watched the stars and they watched each other's eyes. They learned a lot that neither could put into words.

Bad News

Sal watched as Jason greeted José and Simon, and then asked, "How's Colleen?"

"Wonderful!" Jason said. "And by that I mean she fills me with wonder."

"To be young and in love," Sal said wistfully. "Well, we'll put that feeling to rest; Pet's on a rampage."

"She's here early. What's up?"

"I'm pretty sure it's the same thing that caused J.P. to be so upset yesterday."

"And have you determined exactly which hornet's nest we poked?"

"I'm not sure why it's got Pet so worked up," Sal said. "But it must have something to do with the connection between Andrew and Avizales."

"She probably won't leave us wondering too long," Jason guessed. "She has a tendency to share her pain with others."

Jason was correct; Pet returned just as he finished speaking. "What are you two mucking about in?" she asked. "Tess showed up at my door last night and, as far as I know, she's still there!"

"You didn't let her in?" Sal joked.

"Very funny! Tess never shows up unannounced and she never stays at my place... so what did you do?"

"You know what we're doing," Jason feigned. "We're looking into that InSyst thing. Maybe your Uncle Gus is the one who upset her."

"He's in Mexico and she's here!"

"Wow, he must really have upset her if she doesn't want to even be in the same country," Sal said.

Pet's face grew red and she stamped her foot. "Tell me! Just tell me. I'm going to find out, so just tell me."

“If you find out before us,” Sal said, “you tell us.”

“Rrrrrr,” Pet growled. “You two are so infuriating!”

“First your mother and now you,” Sal said. “Be sure to let us know what it is; maybe we can be infuriated too.”

“Come to think of it,” Jason said, “J.P. was a little furious yesterday too.”

“A lot furious,” Sal said. “And he mentioned that Andrew was furious as well. It must be contagious.”

“Contagious fury. I wonder if they have pills for that.”

Sal could smell Pet’s anger. “You’d better go splash some water on yourself; you’ll feel much better when you cool down.”

Pet stomped off. Once she was gone, José came out from the kitchen where he’d been hiding. “I can taking your order now.”

“Pastries for me,” Sal said.

“I’ll have the eggs Benedict she probably ordered but won’t be eating,” Jason said.

José returned shortly. “Simon say you are too smart, Señor Jason, but these ones is Florentine. No Benedict. Still, is very good!”

“Thank you, José. Everything Simon cooks is very good.”

“But when he cook Mexican food is very much even better. I having *chile verde* in kitchen.”

“Let’s finish this breakfast and do some more poking,” Sal said. “Let’s see who else these hornets can get jumping.”

As they entered their floor, Sal and Jason greeted Janice; she handed Sal a pink paper. “His call was on voicemail. He called last night just after six. He said to call him any time at all. He sounds quite anxious to talk with you.”

Sal looked at his watch as he and Jason went into the office and closed the door. Sal dialled his cellphone. “Cedric, something’s come up. I won’t be able to go see Andrew right now. Can you pick up the papers he wants me to sign and bring them back here? No... Do whatever you have to do. I have no other appointments today. Thank you.” Sal dialled again and put the call on speaker. “Hello,” a sleepy voice answered.

“Hello, Mr. Solway, this is Solomon Rosenthal with TechSys Incorporated. I have Jason Johnstone here with me.”

"Incorporated? Since when is the state of Texas incorporated?" Hank asked.

"It's not the state; it's the company. T-E-C-H-S-Y-S Incorporated."

"Oh," Hank sounded disappointed. "Jackson said he was a detective investigating the cinnabar disaster. I thought he was with the State of Texas."

"No," Sal said. "He's a private detective working for us."

"Why are you investigating the cinnabar disaster?"

"We believe there was more to it than just a bad rainstorm."

"Darn right there was! I designed that weir and supervised the construction myself. That excavator did more than just park on top of the dam."

"What are you saying?"

"That Kumar wasn't just an ass; he was a saboteur. He undermined the damn weir!"

"Can you prove it?"

"I know how the dam was designed and how it was built and what kind of loads it needed to withstand," Hank said. "That's proof enough for me. The Railroad Commission just didn't believe the dam was constructed according to plans because I don't have third-party confirmation."

"What more can you tell us?"

"I can tell you what I told them before they railroaded me. Find out what happened from Burkeman Minerals. I knew they were up to something."

"So you suspect someone at Burkeman Minerals was behind the sabotage?"

"I know it was them," Hank said. "I had someone watching Tajima, Burkeman's top engineer. I knew they would play dirty."

"Who was watching?"

"Hector Rodriguez. A private detective out of El Paso."

"What did he find out?"

"Andrew Burkeman seduced one of my employees. He was messing around with her from just before the weir failed until just after. Tell me that's just coincidence!"

"What else did he find out?"

"He paid a lot of attention to Kumar's drug use. We knew about Kumar's drug habit before we hired Hector, but Hector made a very big deal out of it. Kumar didn't wreck the weir, because he was stoned."

"Maybe Hector thought Kumar agreed to wreck the weir because he needed money to buy drugs," Sal suggested.

"Kumar was pretty much a loner," Hank said. "He earned enough money to buy the amount of drugs he used."

"Do you know how we can get in touch with Hector Rodriguez?"

"No, I lost track of him when I stopped being able to pay him. Like I said, though, he was out of El Paso."

"Thank you, Mr. Solway. This information is very helpful," Sal assured him.

"It's Hank, and it's been my pleasure. I hope you can finally get to the bottom of all this so I can get my reputation back."

"We'll keep you posted," Sal promised. "Thank you, Hank."

Sal hung up and immediately dialled again. "Jackson... See if you can locate a private detective in El Paso. Name of Hector Rodriguez... He's the photographer... That's right... And everything... Of course... Sooner than later... Bye."

"So now we know how and why it got started," Jason said, "but why did it keep going?"

"Rodriguez doesn't sound familiar?" Sal asked.

"Avila family tree." Jason was already pulling up the file. "There's more than one Hector Rodriguez. Do you remember Conchita Rodriguez?"

"Sweet sixteen at the hacienda?"

"She has an Uncle Hector."

"Let's see what Jackson finds out before we go jumping to conclusions."

"Or to Mérida?"

"We have too much to do here."

"What? Wait! The DEA has things to do. Jackson has things to do. What do we have to do right now?"

"That phone will ring and we'll have things to do."

Sal was right; the phone rang. "Hello... What!... Where?... When?... How?... Of course... Right away... Thank you."

Sal buzzed Janice. "Call a taxi!"

"A taxi? Where's Cedric?" Janice asked.

"Houston Methodist," Sal said. "He's been in an accident!"

"You'll be faster to just go down and hail a cab."

Jason and Sal rushed out. "Tell him I'm praying for him," Janice said.

Sal dialled his cellphone as they walked. "Mabel... We heard... Yes, we're getting a taxi. We'll pick you up... Don't you dare drive! You're too upset... They'll be at work... Let's just us go there for now and decide that when we find out more... Jason and me... He will... Yes, we do... Don't worry at all about that... He's strong... Good... Yes... Probably fifteen minutes... Yes, I know, I will."

"It was nice of you to think of Mabel," Jason said.

"It's the Cedrics, Simons and Josés I care about around here. The other ones are too busy caring about themselves."

The taxi pulled up in front of Cedric's house fifteen minutes later, just as Sal had predicted. Mabel was waiting on the front steps. She waddled down and met the cab at the curb; Sal got out and helped Mabel in. "I'm sure he'll be okay," he said.

Cedric was in surgery when they arrived at the hospital. The nurse assured them there were broken bones but nothing life-threatening. Once Mabel calmed down enough, one of the nurses escorted her to a waiting area. The other nurse pointed to a corner in the other direction. "Those gentlemen would like to speak with you."

Three policemen were standing watching Sal and Jason. As they approached, one of the officers waved toward a side room. "Solomon Rosenthal?"

"That's me," Sal said. "Cedric is my driver; the car belongs to the company."

To Sal's and Jason's surprise, Bert was in the room. He approached them, hand extended in greeting. "Mr. Rosenthal? Detective Bertram of the Houston Police Department."

"What can we do for you, detective?" Sal asked.

"We'd like to ask a few questions as to the nature of Mr. Cooper's activities this morning," Bert said.

"He picked me up at about five forty this morning and drove me to work," Sal said. "I had an appointment at DBK to sign some papers but something came up. I asked Mr. Cooper to pick up the papers and bring them back to TechSys. He had errands to run for his wife after that. I had no other appointments so I told him to go ahead."

"Had no other appointments," another officer said. "You say you had no other appointments; did that change?"

"And you are?" Sal asked.

"Lieutenant Smallwood," he replied. "Do you have appointments now?"

"Apparently one with you fine gentlemen and hopefully one with Mr. Cooper shortly."

"And who is this?" Smallwood nodded toward Jason.

"Jason Johnstone," Jason answered. "I work with Mr. Rosenthal and Mr. Cooper."

"Did you have an appointment with Mr. Rosenthal?" Smallwood demanded.

"We work together," Sal said. "No appointment needed."

"Are you aware of Mr. Cooper's exact activities at the time of the accident?" Smallwood asked.

"I believe he was driving," Sal said.

"Mr. Rosenthal—" Smallwood began.

Brok and Trevor arrived just in time and flashed their IDs. "Agents Brokowicz and Wyman. This is DEA. Detective Bertram can stay. You three, scoot!"

"What's going on?" Sal asked once the door closed behind Smallwood.

"Cedric's crash was no accident," Brok said. "It appears the Machetes don't like your car."

"They don't like my car?"

"They had it shot," Brok said. "I don't doubt they thought you were inside; if you had been, you would have fared much worse than Cedric."

"You know this for sure?"

"We saw it. What have you been up to?"

"We thought we'd been leaving all the 'up to' to you!" Sal said. "Andrew's mad. J.P.'s mad. Patricia's mad. Teresa's mad. Apparently the Machetes are mad. The whole world's gone mad!"

"Who did you talk to and what did you say?" Brok asked.

"We talked to you about this!"

"What about Jackson? P.I.s and trouble go together."

"He's tracking a lead in El Paso."

"Since when?"

"We talked to him this morning," Sal said. "I'm pretty sure it was a fresh lead, probably today, even."

"The Machetes couldn't have set this thing up that quick," Brok said. "What did you do yesterday?"

"We talked to you, remember? You were there!"

"After that!" Brok demanded.

"J.P. and I had a bit of a set-to at his brother's request," Sal disclosed. "Seems Andrew wants me to stop; J.P. didn't bother finding out the particulars. He just assumed I would know whatever it is Andrew wants me to stop."

"So we've got four players here," Trevor said, "Andrew Burkeman, Patricia Avila, Teresa Avila and the Machetes. J.P. is only upset because he's been drawn into it."

"Three," Sal said. "Patricia is mad because she doesn't like her mother being here."

"Well we can't have people shooting up the streets," Brok said. "We'll have to move soon; we're running out of time."

"Especially when the shooting is at Sal," Jason said. "Do you think they'll try again?"

"I don't know." Brok looked at Sal. "But I'd like to put you in protective custody."

"Absolutely not. If you think they're mad now, try doing that. They'll only change their target and keep shooting, maybe Jason or worse, Colleen. I won't have it!"

"You're probably right. It's easier to protect a target when we know who the target is. We know who's doing the shooting; we're watching him very closely. He won't get another shot at it. Will you at least wear a vest?"

"That's how sure you are that he won't get another shot?" Sal asked. "Could you loan us a bulletproof car too? My car seems to be out of service."

"With a driver?" Jason suggested. "Our driver's also out of service. Who actually took the shot?"

"We're still working on a positive ID," Brok said. "This guy showed up at the clubhouse and we tailed him from there. We had no idea what he planned to do at the time."

"Have you got pictures?" Bert asked. "Maybe I know him; I tend to hang around a lot of lowlifes in this job."

"Ident is working some up for us. I'll make sure you get a copy but don't spread them around. I'm not telling you this, but your IA has concerns about some of your HPD buddies."

"Thanks for the warning," Bert said. "Do you have any names to put to that warning?"

"Don't worry; you're clear. But you'd better watch your back."

"Is it linked to this case?" Sal asked.

"I, even more, didn't tell you," Brok said to Sal, "but, yes it is."

"How deep?" Bert asked.

"You're the only HPD in this room," Brok said. "How good a detective do you need to be to figure it out from there?"

"Jackson!" Sal remembered. "Do you think he might be in danger?"

"Probably," Brok said. "His type usually is; why are you asking?"

"He was in our office. J.P. saw him."

"I'd be worried if it was Andrew that saw him. I think J.P.'s okay," Brok reassured him.

"I have to call Jackson anyway about Hector Rodriguez; I think you'll want to hear this," Sal said. "We suspect Hector's the one who collected all our data."

After a few rings, Jackson answered, and Sal put him on speaker phone. "Jackson, Sal here. I have you on speaker with Jason, Brok, Trevor and Bert. What have you found out about our friend Hector Rodriguez?"

"A few bullets found him before I did," Jackson said. "About a year ago—and get this!—the prime suspect is a Machete, none other than Little Billy."

"What else did you find out?"

"He has a widow, Maria Rodriguez. She moved back to Mexico, lives on Finca Rustica de Gonzales Street in Mérida. I can't find any phone number."

"Are you sure?"

"That's what I found so far," Jackson assured him.

"Watch your back."

"I always do. Why do you mention it?"

"A Machete wannabe took a pot-shot where he thought Sal might be," Brok said. "I don't think it's really all that likely, but Sal's concerned you may be in someone's crosshairs too."

"Thanks for the heads up," Jackson said.

"Heads down might be a better option," Jason quipped. "Watch out for yourself."

"Thanks. I'll call you when I get back," he said, ending the call.

"Do you think Jackson will be able to find Hector's widow?" Jason asked.

"I'm sure of it," Sal said. "Finca Rustica de Gonzales isn't a street. You know it better as Hacienda Gonzales."

"Maybe Carlos and Catalina will know Maria," Jason suggested. "They're Rodríguezes."

Sal kept the speaker on and dialled again.

Jason recognized Ricardo's voice. "Sal, how are things in Texas?"

"A little scary, to be honest."

"That's what I keep telling you," Ricardo said. "How many times have I told you; you need to move down here with Myriam."

"Right now I'm wondering about someone else who moved down there. I need to find a widow who moved there from El Paso about a year ago."

"That'll be Elena; you met her," Ricardo said. "At the sweet sixteen party. She's Hector's widow."

"We have her as Maria Rodriguez," Brok said.

"All the Rodriguez girls are Maria," Ricardo explained. "They all go by their second names."

"I'd like to talk to her," Sal said, "if that's possible."

"I don't know," Ricardo said. "She's very jittery, that one. She doesn't talk to many people and never talks to anyone on the phone."

"It's very important," Sal assured him.

"I can send Luis to go fetch Carlos, her brother-in-law. Maybe he'll talk to you. I'll call you back when he gets here," he said before hanging up.

"We just might get this sorted before you get shot," Brok said. "Things are starting to click."

There was a knock on the door and a doctor came in. "Your friend is out of surgery. Everything went very well and he can expect a full recovery. We'll see him back here in two weeks for follow-up. You can see him now and he can go home whenever he feels ready.

"We'll give you a ride," Brok said. "We've got room."

"Room for six?" Sal asked. "Mabel, his wife, is with us."

"I'll take Cedric and Mabel," Bert offered.

"That would be good," Brok said. "I want to be around when Carlos Rodriguez calls back."

They went off to see Cedric. Mabel cried when she saw Cedric, arm casted, badly bruised and dressed in a hospital gown. "Cedric Cooper! Don't you ever do that to me again!"

Cedric smiled. "I'm fine, Baby. Relax. You just make me some of that old chicken soup of yours and I'll be fit as a fiddle."

"That chicken soup don't heal no broken bones," Mabel said.

Bert pushed Cedric to the parking lot in the wheelchair as Mabel waddled along beside, still chattering away. Sal, Jason, Brok and Trevor followed. They waved goodbye as Bert drove off and then got into Brok's SUV.

"I think Jas' would be in order," Sal said.

"I'd prefer something more private," Brok said. "I don't want whatever Rodriguez has to say broadcast over a speaker in a public café."

"Fair enough," Sal conceded, "if you can promise us a good cup of coffee."

"I'll see if I can pressure Betsy into it," Brok said. "She does a decent job of it."

"And, condition two, you must let J.P. treat us all to dinner at The Tasting Room," Sal said. "It's just around the corner from you."

"Isn't that just a snack place?" Brok asked.

"Only if you don't appreciate fine wine," Sal said. "Make sure you're off duty; I'll educate you!"

Black Sheep

How did you coax this coffee out of that machine?" Sal asked Betsy.

"That's my secret," Betsy said. "It's also my job security, so good luck if you think I'll tell!"

"You know we couldn't live without you," Trevor said.

"Says you until you get back to El Paso," Betsy said. "You seem to get along just fine without me there."

"Why don't you just suck it up and ask her out?" Brok chuckled. "Everyone knows it but you."

Trevor turned deep red; Betsy, a little less.

Sal's phone rang.

"Listen in, Betsy," Brok said. "This might help us." Betsy took out a pad and started taking notes.

"Hi, Ricardo," Sal said. "Is Carlos there?"

"He and Elena are both here," Ricardo said. "You're on speaker."

"You're on speaker too," Sal disclosed. "We're at the DEA. Jason is here and three DEA agents. Mr. Brokowicz, Mr. Wyman, and... sorry, Betsy, I didn't get your last name—"

"Thomas," Betsy said. "But we're Brok, Trevor and Betsy today."

"So Carlos, I'm Brok with the US Drug Enforcement Agency. Do you understand?"

"Yes. Hello to you, Mr. Brok," Carlos said. "What can I to do for you?"

"I understand Hector was your brother."

"Yes."

"And Elena, he was your husband."

"Yes," Elena said timidly.

"So your full name is Maria Elena Rodriguez?"

"Yes," she said in a small voice.

"What can you tell us about him?" Brok asked.

"He is very too good! He is detective to El Paso on Texas," Carlos said. "He having a licence to detective and everything. Everybody is very too sad when did he died because Hector is so more good than to our another brother."

"Who is your other brother?" Brok asked.

"Francisco. He is the older brother to me and Hector," Carlos said. "He is not so much very too good,"

"He is bad very much!" Elena said.

"Is okay, Elena," Carlos said. "He no is come to here anymore."

"Where is he?" Jason asked.

"He is to Texas," Carlos said. "Before he is come here and go in Texas by big truck to his Uncle Ernesto. Now, Uncle Ernesto *esta muerto*. Big truck is gone for Texas so Chico is gone for Texas also too."

"Chico?" Sal asked.

"That is the another name to Francisco, for shorter," Carlos explained.

"So what made him so bad?" Sal asked.

"Chico is too bad since he see much to our cousin; William is very *el mandamus* bad man."

"What is *el mandamus*?" Sal asked.

"Big shot," Ricardo said, "the boss."

"The boss of what?" Sal asked.

"Ride the motorcycle very bad mans."

"A biker gang?" Brok asked.

"*Banda de moteros*?" Ricardo translated.

"*Si*, the one to selling *cocaina*," Carlos said. "Girls too. They doing very bad things on them."

"Are you sure?" Brok asked.

"*Si*, that is for Hector too mad to our brother," Carlos said. "He watching him and make many paper to him."

"What happened to the papers?" Sal asked.

"Some are go when Hector shot," Carlos said. "Too some are for here. Elena bring it; she don't looking until they here."

"Do you still have them?" Brok asked.

"They too more boxes to house for me," Carlos said. "So I put them for barn."

"Can I send someone to pick them up?" Brok asked.

"Why not?" Carlos said. "Maybe you catch my brother Francisco to that papers. Everybody for my family mad to him that he make Rodriguez for bad name. Nobody like to talk on him!"

"Thank you, Carlos," Brok said. "We'll send someone to pick them up. Is it okay, Ricardo, if I have them contact you?"

"Absolutely," Ricardo said. "I'll make sure I know where everything is. When should I expect them?"

"I don't know. It depends on who we have down there. El Paso will contact whoever is closest, and they'll contact you directly."

"Thank you all very much," Sal said. "Elena, I'm so sorry about your husband. Hopefully this will bring his killers to justice."

"Thanks for you too," Elena said. "I am pray too long for that this can happen."

Brok was already on the phone arranging with someone from El Paso to have Hector's papers picked up. "He says there's boxes of it. Let's see how far we can get with this new stuff."

Sal looked at his watch. "Jason, you'd better phone Colleen and have her catch a taxi to meet us," he said. "Betsy, we're going for dinner at The Tasting Room when Colleen gets here; will you join us?"

Betsy looked at Trevor, who nodded. "So that's a yes," Jason said.

The Dinner

Jason called Colleen. "Hi, Hon. I'm with Sal at the DEA building. We're going for dinner with the DEA agents; you're invited."

"Why are you there?" Colleen asked.

"It's a long story I can finally tell you," Jason assured her. "Can you take a taxi here after work? Fourteen thirty-three West Loop South. You should be here between five thirty and six, depending on traffic."

Colleen confirmed the address. "I'll see you when I get there."

Betsy was busy with her laptop; the screen displayed the picture of Simms, the three top Machetes, Chico and Hector Avila. "We've got Francisco (aka Chico) Rodriguez pretty clearly identified now," Betsy said. "If Little Billy turns out to be Cousin William, that would wrap this picture up in a very pretty bow!"

"It won't be very pretty for Hector," Jason said. "It ties him pretty tightly to some pretty bad things."

"Yes, before this, our operation was all north of the border," Betsy said. "We knew the drugs were coming in from Mexico but we had no idea how."

Sal looked at Brok with a sidelong glance. "So before this," Sal suggested, "all you had was the Machetes."

"Not quite all," Betsy asserted. "We had them and we had street level. We were never able to find the Machetes' supplier. They always made their drops in stolen vans and torched the vehicles right after the deals went down. Now it appears we have several Mexicans to track and a cross-border transportation company."

"This was pretty much the break we were waiting for," Brok admitted. "It often goes like that. We watch and watch for years, getting more and more frustrated as we wait, seeing these guys destroy other peoples' lives while they live high on the hog, unable to do much to stop it. Then one thing happens that ties everything together and—bang!—things speed up, they get very fast and all the waiting seems worthwhile."

"It's easy to get very cynical," Trevor said. "We watch bad guys living the good life and good guys getting stomped on. We have to obey all the rules and they don't. We have to dot all the i's and cross all the t's while they just run roughshod over whatever they don't like."

"We really have to thank you." Brok shrank a couple of inches and turned red as he spoke. "And apologize... We see so many bad guys that it's hard to recognize the good ones when they show up to the table. You guys really helped us out. We wouldn't be here without you. I gave you a pretty rough reception that you didn't deserve."

"Thank you for being man enough to admit it," Sal said. "I know from all the times I haven't given my subordinates their due credit that it's not easy to admit. I was every bit as wary of you and just as reluctant to disclose things fully. I'm glad cooler heads prevailed and we were able to work together. It's important to the integrity of Burkeman Holdings that this be completely rooted out and purged from the company."

"My faith in humanity is somewhat restored," Brok said. "I doubt it will ever return completely, but I will always be able to remember you and Jason."

"Don't forget Cedric; he almost died for us," Sal reminded him. "And maybe Jackson deserves a bit of a break."

"I still don't count him a hundred percent on the up and up," Brok said, "but I will put him on the plus side. I may consult with him in the future; he's okay."

"You shouldn't count me and Jason a hundred percent on the up and up either," Sal said. "We may not be doing anything illegal, but business, at our level, often requires us to be on the grey side of ethical... sometimes a very dark grey."

"There's something wrong with a society that expects us to act against our beliefs in order to get by," Betsy said. "I got into this job so I could help make the world a little bit better, but I'm learning that it needs to be a lot better. Sometimes I wonder if we can make things better faster than the other side makes it worse."

"There's that," Jason said, "and also whether we're in the right place to make them better. I think you are—I'm sure you are—but am I able to do what I ought to do from where I am?"

"Why are you there, then?" Betsy asked. "And what, exactly, do you do?"

"I manage information," Jason said. "I chose to make my career here for the noblest of reasons. I thought that, of all the things I could do, this is where I could make the most money. Now I'm here, pretty much, because I'm here."

Someone called to let Brok know Colleen was waiting out front. "Let's go," he said. "We'll continue this conversation over a nice dinner, courtesy of the DEA. I know, Sal offered, but we have a big debt to pay." Brok held the door for everyone as they headed to the lobby. He switched off the light and had a last look around the room before closing the door.

"Burkeman will pick up the wine," Sal promised. "Otherwise you might get fired when they find out how much they paid for what I intend to drink."

"Deal," Brok said. "Burkeman picks up the alcohol; DEA picks up the meal and the tip."

"That saves him telling you we're not allowed to accept fancy dinner invitations or anything that might be seen as a bribe—anti-corruption policy," Betsy said. "The DEA always makes us personally responsible for any alcohol."

"That's happening at our place too," Sal said. "No one wants to be liable for what happens to people who leave the party drunk. Apparently we're still open to corruption."

Colleen arrived, and Jason gave her a hug and a quick peck where her lips were before she turned her cheek. "Hi, Hon."

"Hi, Jason."

He paused long enough for a handshake between each introduction. "Colleen... this is Brok... Trevor... and Betsy."

"What are you doing here?" Colleen asked.

"We've been solving the biggest drug trafficking racket in all of Texas," Jason said.

"Jason," Colleen gave him a smack on the arm, "why are you really here?"

"He's probably telling the truth," Betsy confirmed. "We are very close to solving a crime the DEA has been investigating for years, and it may very well be the biggest drug ring currently in Texas, possibly ever in Texas."

Colleen was bewildered. "Why am I just finding out now?"

"The whole DEA is just finding out now," Jason said. "You expected to find out sooner?"

Colleen smacked Jason's arm again, quite hard. "Jason!"

"It's true," Brok said. "We knew there was something but, until very recently, we didn't know what it was. The DEA is indebted to Jason and Sal for their cooperation. We'd still be a long way back on this file without their help. We'll probably recommend a citation for them."

"Not while there are still any Machetes riding around out there, I hope," Sal said. "Unless you're looking for another homicide to solve."

"Betsy, do you have a car here?" Brok asked. "We won't all fit in ours."

"I'll take Colleen," Betsy said. "I like her already!"

"You know the way?" Brok asked.

"The way and the wine," Betsy assured him.

Brok, Sal and Trevor got into Brok's SUV. Jason and Colleen continued on with Betsy and got into her car. Betsy pulled out onto Post Oak Boulevard right behind Brok. At The Tasting Room, Brok backed into a parking space by the patio. Betsy backed her Prius next to his SUV. The hostess seated them near the far end of the pergola.

"Could we have some truffle fries and a cheeseboard, please?" Betsy asked. "You guys will love these!"

Sal was busy with the wine list when their server brought the appetizers. "Is this the Twenty Thirteen Bussia?"

"Yes," the waiter said.

"We'll have that," Sal said. "People, prepare yourselves for a treat!"

They looked over their menus as they nibbled on the cheeses, grapes and truffle fries. "I recommend the cheeseburger with bacon and avocado," Betsy suggested.

"How do you stay so small?" Colleen asked.

"Chasing bad guys. Lately I've been doing most of that on the computer; though I sense it's about to get real busy out in the field pretty soon."

"What's really going on?" Colleen asked. "Are Jason and Sal really helping you?"

"They pulled the whole thing together," Brok said. "All the pieces we gathered over several years just sort of fell in place once Jason and Sal brought their pieces."

"Our job would be a lot easier if we had more Sals and Jasons out there," Trevor claimed. "They didn't ignore the things going on around them."

Their waiter returned with the wine and glasses. "I'm John. I'll be serving you this evening. If there's anything you need, just let me know." John let Sal taste the wine and then poured six glasses. "Enjoy! Are you ready to order?"

"It'll be real simple," Betsy said. "Six cheeseburgers with bacon and avocado."

"Excellent choice for this wine," John said.

Sal raised his glass. "Here's to good work by good people."

They all toasted. "Good work by good people!"

"Wow," Brok said, "I'm not a wine person, but this is very good. I could become accustomed to this."

"Not on our salary," Betsy said.

"You seem to know this place well enough," Trevor said.

Betsy raised her glass again. "Thank you, Daddy!"

"Silver spoon?" Colleen asked.

"Very," Betsy replied.

"But you seem pretty normal," Trevor claimed.

"I haven't been normal since I left my mother's womb."

"That's the beauty of it," Colleen said. "We're all exceptional in our own way. There wouldn't be much to appreciate in a world where everyone was completely normal."

"That's coming out on your first glass?" Jason held his glass up, swirled it and looked at it carefully. "This is good wine."

Colleen smacked him playfully. "They have good wine at Tink's too.

It's just that Moses has more to say that's worth hearing than I do."

"Not if you have more stuff like that," Betsy said. "Can you repeat that one to my dad? He's not such a big fan of my 'eccentricities,' as he calls them."

"Let me guess, he wanted you to become a doctor," Sal said, "or a lawyer."

Betsy raised her glass to Sal. "Lawyer! I keep trying to put them in and he keeps keeping them out."

"Criminal law?" Sal asked.

"Corporate," Betsy said. "But some of the sharks he swims with are worse than the guys I chase."

"The case at hand being a case in point?"

Before Betsy could reply, eight Harley Davidsons came roaring down Uptown Park Boulevard and pulled into the parking lot. Eight Machetes got off their bikes and entered The Tasting Room. Everyone at the table grew silent. Brok made a discreet call on his cellphone. The Machetes pulled two tables together under the pergola not far from them; they looked pointedly at Jason and Sal and waved.

"This is what you call intimidation," Brok said. "They won't do anything... probably. They just want you to know that they know about you."

Colleen grabbed Jason's hand and pulled her chair a bit closer. "It's working," she said.

"It's a bit futile," Brok said. "It's the paperwork that will convict them, not any testimony from you."

"Do they know that?" Jason asked.

"I say we order more wine," Sal stayed relaxed in his chair, "and enjoy our burgers."

The street out front got very busy; several HPD cars and large black SUVs pulled up. The Tasting Room suddenly had many spectators, and patrons began leaving rather hurriedly. Soon there were only two groups left on the patio. "If they meant us harm," Brok calculated, "it would have been a sniper, and it would have been done already. We wouldn't have seen it coming."

"I say just play it out," Sal said. "We have good wine, good company and good burgers coming; we can't let thugs rule. Is that okay with you, Colleen?"

Colleen plucked up her courage. "I say we send them a round of beers."

Jason patted Colleen's hand. "If you're fine, I think we're all fine."

"I think Texan is more accurate than fine," Colleen said. "Gary Cooper Texan."

Betsy looked reassuringly at Colleen. "You can't be brave until something scares you," she said. "If nothing scares you, that's just stupid."

"Are you scared?" Colleen asked.

"Often, because these guys are stupid."

Eventually John ventured cautiously out to the deck with everyone's burgers and edged toward their table, steering a wide berth around the Machetes.

"We'll have another bottle, and we'd like to buy a round of beers for our friends, over there," Sal said nodding toward the Machetes. "The cheapest draft you've got will probably be better than anything they're used to. They're probably ready to order; they've been here a while."

"Yes, sir," John said very nervously.

"Don't worry," Brok said calmly. "They won't do anything with all of us watching."

"No, sir." John slid over to the Machetes' table very slowly.

"Shall we bless our food?" Betsy suggested.

"Yes," Colleen agreed. "And we'll add a few prayers for our wayward friends over there." She looked over to the Machetes and smiled.

"What makes you think prayers will help these guys?" Trevor asked. "Old superstitions aren't going to turn any of them into angels."

"You never know," Sal said. "Besides, do you think we can come up with anything better than what our ancestors have depended on for four thousand years?"

"I thought Jesus was only two thousand years old."

"He only finished what the Jews started. Besides, even two thousand years? I think I'll trust it to last a few minutes more."

Colleen, Betsy, Sal and Jason crossed themselves; they all bowed their heads and prayed, some more earnestly than others. "It might not help," Brok said, "but it probably won't hurt either, not as much as these guys might."

The standoff continued for an hour longer. The Machetes glared steadily at their opponents but Jason's group largely ignored them. The burgers were very good. Betsy ordered another cheeseboard and an Italian piatto. They were near the end of their third bottle before the Machetes surrendered and left. The parking lot and street cleared and regular patrons began returning.

"That was exciting!" Colleen said in understatement.

"Shall we do it again?" Betsy asked.

"I'd love to," Jason said. "Same company, different audience... if the management will let us back in."

"Yes," Betsy said, "I expect their sales will be a bit off tonight; it's too bad the innocent always suffer."

"We could order a fourth bottle," Sal said. "Bump the sales up a bit?"

"And they have excellent desserts here," Betsy assured everyone, "especially the stilton cheesecake."

"Jason," Colleen said, "we've forgotten in all this excitement that we made Moses a promise; we don't know where to meet him. Do you think he'll still be at Tink's?"

"You're right," Jason said. "I'll call and see if he's there."

Moses was gone but Maria agreed to text the address of where she knew Moses would be the next day. "We may just as well stay for dessert then," Jason said, and Colleen agreed.

John came back to the table. "You guys are amazing! My boss says desserts are on the house." He handed out menus.

The mood was much more relaxed. They ordered more wine, various desserts and coffee. Brok and Trevor drove Sal home; Betsy insisted on driving Colleen and Jason.

Hope House

The next morning Moses was surprised to see Colleen and Jason. "You found me! I thought you'd forget."

"Who could forget you?" Colleen asked.

"Many people who I'm glad did," Moses said, "and a few I wish hadn't."

"Count us among those who won't," Jason assured him.

"That's a legacy that will last but a short while," Moses said. "Most people believe themselves much more memorable than they actually are. I try not to have such pretentions."

"What is this place?" Jason asked.

"Hope House," Moses said. "This is my work these days. We collect things from those who don't want them and give things to those who need them."

Jason looked around the old factory that was now cleaned up and brightly painted. There were rainbows, unicorns and yellow brick roads on the floor and amusing caricatures on the walls. It was a much happier building than it had been as an electronic components assembly business. "There's a lot of stuff here."

"Far too much 'stuff,'" Moses said. "We're so busy shifting and storing 'stuff' that we have little time and little space for necessary things."

"Where does it all come from?" Jason asked.

"It comes mostly from closets and garages. Stuff people get tired of," Moses said, "stuff their kids outgrew, stuff their egos outgrew."

"How does this work?" Colleen asked.

"Poorly, for the most part," Moses admitted, "but we get enough bright sparks to keep despair at bay."

"Are these all volunteers?"

"They're workers; most of them were cast off with less regard than was paid to this stuff. These people know they can get things here, but they also know they earn it. Giving people junk steals their dignity and their ambition. Here, they come with a list of what they need and line it up next to our list of what we need."

"What do they do?" Jason asked.

"They pick things up from where they're not wanted and deliver them to where they're needed. They sort stuff, they clean it, mend it, repair it. Sometimes they look after those who aren't able, for various reasons, to care for themselves. But mostly," Moses said, "they belong."

"Do you run this place?" Jason asked.

"Providence runs this place," Moses answered.

"Are you in charge, then?"

"Love's in charge."

Maria came around the corner with three young teens in tow. "Hi, Colleen, Jason. I see you made it. These are my nieces, Evelyn and Eva, and their friend Evita. Girls, this is Colleen and this is Jason."

"Can you help with the sandwiches?" Moses asked. "I'll get Jason to help line some boxes."

Colleen went off with Maria and the teens; Jason followed Moses. They went over to a long stainless steel table and pulled twelve cardboard boxes out from under it. Moses unrolled a length of butcher paper from a large roll and showed Jason how to form it into a box liner. When all twelve boxes were done, Moses cut shorter lengths from the roll to use as tops. They brought them over to where several people were making and bagging sandwiches. They filled the boxes, keeping tally and stopping according to a list taped to the wall. When each box contained the proper count, they tucked a piece of butcher paper over the top and loaded the boxes into wagons. Groups of people went off with each wagon. After the wagons were all gone and the sandwich prep area was cleaned and sanitized, Moses led Colleen and Jason to an area where arrivals were being processed.

"We get a lot of stuff that's never been used," Moses said, "and a lot of stuff that should just have been tossed. We have a laundry, a sewing room and a little workshop. Over there is our little store and that's our café. All our members have cards; their purchases earn debits and their hours earn credits. As long as one side doesn't get too much higher than the other, we're okay. Anyone can be a member, and the members pretty much regulate themselves. I'll get cards filled out for you."

"It's okay," Jason said. "We don't really need cards."

"This place is for members only," Moses said. "Every member needs a card. We don't check IDs, but everybody needs a card."

"If Mabel brings in some of her pies," Maria said, "you'll definitely need a card!"

"Wander around and see what you think," Moses suggested.

Maria took Colleen and Jason around; she showed them the workshop first. It had separate, well-equipped areas for woodwork, metalwork and electronics. Next to it was a room divided into sewing, pottery and general crafts areas. Then, there was a room where people played cards and board games, a room with pool tables and one with table tennis.

"This is our gym," Maria said as she opened a door. "We have exercise classes and martial arts classes during the day and different programs at night. Monday night is twelve-steps night. Wednesday is basketball night. We used to have soccer, but it got too rowdy. Tonight will be choir night; we have a really good Gospel choir!"

Maria showed them around the commissary; it rivalled many small department stores for selection and presentation. Moses was busy with a man at the counter.

"That's Maxwell," Maria said. "He means well, but you have to be patient with him. Moses is getting him to make your cards. You'll have to bring them back before you leave. Make sure you watch over his shoulder when he files them or you might not find them next time."

Maria saved the cafeteria till last. "Stella is really doing wonders with this place since she took control of it."

"Hi, Stella. This is Jason and Colleen. Moses is getting their cards ready; they're new here."

"Okay, sweeties," Stella said. "Take whatever y'all want, but be sure to get your cards stamped before y'all go."

"Thanks, Stella," Colleen said. "Nice place you have here."

Colleen and Jason each had a bowl of chili and a cheese enchilada. Maria had tacos and a salad. "That's Mabel's pecan pie," Maria pointed out. "Be sure to get some before it's gone! She must have just brought it. I bet she's still here somewhere. We'll look for her after we eat; she's really nice."

The food was really good; they were enjoying it when Stella brought over four glasses of lemon water. "You must be VIPs," Stella said. "Getting the royal tour from Maria herself!"

"We're just friends of Maria and Moses," Colleen said.

"A friend of theirs is a friend of mine." Stella offered her hand. "Let me shake your hand now that I ain't behind the counter, and now I know you ain't food safety."

"I'm sure a kitchen as clean as this can't have any trouble with food safety," Colleen said.

"It ain't the kitchen," Stella said. "It the idea. That nasty little excuse for a man thinks we all cockroaches that inhabits these parts."

"He should eat here and find out," Jason said.

"He ought to stay clean away from here! He ought to take his skinny backside clear over to the other side of town and keep it there! Some of these here folk only had a dumpster for a kitchen before they got their card. He got a nerve to complain about my cooking that there ain't nothing wrong with. Ain't no way I ought to have to put up with that polecat! I bet my kitchen is cleaner than his one back home. I wish my John-Henry was still here and talk to that man! He do his talking with a big stick; that what that man need!"

"Stella has quite a strong opinion about bureaucrats," Maria said.

Moses came in. "Here are your cards. I've stamped them for the work you did. Stella, can you stamp them for the food?"

Stella took out a pen and marked an X on each card.

"Be sure Maxwell gets them before you leave," Moses said. "You might want to watch how he files them."

They watched people come and go as they finished lunch. "I always work in the laundry," Maria said when they were done. "Between the sorting, washing, ironing and storing away, there's always lots to do. It's amazing how fun it is as a group activity; I hate doing it at home."

"I'll go with you," Colleen said. "I actually enjoy it; I'm a bit of a laundry freak."

"That's encouraging," Jason said. "We complement each other perfectly. I'll help in the receiving area."

Moses scurried about from place to place making sure all went smoothly and everyone was happy. Maria excused herself at two thirty. "My sister Corina will be here at four for the girls; you'll like her," she said. "See you at Tink's later."

"Yes," Colleen assured her. "Are the girls okay here by themselves?"

"They're safer here than anywhere else in the neighbourhood. Everyone respects what's going on here."

Maria's sister arrived precisely at four to collect her daughters and their friend; she found the girls and then found Colleen. "I'm Corina," she said, introducing herself. "My sister said you'd be in the laundry; she described you perfectly. It's nice to meet you. I hope I see you again when I have more time to talk."

At four thirty Moses collected Jason and Colleen. "Get your area supervisors to stamp your cards and leave them with Maxwell," he said. "Make sure he files them correctly."

The cautions about Maxwell's filing prowess were well warranted. "Sorry," Maxwell apologized, "I've only been doing this for a month. I'm not use to alphabetical order yet. I wish they would use numbers; I'm pretty good with those."

Jason wanted to call a taxi but Ralph Greener, who had shown him the ropes in receiving, insisted on driving them in his Ram Crew Cab. "This puppy still purrs like a kitten," Ralph said, "even if her muffler does make her sound a little rough." He stroked the dash lovingly. "Yup, Big Bertha's got almost three hundred K on her clock, but there's not a drop of blue smoke. I bet she's got another three hundred K in her."

"Why don't you find a parking spot for Big Bertha, here?" Dust rose from the front bench seat as Jason patted it. "And come in for a beer with us."

"No, thanks," Ralph replied. "I got my Sally and three hungry kids waiting for me back home, and a box of groceries in the back I bought from work today."

"Sorry for keeping you longer from them," Jason said. "Maybe next time. Thank you for the ride."

"Okay, see y'all 'round."

Road to Hope

Hi guys. Hi, Colleen," Maria said in greeting. "How did you like Hope House?"

"It's really great," Colleen said. "I had so much fun there."

"Me too," Jason agreed. "I haven't worked that hard in ages! I'm a little stiff."

"Wait until you sit a while; then it really hits you," Moses said.

"I can hardly wait," Jason said. "I must be some kind of masochist. I'm actually looking forward to going back for more."

"The place is contagious," Moses said. "The more you go, the more you'll like it. Eventually you'll hit a hump and stop for a while, but no one ever really manages to leave Hope House, and Hope House will never really leave them."

"How long have you been going to Hope House?" Colleen asked.

"Actually, Hope House came to me," Moses said, "and never left."

"How long ago was that?" Jason asked.

"The day I decided to make me be me. I can't pin it on the calendar."

"So Hope House was your idea?"

"I can't claim that honour. No one can. It was the fire's idea."

"The fire's idea?" Colleen asked.

"I'm sure you'll need these," Maria said serving their drinks, "and a few more." She winked at Colleen.

"We were standing around a fire in an old oil drum," Moses said, "me, Patches, Griz and Wheezer. We had the rags on our backs and whatever food we could find. None of us wanted to have nothing, so we listed the things we did have. Griz had a new pair of shoes with no holes, but they were a little too big. We all agreed it was better than a little too small. I had enough apples to share. Wheezer had the heat from the fire. Patches had us. We all agreed that what Patches had was best.

"Then we started dreaming of things we might want and discussing the merits of each. We realized that most of what we thought we wanted we could only have for a while. I don't remember who actually said it first, but by morning we all agreed that what we all wanted most was to belong. It was the fire's idea."

"And that became Hope House?" Colleen asked.

"Not right away," Moses said. "The next day, Patches jumped in front of a big truck. Griz, Wheezer and I knew it was because he knew he didn't belong. We made a pact to belong to each other; we went everywhere and did everything together. Mostly, we got chased away together. We were happy. Then Wheezer got sick. They came and took him away in an ambulance. We never saw him again.

"Griz and I realized we couldn't belong alone; if something happened to one of us, whoever was left would no longer belong. We decided it was better to collect a few more people than to keep collecting things that were already long past their best before dates.

"At first we collected people who were sick because they couldn't get away. What little we found, we shared. Eventually, out of necessity, we plucked up the courage to start asking for donations 'to help our sick friends.' At first we got chased away, but eventually word got around the neighbourhood that we really were tending sick people. People started saving things for us and some people even started looking for us to give us things. Our collection of sick people grew quite large; then some people who weren't so sick decided they wanted to help too. We got to be too many for where we were so we found the old factory.

"What people in the neighbourhood disliked the most was the drugs. They tried to chase us away but we just kept coming back. We tried to get everyone to clean up their own drug paraphernalia but that didn't work. Old Geezer decided we should have a vote to ban drugs from the factory."

"Wait," Jason said, "who was the old geezer?"

Moses shrugged. "That was his name. He said everyone called him old geezer so he may as well be Old Geezer. Anyway, we voted to ban drugs from the factory. People still kept coming every so often to chase us away so Old Geezer decided we needed a public relations campaign. We started talking to anyone who'd listen about what was going on and assuring them no drugs were being used there—a lot of people were still using drugs, but not at the factory. Eventually, they stopped chasing us off. Old Geezer convinced us we would benefit by 'formalizing our structures,' as he called it. We began giving people jobs; we became a benevolent corporation."

"A charitable organization?" Jason asked.

"No," Moses said, "definitely not. Charities have been usurped by a corrupt society. People these days give their cast-offs and a few dollars to charity and absolve themselves of any further responsibility. Many charities these days increase a person's dependency instead of helping them become independent. People say, 'Here, this isn't good enough for me, but you should be grateful I'm giving it to you.' What these people want is their right to belong. Belonging is not just having things; it's having dignity, responsibilities and consequences. Poor people don't receive any of those in the same manner as rich people. True charity is shared, not given. Today you two, I dare say, got more than you gave."

"Bangers and mash," Maria placed a plate in front of each of them, "and Caesar salad. This'll go well with Moses' talk—very heavy with a light side."

"I've said all that I'll say of that," Moses promised. "You'll learn far better by being there than you ever can by being here."

"I don't know," Jason said. "I've heard many words of wisdom in here."

"If they only make it only as far as your ears, they won't do much good. You must keep them in mind, take them to heart and allow them to fill your soul. And if you're speaking of my words, you should discard far more than half!"

"Somehow, the words said around this table have more meaning than those said in the TechSys boardroom," Jason said.

"Words can free the mind," Moses said, "but they are often used to enslave people."

"We don't sit around the table discussing how to make our employees do more work. Well, sometimes."

"Do you sit around asking how to bring more truth, beauty and goodness into the world? Or do you, rather, discuss how to bring more dollars into your pockets?"

"Truth, beauty and goodness will not pay the bills," Jason said.

"There are more bills due than those printed on paper. Whose bills are paid by dollars hoarded?"

"How would you suggest a business be run?"

"That depends on the business," Moses said. "A business should do what it's meant to do. What does your business do?"

"We develop management information software."

"And are you able to determine how well that software manages information by how many dollars flow in and out?"

"Sales and maintenance revenues are indicators of how suitable our product is for our market," Jason said. "That's a measure of effectiveness; tracking expenses lets us monitor efficiency and economy."

"Few parts—in the software I knew—need oiling," Moses said. "I recall that maintenance is really fixing or enhancing. High maintenance revenue correlates inversely to satisfaction. Does your board measure success by the reduction of maintenance revenue?"

"So what is your big solution?"

"Business should start with people and end with people. Focussing on money distracts one from the true end," Moses said. "In any business, some amount of labour will be expended upon some amount of resources after which those resources will have more value. To say a business should start with people is to say that once enough people decide they should have resources in one form or place rather than another, a person of enterprise will concoct a plan to achieve that goal. Any added value will provide wages for the labour. To say a business should end with people is to say that, if not enough people agree to provide the necessary labour for the resultant added value, the business will fail."

"And what do you think is happening now?" Jason asked.

"A great deal of coercion, extortion, distraction and distortion."

"Is that a bitter, defeated man speaking?"

"It was for a long while," Moses admitted, "but now it's an optimist. I used to believe I had lost, and I resented those who cheated me. Now I realize I was playing under the wrong rules in a game with no winners, a game that can only end badly for those who lose and go on forever for those who haven't lost yet. No one will ever win, and the further ahead one is, the more desperate the game becomes. Now I follow the rules to a game in which everyone wins; the goal of this game is to see others advance."

"It sounds suspiciously similar to socialism," Jason said, "or communism."

"Not at all," Moses said. "Those just wrest power from one tyrant to confer it on a less capable one. Capitalism, socialism and communism are all different players in the same game. Each focuses on production and consumption from the perspective of a different distributor. To what end do they produce and consume? We know we are here on this earth and we know we will die on this earth. How one produces and how one consumes is but a means of making that journey. Having more of this thing or less of that thing will be inconsequential. One may be more or less healthy before death but not after death. Tall or short, fat or thin, dead is dead. The end I propose as the only one proper is to bring our hearts and souls to that death in a proper state."

"To that end," Colleen said, "I must get up early to go to eight thirty Mass tomorrow; it's been a long day. I did a lot more physical work than I'm accustomed to."

"I probably need to go more than you do," Jason said. "Would you mind if I join you?"

"I'd love that."

"I don't know what 'that' is," Maria said, as she got to the table with their desserts, "but I know you'll love this!"

Maria was right; the lava cake was a perfect finish for their meal.

"Jason and I should be off now," Colleen said. "We'll both be getting up early."

Jason winced a bit and groaned as he rose. "If I'm not too stiff."

Jason suggested a short after-Tink's at Northside High. "If I sit on your nice soft couch I might not get up."

"Five minutes," Colleen said, "and we'll just hold hands."

"Not even three kisses?" Jason asked. "Or five?"

Colleen stayed firm except for one quick peck on the lips at her front door. "Now, off with you! I'll see you back here at seven tomorrow morning."

Sunday School

"You're a little late," Colleen said as Jason approached. "This is my neighbour Cecelia and her daughter Sylvie; we always go to Church together. If we miss our bus, the next Mass is ten thirty."

"You do this every Sunday?" Jason asked. "You're up and out the door by seven to go to Church? What time do you get back home?"

"Usually about eleven."

"Four hours every Sunday morning?" Jason was amazed. "When you could be sleeping!"

"It's important. We make time for what's important to us."

"Like you made time for me last night, after Tink's?"

"We're also responsible with what's important to us," Colleen said. "More time with you last night might have been fun, but it's more important to me that you're here now."

"Take it from me," Cecelia said. "Better take care of the important stuff before the fun stuff. Don't get me wrong; I wouldn't give up my Sylvie for the world, but I sure would have given up that sorry bag-of-bones daddy of hers a lot sooner if I hadn't given up myself so soon. Colleen is doing things the right way and, if you really want to make this thing work, you better do it the right way too."

"I really want to," Jason said. "I've had relationships before, but they were different. They were more now things than future ones. They were more what's normal than anything special. People are expected to have partners; you're weird if you don't. A lot more attention is paid to having a partner than having the right partner. Maybe it's because right partners—or even potentially right partners—are so rare. I didn't really think about what the right partner meant until I met Colleen. I think that's why it took me so long to ask her out. I was still busy entertaining myself; I wasn't ready to be serious. I didn't even think about serious. I guess, somehow in the back of my mind, I knew I wasn't ready for Colleen. I'm not sure I'm ready yet, but at least I'm ready to think about being ready."

"I'm Catholic," Colleen said. "We're taught to be ready, not that all of us pay attention! We're also taught to wait for someone who's ready. There's a lot of distractions to make us forget what we know. That's why Mass is important; it refreshes our memory."

The bus arrived; it was almost empty. They sat and continued their conversation. "There's that Catholic thing again," Jason said. "We keep saying we're going to have the Catholic talk, but we only ever manage little pieces of it. We really ought to do it. Remember, we make time for the things that are important."

"The little pieces are important," Colleen said. "Besides, I don't know if I could put it into words well enough for you to understand. I've been Catholic my whole life. Our faith was always very important at home. I went to Catholic school, and still, there's so much about being Catholic that I don't know how to describe. It's the way we live."

"That doesn't give me much to go on," Jason said. "It sounds more like an excuse for not talking about it."

"You're not Catholic. Can you tell me what it is to not be Catholic?"

"I don't believe there's a God who's in control of every little thing. I believe things happen in a particular way because the conditions are right for them to behave that way. If we can determine the conditions, we can anticipate the results. If we create the conditions, we will cause the results. Life's about deciding what results we want and lining up the right conditions to make it happen."

"How do you decide the best results to cause?"

"We look at the options and pick our favourite."

"That's what we call free will," Colleen said. "God created us with free will so we can choose to do what's best. That's a little bit different from doing what we like, because sometimes we may not like what's best."

"We believe that God created everyone for a purpose," Cecelia said. "We live well when we follow the purpose God created us for. If we choose to follow our own desires, we are sinning."

"What if your will is the same as God's will?" Jason asked.

"Then you're a saint," Cecelia said.

"Sometimes our will is the same as God's will for us, but often it isn't," Colleen said. "We believe that Adam and Eve were the first people and they ate the apple when God told them not to. That was the first sin and it broke our relationship with God so now people have a tendency to sin."

"That's a pretty outrageous claim," Jason said. "Because two people sinned, everybody sins?"

"It's not that outrageous. We learn by example. You've heard the saying, 'The apple doesn't fall far from the tree'? Think about it. If their parents lied and cheated, would it surprise you if their kid's lied and cheated too? If their parents drank too much or used drugs, would you be surprised if they did the same? Wouldn't you be more surprised if they didn't?"

"So how do we know what purpose God made us for?" Jason asked.

"To love one another as He loves us," Cecelia said.

"That's right," Colleen agreed. "That's the general rule, but we also believe that, since God is all-powerful and created us for a purpose, He wouldn't create us without everything necessary to fulfill that purpose. Your talents and abilities are clues to your purpose. Your best talents and your keenest interests will be those needed for you to fulfill your purpose."

"You don't need to be Catholic to figure out that it's a good idea to do what you like to do and can do. Also, they forgot to mention that it has to pay the bills."

"Paying the bills is part of the 'everything necessary' that God provides. For us it's a consequence of doing the right thing, not the motivation to do it. Our motivation is always love of God and love of neighbour. Actually, loving our neighbour is part of loving God because we see God in our neighbours. It's the same for the environment; looking after God's creation is a sign of loving Him."

"So, according to what you're saying, you believe that God created you to be an accountant and you are being a good Catholic by being an accountant."

"Actually it's the other way around. Being a good Catholic helps me be a good accountant. Being Catholic is a means—we believe the best means—of fulfilling God's purpose. We believe God comes to us through the Catholic Church and that the Catholic Church is the most effective and efficient way to go to Him."

"I was never interested in the Catholic Church until I found out you are Catholic," Jason said. "So I didn't pay a lot of attention, but the way I remember it, there are a bunch of thou-shalt-nots and, if you do, off to hell!"

"That would be the Ten Commandments," Colleen said. "They aren't really threats; they're more like an instruction manual. God made us and he knows how we operate. If an engineer said, 'Thou shalt not let your car's gas tank be empty,' you wouldn't complain. You're free to let the tank get empty, but if you do, you'll suffer the consequences. It's the same with the Ten Commandments. If you choose to do what they prohibit, you will suffer. The hell option is only if you know what you're doing is wrong, you do it anyway and you had the option not do it, full knowledge, full intent and freely chosen. Even then, if you repent, confess, make atonement and have a firm resolve not to repeat the sin, you'll be absolved. Jesus became man so he could pay for our sins."

"This is not something I can just hear and accept," Jason said. "I know that you believe all this stuff, and I know you're pretty smart, but I need some time to wrap my head around it all. It still sounds a bit hokey pokey to me."

"That's good," Colleen said. "I don't want you to go along just because you think I want you to. I want you to be part of the Church because you believe it's true. It will help if you give some things the benefit of the doubt while you're figuring them out, but don't say you believe them unless you really do believe them. I have to admit, one thing that bothers me is people who say prayers without knowing what they're saying; they memorize prayers and repeat them, but they don't really mean them. It becomes more superstition than belief. If you become Catholic, I want it to be because you understand enough about it to believe it's the best thing to be. I'm glad to be an influence—I hope I'm a big one—but I shouldn't be the reason; maybe the reason you thought about it, but not the reason you're Catholic. That's God's job."

"I'm pretty sure lying is one of those thou-shalt-nots. It would be grossly hypocritical to falsely state I believe all things Catholic when that's a pretty basic part of all things Catholic."

"That brings up another point," Colleen said. "The Catholic Church has dogmas that are pretty much a take-it-or-leave kind of thing. They are teachings that are so basic to our faith that they must be believed."

"That's a bit awkward, isn't it?" Jason asked. "Only believe if you believe, but you must believe this?"

"No," Colleen said. "It's like physics, or math; you must accept certain rules or they don't work. Dogmas are things that are so central to our faith that, if you can't accept them, you won't be able to accept the rest. The dogmas are sort of the foundation the Church is built on; if you take them out, the whole thing falls down—or at least a significant portion becomes unstable."

"This is our stop," Cecelia said.

"That's good," Jason said. "I think it's time to stop. I can see that there's a whole lot more to being Catholic than can be explained on one bus ride. I have to do a lot more thinking before we do more talking."

"I haven't scared you off, have I?" Colleen asked. "I'm not a catechist."

"I know, you're a Catholic!" Jason quipped. Colleen smacked him.

"You know a lot more about the Church than I do," Cecelia said. "I just know that God has always been there to see me through whatever tough times I was facing."

"Couldn't He just have steered you around them?" Jason asked. "After all, He's God; He can do anything!"

"He steered me through them to make me who I am," Cecelia said. "If he just steered me around them, I wouldn't have my Sylvie; she's the best thing that ever happened to me."

"I guess every cloud has a Sylvie lining." Jason got a bigger smack.

"Our troubles aren't sent to annoy us," Colleen said. "They're sent to form us. Everything God gives us is a gift. If we cooperate, it helps; if we fight, it hurts."

"That one hurt!" Jason said. "Maybe we could talk about the weather."

"Whether you're going to cooperate or whether you're going to fight?"

"Whether my arm will survive. Do you want to go through life with a one-armed man?"

"Is that a proposal?"

"You haven't beaten me into submission yet."

"Good," Colleen said. "I'd rather have a proposal that comes from the heart than from a sore arm."

"You wouldn't say yes if I asked you right now anyway," Jason said. "And you'd be right; we're not ready. Like Cecelia said, it's better to do it the right way—one marshmallow now or two later."

"So you have been listening," Colleen said.

"When did I talk about marshmallows?" Cecelia asked.

"Look at that," Jason said. "Not a cloud in the sky!" He got another smack.

"Come on," he said, "it's still very early. You said Mass starts at eight thirty and it's barely seven thirty now. We still have almost an hour."

"We're always early," Colleen said as they turned left on Seventh. "We usually go to Donovan Park for a while."

"But can we talk about something else?" Jason asked. "My head is spinning from all this Catholic stuff. I have to let it settle down and settle in. I've already figured out that it would be very hard for you to be with someone who couldn't share your faith, but it would be worse yet if you were burdened with someone who only pretended to share your faith. If that's not one of those thou-shalt-nots, it should be."

"There's nothing that prohibits a Catholic from marrying a non-Catholic," Colleen said. "But I have to admit, it would be difficult for me."

"I wasn't talking about that," Jason said. "I meant pretending to believe something just to get something—someone, more precisely. That just wouldn't be right."

"That's a very Catholic thing to say," Colleen said. "The ends don't justify the means."

"That's not a 'Catholic' thing," Jason said. "It's a real thing." He thought about it for a few seconds. "It might not be a work thing."

"Catholic thing, real thing, work thing," Colleen said, "what matters is, is it the right thing?"

"So according to that, it's more important to do the right things than to be Catholic," Jason said.

"Right things and Catholic things," Colleen said. "Catholics don't hold that right things are exclusive to Catholics. It's more that right things are inclusive to Catholics and wrong things are excluded."

"Does that mean you believe that Catholics don't do wrong things?"

"Not at all. Many Catholics do bad things; I do bad things," Colleen said. "What it means is that, when a Catholic does bad things, they are not behaving consistently with their faith."

"So if non-Catholics can do right things and Catholics can do wrong things, why be Catholic?"

"So you'll know when you're doing wrong things."

"It still doesn't make sense," Jason said. "If Catholics know when they're doing the wrong thing, where do they get this knowledge so they can become Catholic?"

"Being Catholic is a journey. To say you're Catholic is to say you believe the right things are there and you'll try to find them and do them. We don't believe that anyone, other than Jesus, knows or does everything right."

"So why not just try to find the right things and do them without being Catholic?"

"So why not try to get a PhD without a university or professors?"

"Not everybody can get a PhD even with universities and professors," Jason countered.

"Catholics are the students," Colleen said. "The PhDs are the saints."

"So becoming Catholic is more like picking the university of life."

"I guess that's a pretty good analogy."

"So how do I enroll?"

"We can talk to Kelly," Colleen said. "We have classes on Thursday nights from seven to nine, starting in September."

"Uh, that was a rhetorical question," Jason said.

"Be careful what you ask for!" Colleen squeezed Jason's arm. "You might get me."

"We'd better go now," Cecelia said. "Sylvie is altar serving."

They walked back to Harvard Street and up to Tenth. "How old is this church?" Jason asked.

"The Parish goes back over a hundred years," Colleen said. "The church itself was finished in nineteen twenty-something."

They went in. Sylvie rushed off, and Colleen, Jason and Cecelia went into the main part of the church. There were several stylized pictures of people at the front. "Who are they?" Jason whispered.

"Those are icons of various saints," Colleen said. "The big one at the top is the Holy Trinity."

"Okay," Jason said. He didn't understand, but he also didn't want to disturb the people sitting and kneeling quietly. "Who are the people in the windows?"

Cecelia pointed to one of the windows. "That's me." Jason looked at her in surprise.

"Saint Cecelia," she explained. "The ones on the sides are saints, and the ones over the altar are the apostles."

The only thing Jason gained from the explanation was that Cecelia had been named after the person pictured in the window. He decided not to ask anything more until after Mass. He listened as best he could but there were a lot of distractions: the little boy getting animal crackers from his mom's purse, an older lady having trouble keeping her polyester dress where it belonged and the mom who jabbed her son in the ribs each time she caught him looking away. It didn't help Jason's concentration that he understood so little of what went on. Jason stood, sat and knelt as instructed. He followed Colleen up to the front where she ate something she received, which he didn't receive. He followed her back to their bench where he knelt, stood and sat some more. They sang one last song while the priest and his group left; then everyone left.

"What did you think this time?" Colleen asked as she led Jason to the parish hall for coffee and snacks. "Any different from Mérida?"

"Not quite so hot," Jason said. "I didn't understand it any better. I kind of got that the Egyptians and Israelis were fighting and some rich kid figured out he was dumb to leave home. I guess things haven't changed that much in two thousand years."

"I was hoping you'd get the part about Jesus dying for our sins," Colleen said. "That's pretty much the central point for Catholicism, for all Christians, really."

"I think I really need to pause for now," Jason said. "I'm already going to forget so much of what we've talked about. There's no more room between my ears right now. I need to sort out the inbox and file a few things away."

"And toss the junk mail?"

"You said that, not me!"

"Do you have plans for the rest of the day?"

"How about a just-the-two-of-us day?" Jason suggested. "Just the two of us with nothing to do except relax and enjoy each other's company. We don't need to say anything, just be together."

"Tink's tonight?" Colleen asked.

"I don't know if I could handle this much Catholic stuff and Moses on the same day," Jason said. "I'm not done figuring out yesterday's stuff."

"It has been quite a weekend with Hope House, Moses and Church one after the other."

"On top of a crazy week at work!"

"That standoff with the Machetes was so intense; I was so scared!"

"You were very brave," Jason said. "I've been trying to keep you out of all that work intrigue."

"I don't want you to," Colleen said. "If it's too dangerous for me, it's too dangerous for you."

"I know, but I don't have any choice. I'm in it whether I want to be or not. You don't have to be in it."

"Shouldn't it be my choice? Actually, I'm already a part of it, no matter what. We're only discussing how big a part. Maybe it's too soon yet to know one hundred percent how things will work out between us, but I've invested a lot in the possibility of us. Us has to be us—all or nothing!"

"Isn't that a part of the Catholic thing?" Jason asked.

"Well, yes, it is."

"That part of Catholic," Jason said, "I do know I agree with."

"That part of Catholic," Colleen warned, "includes kids."

"I'd like kids," Jason said, "and kids deserve parents who've already made the all-or-nothing choice."

Cecelia and Sylvie came to collect Colleen and Jason. "We'd better get going or we'll miss our bus," Cecelia pointed out.

They headed down Harvard Street to their bus stop. "Would you guys like lunch at Revival Market?" Colleen asked. "My treat."

"Yes, Mom, yes!" Sylvie hopped up and down and held her hands in prayer. "Can we, can we? Please!"

"How can you say no to that?" Jason asked.

"Thanks," Cecelia said, "but Sylvie has homework to do."

"Mom!" Sylvie said. "I already did my homework. Last night!"

"You have a math quiz to study for," Cecelia reminded her. "Studying's not done until after the quiz."

"Mom!" Sylvie stamped her feet.

"You still have to have lunch," Colleen reminded her. "At home or at Revival Market."

"Okay," Cecelia relented. Then she looked sternly at Sylvie. "But I don't want to hear any squawking once we get home."

Colleen hugged Jason's arm and pulled his ear closer. "This is what we're discussing. Kids are more than just cute photos for your wallet; sometimes parents' plans have to take back seat."

"Right beside the car seat?" Jason earned a solid jerk on his arm.

"Kids are a serious responsibility."

"So are wives. We've both been living on our own for a long time; I know we're both in for major changes if we decide we'll do this."

"There will need to be a lot of give and take."

"Charles' dad says give and take doesn't work; it only works when it's give and give," Jason said, remembering. "Pops said husband and wife both get more than they give, but they're not allowed to take it. He said the only time you should take anything is when you forget to give; then you'd better take cover because bad things are coming at you!"

"You like him," Colleen observed. "He sounds like a smart man."

"He had a lot of practical wisdom," Jason said, "a simple way of seeing complicated things."

"You wait for us before you cross White Oak," Cecelia called out.

"Mom! I'm a big girl already!" Sylvie protested.

"Not too big to get grounded!"

Jason tapped Colleen's hand and smiled; Colleen blushed. They all managed to arrive safely at the café. They ate their meal leisurely until

Cecelia noticed the time; then they gulped down their last few bites and rushed to the stop just ahead of the bus. "Did you thank Auntie Colleen?" Cecelia asked.

"Thank you, Auntie Colleen," Sylvie replied.

The bus ride took eleven minutes followed by a five-minute walk. Colleen and Jason said goodbye to Cecelia and Sylvie outside their gate. "Thanks again, that was really nice," Cecelia said. "Nice to meet you, Jason."

"Nice meeting you too," Jason said, "and you, Sylvie."

"Bye, thanks for coming with us," Sylvie said. "You coming next Sunday?"

"We'll see," Jason said.

They watched mom and daughter disappear through their front door. "What shall we do?" Colleen asked.

"Can we just sit in front of the TV and watch a movie?" Jason asked.

"And cuddle?"

"And cuddle."

"Only cuddle!"

"Until we know for sure," Jason promised.

"One only knows for sure at the altar. Even with an engagement, things can happen. Do you want to watch a new movie or a classic?"

"Classic," Jason said. "What do you have?"

"*Sound of Music?* It's one of my favourites."

"Kids again?"

"Triumph over adversity," Colleen said, "but kids too."

"She was a nun, right?" Jason asked.

"Planning to be," Colleen corrected, "until she met Captain Von Trapp."

"So she changed her mind."

"She was discerning. Much like we are. She decided God was calling her to marriage, not sisterhood."

"Things happen."

"Even when you're very sure they won't," Colleen cautioned.

"How about if they happen after the altar?"

"That's the whole point of waiting," Colleen said. "Make sure you're committing to the right person; it's a covenant, not a contract."

"What's the difference?"

"If you break a contract, you pay a penalty. If you break a covenant, everyone pays a much bigger consequence."

"I've experienced it," Jason claimed, "and I don't want my kids, if we have any, to suffer the same way."

"Marriage is more about what the kids need than what the parents want," Colleen said. "If the parents can't solve their problems, how will the kids learn to?"

"Or commit themselves to," Jason pointed out.

"Did you learn to?"

"From Pops and Mrs. Jackson. Occasionally they'd get into some nasty fights that would scare the kids. After a few minutes of nattering at each other, one of the kids would go over and hug Mrs. Jackson. They'd stop fighting right away. Mrs. Jackson would stoop down, grab the child's head in her hands so they were looking eye to eye and say, 'Don't worry, Baby Bear, Pops and I are just working things out.' Then she'd go over to Pops and say, 'Right, Poppa Bear?' He'd answer, 'Right, Momma Bear." Then they'd kiss and Pops would give Mrs. Jackson a smack on her butt. They only called each other that when they argued."

"Nattering?"

"Almost every fight, Pops would say, 'Woman, why are you always nattering at me?' and Mrs. Jackson would say, 'Because nattering is the only time you listen!'"

"Do you think we'll natter?"

"I think we'll kiss and I'll give you a smack on your butt."

Colleen put in the Blu-ray disc, and they sat together on the couch. "This is nice," she said as she leaned against Jason. After *Sound of Music*, they watched *Mary Poppins*. "Should I make soup and a sandwich?" Colleen asked.

"We could go to BB's," Jason said.

"More time for cuddling if we stay here."

"Soup and sandwich sounds great! Can I help?"

Colleen pulled out dishes and cutlery. "You can set the table." She sautéed portobello mushrooms and added them to some cream of mushroom soup. As the soup warmed, she made two sandwiches. "I think I have wine, if you'd like."

"Are you planning to get me drunk and take advantage?"

"What was that Pops and Mrs. Jackson used to say when they were fighting?" Colleen asked. "No wine!"

"I'll behave," Jason promised.

"As long as you promise!" Colleen relented. She disappeared down the hall and reappeared with a bottle raised victoriously in her hand. "You're in luck!" She got a corkscrew and two glasses and brought it to the table; Jason pulled out her chair for her. As she sat, she handed him the wine. He opened it and poured her a taste.

"That will be fine, waiter," Colleen teased.

They talked about Colleen's childhood as they ate. It was so much more normal and pleasant than Jason's. "I want our kids to be able to remember things like that," Jason said. Colleen blushed and looked down.

When they finished eating, they took their wine to the couch. They sat, cuddled and talked a bit more. Jason looked at his watch and noticed it was already eight o'clock. "Tomorrow will come early again. I'd better go. This is getting much too comfortable." They had a quick kiss at the door and Jason walked home.

The Ultimatum

Sal looked extremely tired and worried when Jason got to the executive lounge. "Good morning, Jason. How was your weekend?"

"Much better than yours by the looks of things."

"What did you do?"

"I spent all weekend with Colleen. I thought very little about work," Jason admitted.

"I thought very little about anything else," Sal said. "I guess it wasn't technically about work. It was about all the shenanigans going on between Avizales and Andrew."

"And the Machetes?"

"Especially the Machetes. When I got home on Friday, I found Stinky hanged from my driveway gate. He was locked inside when I left Friday morning, so I wasn't able to go in myself until Brok and Trevor finished investigating. Bert was there too; he brought a whole team with him. It was very dramatic."

"That's terrible!"

"Yes, it was horrible. It might turn out to be even worse for whoever did it."

"Why?"

"Bert's forensic guy recognized the rope and the knots. It was just like the one that hanged Ernesto on Andrew's front gate. The noose and clove hitch were left-handed; apparently they can tell by the direction the loops turn and which way the tail hangs out. Poor Stinky's tail just hung straight down. Originally, the left handed knots supported the suicide theory because Ernesto was a lefty. But Ernesto couldn't possibly have tied Stinky's so now they think someone else tied both—ergo, Ernesto didn't commit suicide."

"Add another murder."

"Whoever hanged Ernesto and Stinky may just have hanged himself. The police spent all weekend at my house; I stayed in our hospitality suite here. I couldn't have stayed home anyway, not with that image of Stinky dangling in my head."

"Why didn't you call me?"

"I planned to, but Myriam deserved to know about Stinky's demise; she loved that cat even though she claimed not to. We wound up talking for ages. Then I called again on Saturday and again on Sunday. It was good, very good. We talked mostly about me, because I'm the wreck. I realized how well Myriam is doing down there without me and how badly I've treated her over the years."

"You came to terms with that quite a while ago," Jason said. "We've talked about it at some length."

"I accepted it in my mind," Sal said. "I knew I did terrible things—I admitted a number of them—but I never really talked to Myriam about them. Discussing all those things with her struck me in the heart; I felt the full ramifications. I needed those talks with her, not just in my mind and not with someone else. It was pure agony! Before, when I thought about my poor treatment of Myriam or talked about it with others, the pain would subside but it never went away. I think now I might really be able to be with Myriam. I won't have to pretend I'm the Sal I imagined she wants me to be. She really does love me, after all I've done. Anyhow, one upshot is... I'm not going to Bermuda."

José came over with coffee. "I see you are very busy to Mr. Sal so I don't come for bother you to hello. Mr. Sal is too much sad, I think, for his died *gato*."

"Thank you, José," Jason said. "How was your weekend?"

"Very much better for Mr. Sal weekend, I think," José said. "I am too sorry to him. You like to having some breakfast?"

"A nice Mexican breakfast, thanks, José."

"Okay, I ordering for you."

"Good morning, Simon," Jason called out.

"A sad morning," Simon said more correctly.

"So what now?" Jason asked Sal.

"It turns out that Hector Rodriguez was a very good detective. DEA found all kinds of documentation tucked away in the barn at Hacienda Gonzales. Hector documented everything; he even shot video. The only mistake Hector made was going to the El Paso Police Department when the wrong detective was sick. He wound up presenting his evidence to a detective who was in the Machetes' back pocket. Fortunately, he kept copies and got signed receipts for everything he handed over. He attached the receipts right onto his copies of everything. There's more than one dirty cop in El Paso and a couple in Houston who are going to be in for a very nasty surprise. There will be simultaneous arrests in Mexico City, Monterey, Laredo, El Paso and Houston sometime today; they may already have started."

"How will that affect us?"

"Certainly Andrew will be arrested." Sal started imagining a sequence of events. "That means J.P. will head over to Burkeman Holdings and he'll leave J.J. in charge here. I don't know how much will be revealed to the press, but they'll have a field day with Andrew's arrest. Avizales will have a rough go just to survive; I don't know how long it will take some reporter to link all this to TechSys, probably not very long at all. We'll be okay, maybe good, because we'll point out you and I were instrumental in uncovering the crimes. That gives us leverage."

"We should do something concrete to show TechSys' commitment to integrity, maybe appoint a director of corporate ethics and social responsibility or something," Jason suggested.

"Yes, and the cinnabar affair is likely to get dredged up too," Sal said. "Maybe pre-empt with a director for environmental affairs. I could do that and still be the Sal I really am."

"No more dichotomies between our work selves and our rest-of-the-time selves."

"Would that it could be thus for all," Sal rued.

"That sounds like a project for the director of corporate ethics and social responsibility," Jason suggested.

"Good luck with that!"

Pet came rushing in. "Have you heard what's happening?"

"What brings you here this early?" Sal feigned.

"You haven't heard?" Pet was panicking. "They arrested my parents and Andrew, and a whole bunch of people. The DEA! They say it's a huge narcotics ring."

"We'd better call an extraordinary board meeting, wouldn't you think?" Sal said. "Aren't you in charge of scheduling those things?"

"How can you be so calm?" Pet demanded.

"Calm heads prevail," Sal said. "You and Janice should get things underway."

"Isn't that 'cool heads'?" Jason asked.

"Not this time of year in Houston," Sal jested.

"Ooh! You two are infuriating!" Pet stomped out.

"Well, that's set," Sal said. "She won't be able to set that up any earlier than Wednesday morning; we have until then to set things up ourselves."

"What are we setting up?" Jason asked.

"J.J., and I don't blame you for calling him a 'what.'"

"Okay, what are we setting J.J. up for?"

"We need him, Pet and Marco to support our resolution to add the new directors."

"How?"

"Point out the obvious. We need to avoid the negative PR from this mess, and you and I are the best currency this company has for that."

"When?"

"We need to give him enough time for our ultimatum to sink in but not enough for him to reconsider." Sal calculated. "Dinner tomorrow. We'd better make it a couples' event. Myriam's coming up today to spend some time with me. Having ladies present will help keep J.J. in check."

Jason called J.J. "Colleen and I would like to invite you and Alice to dinner tomorrow."

"I'm afraid I can't make it," J.J. said.

"You should be afraid," Jason said, "and yes, you can make it. Vic and Anthony's, tomorrow, seven p.m."

"I'm meeting someone tomorrow."

"Bring Alice, bring Cynthia, doesn't matter as long as you come."

"I really can't, Jason."

"You really can, J.J. Turn on the news." Jason hung up.

"I guess Pet wasn't in such a big hurry to tell J.J. as she was to tell us," Sal said. "That's telling."

"Do you think J.J. will be able to control Pet and Marco?"

"His father's only away, not dead," Sal assured him. "Everyone's fear of J.P. is still the big play."

"Are we still being bad?"

"This is our end game in that game. After the board meeting, we can start being good."

"Do you think Charles could be the new director of development?" Jason asked. "I really think he'd be good at it."

"We can nominate him, but we can only forward a notice of motion. Our bylaws are quite precise about changes to the board."

"How does that work with what we're doing? We're proposing changes."

"Technically, we're proposing additions, not changes."

"And you had all this bylaw information at hand even though I'm the one who suggested the new directorships?"

"I've been thinking about a director for the environment for a while," Sal admitted. "I think the loophole I found seems like an oversight the new director of corporate ethics ought to take care of, preferably at the same meeting."

OOPS!

Jason got to the lobby before Colleen. She rushed out of the elevator and ran to hug Jason. "It's all over the news!" she said. "It must have been horrible for you up there!"

"Actually," Jason said, "most of the horrible happened to Sal over the weekend. Someone broke into his house while we were at The Tasting Room. They hanged Stinky on his gate; who knows what they did inside."

"That's awful! It's a good thing Sal wasn't home."

"I'm afraid I did something bad too."

"What did you do? And when? I was with you all weekend."

"This morning," Jason said. "I'm afraid I committed you to dinner at Vic and Anthony's tomorrow night without asking you. Myriam's coming up today and Sal wanted to make it a couples' dinner."

"That's not bad. That's good! I'd love to see Myriam again!"

"The bad part is J.J.'s coming. We're going to ambush him."

"What are you making me party to?"

"We got Pet to call a board meeting to deal with all this, and we're about to coerce J.J. into supporting the creation of two new board positions: director of corporate ethics and social responsibility and director of environmental affairs. We also have to make sure he gets Pet and Marco on board."

"I'm okay with that," Colleen assured him. "Those positions sound like a good idea. I'm not so happy with twisting J.J.'s arm to do it."

"Corporate politics. Somebody's always twisting somebody's arm. If you don't count the votes until after the debate, you've already lost."

"That sounds like something the director of corporate ethics should look into," Colleen suggested.

"You're right. Nobody breaks rules that don't exist. Perhaps it's time for a few new rules."

"After you and Sal finish breaking them."

"That did come up in our conversation," Jason admitted, "and we decided better sooner than later."

Colleen snuggled against Jason all the way to Quitman Station, neither of them saying anything; they were comfortable.

"At least we can tell Moses in advance this time," Colleen said.

"Yes," Jason said, "we—I—do seem to take him for granted at times. I really shouldn't."

"He's really a nice old fellow, very odd, but very nice."

"I can't help thinking how different things are now than they were last month," Jason said. "Last month I was only concerned that my team was staying on track and on budget. I cared about scope creep more than anything else. Moses was still 'that homeless guy' in the corner. You were still 'the girl on the elevator.' None of this other stuff even existed. How can things change that much in one month?"

"And I was more like a spectator to my own life," Colleen said. "I didn't really have that much input in its direction. I just kept going from day to day without much thought of changing. I guess we need a bit of chaos chasing us to make us move."

"Now I'm completely caught up in things that I didn't even know existed a month ago," Jason said. "I'm not depending on immature jokes and pranks to keep me entertained."

"I wouldn't write off those immature jokes just yet," Colleen advised, smiling. "Do you think we'll wind up bored when this is all done and things settle down?"

"No, I think I'll wind up like Charles: content. If we're lucky, maybe a fair bit of Moses will get thrown in. I don't think we'll be able to forget about Hope House. I'm already thinking about some things we might be able to do, technology-wise."

As Colleen and Jason walked into Tink's, Maria called out, "You must have had quite the day!"

"Hi, Maria," Jason and Colleen greeted her.

"His nibs is waiting for a blow-by-blow."

As Jason and Colleen approached his table, Moses declared loudly, “You must have had quite the day in that concrete tower!”

“Not as much as you’d think,” Jason admitted. “TechSys is on the periphery for now. I guess everyone is too focused on the eye of the storm. This thing hasn’t filtered down to us yet.”

“There must be some activity,” Moses guessed.

“Just a few minutes’ worth early this morning. I don’t expect much else until tomorrow evening, which reminds me... we won’t be able to come here tomorrow. Colleen and I will be at dinner with John Patrick Burkeman Junior.”

“I’d sure like to be a fly on that wall!” Moses enthused.

“Why don’t you and Maria come?” The words popped out of Jason’s mouth unbidden. He tried to think of a way to retract the invitation but knew he couldn’t reverse it without offending Moses. “Do you think you could find something to wear down at Hope House?”

“I’m sure I could,” Moses said. “I don’t like pomposity, but for this, I’ll dress up a little!”

Since there was nothing else to do but dig himself deeper, Jason added, “Do you think Maria will be able to get tomorrow off?”

As Maria was delivering their drinks right then, Moses asked, “Maria, Jason has invited us to dinner with Junior Boss tomorrow. Would you like to go?”

“Are you up to it?” Maria asked Moses.

“Absolutely!”

“I thought you weren’t interested in this sort of thing anymore,” Jason said, trying to backpedal.

“*Au contraire!*” Moses said. “I’m exceedingly interested in it; I just don’t want to do it anymore. Front row seats to watch it? That I’ll do!”

“Of course I’ll accompany you, Moses,” Maria said. “I haven’t seen you this excited in ages.”

Colleen sensed Jason’s predicament and was obviously suppressing laughter as she watched it evolve. “We’re meeting at Vic and Anthony’s Steakhouse at seven. This will be perfect!” she said as Jason poked her in the ribs.

“We’ll be there,” Maria assured her.

"I thought things were bad before," Jason whispered to Colleen. He could feel her giggling. "You're enjoying this, aren't you?"

"Things always happen for a reason," Colleen whispered back. "You'll see."

"Is that one of your Catholic things?" Jason asked quietly. "I'm not sure I trust that one."

"It just might be divine intervention. Sometimes things we'd never choose, things we think are the worst possible, turn out to be the best."

"What are you two conspiring about?" Maria asked.

"Jason wanted me to clarify one of the finer points of the Catholic faith."

"Do you have it figured out?"

"I heard Colleen's explanation," Jason said, "but I'll have to see it to believe it."

"Sometimes it takes things that are most unexpected to make us believe," Moses said. "For example, I wasn't expecting you to show up tonight, with all that's going on, yet here you are and now Maria and I are invited to dinner with a Burkeman."

"Yes," Jason said, "that's pretty incredible. It wasn't my plan when I came here."

"It will be great," Colleen assured him.

"The food and the wine will be," Jason agreed. "We'll see about the rest."

"Keep your mind open, just a crack, about J.J. Nobody is one hundred percent bad," Moses advised. "How certain are they about Andrew's involvement with this Mexican group and the outlaw bikers?"

"Very," Jason said. "But let's save that for tomorrow when we have a Burkeman to voice his defence. Why don't we talk about Hope House?"

"What would you like to know?"

"Colleen and I really enjoyed it and we'd like to go again, but I'm not sure my back enjoyed it as much. Is there anything that needs to be done that's more in our line, more management?"

"Things aren't too formal there," Moses said. "People get attached to one thing or another and step up to the plate to run it. Stella's a good example of someone who's very capable. Maxwell may represent the other end of the scale; he's someone we're trying to help along. There are so many levels of competence and so many personalities that it would be hard to introduce one integrated management system. One size fits all won't fit Hope House."

"I was thinking of a separate analysis for each department," Jason said. "Determine what's being done and how. I think Hope House is definitely a place where a system will need to be tailored to fit the client, no forcing Hope House to fit a package."

"I'd better get back to work," Maria said, "and find someone to cover my shift tomorrow."

"What's the special today?" Jason asked.

"Pork pie," Maria said. "I know you'll enjoy it. Save the fancy stuff for tomorrow."

"So what do you think, Moses," Jason asked, "about Hope House? Colleen and I can work on it together; it's right up our alley."

"And easier on Jason's back," Colleen said. "I actually enjoyed the laundry, but it might not be your best use of resources. Even if we determined that changes aren't warranted, or perhaps even possible, that in itself would be useful."

"I'll run it by a few people," Moses promised.

"We're trained to be sensitive to protecting our clients' sense of control. There's a change management program developed with each client."

"In plain English, you don't intend to bully anyone," Moses said. "Most people at Hope House have been bullied and harassed for years; they become hypersensitive. Hope House is not a traditional business and things cannot be done in the traditional way."

"Perhaps it's exactly the type of place where we can find a better way," Jason said. "Maybe instead of making Hope House work like other places, we can convince other places to be more like Hope House."

"Maybe," Moses said. "But there will be a lot of people fighting that. The current system is very entrenched. Even if you can convince ninety-nine percent of the people that change would be better, the other one percent has the say."

"It might have only a very slim chance of success," Jason said, "but it will have zero chance if no one puts it out there."

"That's a project for another day," Moses said. "Tonight I want to prepare myself for tomorrow. What's on the menu tomorrow besides steak?"

"It's a little related to our discussion about Hope House," Jason said, "changing how other businesses conduct themselves. Our plan is to convince Junior to support adding two directors to the board: one for ethics and social justice and the other for the environment. That's a start. We plan to propose it as a PR move to counter the negative publicity our association with the Burkeman drug scandal will generate."

"So are you going to leave Andrew Burkeman hanging out to dry?" Moses asked.

"It's not really our call," Jason said, "but I don't see how anyone can do anything else; he's been caught on video, as I hear. Our job is to insulate TechSys from that action and save as much of Burkeman Holdings as possible. I think any criminal activity is limited to the personal involvement of a few individuals at DBK and Houston Long Haul. I don't think there's corporate involvement—a few bad apples in the barrel, as it were. I don't know if the same can be said for Avizales; their involvement runs much deeper and much longer."

"So what's your plan?"

"Our reputations will be untarnished, maybe even burnished, because we helped uncover the corruption; we became a valuable asset for TechSys. We'll leverage that into creating the new board positions as further evidence of TechSys commitment to ethical corporate behaviour. Sal and I will then present ourselves as eminently qualified for those positions."

"And then we'll all watch to see how well Junior takes his castor oil?" Moses asked.

"Yes," Jason confirmed. "I suspect he might leave before the rest of us."

"This is going to be a very fine spectator sport," Moses predicted. "I'm looking forward to it!"

Maria arrived with their pork pies. "You're all looking very content," she observed.

Jason looked at Colleen and then Moses. "We are," he said.

"Well, this will make you even more content," Maria said as she set down their plates.

"Thanks, Maria," Colleen said. "This smells delicious!"

"Now that all the work turmoil is as settled as it can be for tonight," Moses said, "how are you coming with why?"

"I've settled that why should be the same no matter where," Jason said. "The why at work shouldn't have to hide from the why elsewhere."

"The more our why's agree, the better we'll be," Colleen said.

"Your why's are becoming wise," Moses quipped. "And how do you suppose that may be?"

"Because all the bad things that are happening are making us notice the good things," Jason said.

"Which is one way the worst can become the best," Colleen pointed out.

"When the bad gets gradually worse, we tend to succumb to its allure and become complacent," Moses said. "But when bad takes a sudden leap, we finally recognize it for what it is."

"And hop out of its way," Jason said.

"Speaking of hops," Moses said, "do we have time for another round?"

"I did a lot of laundry this weekend, but not my own," Colleen admitted. "I need to get it done, and I need to make sure I have everything ready for dinner tomorrow. It sort of hopped up on me unexpectedly!"

"In plain English, that's no," Jason said. "I don't have any laundry at home, but my day will start early."

"Your dirty laundry is at work!" Moses joked.

"We'll see you tomorrow at Vic and Anthony's, then," Colleen said. "Seven o'clock!"

Getting Ready

Sal, Myriam and José were all sitting together when Jason arrived at the executive lounge. Myriam and José were chatting away in Spanish. "*Hola, mis amigos,*" Jason said.

"*Hola*, Señor Jason!" José was very excited. "You see Señora Myriam is here of Mexico! She is speaking Spanish very well."

"She is speaking Spanish so well that Señor Sal had to make the coffee this morning," Sal said. "Myriam spoke very little Spanish last time she saw José."

"It pass much years that she no see José. She is a very good friend for José on those time and for my wife also too."

"*Nos prometiste un muy buen desayuno Mexicano cuando Jason llegó,*" Myriam said.

"*Si!*" José said as he scurried off to the kitchen.

"I take it our 'very good Mexican breakfast' is coming," Jason said.

"Yes," Myriam said. "José is so excited that I'm here."

"So is your husband," Sal said. "I need you here much more than I have for a very long time."

"Not really. It's just that you finally know you need me."

"It takes things getting much worse to show us how good things were. I kept chasing more and almost lost best."

Myriam took Sal's hand. "Except that best will never lose you."

"So are you back, Myriam," Jason asked, "or are you visiting?"

"If Sal's back, I'm back," she said. "My home is where the man I married is. For a long time he was nowhere. It would be very nice if the world was more like Hacienda Gonzales, but Mérida was only ever my compromise. Besides, the people make the community, not the location.

I expect we'll find enough good people here to make a good community, now that we realize we'd like one."

José brought breakfast. "We have José and Simon and Jason and Colleen," Sal said. "That's a good start."

"There still needs to be a place where these people can gather," Jason said. He thought about Hope House but it was too soon to know whether it would live up to his first impression, so he kept it to himself.

"I predict there will be a lot of people gathering here today," Sal said. "It would be much better if they didn't show up until tomorrow, but I think that's too much to ask for. I also predict they will be more intent on tearing down TechSys than in building up a community."

"We have to make sure they tell our story instead of one they make up for themselves," Jason said.

"But at the same time; we need to keep our plan to ourselves for today," Sal said. "We don't want to give our friends time to come up with a counterproposal."

"I know our friends well enough to guess they'll only be thinking of defensive strategies. They won't think of anything proactive."

"I've been guilty of that also, too busy worrying about bad things others might do to be thinking about good things we might do."

"The ones who most fear bad things," Myriam said, "are also the ones most ready to do bad things. We tend to see others as we are ourselves."

Pet burst into the executive lounge, all in a panic. "We have to warn Brew! I came in extra early, just in case, but there are already reporters out there. I had to sneak in the back way!"

"Perhaps it would be better to prepare him than warn him," Sal said, "give him a sound bite."

"Perhaps someone could point out that the bad guys work for a different company and the good guys work here," Jason suggested.

"I know it's J.J.'s responsibility," Sal said, "but Brew could promise an official statement after tomorrow's board meeting."

Pet took Jason's napkin, fished a pen out of her bag and wrote a few notes. "I'll call Brew; tell him what's up." She rushed out as quickly as she came in.

"You boys are still being bad," Myriam said. "Does she really not see what you two are doing?"

"She's too busy being important," Sal said.

"So what important things do we have to do today," Jason asked, "besides waiting for tonight?"

"Hide," Sal said. "If the reporters find us, they'll expect answers."

"Yes, at least the others will only be able to admit they don't know anything."

"They'll likely be pressured into divulging who does know, and that will only strengthen our position."

"How will we get out?" Jason asked. "Cedric and the limo, with its dark-tinted windows, are still out of commission."

"That was terrible!" Myriam said. "Sal told me what happened."

"Maybe we should call Brok," Sal suggested. "The DEA has a lot of dark-tinted windows."

"Seeing the DEA here will heighten the frenzy," Jason said.

Sal was already dialling. "It will also reinforce our credibility when we finally do say something."

Brok agreed to meet them at five o'clock. Jason phoned Colleen to tell her the plan.

Myriam recounted the DEA's activities in Mérida for Jason, and Sal reminded her, every now and then, of things she left out. Myriam finished by announcing, "Elena is so glad that Hector's killers will finally face justice. She promises to host a banquet for you and Sal once they're in jail."

Breakfast was long finished and everyone had had too much coffee when Sal suggested they go to their office. "Good morning, Janice," he said as he walked to his office. "We need you in my office."

Janice rose and followed them in. "What do you need?"

Sal pulled out a deck of cards, a pad of paper and a pencil. "It's time Jason learned to play bridge. We need a fourth player—boys against girls."

"I hope you plan to stay a while," Janice told Myriam. "I haven't seen him like this for ages."

"Neither have I," Myriam said. "That's why I've been in Mérida."

"Welcome back to both of you."

About three hours later, Sal and Jason were able to win a game with the help of two favourable deals in a row—one that guaranteed seven no trump and another that assured seven hearts. "That's a fine place to stop," Myriam suggested. "Sal and I should go and get ready." They left the room holding hands and smiling.

"I remember when Sal was always like this," Janice said. "It was so much fun around here when we started."

"I think it might be again," Jason said.

"I'm afraid the kids won't like it much," she said. "They seem to think that anything enjoyable can't be work."

Jason sat and thought about what a director of corporate ethics and social responsibility ought to do; it wasn't as easy a task as he'd first imagined. *How does one find what ought to be done? How can it be quantified, measured and tracked? What is the goal?* Jason still knew it was a worthy goal even though he didn't know quite what it was or how to find it.

Myriam and Sal came down and rescued Jason from his enigma. Myriam wore a loose-fitting white dress that came to mid-calf; the bodice was embroidered with red and yellow flowers on a winding green vine. Sal had on a dark blue suit, pale blue shirt and blood red tie with matching hankie. Jason thought about the clothes in his closet; he was glad he bought, rather than rented, the black pinstripe suit he wore to Charles' wedding. The trio went down to meet Brok and wait for Colleen.

"It's too bad you won't be able to join us for dinner," Sal said as they waited for Colleen.

"Actually," Brok said, "Trevor, Betsy and I discussed things and decided that protective surveillance would be appropriate.

Colleen came down just after five and the celebrities snuck past the reporters, hidden behind the dark windows of Brok's SUV.

"Knowing J.J., he'll either be early or late," Sal said. "What he won't be is on time. I don't want him to be there before us, so I suggest we arrive by six." The others agreed.

The Dinner

It was just past six when they arrived at Vic and Anthony's. They were surprised to see Moses and Maria already there. Maria's dress was amazingly similar to Myriam's. Moses was dressed in a blue pinstriped three-piece suit. He had a carnation boutonnière and bright red tie to match. His hair was still long and his beard still full, but they were neatly trimmed; he looked very dapper. Jason looked over; Sal was crying.

"Gerry," Sal said.

"Rosie," Moses replied, "you look like you've seen a ghost."

"I thought you were dead! I'm very sorry; I really am."

"I wanted to be dead, for a while," Moses said, "and I wanted you to be sorry for a longer while. I hated you for too long a time. I kept tabs on you through a few mutual acquaintances who hated you for similar, if not as drastic, reasons. Your remorse over my death was the only vengeance I could muster for a long time, so I let you believe the rumour until I didn't care anymore. Then I forgot to care again until just recently."

"I destroyed you," Sal said. "I still hate myself for what I did to you."

"The one thing you won't admit?" Jason asked.

"Yes."

"Actually, it was my hatred that destroyed what was me," Moses said, "but past is past. You really are looking well, Rosie."

"And you still look like Charlton Heston. That used to make me quite jealous."

"You should still be jealous of my looks, but at least you can stop feeling guilty for killing me. I should thank you for what you did for me. I'm sorry that I let you suffer with your guilt this long."

"I took everything from you."

"Yes, every 'thing,' but we all occupy ourselves too much with things—getting things, doing things—so much so that we stop being. Have you ever noticed that when you ask someone who they are, they will tell you either what they do or what they own?"

"Lately, I've been coming to terms with that very thing," Sal said.

"We value things much more than we value people; we even expect people to thank us when we treat them like things."

"I'm not inclined to go quite that far," Sal said. "I do see that we set up a dichotomy within ourselves—one self that allows us to mistreat our neighbours and another self that still respects our neighbours—roughly along the lines of work self and other self."

"And the higher we grow in social esteem, the more of that other self we have to shift into our work self. When one gets to the heights we got to, that other self becomes negligible," Moses said. "Our buildings are a good reflection of society today. Our biggest and most impressive towers are built for our work; they are no longer built for our faith or our government. Our work is what's most important to us today. We stack up a great many plain floors into great towers and put shiny façades on the outside. Then we divide each floor into tiny cubicles. We put the little people at the bottom; with each floor one climbs, the people and cubicles get a little bigger. At the top of these great pedestals reside the titans. Their cubicles are far bigger than necessary and ornately filled with treasures to reflect the value we place on the occupants.

"When we take a person," Moses continued, "we stuff them into a cubicle. If they don't quite fit, we adjust the person, not the cubicle. We pare them down or pad them out a bit, but we don't allow them to differ from their cubicle. 'This is your job description; you must not do more, you must not do less and you must not do other.' Professional development molds them ever more into what the business needs rather than who they are. I built a very high pedestal and climbed to the very top. I molded myself to fit the biggest corner office on the top floor. I looked down on all the people I had stuffed inside and I made them look up to me. Then you came along and knocked the whole thing down. The thing that got knocked down furthest was my pride."

"What I did was very wrong," Sal admitted. "Andrew's position was no excuse for his behaviour that night. We deserved to be thrown out; we should have apologized rather than retaliated."

"He had become inured to treating people as things, and I had inured those poor girls to being treated as things. We both treated those women as things; we were both wrong. I'm the one who packaged them up—or unpackaged them, more accurately—and presented them as objects to be used. Andrew merely exceeded a limit that was poorly set from the start."

"Nonetheless, you were far more justified in your actions that night than I was in my response."

"And yet that night, probably in greatest part, led us to this," Moses said. "Perhaps we take too much credit for the bad we do. Consider the good that has come from that night despite all our intentions. In my case, instead of remaining the Scrooge I was, I'm the me I am. In Maria's case, the story is a little longer; I was tinkering with the books at Diablo's Den to evade taxes and protect the club from some very bad characters. Part of that tinkering put Diablo's in Maria's name. It turns out that my lawyers did such a good job putting it in her name that no one could un-put it, not even the government. Once Maria discovered she owned my club, she got rid of the exotic dancers and turned it into The Tinker's Table."

"Things worked out better for me than anyone could have planned," Maria said.

"You own Tink's?" Jason asked.

"Yes," Maria admitted, "but I like being the waitress much better than I like being the owner."

"You have to admit that Tink's is far better than Diablo's Den," Moses said to Jason.

"I think Tink's and you, Moses, deserve a lot of the credit for me being me." Jason looked over to Colleen. "And us being us."

Colleen blushed and took Jason's hand. "Tink's is very special."

"How about you, Rosie?" Moses asked. "How did that night affect you?"

"Of course you know I got angry, even angrier than I always was," Sal said. "And you know what I did to you. But when I heard the rumour that you died, and the rumour persisted, I learned guilt. I was a no-holds-barred businessman. Everything was fair; yet, somehow, I knew I had killed you and that it was wrong. That realization opened the door just a crack. I got a tiny bit better. It wasn't until my sister found out how I destroyed you, though, that the full repercussions of the evening hit me. She threatened to tell Myriam what I had done. I was still under the illusion that Myriam's faith in me was licence for what I was doing, but I knew Myriam would never stand for that. Rebekah threatened that, if I didn't resign, she would tell Myriam everything."

Myriam took Sal's hand, smiled lovingly and said, "Poor Sal had no idea that I already knew everything, that no matter what, I could never leave him."

"Anyhow," Sal continued, "the thought of Myriam leaving me was too much. That defeat at the hands of my own sister is what forced me to face who I had let myself become. So, yes, even though it happened far too many years later, that night is what finally made me a better man."

"The worst can become the best," Jason recalled.

"In God's hands," Moses claimed.

"Perhaps it's just fate," Jason said.

"And is fate chance or design?" Moses asked. "And if design, who's design?"

Time leaped forward to seven thirty over the course of their discussion. J.J. walked in with Cynthia clinging to his arm. "Sorry I'm late," he said. "I was busy."

Cynthia blushed. "It took me longer to get ready than I thought it would."

"So what's so important that you have to summon me here instead of talking to me at the office?" J.J. asked. "I was there all day, you know."

"And now you're here," Moses said. "So you must know that there is something important."

"Who are you?" J.J. demanded.

"Gerald Foster," Moses replied. "I'm a long-time friend of your father."

"And that matters why?"

"That's for you to ponder," Sal said. "What does it matter? Perhaps it matters that you know that we know something you don't know. Perhaps there are others who should also not know. Perhaps that's why we're meeting here instead of at the office."

Sal's response was confusing and concerning enough to curb J.J.'s flippant responses. "What do I need to know?"

"TechSys shares are in a bit of a free fall due to its Burkeman connection to the drug scandal your Uncle Andrew got involved in," Moses explained. "You need to do something at tomorrow's board meeting to restore confidence in TechSys, something substantial. Sal and Jason will propose something, you will support their motions and you will make sure the other board members also support their motions."

"You're not going to tell me more than that?" J.J. asked. "I'm supposed to jump because someone I've never heard of before now says jump?"

"No, you're supposed to jump because someone who's known your father since before you were born also knows something your father would not like you or anyone else to know," Jason said. "If you want to know more than that, tell your father that you met with Gerald Foster tonight. Ask J.P. what else you need to know."

"Just don't expect to like what you hear," Sal warned.

"And don't expect J.P. to like that you know there's something to ask about," Jason added. "What we'll propose will be good for TechSys. This meeting is more to ensure debate on our proposals is limited; we must act quickly in light of the current situation."

"We'll propose increasing our board by two members to deal specifically with ethical and environmental issues," Sal explained. "Lateral moves for Jason and myself. The cost will be the additional directors' salaries, support staff and offices. Details can be worked out later, but it should only be a fraction of a percent of TechSys expenses."

J.J. sensed wisdom in the proposal and feared his father too much to ask more. "Okay," he conceded, "I'll make sure your motions are approved."

"Now, you may stay and join us for a delightful dinner," Sal said, "or find another table and enjoy the company of your friend more privately; the choice is yours. We won't feel offended either way." J.J. chose to leave.

"You did a good job finessing our trump," Sal said to Jason. "There may be hope for our bridge partnership yet."

Jason raised his glass. "And even more hope that I will join your wine appreciation club."

Resolutions

The next morning, Sal and Myriam sat in the executive lounge having coffee while they waited for Jason. José was chatting with Myriam when Jason entered the room. "*Hola*, Señor Jason," José said.

"*Hola*, José, Myriam, Sal," Jason replied. "Are we having a good Mexican breakfast today?"

"Of course," José said. "Señora Myriam very like it!"

Pet came storming in; José scurried off to the shelter of the kitchen. "*Bonjour*, Simon," Jason called out loudly.

"*Bonjour*," echoed the reply.

"Hello, Pet," Jason said.

"Cut the crap," she said. "What did you two do to J.J.?"

"We just invited him for dinner," Sal said calmly, "but he wasn't able to stay. What did he tell you?"

"He wouldn't tell us anything. But he was sure in a big hurry not to tell us. I think he knows more than you think he knows. Brew and I are on side for now, but don't think this is over... and there are limits. Don't stretch them too far!"

"Will you join us for breakfast?" Myriam invited.

"You're no better than they are!" Pet scoffed as she turned and stomped off.

"No wonder you like it here so much," Myriam teased Sal.

They ate leisurely and discussed Mérida more than TechSys as they waited for nine o'clock. Sal kissed Myriam on the cheek she offered as he and Jason rose to leave for the boardroom.

J.J. chaired the meeting in his father's absence. Jason and Sal presented their motions; Marco proffered the expected challenge. He scrolled back and forth through the corporate bylaws for several minutes before finally acknowledging that Sal's loophole was, indeed, valid. During discussion, Sandy convinced the others that "corporate ethics and social responsibility" was too long a name and that social responsibility could be considered redundant to corporate ethics. Pet and Brew offered nothing more than evil looks.

Within an hour, Jason and Sal were the newly minted directors, of corporate ethics and of the environment, respectively.

To Jason's and Sal's satisfaction, Marco then moved to amend the corporate bylaws so that the loophole they'd just slipped through would be shut tight—so tight, ironically, that Jason and Sal could not be slipped back out again.

The remaining time was spent crafting a press release that rued Andrew Burkeman's behaviour while distancing him from TechSys. It praised Sal and Jason for their diligence, announced the new directorships and assured TechSys shareholders, customers and employees that the company would continue to serve them proactively.

After J.J. read the announcement, he fielded questions, along with Sal and Jason, for another forty minutes.

Sal and Jason became minor celebrities for the next while. The executive lounge was a secure retreat at work, and Tink's proved to be a safe refuge for the evenings. Sal and Myriam filled out Tink's corner booth nicely.

"This has been quite the ride," Jason said. "A month ago I didn't know any of you; I didn't know myself. I sat here at Tink's, missing my friend Charles and missing my childish antics. I asked why not a lot more than I ever asked why. I never even considered there was a why. I just let today drift into tomorrow, just let be whatever might be. I never appreciated what a great gift free will is, and I certainly never gave it much exercise.

"Now, thanks to all of you and all that's happened, I know it has great value; I know also that it comes with responsibilities and consequences. Sometimes we suffer worse consequences when we use our free will to avoid making choices. It's the exercise of our free will that forms us into who we become. If we use it well, we become who we ought to be, and if we use it poorly, we become who we ought not to be. I was definitely on the road to ought not, and I thank you all for helping me see that."

"See what comes of asking why," Colleen said. "It's more dangerous to ask than it first appears, but it's far more dangerous to ignore."

"So what do you make of why now?" Moses asked.

"Why is because there's ought, ought is because there's purpose and purpose is because all is not random," Jason said. "When there was nought, there was no ought. But now that there is, there is."

"The scary thing is," Colleen said, "I understood what you just said!"

"Another scary thing is, now that we know there is ought, we have a responsibility to do," Jason pointed out.

"Not only that," Sal said, "but you've just accepted a position that ties a lot of other people's oughts to your tail."

"You must use your free will to guide the free will of many others," Moses said.

"I'm afraid you've accepted the position of navigator for a captain who prefers to steer a rather reckless course," Sal said, "and you're sailing in a rather narrow channel with strong currents and many obstacles."

"But tonight we're in a safe harbour," Jason said. "Let's enjoy tonight. We've all survived one perilous journey!"

"And how perilous is the journey that lies ahead," Colleen asked, "now that you have yourself and all of TechSys to answer for?"

"I guess that will depend a lot on whether TechSys' conscience is strong enough to keep her focused on truth, beauty and goodness while worldly desires pull her in other directions."

"And how will that conscience know the way to truth, beauty and goodness?" Moses asked.

"By asking why and how, and considering the true natures of God, man and the universe," Jason said. "And I think I have a pretty good advisory council right here, one that will contemplate much more meaningful problems than the ones considered by the Bachelors of Ales."

Printed in Canada